Rave reviews for Dave Bara's novels of
The Lightship Chronicles:

"Enthusiasm reinvigorates familiar material in this lively space opera. . . . This energetic mélange of tried-and-true elements—futuristic jargon, military and romantic tactics, and multiple levels of skullduggery—easily grabs the reader's attention; more impressive is that Bara's story holds that attention all the way to the end."
— *Publishers Weekly*

"*Impulse* is fun, fast, and proper science fiction. Where the stakes are big, and things matter because the characters matter. I enjoyed the hell out of this. *Impulse* should be an impulse buy."
—Simon R. Green, *New York Times* bestselling author of the *Deathstalker* series

"Totally convincing space navy . . . check! Perfectly realized characters complete with depth and heroism navy . . . check! Plus, a fascinating story with an Ahab of a captain determined to complete his mission, and a fledgling lieutenant who comes into his own in the midst of interstellar conflict. Oh yeah: exploding spaceships . . . double check!"
—Tony Daniel, national bestselling author of *Guardian of Night*

"*Starbound* confirms what we suspected when *Impulse* hit the shelves: Bara has created one of the most thought-provoking visions of the far, far future we've seen lately, taking the best elements of military sci-fi, space opera, and good old-fashioned adventure stories, and fashioning them into something both familiar and unique."
—The B&N Sci-Fi & Fantasy Blog

"If you liked *Star Trek Into Darkness*, you'll like Dave Bara's *Impulse*."
—Jack Campbell, *New York Times* bestselling author of the *Lost Fleet* series

"*Starbound* ulti̶‌‌‌‌‌‌‌‌‌‌‌‌ and engaging universe, bu̶‌‌‌‌‌‌‌‌‌‌‌ shioned fun."
— *Magazine*

"This guy is the ̶‌‌‌‌‌‌‌‌‌‌‌"
—T. C. Mc̶‌‌‌‌‌‌‌‌‌‌ *ar* series

D0595157

DAVE BARA
STARBOUND

Volume Two of the
Lightship Chronicles

DAW BOOKS, INC.

DONALD A. WOLLHEIM, FOUNDER

375 Hudson Street, New York, NY 10014

ELIZABETH R. WOLLHEIM
SHEILA E. GILBERT
PUBLISHERS

www.dawbooks.com

Published by DAW Books, Inc.
375 Hudson Street, New York, NY 10014.

First paperback printing, January 2017
1 2 3 4 5 6 7 8 9

This one is for Janaan, my Mamouna,
wherever you are.

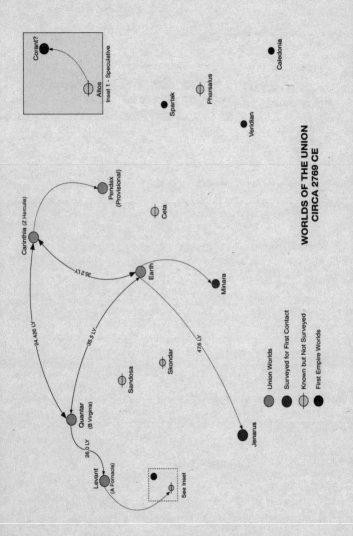

WORLDS OF THE UNION
CIRCA 2769 CE

Inset 1 - Speculative

Corant?

Altos

Caledonia

Spartak

Pharsalus

Veridian

Pendax
(Provisional)

Carinthia (Z Herculis)

Ceta

35.2 LY

Earth

Minara

24.426 LY

38.5 LY

Quantar
(B Virginis)

Sandosa

Skondar

4.76 LY

26.0 LY

Jenarus

Levant
(A Fornacis)

See Inset

Union Worlds

Surveyed for First Contact

Known but Not Surveyed

First Empire Worlds

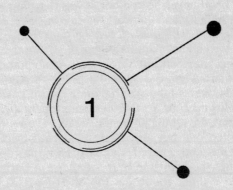

At High Station Candle in the Quantar System

I circled my opponent, foil raised and held at the ready. She circled me in return, but with her foil casually at her side, each of us making our way around the perimeter of the pen. I had faced her before, and felt the sting of her treachery more than once. *But not this time*, I thought. This was one-on-one combat, no mercy given inside the pen, none asked for.

A large crowd had gathered, as was typical for our daily fencing matches. Both Quantar and Carinthian sailors alike had proven to be great fans of our once-private sporting spectacle. They came to watch, hoping that I could finally break through, hoping I could finally best my superior officer, Commander Dobrina Kierkopf of the Royal Carinthian Navy, a former military fencing champion of her world.

I had never beaten her, it was that simple, but I had my military and my world's pride at stake. *For Quantar*, I thought. *This time I'll beat her for Quantar.*

We had been at this almost three months. I had taken it up after concluding physical rehabilitation from my numerous injuries after the Battle of Altos, where we had traversed the artificial jump gate at Levant with our Lightship *H.M.S. Starbound* and fought an ancient Imperial dreadnought to the death. Their death, it had turned out, but also likely the death of many of our friends and comrades aboard Dobrina's former command, the Lightship *H.M.S. Impulse* of Carinthia. I tried not to think about that too often—a reckoning would come soon enough—but right now I had only one goal, to defeat the commander in the fencing pen for the first time. I watched her dip her right shoulder subtly, just a dip, and then—

"En garde!"

She charged across the mat at me, whipping her foil back and forth in a flurry of motion that it had taken me weeks to even learn to track. I parried, I hoped successfully, then quickly fled to open space to regain my bearings. I was doing better today than most. We were tied 2-2 in the match, but the next score would seal it for one of us.

I continued circling away from her, retreating as she pursued, fending off her occasional testing of my defenses with her foil.

"Growing bored again, Cochrane," she said.

"Is that what you call it?" The truth was I had to bore her with my defensive strategies. My only scores against her invariably came when I was defending. Attacking such a skilled swordsman was pure insanity. She never seemed to make the same move twice, and it was difficult to learn her style, because she didn't really have one. She would use any manner of strategy to win, whether inside or outside the rules. As she had told me once before, this wasn't really fencing, it was sword fighting.

She attacked again, probing my defenses high and low, our foils clattering as they clashed. She moved inexorably closer with each step. I was barely able to hold her off and was completely unable to gain any positive ground under her relentless assault. It was only a matter of time now before I made a mistake.

I took a wild chance and lunged at her, getting inside her foil range and holding her off by grasping at her wrist, using my superior physical strength to my advantage. To my surprise she dropped her foil instantly and then pulled me close to her before spinning me around in a circle, using my own momentum against me. I tripped over her extended leg and fell on my back, sprawling on the mat. By the time I got my bearings back she had her foil in her hand, poised over the scoring zone at my chest.

"And now you've fallen for the dropped-foil technique," she said.

"It seems I have," I replied. She pressed her foil tip to my defenseless center.

The scoring bell sounded.

The crowd let out a groan of disappointment. She walked casually back to her bench, as she always did after defeating me. I took off my safety mask, went toward my own bench, and sat down. To my surprise, I saw a Carinthian sailor trading Union crowns to a Quantar sailor while his friend chided him.

"He has to win sometime," I heard the losing Carinthian mutter.

"No, he doesn't," said his friend. Then they all walked off together, laughing.

Commander Kierkopf came across the mat. She looked down at me, her hair pulled harshly back in a knot, sweat pouring from her brow.

"Good match today, Peter," she said.

"It's always good when you win," I said back to her.

"Yes, well, you've come a long way from our first match," she said. It was a compliment, and I took it as such, but I really wasn't sure if I was getting any better.

"Thank you, Commander," I said. She nodded.

"Don't be late for staff. Captain Maclintock's notes said he should have news on our redeployment today," she said.

"I can't wait," I replied, wiping my own sweat-soaked face with a towel. Then she was off without another word. The deployment was welcome news. After the battle at Altos, the Historians of Earth had decided *Starbound* needed not just repairs but upgrades, and she had been under repair or refit for most of the last six months. I was itching to get out into deep space again.

I looked down at my watch. 0713. I had forty-five minutes or so. I lingered in the pen for a few more minutes, then made my way back through the men's locker room and out into *Starbound*'s broad main hallway, the galleria, there to take the walk of shame back to my cabin as I'd done almost every day for the last three months.

•———•——•

I was out of my fencing gear and into the shower by 0725. It was a Saturday aboard ship, so Maclintock's staff meeting had been moved from its traditional 0530 to 0800 as a gesture of kindness to the senior officers. Sunday was the only day we didn't have a full staff meeting, relying on informal contact, coms and messages, to stay up on current issues with the ship.

I let the water run over my hair and started shampooing, and inevitably got some in my eyes. I reached for my towel but found only empty space, followed by a burst of cold air for my trouble. I was sure my towel had fallen from the shower door, and now I would have to scramble to find it on the floor, half blind with my eyes burning. Suddenly a warm towel covered my face and a pair of firm hands cleaned the shampoo from my eyes for me.

I felt a warm body slide into the shower behind me. She handed me the towel and I hung it back on the door rack.

"I should have suspected," I said.

"Christ, I thought you'd never get back here," said Dobrina. "You're cutting it pretty tight."

"I'm not the one invading someone else's shower." She laughed and started rubbing my back with soap, lathering me up. Then she rubbed herself against me, too. "I'm not sure we have time for this," I said in mock protest. I was pretty damn sure that I'd make time for whatever she had in mind, but I didn't want her to think I was too easy.

"You should have thought of that before you gave me your door security combination," she said. Then her lathering started getting very direct.

"Are you *sure* we have time for this?" I repeated. She responded by sliding her body around mine until she faced me in the tight confines of the shower. Then she put her arms around my neck and kissed me passionately.

"Oh, I'm sure we have time," she said between kisses, "for what I have in mind." Then she slinked her way down my body, and the staff meeting became the furthest thing from my mind.

———

There were six of us on call for the Saturday staff, and I was there two minutes early to load my plate with a croissant and my morning coffee. I took my place to the left of the captain's chair in the Command Briefing Room and nodded good morning to Colonel Lena Babayan, *Starbound*'s marine commander, George Layton, our chief helmsman, and Jenny Hogan, our astrogator and the lone survivor besides Dobrina of the doomed ship *Impulse*. Maclintock came in and took coffee before sitting in his customary place at the head of the table. Dobrina was last in, and took no refreshment at all. I fancied I'd just given her all the refreshment she'd need for the day.

I smiled and nodded slightly to her as she sat down, her face giving away none of the deviousness of her true character.

"Let's begin," said Captain Maclintock. "There's news about our new deployment. We leave Monday morning at 0700 for the Jenarus system."

"First Contact mission?" I asked, excited at the prospect. Maclintock nodded.

"Jenarus has been surveyed by *Valiant*, but there has been no contact with the government as of yet. From what we can tell from eavesdropping on their communications network the government there is in a rather regressive state of crony socialism. A lot of government-controlled media and an oppressive police state," said Maclintock.

"Not ideal for inclusion in the Union," I stated.

"Not ideal, no, but still, they meet the standard for First Contact, a seven on the Technological Development scale if only a six on the cultural scale. Not as high as Levant, but they rated out very closely to Pendax, so they're in the ballpark," he continued.

"What's the status of the survey teams left by *Valiant*?" asked Dobrina.

"Two teams of six were dropped surreptitiously on the planet sixty days ago, and we're coming in to pick them up. If all goes well we can begin the First Contact protocol. But here's where it gets interesting," said Maclintock. "There's apparently a First Empire station orbiting the fourth planet, which is basically an airless rock. They were mining something there, but we don't know what. *Valiant* didn't have time to explore the station in detail, but they listed it as both 'abandoned' and 'operational.' Best guess is that it's been running on automatic protocols since the war ended."

"Active but not occupied?" I said. "That's curious." Maclintock nodded. He looked down the table at Lena Babayan.

"So this looks like an opportunity for your marines to stretch their legs, Colonel," he said.

"We welcome it, sir," she replied.

"Good," he said, then continued. "The Jenarus government seems to have little interest in space exploration at this time, even though they have the technology for it. They seem much more inclined to spend their capital on orbiting satellites to monitor their populace and doling out meager social programs than in exploring their own star system any further. We'll go in undercover, which shouldn't be too much trouble since they spend almost all of their time with their cameras turned on their own people, explore the station, determine its function, and then disable it before we make contact. Admiral Wesley wants no repeats of what happened to *Impulse* at Levant."

I looked at Dobrina across the table. She remained impassive but there was no doubt her feelings for her lost command still weighed heavily on her, as they did on me.

"And as for *Impulse*," continued Maclintock, "there is more news I'm afraid, for both Commander Kierkopf and Lieutenant Commander Cochrane. Admiral Wesley wants you both back on Quantar inside two weeks. There's going to be an inquest over *Impulse* called by the Carinthian Royal Navy next month, so you'll both have to be briefed before you go. I'm sure we'll find a way to get you there well ahead of schedule."

"Thank you, sir," said Dobrina, again showing no signs of the internal turmoil she must be feeling. I sympathized with her. At least I would be there for support.

"Now, back to Jenarus. Lieutenant Hogan, what's our ETA to the system?" asked Maclintock.

"Well," said Hogan, clearing her throat before starting in. "It's a much further jump than the local hops we've been making to Levant and Pendax, sir. Probably at least two days of traverse in a hyperdimensional bubble before we emerge at the other end of the line. Jenarus is forty-seven point six light-years from Quantar, a G-IV-type star, binary, six rocky planets and ten gas giants. The Jenarus system has an unusual landscape in that there appears to be a jump space tunnel within the system, which we'd like to avoid. So given all that, I'd make it a two-point-four-day traverse in the hyper-bubble, and if we emerge into normal space at the same jump point that *Valiant* did, another day to the First Empire station around Jenarus 4, sir."

Maclintock turned to Layton. "Can we avoid that jump space tunnel, Mr. Layton?" he asked. Layton leaned forward.

"I think so, sir. It could be tricky on the jump-out, though. As long as Mr. Cochrane can provide me with accurate longscope data, we should emerge near the exit of jump space and be able to leave the tunnel without incident, sir, but it could be tricky. If our HD drive is engaged at all, even one ten-thousandth of a point, we could find ourselves sliding back into the tunnel and emerging at the other end of the line," said Layton.

"And where is the other end, Mr. Layton?" asked Maclintock.

"Almost in the corona of the Jenarus star, sir."

Maclintock looked at me.

"So we'll have to completely disengage our HD drive, cool it down to zero, disengage our Hoagland Field and fire the chemical impellers to get us out of the jump space tunnel to avoid ending up in the furnace of Jenarus Prime, all within how long, Mr. Cochrane?" asked the captain.

"I'd say we have about five seconds," I replied. He looked at me incredulously. "With Serosian's help, that's practically an eternity, Captain," I reassured him. "And besides, *Valiant* did it."

He took a long draw of his coffee.

"Let's make sure *we* do it, Commander. I'm holding you responsible."

"Aye, sir," I said, confident but not cocky. I was anxious to get back into space and spread my wings some, and this seemed like an excellent opportunity.

"Well then," Maclintock said, "let's do it. The twenty-four-hour launch clock starts at 0700 tomorrow. Recall the crew and button her up by 2300 tonight. No screw-ups, and no delays, gentlemen."

"Yes, sir!" came the enthusiastic chorus all around the table. Maclintock stood and departed, and we were all left to our duties, ready to tackle the day.

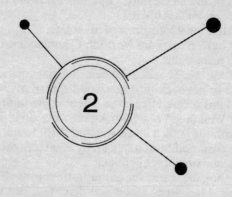

Departing Candle

Starbound's Earth Historian, Serosian, was back aboard the ship by 2100. I joined him in his library, which was also part of a separate vessel, the Historian's Yacht, to go over the last-minute upgrades to our newly trimmed-out and fitted-up Lightship.

"And what do you have to report on your work on the new longscope station?" he asked me in his distinctive baritone.

"I'm pretty comfortable with it," I said, and that was true enough. The new unit had a reduced footprint on the bridge and a drastically smaller hood. Instead of covering my whole upper body as it did before, it now had just a small cowl for me to lean into. The privacy of the displays was handled by an upgrade to my coronal overlay, which allowed me to see any display I chose, or any display the Historian chose to share with me. A casual observer without the upgrades or security clearance would just see a blank gray screen. "It makes me feel like I'm part of the command deck again, with the captain and the tactical station available and easy to talk to. Plus of course your station is more readily available." I said.

"That was one of the goals of the upgrade," he said, "but we will still be doing much of our communication through the private com and via your displays."

I nodded. "Understood. What about the new weapons systems? Any surprises there?" He shifted in his chair, seeming a bit uncomfortable at my question and perhaps reluctant to answer, but he answered anyway, at least partially.

"The primary coil cannon arrays have been upgraded to six hundred and sixty exajoules per volley, enough to shake up a continent. After our encounter with the Imperial dreadnought at Levant it was clear we were severely underpowered compared to old Imperial technology. Likewise, we've upgraded the Hoagland Field array to match, as well as the warheads on our atomic torpedoes to increase their yield. The field will now be able to diffuse the effects of any anti-graviton plasma weapons we might encounter, like those at Levant. Our pace through normal space is still limited by Newtonian physics, but we've upgraded the impellers and the sublight hyperdimensional drive output to give us quicker acceleration and more escape speed, if we need it," he said.

I was a bit disappointed at this. "What, no new super-weapon? A planet-melter or something?"

He looked at me, nonplussed by my attempt at humor. "That's all I'm willing to discuss at the moment, Peter. The rest will depend on our circumstances," he replied coolly. I eyed my friend and mentor. He was throwing up a stone wall at me, but I wasn't ready to concede just yet.

"The anti-graviton device the Imperial HuK used at Levant is the most worrisome to me. That is a potent weapon. Let's hope the First Empire didn't develop any capabilities of that weapon beyond what we've already seen," I said.

"The new field will protect the ship," Serosian said flatly. Again, I wasn't ready to concede and let him off the hook.

"But what about planets like Levant?" I asked. "Who or what will protect them?"

He shifted again in his chair.

"We have developed and deployed a drone network at Levant, Quantar, and Carinthia that will diffuse any anti-graviton energy if they try to use it on a planet," he said. "I know you have a particular interest in the welfare of Levant, Peter, but the Church has the Founder gateway device there under control and she is safe enough for now."

I wasn't sure if by "she" he meant the planet itself or its most intriguing resident, the Princess Janaan.

"Thank you for your reassurances," I said. "But that doesn't answer my question."

"No," he said, finally smiling but not giving in, "but it is all I'm willing to tell you for now."

I nodded. "Very well. I can see your stubborn streak has kicked in."

"That it has," he said, then quickly changed the subject. "So, how are things with Dobrina?" he asked casually.

The question caught me off guard. I'd been in a personal relationship with the Commander since my rehab stint on High Station Candle had ended and I'd returned to *Starbound* three months ago, but he and I had never discussed it.

"Things are . . . progressing," I said cautiously. "Are you going to be the latest to warn me off of personal relationships with superior officers?"

He shook his head. "No. In fact I'm glad you two are enjoying each other's company. Just be aware that it can't interfere with the smooth running of the ship."

"It hasn't yet," I said. "And it's been three months already."

"Three months of repair and refit," he countered. Now it was my turn to give him the steel-eyed stare.

"Do you have doubts about me, Serosian?" I eventually asked. No one out-stared *Starbound*'s Historian. Again the negative shake of the head.

"Doubts, no. But I do have a warning. Like it or not, you have two roles aboard *Starbound*, Peter. One is as a navy officer, which you handle quite excellently. The other is as a young royal representative of the Union who might be called to assume the mantle of diplomat at any time, as you were on Levant," he said.

"I understand that."

"Then please consider one other thing; you are engaged in a personal relationship with a valuable fellow officer. At any time you may be called by duty to relinquish that relationship for the sake of the Union. Are you prepared to do that?"

I thought about that. I had feelings for Dobrina, feelings of romance and respect and possibly even of love, but my standing as the heir to Quantar's royal titles was never far from my mind. "I think so," I said.

"Then also keep in mind that Dobrina has feelings as well, and though you may be prepared to sacrifice your relationship with her, she may not feel the same way about you. Tread lightly, Peter. She is still a woman underneath the uniform and the duty and the honor," he finished.

And I had nothing to say to that, so I didn't. I thanked him for the conversation and made my way back to my own cabin to rest. Alone.

⋅—•——•———•

Ship's Sunday was filled with checking in on the marines, including my friend Sergeant John Marker, who was now leading a fully integrated team of equal numbers of Quantar and Carinthian troops. Colonel Babayan had overall command (and I had responsibility over her) and her own integrated team. Together the two of them made friendly rivals. I ran the marine teams through several drills and even had them run one in their full EVA suits with the gravity off in the landing bay, deploying out of their shuttles by tether. I wasn't sure they would ever need it, but I wanted them to be prepared just in case. Deploying on the First Empire station orbiting Jenarus 4 could be tricky, and I wanted to prepare them for any eventuality.

After a couple of hours of drills I let the teams have the afternoon off, but not before heading down to the ship's firing range to get in some practice time. Usually on Sundays I was alone, but today one of the nine ranges was occupied. I checked out a coil rifle and pistol and loaded them with plasma packs before heading over to see who the other shooter might be. I found a small and scrawny young lieutenant practicing his target shooting. He immediately snapped to attention when he saw me coming, but I waved him to at-ease.

"Lieutenant . . . Daniel, isn't it?" I said.

"Yes, sir," he snapped in reply.

"Practicing your target shooting?"

"I am, sir." I paused for a second to recall what I knew of the young man. All I could remember was that he was responsible for ship's accommodations and supply, not an active combat role of any kind.

"Aren't you the ship's purser?" I said. He nodded.

"I am, sir," he repeated.

I smiled as I loaded my rifle. "What brings you here?" He hesitated at this.

"Well, Lieutenant?"

"Sometimes Sergeant Marker lets me come down and practice with the marines, sir. I like to keep my shooting skills fresh, sir," he finally said.

"So are you looking for a more active combat role?" I asked him. Again he hesitated.

"Being the purser has its perks, sir. But I've always wanted to have a combat role," he said. I appreciated his honesty.

"Well, if that's what you want, you should have come to me. I've got final jurisdiction over the marine detachments."

"Yes, sir." I looked at him again. Physically there was no way he could measure up to the marines *Starbound* had. Ours, whether Quantar or Carinthian, were the best of the best. Still, I admired his ambition.

"Let's see you shoot," I said. He activated a new target and completed ten out of ten on his first run, but missed two on the second. I set it up for a two-man challenge, pistols and rifles both, and set it for a three out of five game. I won the first two rounds in each category easily, but he showed determination and took the third legitimately before I dispatched him in the fourth round. Still, for a noncombat officer, he showed promise.

"I'll recommend to Sergeant Marker that he let you drill with the teams on your off hours, Lieutenant. But no skimping on your regular duties," I said afterward as we cleaned our weapons.

"Thank you, sir!" said Daniel, quite enthusiastic.

"You're welcome, Lieutenant," I said as I departed, making a note on my com pad to talk to Marker about him.

I turned down Dobrina's offer of an afternoon fencing match via my com, I hoped politely. Serosian's lecture was affecting me, and I was concerned that perhaps I had let things between us go too far, considering all my other responsibilities aboard *Starbound*.

I ate with my senior reports, Marker, Hogan, Layton, Babayan, and Duane Longer of Propulsion, for both lunch and dinner. Satisfied we were all ready for launch at 0700 Monday, I headed back to my cabin at 1930 hours to rest and relax before the next morning's events.

I opened my door to find Dobrina on my couch, reading her reports on a plasma display and drinking a bottle of my favorite Quantar shiraz. She was also wearing a one-piece, skin-tight black bodysuit that was no doubt designed to get my attention. That it did.

"Have I no privacy anymore, madam?" I said as I entered and then quickly shut the door behind me.

"Not today you don't," she said. "Not after giving me the brush-off on fencing."

"I was busy," I said, defending myself and taking off my duty jacket as she poured wine into a glass for me.

"Not good enough, Commander. You'll have to do better with those excuses," she said. I had the rest of my uniform off in a few more seconds, then put on a pair of casual duty coveralls and sat down in a chair as she handed me my wine from across the coffee table.

"And how was your day?" I asked her casually, like we were an old married couple. She smiled and it lit up the room, for me anyway. I found that my ability to hold her at arm's length emotionally evaporated when I got near her. I wondered if that was what love was like.

"My day was full of reports and system failures and general to-doing that should never have happened. I spent two hours down in Propulsion kicking some ass on their preflight performance drills," she said.

"They aren't ready?" I asked. "Duane Longer reported to me otherwise."

She shook her head. "Not even close as far as I'm concerned. I put Lieutenant Longer on notice. But it doesn't matter. We launch at 0700 anyway. Maclintock won't stand for anything else."

"That he won't," I said and took a drink of my wine.

"You seem pensive," she said. It was as if she could read my mind. "And I could tell you were avoiding me all day."

I circled the rim of my wineglass with my thumb, looking down at the table.

"Come on, out with it. That's an order," she said. I laughed, then sat back.

"I had a talk with Serosian today."

"Well, it wouldn't be a conversation with our esteemed Historian if it didn't involve warning you about me again, would it?" she said.

I shrugged. "You shouldn't be so hard on him. He's actually trying to protect you," I said.

"So he thinks," she replied. "I'm a big girl, Peter, all grown up. I think by now I've proven that I know what I'm doing in this relationship, as well as with my career."

"He's just concerned about my future political responsibilities, and how they might end up hurting you if we get too close," I explained. She sat back at this, increasing the distance between us.

"I appreciate his concern, but I'm well capable of taking care of myself, thank you," she said.

"I'm not taking his side, you know. Just relaying his concerns," I answered.

"And so you have. Perhaps it's time we moved on to more pleasant activities than arguing about Serosian." With that she put her glass down and came across the room. She took my glass from me, then straddled me on the chair, her hands on my shoulders. I looked up at her. She had a magic about her, though it certainly wasn't about her external beauty. It was something more, something deeper, that had its hooks in me.

"I learned a long time ago that I could get hurt in love, Peter. It hasn't stopped me from pursuing it, and it won't keep me away from you, unless that's what you want," she said. "Right now I'm enjoying every minute we have together, and I'm taking it just that way, moment to moment. Don't let Serosian worry you. Do what feels right in the moment, and we'll both be safe, and happy, okay?"

"Okay," I said. Then she started kissing me, and the body suit started to come off, and I was reminded again just why I thought she was such an extraordinary woman.

We were set and ready for launch by 0630. All of my system responsibilities checked in green a full forty minutes prior to departure. Dobrina's reports took a bit longer but we were green to go with thirty minutes to spare.

Maclintock started the launch clock at 0645.

Serosian came up to his station five minutes before the hour. I took to my longscope station and clicked into our private com channel as I fired up my systems displays.

"You're nothing if not prompt," I said sarcastically.

"There's always a critic," he said back. That made me laugh, but only for a second. Maclintock demanded a final departure report.

"All systems green, Captain," I said in response.

"Regretfully, Captain, I must disagree." This came from Dobrina, seated next to the captain at her XO's station.

"Explain, XO."

"We are green, but we are not optimal, sir. The performance of the Propulsion team has been below accepted norms for the last two ship's cycles," she said.

"Mr. Cochrane?" asked Maclintock, turning his attention back to me. I stepped away from the longscope and approached the captain's chair, looking down on Maclintock and Dobrina.

"Propulsion Officer Longer has reported both chemical impellers and sub-light HD drives are above acceptable minimums, sir. I trust that evaluation," I stated.

"But the fact is that the unit as a whole is testing out at just eighty-four percent efficiency, isn't that true, Lieutenant Commander?" said Dobrina. I took her challenge.

"Your test evaluations are correct, XO. But I prefer to measure performance by actuals, not test evaluations," I replied. Maclintock mulled this.

"Lieutenant Longer," said the captain to the slightly pudgy, ginger-haired lead propulsion officer. Longer stood and faced the captain's chair from his post one level below the Command Deck. "Can you guarantee we will outperform the XO's test evaluations in actual flight?"

Longer looked to me, and I gave him an assenting nod, guaranteeing him my support.

"I can, sir," said Longer. "XO's evaluations are based on assumptions that we cannot compensate for a filtering problem with the chemical fuel infusers, sir. I believe we solved that problem late last night."

"So you're *guaranteeing* that we will outperform the eighty-four percent threshold?" asked the captain. Again Longer looked my way. I held my gaze firm.

"Guaranteed, sir," he said.

"Good. I'll hold you to that. But as a matter of course, whenever a challenge is raised on my bridge there must be something put on the line as compensation to the winners. I propose that the loser of this little bet must provide the winners with something of value, perhaps dinner at the Cloud Room on Candle when we return," he said. That was no small bet, especially for a junior officer. The Cloud Room was expensive.

"I'll take that bet, and I'll back the lieutenant on this one, sir," I said.

"Done," said Maclintock. "And so as not to leave the XO flailing alone in the wind, I will back her side of the bet."

"Also done," I replied, eyeing them both with a smile on my face. Maclintock smiled back.

"Very well then," he said. "You have to keep your propulsion efficiency average over eighty-four percent for the duration of the voyage to Jenarus, gentlemen.

Stations!" he called out. Then we all broke back to our duties, with George Layton taking us away from Candle and making for our jump point exit from our home system.

We were good on impellers for the two light-hours it took us to reach the exit of the Quantar system, but when we started to decelerate to the jump point, our propulsion efficiency began to drop. Lieutenant Longer sent a note of it to my systems display as we slipped below our minimum. The damned infuser filters were probably clogging again. I looked over at Dobrina, who smiled and winked back from her monitoring board. I switched the com to Longer's channel.

"What are we gonna do?" he said, a bit panicky. "We're already dropping in performance."

"Buck up, man. We stay the course. Once we enter the hyperdimensional bubble we'll engage the sub-light HD drive and that will carry us through until we exit into normal space again. You'll have almost two days to fix those infusers," I said.

"But if we engaged the hybrid drive—"

"No." I cut him off, looking around the bridge to see if Maclintock or Dobrina was eavesdropping on our conversation. When it was all clear, I said, "That's our ace in the hole. We're not using the hybrid drive until and unless we *have* to. Clear, Lieutenant?"

There was silence for a moment, then, "Clear, sir."

"Good."

The hybrid drive was something I'd had Longer working on for a couple of months, a way to increase the chemical impeller drive output by running the HD sublight drive at the same time in standby mode. The impellers could then cultivate the electrons from the excess HD plasma, convert them to a gas, and run more efficiently. Basically it was a kinetic energy reclamation system. Of course there was the *slight* possibility that the resulting energy intermix could destroy the ship, but that was a less than .000086 probability. Those were numbers I was going to hold on to, for now.

Twenty minutes later, we shut down the impeller drive with our efficiency score running at 84.56 percent, barely over the bet minimum. Switching to the sub-light HD drive inside the bubble would help us, but our margin was razor thin.

Longer turned over control of ship's propulsion to Jenny Hogan at Astrogation with five minutes to go on the jump clock. She had plotted our path to Jenarus through the hyperdimensional aether, and once we jumped, we wouldn't be able to exit traverse space until we reached our destination. I quietly hoped she was as good at interstellar geolocation as I thought she was as I strapped in for the transition. We were, after all, essentially jumping blind to a point in space 46.9 light-years distant.

"All systems green for the jump, Captain," said Dobrina.

"Thank you, XO. Mr. Cochrane, a countdown if you please," said Maclintock.

I checked my board one last time. Serosian had transferred jump control to my station, I had entered Lieutenant Hogan's calculations, and Longer had the interstellar hyperdimensional drive warm. We were cruising through jump space in our own star system and preparing to enter an alternate dimension before exiting two and a half days later at a point trillions of kilometers distant, without actually traversing the space in between. It was a terrible responsibility.

I looked down at my jump controller.

"Five . . ." I counted down.

"Four . . ."

"Three . . ."

"Two . . ."

"One . . ."

"Jump!" ordered the captain.

"Jumping!" I engaged the Hoagland Drive, and colors that had never been seen filled my mind, and I found myself wondering, as I always did, if I would awaken in this life, or the next.

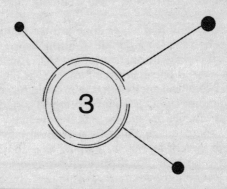

The Traverse

It seemed like days later, or seconds, I was unsure, when I came back to my senses. My mind felt like pieces of a puzzle being put back together in random order, but then suddenly there was clarity, as if some unseen hand had guided everything that made up my being back into its proper place.

I looked over at Serosian's station. His eyes were closed in deep meditation, as was his practice during jumps. I tried to focus on my board as the bridge crew started coming out of their joint trance.

The Hoagland Drive was operating in perfect sync within the protective field of the same name that kept us safe. Longer had timed the sub-light HD drive activation perfectly, and we were making .88 light within a bubble of space made of our own universe/dimension. What was outside that bubble was completely unknown, and I found myself uncurious about it. As long as the

Hoagland Drive and Field kept *my* ship safe, I was happy.

Starbound had never done a traverse this way, with extended time in a bubble of normal space while actually traveling through another space/time dimension that existed outside of the bubble. Our previous jumps had been local enough that they could be accomplished by jumping from one point in our host system to another point in a nearby star system. But the navy had discovered some time ago that the maximum safe distance for direct system-to-system jumping was about thirty-five light-years, and thus the need for long-distance traversing technology had arisen. Fortunately, the Earth Historians had just such a technology available, and had integrated it seamlessly into the Lightships at the design stage. *Valiant* was most experienced at the technique, as she was the navy's primary Survey and First Contact vessel. *Impulse* had also made a traverse or two before her untimely demise, but this was our first, and we aboard *Starbound* were proud of the opportunity.

"Systems status," demanded Maclintock of me.

"All green on my board, sir," I said.

"Tactical," he called.

"Safely inside the traverse bubble, Captain," replied Dobrina. "All tucked in for the voyage to Jenarus."

Maclintock nodded. "Just out of curiosity . . ." he started.

"I've got the visual display coming up now, sir," I said, having anticipated his request. We all wanted our first look at traverse space. The primary display on the front of the bridge wall showed a charcoal gray backdrop with faintly visible black ripples passing through it in regular waves. I ran through all our external views and they showed the same pattern.

"Well, so much for that," said Maclintock. I agreed with him. It was disappointing.

"And once again we have humanity's typical reaction

to the miracles of the universe," chimed in Serosian. The captain looked to him.

"Forgive me if I'm an aesthete," he said. Serosian shrugged.

"It's typical, Captain, as I said, and not unexpected. Beyond that barrier are sights no man should see, and miracles no man could describe," said the Historian.

Serosian's words, spoken in all seriousness, sent an involuntary chill up my spine. Maclintock just stared at the Historian.

"Thank you, Lieutenant Commander," said Maclintock to me. "That's enough for now."

"Aye, sir," I said, and shut the display off, returning to a standard systems display. Maclintock stood.

"XO, you have the con. I've got a couple of dozen novels to catch up on," he said. Dobrina rose to acknowledge.

"I have the con, aye, sir," she said. "Enjoy your reading."

With that the captain was gone off the bridge. I came and stood next to Dobrina.

"Looks like we'll have plenty of time for fencing the next two days," I said quietly to her.

"Or other activities," she deadpanned.

"Umm. Yes, well, I'd prefer to stay focused on my fitness for the moment. It makes those 'other activities' even more enjoyable," I said.

"Speak for yourself," she said, then headed off to do a station-by-station walkthrough. I smiled. I decided getting in plenty of both wouldn't be a bad way to spend the next couple of days.

Two days later, we were four minutes from exiting traverse space into the Jenarus system. I was at my duty station sweeping across my boards looking for trouble, but finding none. That made me uncomfortable. I made a quick com call down to Duane Longer.

"How are we looking?" I asked, fishing for information.

"All nominal, sir. The sub-light HD drive is scheduled to cut off the moment we break the bubble in the Jenarus system. The chemical impellers will activate automatically and propel us out of the jump space tunnel and into normal space. From there our only concern should be winning the bet," he said.

"Which you had better," I replied. "Thanks, Duane." Serosian chose just that moment to enter the bridge and take his station, firing up his board with a sweep of the hand. The confusing glut of shapes and colors were a complete mystery to me, and I was glad I'd never had to learn them.

We all buckled in with one minute to go. Maclintock turned the countdown over to Jenny Hogan at Astrogation.

"Thirty seconds," she called on the shipwide com from her second-tier station. "All systems green. When we exit jump space we will have traveled farther than any Quantar ship in more than two centuries. We are making history." That was something we could all be proud of.

I looked to Dobrina, our highest-ranking Carinthian officer, but she had her eyes fixed to her board. Although we had similar duties, monitoring systems and such, I was much more engaged in the smooth running of the systems and she much more in the application of those systems to overall ship's status. If she saw something she didn't like, it was within her prerogative to shut that system down. I didn't have that power, only the power to report problems and then to ride the lower ratings to get things running to her satisfaction.

"Ten seconds," counted down Jenny Hogan. In that short amount of time she would disengage the hyperdimensional drive and shut down our protective Hoagland

Field in the same instant, "dropping" us from a bubble of space in an unknown higher dimension and back into our dimension. Then our sub-light HD drive would cut out and our chemical impellers would kick back in, reengaging our mass in a forward motion to exit the large and unusual jump space tunnel at Jenarus. Only when we had exited the tunnel would we find ourselves totally in normal space again and able to navigate normally to the system's home planet.

I gripped the arms of my safety couch as Hogan counted down to zero. The cerebral scattering associated with entering a jump was much different than when exiting. While all of our maneuvering actions of the ship were preprogrammed, we were not. We still needed a few seconds to reassociate ourselves to our own dimension, but it wasn't as profound an effect, for some reason, as when we jumped out of our own dimension.

I was quickly on my board demanding reports. Everything looked green except ...

"Lieutenant Longer," I said. "Why is the sub-light HD drive not shut down?" I watched him scramble his hands across his board.

"Unknown, sir," he responded.

I unbuckled from my seat and was at the railing in a second.

"If that drive is still engaged we could be pulled back into the jump space tunnel, mister," I said.

"Understood, sir. The HD drive is shut down but ..."

"But what, man?" I demanded.

"It looks like residual neutrinos were generated by the full stop, sir. It kept the drive engaged for a few microseconds longer than planned, sir," he said.

I turned to George Layton at the helm. "Where are we, Lieutenant?"

Layton's hand played across his board. "Point one five three AUs further into the tunnel than expected, sir," he said.

"And what's our heading?"

"We're not in normal space, sir, we're in jump space, so it's difficult to tell, but it seems we're losing ground to the star."

I spun around and reported to my captain. "Our position is not as expected, Captain. We're still in the jump space tunnel and appear to be drifting away from the exit, sir," I said.

"How long until the impellers can pull us out?" asked Captain Maclintock. I looked to Longer, then over to Serosian.

"Uncertain that they can, sir," I said honestly. "The chemical impellers are designed to work in normal space primarily, sir. We are significantly further inside the tunnel than anticipated. Excess neutrinos generated when the HD drive didn't shut down properly appear to have displaced us from our landing point, sir."

Dobrina stood up from her station. "Are you saying that the gravimetric energy of the Jenarus star is pulling us deeper into the tunnel?" she said.

"Yes, XO," I replied. "The jump space tunnel magnifies the gravity pull of the star by a significant amount." Maclintock looked to Serosian.

"Can we survive if we exit the tunnel inside the envelope of the star's corona?" he asked.

"Very uncertain, Captain. Even with the Hoagland Field," said the Historian.

"Solutions?" asked Maclintock. The Historian shook his head.

"None readily available, Captain," he said. "The impellers aren't strong enough to fight the pull of a star the mass of Jenarus. The jump space tunnel acts as a field magnifier for the gravity of the star. The more ground we lose to the exit point, the stronger the pull will be."

"What about reengaging the Hoagland FTL drive?" asked Maclintock.

"That would actually make our situation worse. The

gravitons generated by the drive spooling process would bond with those of the star, resulting again in a magnifying effect," stated Serosian.

"And the sub-light hyperdimensional drive?"

"The sub-light HD drive generates neutrinos, which would cancel out the star's gravimetric pull to a degree, but not enough to pop us out of this jump space tunnel. It's highly unusual stellar topography," commented Serosian.

"Are you implying that this tunnel might be artificial?" asked Dobrina. Serosian nodded.

"A possibility, Commander. But it would take a lot more study than we currently have time for," he said. Maclintock stood and rubbed his face.

"So what you're all telling me is that we have three drives on this ship and none of them can get us out of our predicament?" he said.

"Four, actually, sir," I said, and instantly regretted it. Maclintock, Serosian, and Dobrina all turned their eyes on me.

"Explain, Commander," said Maclintock. I shuffled my feet and took in a deep breath.

"I've been working with Lieutenant Longer on a hybrid drive, mixing the impellers with the sub-light HD drive. I had intended to use it only if it was required to win the bet, sir," I said.

"Well, that won't happen now," said the captain. Then he motioned Longer to come up to the command deck and join us.

"Will this thing work, Lieutenant?" he asked. Longer's face went a little pale, but he answered readily enough.

"Theoretically, sir," he said. "Essentially, it's a KERS, Kinetic Energy Reclamation System. The electrons generated by the HD drive can be processed in such a way that they can be mixed as a plasma with the chemical propulsion fuel cells. Sort of like a hyped-up hydrazine fuel source. In our tests we achieved almost a fifty-percent boost in output from the impellers, sir. But there is a risk of . . . a more explosive result, sir."

The captain looked annoyed at that. "Say what you mean, Lieutenant. We don't have time for mincing words right now." Longer swallowed and cleared his throat.

"There is a twenty-one percent chance the mixture will cause a burst from the mixed plasma, sir, a sort of 'Big Bang' of energy before the plasma flow integrates and settles down. Theoretically it *should* be a powerful enough burst to get us out of this jump tunnel space, just a lot more violent than the impellers in a normal mode, sir," said Longer.

"How long will it take to hook this thing up?" asked Maclintock. Longer looked to me and all eyes were focused in my direction again.

"It's already hooked into the impeller drive, sir. Just waiting on your orders to activate it, sir," I said.

"You hooked up something that dangerous to our propulsion systems without permission?" said Dobrina to me. Her tone was even and controlled, but underneath I could see she was fuming.

"Only for testing, XO," I responded.

"Who gave you that authority?" she said, pressing.

"With respect, XO, I don't need your authority to implement process improvements to systems under my supervision. I only need permission to test those systems from the captain, and since we had no intention of using this device without proper testing, I've done nothing that I have to apologize for," I replied.

Maclintock stepped in then. "Enough. The system is in place. We don't have time to test it." He turned to the Historian. "Serosian, could you please review this thing before I light a firecracker under my own ship?"

"I can be ready in twenty minutes," he replied.

"Good," said Maclintock. "Then let's get to it. Mr.

Cochrane, you'll either be on my report or getting a commendation from this."

"Yes, sir," I said. Maclintock waved us away and we went back to our stations. I followed Serosian to his. Once he had sat down he turned to me and smiled privately.

"I hope this works, Peter," he said.

I leaned in close to him and whispered, "Me, too."

Twenty minutes later my Historian friend reported to the captain that our hybrid drive was theoretically sound. He also reported that if we weren't out of the jump space tunnel in twenty-seven minutes we never would be. We had all gathered around the captain's chair for a final conference.

"So you're saying this hybrid drive will work?" asked Maclintock.

"I'm saying that, *theoretically*, it appears to be within functional safety margins," replied Serosian. "But that doesn't insure it will operate as theorized."

"And the possibility of a plasma mix burst?"

"Higher than twenty percent, sir. But with our Hoagland Field engaged, it should be nothing more than a rough ride," concluded the Historian.

"XO?" asked the captain.

"I'm against it, sir, but it seems the performance of Commander Cochrane and Lieutenant Longer in this situation has left us no alternative," said Dobrina. That hurt.

"Sir, I have every confidence—" Maclintock cut me off with a hand gesture.

"I know you do." He turned to the fifth member of our group. "Lieutenant Longer, how long until we can fire this drive up?"

Longer shifted his feet but answered. "Seven minutes to power it up, sir. Any time after that we can be ready when you give the command." Maclintock nodded.

"Start the engines, Mr. Longer," commanded Maclintock. He turned back to Serosian.

"What will actually happen when we fire that engine?"

"Most likely the mix will result in a small bubble of HD space being created inside the jump tunnel, which will act as a medium for the mixed fuel. The resulting intermix will burst us out of the bubble, but also likely propel us more than far enough to clear the tunnel and end up back in normal space. It will be like making a mini-jump," said Serosian.

"Let's do it," replied the captain.

We all went to our stations and Maclintock ordered a lockdown of the ship. Duane Longer reported he was ready seven minutes and ten seconds after he had started his warm-up process.

"Reports," demanded Maclintock.

"All go here, sir," I reported. Dobrina likewise gave a qualified green light, and Serosian also chimed in that we were ready. Finally Maclintock turned his attention to his chief propulsion officer.

"On your mark, Lieutenant," he said to Longer.

"On my mark," called out Longer confidently. "Five . . . four . . . three . . . two . . . one . . . mark!" He hit the hybrid drive switch and the ship shook violently, lurching from side to side in a much more radical motion than the inertial dampers usually allowed. After a few uncomfortable seconds of this, things calmed again. I brought up the main analytical display to see where we were. The display flickered off for a few seconds, and we all anxiously waited for it to come back online. When it finally did, the data showed us at 2.2 AUs from our previous position and comfortably in normal space.

"All clear of the jump space tunnel, sir," I reported. Maclintock unstrapped himself and stood.

"I can see that, Commander. Good work," he said. Dobrina unstrapped and stood next to him, rubbing her neck.

"And good work on my neck as well, Commander," she said.

"Injury reports?" Maclintock asked of his XO.

"Minor, sir. We broke clear with minimal damage as well," Dobrina said.

"Lieutenant," called the captain. Duane Longer turned to face his commanding officer. "Well done. You and Cochrane will get a commendation for getting us out of the tunnel, but I'm afraid you'll be buying dinner on our next stop at Candle."

Longer smiled. "Yes, sir," he said, then looked to me. I nodded. I'm sure the smile was because he knew I would cover more than my share of the dinner bill. It wasn't something that a spacer on lieutenant's pay could normally afford.

"Request permission to dismantle the hybrid drive, Captain," said Dobrina.

"Sir, I respectfully disagree," I chimed in. "That drive just saved us from a very uncertain destiny." I was right about that. As clunky as it may have been, the hybrid drive had saved our collective asses.

Maclintock looked to Serosian, who smiled and merely shrugged from his Historian's station.

"It did indeed save us, Commander," Maclintock said to me. "But I think it needs some proving out yet. Shut the hybrid drive down and disconnect it from the main propulsion units, Mr. Cochrane. But keep it handy in case we need to hook it up again in the future."

"Sir, I have to protest—" started in Dobrina. This time Maclintock cut her off.

"I hear you, XO. But for now let's see what we can do about improving this thing, rather than just scrapping it because it *might* be dangerous," he said.

"Understood, sir," she said, accepting her captain's

decision. I could tell she didn't agree, but she was too professional to let that show.

"Carry on."

I gave Duane Longer his marching orders for the hybrid drive, then turned my attention to our original destination. The station orbiting Jenarus 4 was about 53.2 AUs inbound from our present position, which was nearly equidistant between the fourth and fifth outer gas giants of the system, planets J-12 and J-13 on the system survey. I asked George Layton for an ETA.

"I make it about nineteen hours at point four-oh light, sir," he estimated. The chemical impellers topped out at about .25 light for any 24-hour time frame, due to their limited acceleration curve. We'd have to use the sub-light HD impeller system, which should be operating normally despite our little side adventure. I took that recommendation to the captain. He pulled an old-fashioned pocket watch from his jacket pocket. It was a completely archaic instrument, but one that accompanied any captain's commission in either the Quantar or Union Navy.

"That puts us in at about 1440 hours tomorrow, ship time," Maclintock said, then repocketed the watch. "Make it happen, Commander," he finished.

And so I did.

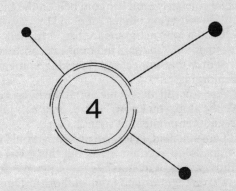

At the Jenarus 4 Station

After a day spent overseeing the mothballing of the hybrid drive and a series of maintenance issues caused by our rough exit from the jump space tunnel, I found myself soaking under a hot shower in the evening. I had begged off dinner with the command staff due to the heavy maintenance schedule, and by the time I had arrived back at my stateroom my knee and back were aching. I had apparently taken more personal damage than I had first thought from our little adventure.

After showering I sat on my sofa with a towel draped over me, rubbing ointment into my sore right knee. I had injured it a couple of times during my soccer apprentice-ship with New Briz Blues, but never hurt it enough to require surgery. I probably should have iced it, but the warmth from the ointment felt good. I tried to get to my sore midback with the same treatment, but found I couldn't quite reach the spot. Then I got an idea.

Dobrina answered her com bell on the third ring.

"You weren't at dinner," she said by way of a greeting.

"I had a long maintenance list," I replied.

"No doubt," she said in her always professional manner, "after that unnecessary shaking you gave the ship this morning."

"Are you still mad at me about the hybrid drive? I did save the ship, you know," I said, only half joking. There was another moment of silence, then:

"I am still mad, Peter. We probably would have found another solution to the crisis, but this going around my authority, it's got to stop."

"I didn't 'go around your authority,' Dobrina. I was innovating."

"Your innovation almost cost this ship dearly," she said. Now I let things hang in silence for a moment.

"You're being very Carinthian right now," I said.

"It's part of who I am, Peter, you know that. But, yes, I do believe in going by the book when in doubt. And I am still your superior officer."

"You are," I admitted, "and I respect that. But I need flexibility to do my job properly." She sighed audibly at this over the com line, then silence.

"Your flexibility—"

"I embarrassed you," I said, by way of confession.

"Yes."

I let the air hang open a bit more. "It won't happen again. You are my ally, I know that. From now on I will clear all my 'innovations' through you before I start the projects."

She still stayed silent for another moment but it eventually seemed to satisfy her. "That would be acceptable," she finally said.

"And . . . I apologize for embarrassing you."

"Also accepted. Now was there anything else? I'm still nursing a sore neck from your little experiment today," she said. I hesitated a moment, but decided to press on.

"Actually, I was hoping to trade you a bit of massage on your neck for some of the same treatment on my back."

"Ahh . . . now we get down to it," she said. Again the silence as she was considering her options.

"I could just go down to sickbay," she said.

"And they'd never be done with you. Probably insist on a brain scan," I replied.

"True."

"Plus there's the added benefit of my personal touch."

"Not sure how much of a benefit that is."

"Now, now," I said. It took me five more minutes of back and forth to convince her to come over for mutual "treatment." Our joint session lasted for over two hours, and when we were finished, all of our aches and pains had been massaged clean away.

I drilled the marines under my command for two hours in the morning until I was satisfied they were ready, as were John Marker and Lena Babayan. We went over our proposed station ingress procedures, but they were really irrelevant until we actually got to the station. *Valiant* had surveyed it, but they had not sent down any teams or probes to fully map the layout. We would be going in blind, basically, and that made us all uncomfortable. I broke off one hour before our arrival in orbit around Jenarus 4 to join Maclintock's final sitrep staff review at 1300. Colonel Babayan joined me.

Inside the Command Briefing Room all senior staff and lower department heads were present. Maclintock looked up and down the table and then started in by asking for status reports. Each system's chief gave their report until it eventually came down to the senior members at the head of the table. Maclintock turned to me for a report on the plans for exploring the station.

"We'll take both shuttles over. I've located what looks to be a landing bay, based on what the *Valiant* survey showed, but they never went inside. After that we have about three hours to do our exploration, determine what's running, what's not, and why the lights are still on," I said. Maclintock turned to Colonel Babayan.

"Do you concur, Colonel?"

"I do, sir. This is an excellent opportunity for our teams to practice this kind of operation. And we need the practice," she said. Maclintock turned next to Serosian.

"Any insight, Historian?" he said. The tall man nodded.

"Just that the configuration of this station is unusual. It doesn't follow standard First Empire designs for any known function, especially mining. There are parts of it that seem to be additions to the original configuration. If it's First Empire, it could be . . . uh, many centuries old," he said, hesitating.

"As always, caution is the buzzword for the day, gentlemen," finished the captain. "We'll go in as soon as we reach an optimal safe distance."

"Which is?" asked Dobrina. Maclintock looked to Layton.

"One thousand kilometers recommended, sir," said Layton. The captain nodded.

"Off you go then. Senior staff, please stay," he said.

We waited as the room cleared, leaving only the captain, myself, Dobrina, and Serosian. Once the door was shut, Maclintock turned to our Historian again.

"So what's with the 'could be many centuries old' statement?" he asked.

Serosian leaned forward. "My initial longscope readings indicate parts of the station could be much older than that, sir. Most of it almost certainly dates from the Early Empire period, between three and four hundred years ago. But the other data I'm getting on my scans indicate carbon readings that could be in the multiple thousands of years," he said.

"A Founder station?" I asked. He nodded.

"Possibly. Or it could be a Founder station that was abandoned and then taken over by the First Empire and used for their own purposes, modified to suit their needs. Either way, it looks to be an intriguing place."

"Or a dangerous place," said Dobrina. She turned to Maclintock. "Captain, given the likelihood that this station is active as well as of dubious origins, I recommend we move much closer than a thousand clicks. More like ten, in case we have to conduct rescue operations."

"We'll be able to handle ourselves on that station," I said. "Rescue will not be necessary."

"This is an unknown scenario," said Maclintock, turning to Dobrina. "One hundred clicks, XO. I want us close enough to act but far enough away to stay safe if something bad goes down. We'll come in for you if you get in trouble, Mr. Cochrane, but I won't be foolhardy with my ship either. Agreed?" he asked.

We all nodded assent, even Serosian. "Recommend longwave coms for Mr. Cochrane and Colonel Babayan, Captain. I can keep in touch with them if conventional communications are knocked out or blocked," he said.

"Agreed. It seems we have a plan. I want to make it clear, Mr. Cochrane, if you encounter operating First Empire or Founder technology, your orders are to survey and catalog. Don't touch a damn thing. Let's just find out what this station is and what it does. Then we can determine if it's an obstacle to First Contact with Jenarus, which is still our primary mission. Understood?" Maclintock said.

"Understood, sir," I replied.

"Then let's get to it."

I outfitted both units with hip-mounted cone jets just in case. The marines didn't like them, as they added bulk, but I felt they might be essential if we encountered any zero-G areas on the station.

We were wrapped up in our shuttles fifteen minutes prior to Layton's signal that we had obtained a geostationary harmony with the station orbiting Jenarus 4 at a distance of one hundred kilometers. I checked my standard com links with Dobrina on the bridge and then with Marker and Babayan in the second shuttle, then switched to the longwave channel and confirmed the link with Serosian. The longwave link used a lot of EVA suit power to operate. I hoped we wouldn't need it.

Right on the dot I gave the signal, and both of the marine heavy bulwark shuttles started to move, each carrying sixteen marines, a commander, and a pilot: thirty-seven personnel in all, including me. We made our way out of *Starbound*'s landing deck and into space, making for the mystery station. Twenty minutes later and we were approaching close to what we *thought* was the station's massive landing bay.

The station seemed dark and abandoned from the exterior as we approached. I ran several scans with the limited longscope technology available aboard the shuttle but got back no readings of power anywhere. I posited that this could be because of an energy-signature dampening field as a possible defense mechanism, or it could be that *Valiant* was simply wrong and the station was dead. But I doubted that *Valiant* and her Historian could miss something that important.

"Send out a probe," I ordered our shuttle pilot, Lieutenant Page. We all watched on the monitors as the probe ran over the face of the station, bouncing blue light waves off the surface both to map it and to take telemetry readings. A second later, John Marker, my marine commander, stuck his head into the cramped pilot's nest.

"Are we going in or not?" he asked in his usual gruff way. I turned to my friend, the descendant of fearsome Maori warriors.

"Not just yet, Sergeant," I said. "We're going to let the probe do its job first."

"My marines are getting bored, Commander. Best hurry it up before they start chewing on the bulkheads."

I smiled at him just a bit. He was a comrade as well as a friend, but I wouldn't let that sway me. "Station please, Sergeant," I said back.

"Sir!" he said and popped his helmet back on, disappearing back into the hold. I smiled and turned back to my shuttle pilot.

"What have we got, Page?"

"The probe has penetrated the landing bay's environmental field and made it inside, sir, holding position there. Scans indicate the deck material itself is a metal alloy in some places and an indeterminate material in others, something like ceramic. The deck has gravity, but there's no air or heat inside the bay. It's a vacuum, sir," she said.

"An environmental field but no environment? That's curious. That and the gravity field indicates there's power on somewhere inside, even if we can't detect it," I said.

"The environmental field could indicate that the bay was decompressed to vacate something unwanted, and then restored afterward, but the environment wasn't," Page said. I took in a deep breath, thought about Marker and his men back in the hold and Colonel Babayan's troops in the other shuttle, and the risks to them. Then I made my decision. "We're here to explore. Let's go explore. Take us in, Lieutenant, and order Colonel Babayan to follow."

"Aye, sir," she replied. I took one more look at the station, dark and foreboding on my display, and sighed. I hoped we were doing the right thing.

We breached the environmental barrier without incident, a static field hugging the contours of our shuttle as we came in and landed on the debris-littered deck. I watched as the second shuttle joined us, then ordered Sergeant Marker to deploy his troops.

Two minutes later and I was on the deck myself, surrounded by our units. The deck was strewn with debris, smashed machinery, and wrecked equipment panels. There were dark streaks of fire damage on the walls, as if there had been a pitched coil rifle battle here in the past. Whether that past was recent, old, or ancient remained to be discovered. The main hangar doors leading inside the station were blown off or disintegrated, with no trace of them except jagged edges of scorched metal near the threshold. It was enough to give me pause.

"I want a squad to reconnoiter that hallway. Two guards each at the shuttles. The rest of us are moving out," I ordered. Marker and Babayan barked out their orders and a squad of five went to the door threshold and then out into the darkness. The unlucky pairs of guards took their defensive positions on the shuttles, the pilots also remaining inside as a precaution. You didn't want to risk losing your way off a hostile station on a reconnoiter. The rest of us formed a single rank to enter the hallway with a squad in front, followed by Marker and Babayan, then another squad, then me, and the rest spread out behind.

After thirty seconds our original reconnoiter unit signaled it was safe for us to move up, and we did.

The hallway was broad and wide, the kind of thing you'd expect of a utility corridor designed for moving cargo, but it was massive in scale and very, very dark. The gravity was consistent with the landing bay, and near as I could tell it was close to one Earth gravity. We'd have no need to activate our own gravity units to stay stuck to the deck.

I let Marker and Babayan deploy their troops as they felt comfortable doing, following along in my place with the pack. I flashed my helmet lights on the walls, and saw that the same dark streaks of singed metal or some other material were present all along the hallway. We progressed about thirty meters at a time, taking our time to make sure we stayed together. I watched as the helmet lanterns of the marines would push forward in groups of five and then stop, being passed by a second group, and so on, until their light vanished in the encompassing darkness. After ten minutes of this I got a private call from Marker, who was running the point for our expedition.

"I'm here," I said into my private command com.

"I'm about fifty meters ahead of you, sir," started Marker. Then he hesitated. "I think you're going to want to see this."

"I'll be right there," I said. I ordered a full stop for our entire unit and then started forward alone, using my helmet lantern to illuminate the few meters in front of me as I passed by several members of the excursion squad. Up front a cluster of five marines had their lanterns running over something large blocking the hallway. Except for the lantern lights of our marines, there was nothing illuminating the hall.

I came up and pushed between a pair of marines and in next to Marker, who was closest to the object. I walked slowly, flashing my lantern over the surface of the thing, running it back and forth. After a few moments I focused on one particular area. The object was made of a dull greenish metal, covered in singe marks and the gray/green glitter of metal exposed to vacuum for too long. But what I saw was indisputable.

"Is that an eye?" I said aloud.

"Looks like it, sir," said Marker reluctantly. I ordered Babayan and another squad of five marines forward. Together we bathed the object in light with our lanterns.

It was a head. A human-looking head, but clearly made out of metal and laying on one side of its face. It had to be ten meters tall. The head was cut off at the neck, which was singed and burnt, its twisted metal protruding and sticking to the left wall. To the right, there looked to be an opening that humans could squeeze through between the head and the outer wall of the corridor.

"This is a mechanism, a humanoid automaton of some kind, but on a scale . . . it would have to have been fifty meters tall, at least," I said. Marker lit up his light to max and went to the ceiling.

"Plenty of space for it in here," he said. "The ceiling is twice that high."

"Do we go forward?" asked Babayan. I hesitated only a second.

"We do," I said. "Those are our orders. Survey and catalog." Then I switched back to the unit com and ordered the marines through the "hole" near the wall. I squeezed through behind Marker and Babayan, determined to stay closer to the front the rest of the way.

We walked through what could only be described as a corridor clearly blasted through the body of the fallen machine. We went on this way for nearly seventy meters as we weaved and ducked through the broken machinery. The mechanisms that we saw inside the "body" of the automaton were so advanced as to be indecipherable, to me anyway, and I fancied myself as a bit of a technology buff. What we were looking at was very ancient, that much was clear, and had been frozen by the vacuum of space for a long, long time. When we finally reached the end of the machine's body, we encountered something even more disturbing.

Dead bodies. Many hundreds of them, in space suits. I ordered a squad to both our left and right to investigate while Marker, Babayan, and I took our own survey, our digital recording equipment taking in as much as possible. The bodies inside the suits were black with age and desiccation, and some had undoubtedly decayed inside their suits while they maintained some environmental integrity. Others were nothing more than dead bones or large piles of ash, indicating they had been vaporized. The one distinguishing mark on all these men was the gold stripe of the Imperial Marines on their black helmets. A pitched battle had been fought here, and the Imperial Marines, the best fighters the First Empire had to offer, had lost.

Beyond the battle scene there was an empty chamber with no doors nor any other remaining mechanism.

"Reconnoiter that chamber," I ordered, more to get our marines out of shock and awe and back into action. I switched to the command com channel and took up a position facing Marker and Babayan.

"What the hell is this place?" asked Marker. I looked to both of my marine commanders, and made a decision.

"I can't tell you at the moment, Sergeant," I said.

"That's bullshit!" said Babayan, then followed after a beat with a pointed "sir."

"These are Imperial Marines," said Marker. "This battle must have happened hundreds of years ago. And that thing, that robot, what technology is that?"

I shook my head. "Again, I can't tell you." At this Babayan started to protest but I cut her off. "That doesn't mean I don't have my suspicions. I do. But I'm not authorized to share that information at the moment. Stay ready. Let's assess the situation so that we can report back to the captain." Then I ordered them off to command their squads while I switched to the longwave com and called up Serosian.

"What have you got, Peter?" came his low baritone through my earpiece.

"Just what you see from your monitors, several

hundred dead marines. Imperial Marines. There was a battle fought here, a long time ago. Are you still reading active energy from this place?" I asked.

"We are, but it is general in nature and we're unable to pin it down directionally other than to say it is several decks above you. Do you see any way to go up?" he replied.

"Not yet. And that energy field isn't showing up on any of our monitors here. Is it possible it's some form of Founder or First Empire shielded stealth tech?"

"Very possible," said Serosian. "Be cautious, Peter."

"That word is not in our vocabulary. I'll report in again when we've found a way up," I said, then dropped the line. The longwave chewed up more energy from my EVA suit than the regular com, but it also provided much needed privacy, and the signal would travel through any known stealth field.

I went up to Marker and Babayan.

"What have you got?"

"Come take a look," said Marker. I followed them both up to the chamber, which I could see was not a chamber at all but an empty lifter shaft that dwarfed what I had seen on the Imperial dreadnought we had destroyed at Altos. And that one was massive.

"Look down," said Babayan. I walked to the edge. The empty shaft went down hundreds of meters into the dark. As I flashed my helmet lantern down the shaft I could see it was filled with more dead bodies of Imperial Marines, piled on top of each other.

"Careful," said Babayan. "The shaft from this level up appears to be a zero gravity zone. If you toss something in it floats, but if you throw it just a few meters down, the gravity is active and the item will get heavy again and fall." I reached over and grabbed an empty Imperial Marine helmet and threw it down the shaft. It moved slowly against the zero-G field and then accelerated onto the pile of detritus far below once it hit the gravity well.

My next decision would be critical. If we continued up, we might find out what this battle was all about and discover the source of the energy field. Safety dictated, however, that we withdraw. I called Commander Kierkopf on the command com channel and explained the situation, which she would no doubt be aware of from monitoring our unit cams.

"Serosian reports the energy source is still active, and it's up there, on the decks above us," I said. "Request permission to proceed to the source with an exploratory squad."

"Denied, Commander," she said. "Be practical. You have one hour and forty minutes of environment left in your suits. I doubt that's enough time to properly investigate. And ancient or not, these remains give me pause. Quite frankly, they scare me, as they should you." She was taking a hard line, which I respected, and reminding me of my duty to the marines. Nonetheless, we were here for a reason.

"Request permission to take up a single squad and Sergeant Marker to at least attempt to identify the energy source, sir," I said. The line stayed silent for a moment longer.

"Also denied," she said, with a professional finality that seemed inflexible.

That upset me. We were here to explore, and my intuition told me the answers to this mystery lay with that unknown power source. "XO, we came here for a reason. If you're not going to let us investigate the energy source, then why did we come to this station in the first place?" I argued.

"I'm not convinced of the safety of this expedition, Commander," she replied. "And you and your force's safety is my primary responsibility."

"Then I request environmental supplies be sent over so that we can revise and extend our mission under pertinent safety protocols," I said. I was pressing her. With each of my requests I knew it would be harder to say no, and I wanted to find out more about what had happened here.

"The captain advises we are already pressing our schedule and deviating from our primary mission objectives," she said back to me.

"All the more reason to at least send up a small team to investigate," I said. "And quickly."

There was another moment's hesitation. Then, "My answer is still no, Commander."

Now I was frustrated. What we had discovered here merited more exploration, and since we were already here and deployed . . .

"Request the captain make that decision, sir." Now I was openly challenging her authority again, after I had promised I wouldn't. That wouldn't go over well on either a personal or a professional level. "Respectfully, sir, we are here, now. The shaft only looks to be a few hundred meters high. We can reconnoiter it in thirty minutes, max," I said, making my final case. There was no response for a good thirty seconds, then Captain Maclintock's voice came on the com line.

"Six marines," he said. "That's including you and Marker. Colonel Babayan stays with the rest of the team and implements a safety protocol. If something bad happens I want a clear path back to your shuttles. Understood, Commander?"

"Aye, sir," I said, then cut the com and started barking orders. We had our window, and I was going to make sure we took advantage of it.

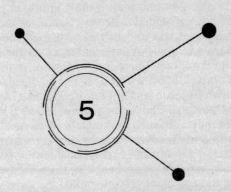

5

I let Marker pick the four marines who would go up the lifter shaft with us. Once we had gathered together at the shaft entrance I left Babayan in command and ordered a line-of-sight dispersal all the way back to the shuttles. She wasn't happy at being left out of the ascent, but we could only risk two command officers to explore the energy source, and I was definitely going to be one of those two. Besides, Marker was a great tactical fighter, and much better suited to the mission and its potential dangers than Colonel Babayan.

I looked at our team. They were all very young in appearance. Marker had picked two Quantar marines: a female private named Jensen and a male named Horlock. The two Carinthians were a female private, Verhunce, who seemed too slight to be a marine to me, and a huge male named Rosler. Rosler was darker skinned, almost like an aboriginal descendant of Quantar, the first one I'd seen among the Carinthian marines. The Carinthians tended to be very Caucasian as a rule, which I supposed was due to their Austrian roots on Earth. There was some Asiatic influence in their bloodlines from the Mongol invasions of Europe more than a millennia ago, but it wasn't as strong as the aboriginal Australian traces in some of our people, like Marker.

One thing about our marine-issued EVA suits was that they enhanced and equalized physical strength so that no marine was stronger or more capable than any other, regardless of gender, bone density, stature, or any other variable. It brought us all up to about 125% of standard so that everyone pulled the same weight, literally.

I looked to Marker. "How should we deploy, Sergeant?" I asked, deferring to his marine experience.

"Horlock's great with the jets, so he'll go first. Then Rosler, Jensen, me, you, and Verhunce," he said to our group, pointing to each of us in turn. I nodded agreement.

Horlock went out into the zero-G well first, pushing off the deck and floating up slowly a few meters. We all watched as he ascended with short micro-bursts from his cone jets. He was by far the most skilled zero-G flyer I had ever seen, maneuvering up and back down to us at will, getting a feel for the shaft and any gravitational eddies there might be. Rosler came next, and then the rest of us in order. Horlock had to slow up several times so that we could stay a cohesive unit. I did my best to keep up, but it seemed as though everyone else in the group was better at flying than I was. I even got a push in the butt from Verhunce when I couldn't get my ascent speed up fast enough.

Within two minutes we were all rising slowly but steadily up the shaft, mostly together. Despite my assurances to Maclintock, the shaft seemed to go on forever. I measured our rise at one hundred meters in the first three minutes. Then Horlock began to pull away from the rest of us.

"Hold up, Private!" yelled Marker to Horlock, who slowed, turned, and responded with a "Sorry, sir."

A second later and an energy weapon blast cut a hole in his chest the size of a football. The next shot took Rosler's head off at the neck with a precision that was frightening.

"Cover!" I yelled into the com, adrenaline rushing and my heart suddenly pounding as I pushed Verhunce down and back to the wall of the shaft. There were some metal support beams that looked like they could provide some cover from the incoming fire.

A second volley came, this time in multiple bursts, and we all scrambled to the walls, Marker returning fire as he jetted to the near side with Jensen. Verhunce and I were stuck to the far wall. I looked up and saw dark figures emerging from the mist, perhaps a hundred meters above us and descending quickly. From the glint of coil rifle fire off of their bodies they seemed undoubtedly made of metal. Automatons, and from the looks of them they could make quick work of us.

"Fire at will!" I ordered, and the shaft lit up with an exchange of brilliant orange and green rifle fire. I ordered retreat back to the shaft entrance into my com just as a green volley skimmed past my head so close I could feel the heat through my helmet visor. I tried to order the retreat again, but got no answer.

The main coms were knocked out. The automaton's energy weapons had a disruptive effect on our com equipment, like an EMP burst. Whatever these damn things were, they were highly efficient. We came under heavy fire again from the advancing automatons as they propelled themselves down the shaft from high above us. I sent Marker a hand signal, ordering him to suppress and retreat with Jensen to the shaft entrance on my mark. He signaled back negative. I repeated the order, this time with emphasis. I got a reluctant affirmative. I switched to my low-frequency backup radio transmitter, primitive but effective within a range of about ten meters.

"We're falling back," I said to Verhunce amid the flashing din of the rifle fire. "Sergeant Marker and Private Jensen will cover us. When I give the signal, you go, full out jets for the deck. And when you get there warn Colonel Babayan that trouble is coming."

"I need to stay with you, sir," she protested.

"Negative, Private. You go first. I'll be right behind you," I said. The cacophony of energy fire was lighting up the entire shaft. I looked down to the deck floor and saw marines taking up firing positions near the opening. I wanted them to retreat, not cover for us, but at this distance my low frequency com was useless. I turned to Marker and gave the signal. He, Jensen, and I filled the lifter shaft with rifle fire.

"Go," I yelled to Verhunce. I saw her push off, making for the deck, her cone jet vapor spilling into my visor's view. I signaled Marker again. Private Jensen was next. She pushed off and flew down the shaft, chasing after the weaving Verhunce. Then Marker gave me the signal and I went without hesitation, hoping that my friend was coming close behind me.

I watched as Verhunce cleared the shaft and landed on the deck. I was closing on Jensen, and looked back to see Marker in turn closing on me. I was about to order Jensen to turn her jets toward the deck to slow down when a lance of green energy shot past me.

"Shit!" I said and twisted around to look back up the shaft.

I could now see a half dozen bronze-colored automatons coming down at us, firing all the way from perhaps fifty meters back. The way they were coming, this was going to be close. I hit my jets again and shot past Jensen, grabbing her arm on the way by. "Hang on!" I said. She nodded as Marker caught up to us and took her right arm from the other side.

I nodded at Marker and we made one last course correction burst for the deck, then we both sent out max bursts to take us through the opening. About a half dozen marines, including Babayan, were standing on the deck about ten meters below us. A burst of green fire came very close to me and I flinched instinctively. When I looked back Marker was falling away from me, but still on course for the deck.

Private Jensen had been sliced in half.

I let go of her body in the shaft as I fell, heart pounding as Marker and I pierced the gravity field and fell onto the deck hard. I rolled and popped back up quickly. Babayan yelled to me over the low-band radio com.

"How many?"

"Half a dozen," I replied. "But they're very formidable." She armed her rifle. I grabbed her by the arm.

"No! We're outgunned. Full retreat, Colonel, that's an order!"

"But—"

"No!" I insisted. "Look around you! Staying is suicide." She looked around the deck at the piles of Imperial Marine bodies. Then I pushed her backward hard. She switched to the general com channel, which I couldn't hear, and ordered everyone to fall back. I sent Verhunce up ahead to prep the shuttles.

I looked back as we headed toward the path through the fallen robot. The first of the automatons was just touching down on the deck. I turned and ran.

We'd be lucky to make it out of this alive.

* ● ● ●

We dodged and ducked all the way back to the landing bay, the automatons in a deliberate and determined pursuit. The fire from their rifles frequently vaporized parts of the massive robot body as we ran through the channel. Their weapons were clearly superior to ours, as was their aim. Occasionally, they got one of my marines. My every instinct was to stop and help, or at least recover the body, but we had no time. If we did stop, we'd all be dead.

When we got to the landing bay I counted twenty-six marines, including the pilots who were firing up the shuttle engines. I'd lost ten men and women so far. Too many.

I frantically waved the marines back to their shuttles, then ran onto the nearest one. It was chaos. There was no time for grief, no time to even strap in. I ordered us off the deck immediately.

I took a quick census and found that somehow Marker, Babayan, and I had all ended up on the same shuttle in the confusion. I was heading forward to the pilot's nest where Babayan and Marker were already getting us away when I saw a green energy burst outside our window.

I looked out and saw the second shuttle, the one I was probably supposed to be on, trailing a few dozen meters behind us as we accelerated off the deck. In the next instant three beams of green energy intersected on the shuttle's hull. It was instantly vaporized. The explosive energy knocked us off our path, which is probably the only thing that saved us—a similar combined beam of energy intersected just seconds later in the space where we would have been.

"Evasive maneuvers!" I yelled. "Marker, raise *Starbound*!" Before he could even respond a second burst hit us and I found myself holding on to the bulkhead wall, but there was no longer any shuttle behind me. Marker, Babayan, and I were spinning away from the station inside the wrecked pilot's nest. The rest of the shuttle was completely gone. I looked over to see Private Verhunce also gripping the bulkhead. Somehow she was still alive.

"We've got to get out of here! Abandon the shuttle!" I ordered.

"But how will we get back to *Starbound*?" said Marker.

"We'll use our cone jets," I said. The tiny units probably had only one to two minutes of fuel left at best, but it was all we had. I pulled Verhunce off the bulkhead wall and spun her away. Then I followed suit. Marker and Babayan followed me. "Form up!" I ordered over the low frequency radio. I didn't know if they could hear me or not, but we quickly had a tight formation, spaced at about ten meters apart as the shuttle wreckage tumbled away from us.

"What direction is *Starbound*?" I asked Babayan. She read off spatial coordinates and I ordered a thirty second burst in that direction, away from the damnable station.

"Commander," said Marker after we had completed our maneuver, his voice deep and grave. "Looks like we have company."

I looked back and saw a cluster of amber dots coming from the direction of the fast-fading station, in pursuit and closing fast.

"Shit," I said to him. "If we don't get help soon—"

"Then we're dead," finished Marker.

"I sent out an automated distress to *Starbound* when we launched," said Lena Babayan. "But I don't know if they heard it through the interference those weapons put out or not."

The cluster of dots, the automatons, was closing on us. I estimated we had maybe three minutes left before they could target us.

"How much fuel do each of you have left in your cone jets?" I asked. They all replied with a different answer. Babayan had forty-six seconds, Marker twelve, Verhunce had sixteen, and I had nine. Nine seconds of fuel left.

There wasn't much else to it. If we weren't going to be rescued, then we had to find a way to survive.

"Everyone rotate and face the robots," I ordered, "but keep your fuel use to the absolute minimum." I managed to turn toward the approaching automatons with minimal effort and expending only a tiny fraction of fuel. Once we were positioned, I gave my tactical orders. We were all spread out a bit and I wasn't sure everyone was in range of the low-F radio. Once we completed our maneuvers, it was a certainty we wouldn't be.

"Each one of you relay these instructions to the next man. I won't be repeating them. By my estimate we have barely a minute or two at best before those things can fire on us. The only way to maximize our survivability is to use our remaining cone jet fuel to propel ourselves into a stagger formation, each of us a bit further distance from the last man. Keep your rifles drawn and focused on the robots. As they come into range I will open fire first and take out as many as I can. Then Marker will do the same, then Verhunce, and then you, Lena," I said.

"No," Babayan said. To my surprise she was still in radio range. "We can form a cluster and go as far as our total fuel will carry our mass."

"And then we'll be a big pile, a single target. In short, we'd be sitting ducks. No, we'll follow my plan. It gives each of us the optimal time to hope for a rescue from *Starbound*," I said.

"But you have the least fuel. You'll be killed first," said Babayan.

"I'm well aware of that, Colonel," I said. "Believe me, it's not my desired outcome, but it's what we have to do to maximize our survivability. And the more time we spend here talking about it the closer those robots get. You will carry out my orders. Sergeant Marker will begin the countdown from five."

Marker did as he was ordered, and we all fired. I watched as the distance between me and the robot cluster lengthened just a bit, but I soon expelled the last of my fuel and began drifting. The automatons compensated, then began gaining on us again. I calculated that my nine-second burst saved me about thirty seconds before they could fire on me. But that meant forty-five seconds for Marker, a bit more than a minute for Verhunce, and maybe three minutes for Babayan. It wasn't much, but I'd take it in this situation.

I aimed and charged my rifle. It looked like I had enough power for three to four ten-second bursts of coil fire. Probably not enough, and their guns had already proven they had a better range than mine, but I was going to give it all I had.

The cluster was close enough now for me to see them in individual detail. They were still ten seconds out of my range when they started firing. I attempted to dodge and dip, anything to keep their green fire off of me, and for a few seconds it actually seemed to be working. Their aim was not as good in space, it seemed.

Then a strange thing happened. They started firing past me, over my shoulder toward something, or someone, else. My guess was that it was Marker, disobeying me and coming to my aid with some kind of jet fuel reserve.

I was wrong.

"Whoo-hoo!" I heard the Maori warrior yelling through my radio. I looked up just as I fell into the shadow of *Starbound*'s Downship, a light shuttle usually used for diplomatic missions. I watched as it came between me and the robot cluster, firing away with its wing-mounted coil pulse-cannons. It wasn't close to the firepower that one of our military shuttles carried, but it was probably equivalent to two dozen marines firing in a single connected burst.

The first shot broke up the robot cluster, with amber body parts flying every which way. The rest came so fast that I had to turn away from the laser flashes. When they subsided I could see the Downship slowly floating

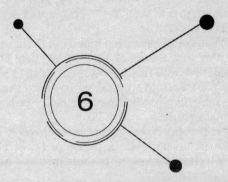

6

The man flying the Downship turned out to be George Layton. I called in by com to *Starbound* and immediately put him in for his lieutenant commander's clusters, but Maclintock said we already had our full complement, so in lieu of that, or until one of us got killed, he was promoted to Lieutenant Grade III, or Super-Lieutenant. He would be the only one on the ship wearing three bars on his collar and everyone below him would have to salute him. That plus the pay raise wasn't enough in my book, but it would have to do.

The more difficult part would be the debriefing. Maclintock would want answers as to what had happened to his marines. But before I could tell him, Dobrina got to me first. She buzzed into my stateroom com as I was changing out of my EVA suit and back into my uniform just prior to the debriefing. "Come in, XO," I said over the com. She opened the door and came through the threshold, then shut it behind her and stood across the room, staring at me. "Yes?" I prompted her as I continued dressing.

"You could have been killed out there," she said.

"I'm well aware of that. More than you know." I thought about Private Jensen, cut clean in half.

"You've got to stop taking so many chances, Peter," she said, then put her hands behind her back in a very formal gesture.

"Is that my XO speaking, or my lover?" I responded as I bent down to slide on my shoes. I wasn't in the mood for a lecture. I'd lost thirty-three men and women under my command.

Now she looked cross at me. "I'm speaking for us both," she replied. "You don't understand how much risk you take sometimes. You can be brilliant, like with that damnable hybrid drive. But other times your intuition has a price. This time it was too high a price."

I stopped. "I'm well aware of that, Commander," I said. "We left enough dead bodies on that station to remind me every day for the rest of my life." I sat there on the edge of my bed, hunched over. I put my hands to my head and rubbed my face, holding back tears. I couldn't get visions of Rosler being beheaded, of Horlock taking a deadly blow to the chest, or of Aydra Jensen out of my head. I took in a deep breath. The next thing I knew Dobrina was standing over me, her hands rubbing my shoulders and neck, trying to comfort me.

"Your intuition told you that the mystery power source was above you. You wanted answers, so you convinced Maclintock and you went. But your intuition can't tell you if that decision is good or bad, only that you're correct in your assumption. This time it cost us many lives. Most of all, it almost cost us *you*," she said quietly.

I rubbed the tears out of my eyes. She pulled me close to her, my head resting against her body while I sobbed quietly.

"My heart aches at how many we've lost, here and on *Impulse*," she said quietly. "But it would break if I ever lost you."

We stayed like that for a few minutes more. Then I stood and started buttoning up my uniform jacket. "The captain is waiting for me. He'll want answers," I said.

"He will," she replied, looking up at me.

"Then let's go give them to him," I said.

"So you were completely overwhelmed by a superior force of automated . . . robots?" Maclintock said, incredulous. He, Dobrina, Serosian, and myself were the only ones in on the debriefing, held in the command deck staff room. Marker, Babayan, and Verhunce had been sent down to console the remaining marine PFCs on the loss of so many of their comrades, more than half our full complement of sixty. I thought about that.

Thirty-three marines.

"Yes, sir," I replied, stating it as a matter of fact. "In my opinion, that base should be destroyed as our first course of action."

"That's to be determined," snapped Maclintock. "Describe these . . . robots." It was almost as if he couldn't bring himself to say the word.

"Gold in color, bipedal, similar to humans in shape, but large, two and a half meters tall I'd say. And they carried a type of coil rifle that emitted a green energy beam that was incredibly destructive. I saw marines dismembered, cut in half right through their armor and shielding, and a combined volley from just three of them destroyed both of our shuttles as we exited the landing deck. It was devastating," I finished. In addition to our regular armor, the new marine EVA suits also had a static energy field that pulsed at variable frequencies as a protection against energy weapons fire. It hadn't made a bit of difference in the firefight.

Maclintock looked to Serosian. "Are these robots an Imperial design?" The Historian shook his head.

"Unlikely," he said.

"And of course there's the fact that we discovered hundreds of dead Imperial Marine bodies, enough to nearly fill a massive lifter shaft," I interjected.

"So if not Imperial," said Dobrina, looking at Serosian. "Then what is this station?"

The Earth Historian clasped his hands in front of him, looking pensive. He clearly didn't *want* to answer the question, but his duty to us demanded that he did. We all watched him, waiting for an answer.

"There are stories, myths really, that at the end of their cycle of time, the Founders created an advanced group of machines to conduct much of their menial labor, deep-space exploration, even military missions. It is also said of these myths that these machines had much to do with the Founders' downfall. We have never encountered functioning machines of this kind before, and what we do have is just bits and pieces of technology. It's almost as if when the machines turned on their creators, the Founders had some sort of self-destruct they activated as a fail-safe. This has left very little trace of the technology of these machines," he said.

"And you think these robots could be an active remnant of those machines?" asked Maclintock.

"The description fits. It seems likely," admitted the Historian.

"You know, I don't care about any of this. I just care that I lost thirty-three marines, and I want that station destroyed to keep that from ever happening again," I said, rather pointedly.

"You need to keep your emotions in check here, mister," said Maclintock. "Those marines were under your command. I'm not blaming you directly for their deaths, but their lives were your responsibility. You'd do well to set your emotions aside for the time being and try to think and behave rationally, like a senior officer should."

That stung. I took a deep breath. "Aye, sir."

"This station could become a very valuable artifact for our research into the Founders and what destroyed them," said Serosian. "Clearly at some point in the past the First Empire tried to take over the station."

"And failed," said Dobrina. She tilted her head toward me just slightly, a show of support in her body language, then looked past me to the captain. "I'm inclined to agree with Commander Cochrane, sir. We should destroy this station," she said to Maclintock.

"But it could be invaluable," said Serosian in an argumentative tone. It was as emotional as I'd ever seen him. "We could learn how to avoid the mistakes the Founders made, critical mistakes." Dobrina was about to respond when Maclintock raised his hand to interrupt the debate.

"I appreciate your position, Mr. Serosian. But the fact is that we have thirty-three dead here. That station is a menace, and I'm ordering its destruction. The only question is how," said Maclintock.

"It's quite a massive thing," said Dobrina.

"And likely hardened against atomic attack or energy weapons," added Serosian. I could see he was upset about losing the station, but that he also understood that this was Maclintock's decision.

The captain looked at me. "Suggestions, Commander?" he said, giving me another chance. I appreciated the act. He didn't have to consult me, as I was the lowest ranking officer present.

"We could tow it into the jump space tunnel and let its mass suck it into the Jenarus star," I said. Serosian shook his head.

"We would have a power curve issue with that maneuver," he said.

Maclintock eyed the Historian. "I understand we

went through several weapons upgrades during our stay at Candle. Care to share any of the new technology we've added?"

Serosian looked reluctant to answer. Then: "There is one possibility," he said. We all waited for him to continue, but his silence said volumes. I knew this meant he didn't want to share a new weapons technology unless he absolutely had to.

Maclintock leaned back deep in his chair. "I'm waiting, Historian," he said quietly. Serosian looked at me.

"I'll need the commander's help to deploy this technology, Captain. And I would prefer to wait on discussing its function until it's ready for use," he said.

Maclintock nodded, then looked at me. "Work with him, Commander. Then report back to me when you're ready to move."

"Aye, sir," I said. Maclintock stood abruptly and strode out of the room. Dobrina followed him without a word to me.

"I appreciate your help on this, Peter," said Serosian. I looked at him. Thirty-three marines. This was grim business.

"Let's just get this done," I said.

Twenty minutes later we were ensconced in Serosian's quarters, which was in actuality part of an entirely separate ship from *Starbound*, the Historian's yacht. That fact, however, was not known to the vast majority of the crew, and Serosian much preferred to keep it that way. The yacht had served us well during the *Impulse* incident at Levant, functioning as both a rescue vehicle and a diplomatic vessel, and in the end a warship in the fight to save our doomed sister ship. We were a full deck below the public spaces of his quarters, inside the command deck nerve center of the powerful vessel.

Serosian motioned to a chair at the main console and I joined him as he activated the main viewing display, a full three-dimensional holographic projection that took up the entire forward wall of the yacht's command deck. On the screen there appeared a set of what looked like 2-D schematics to me, though what technology was being represented I couldn't be sure. There were some electrical symbols I recognized but others I had never seen before. I wasn't unfamiliar with technical drawings, especially of electrical interfaces, but this one baffled me.

"What am I looking at?" I blurted out as Serosian swept his hands across the smooth display console, his fingers sinking under the surface as if it were liquid, though he had never pulled back a wet finger from the console that I had ever seen.

The technical schematics on the screen dissolved and were replaced by a three-dimensional representation of parts in an exploded view. There were perhaps two dozen. Then just as suddenly they swarmed together and formed a completed unit. It looked for all the world like a small, flat, metal box with serrated edges and what I could only describe as a toilet plunger sticking out of one end. After a few more finger swipes by Serosian, the projection of the device started rotating.

"What am I looking at here?" I repeated. Serosian leaned back in his couch and looked at me pensively, one hand to his face, as if trying to decide if I was worthy to receive the Knowledge of the Gods or not.

"In the simplest terms," he finally said, "it's a gravity accelerator."

"A what?"

He sat up. "A gravity accelerator. As in, a device that increases the gravitic energy within a specified harmonic field. It can be used in a variety of ways. One use would be to slow down or redirect an enemy by increasing the gravity field around a specific moving object, such as a ship. Another would be to use the field to push objects in a specific direction by projecting a higher gravitic field toward it, like a wave of gravity moving an object. A third use would be as an enveloping plasma that essentially increases the weight of an object, eventually crushing it," he said.

"Impressive," I replied. "How do you propose we use it in this instance?"

Instead of answering he swept his fingers across the board again. A second later, a thin filament of plasma raised up on the console in front of me. I took in the small object; it felt like a thin slip of paper with a laminated surface between my fingers. I swept my hand across it, and it grew in size concurrent with my motion. Then it lit up with letters and illustrations. I recognized the forward coil cannon array.

"Installation instructions?" I asked. He nodded.

"I'd like your help. It should take no more than thirty minutes for each of the two cannon ports," he said.

I swept the sheet back down to its original size and then stuck it in my jacket pocket.

"Let's get started," I said. He nodded to me and we were off.

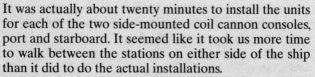

It was actually about twenty minutes to install the units for each of the two side-mounted coil cannon consoles, port and starboard. It seemed like it took us more time to walk between the stations on either side of the ship than it did to do the actual installations.

I was shocked by how small the units were, and how light. Serosian wouldn't tell me if they were Founder technology or Imperial, but the units were clearly more advanced than anything we in the Union could produce. Once they were installed we headed for the bridge and I took up my station under the longscope.

"Check your displays," came the Historian's baritone

voice. "You should find a new icon for the gravity weapon."
I found the icon quickly in my menu and dragged it onto
my main display with a finger. The display popped up with
three options, two of which were dark. The one that was
available for me to select was entitled "Gravity Projector."
I tapped it and it opened a full set of options on the right-
hand side of my display.

"So we're going to be using the gravity projector?" I
said, as casually as I could.

"Obviously," he replied in my ear com. "Now activate
the system and let me know when it reaches nominal for
use." I did as instructed. It took less than ten seconds to
fully power up.

"That was fast," I said into my com. To my surprise, he
replied.

"One of the advantages of pulling in energy from a
higher dimension," he deadpanned. I opened my mouth
to ask him another question about that subject, but then
decided against it. This was ship's business. I could satisfy
my curiosity later.

"Time to conference with the captain. Lock down
your display and join us in the command staff room,"
Serosian said. I did as instructed, arriving just a few seconds after Maclintock, Serosian, and Dobrina.

"Report," said the captain as I sat down in the chair
nearest the door. He was anxious. Serosian responded.

"The weapon I've authorized for our use in this cir-
cumstance is a gravity projector. Using the forward coil
cannon ports, we will be able to activate a field of gravimetric energy and project it onto the station, essentially
bombarding it with a field of heavy gravitic energy that
will push the station down to the surface of Jenarus 4.
The station will be destroyed and as a result the entire
Jenarus system should be safe again for the Union Navy
to explore," he said.

"And what if the robots on the station protest?" asked
Dobrina. Serosian shook his head dismissively.

"That shouldn't be a problem. That much G-force would render an energy weapon useless. It will be completely enveloped by the field. There is virtually no chance of a retaliatory strike from the base."

Maclintock looked to me. "Are you comfortable using this technology?" he asked. I shook my head no.

"Of course not, sir. You're putting the power of the Gods in my hands. But I know my longscope, sir, and I know Mr. Serosian will effectively guide me through its use," I replied respectfully.

Maclintock nodded at this. "How long until we can be ready?" he asked the Historian.

"We're ready now," replied Serosian.

"Very well," said the captain. He turned to Dobrina. "Set ship's status on yellow alert, be prepared for anything that might throw a curveball into this."

"Aye, sir," she replied, then got up to leave. Maclintock looked to Serosian and me.

"The XO and I will be monitoring your com link. Let us know the minute there's any sign of a problem," he said.

"Aye, sir," I answered. Serosian merely nodded. With that, Maclintock and Dobrina were gone back across the hallway to the bridge. I stood next to Serosian.

"Ready when you are," I said. He only nodded in response.

Five minutes later and Serosian signaled our readiness to the captain. At his signal Dobrina abruptly stood and called *Starbound* to yellow alert. There was a flurry of activity as individual officers and combat teams moved into place, activating weapons and defense systems that had previously been dormant. The crew of *Starbound* was ready to go to battle at a moment's notice.

Maclintock stood and gave the orders. "Set all

displays, scanners, and telemetry systems to monitor the station. Be prepared to go to battle stations at my command." He let that sink in as the main viewing plasma display switched to a real-time view of the space station in orbit over Jenarus 4, a good thousand clicks away from us. "Mr. Serosian," said Maclintock, turning to the Historian after he was satisfied with preparations, "will you need us to move closer?"

Serosian shook his head. "We're well within this weapon's range," he replied. Maclintock sat back down in his chair.

"Then you have the bridge, sir," he said. Serosian nodded to me and I took up residence under the longscope hood, activating my stealth protocols so the bridge crew would not overhear my conversation with the Earth Historian.

"Power up the projectors," came the first command from the Historian through my ear com. That was simple enough, I hit the "POWER" icon and watched it fully charge again.

"Set your 'scope monitor to long range and calibrate for the station," came the next. I did as instructed. Nearly a thousand kilometers distant, the image of the space station appeared in my viewer, crystal clear. I made a mental note to one day ask my tall friend how this device actually worked.

"Now begin the power transfer to the projector system. Bring the power up gradually, no more than ten percent every five seconds," he commanded.

I did as I was told, sliding my finger from left to right on the display, a virtual power bar moving with my motion. I monitored my pace as the power output increased, taking slightly less than a minute to reach full capacity. I watched on my viewer as a glittering wave of plasma shot out and impacted the station. It began an almost imperceptible movement on my screen, slowly accelerating as my viewer tracked it.

"It's moving," I announced.

"Affirmative," interjected Dobrina. "We're monitoring it out here as well. Telemetry makes the acceleration five hundred meters per second."

My telemetry told me the same thing, but I chose not to acknowledge it verbally. The acceleration continued on an ever-increasing curve. After two minutes it had doubled its pace. Another minute and it had doubled again, and so on.

Five minutes in and the station, still as big as ever in my longscope viewer, was showing signs of distress, her outer members curling in at the force being exerted on her. One thing was for sure, whatever was inside that station now knew they were in imminent peril.

"You may begin the countdown to impact," came Serosian's calm voice in my ear. On my display a counter popped up, rolling down rapidly.

"Two minutes to impact," I announced. Dobrina repeated the same to the crew. This proceeded apace until the one-minute mark. The station was starting to glow.

"Is that atmospheric contact on the station?" asked Maclintock.

"No," came Serosian's quick reply in my ear, and the warning in it was evident. "Jenarus 4 has no atmosphere."

When I looked down on my screen I was alarmed. The telemetry showed me something familiar, a wave pattern I had seen once before, at Levant. "There's a hyperdimensional displacement wave building from within the station!" I said urgently.

"Red alert!" called out Dobrina. "Screens and shields! Activate the Hoagland Field!" she commanded.

"What is it?" demanded Maclintock.

"That wave is not a weapon, Captain," said Serosian in a concerned voice. "It is far more dangerous. I believe the station has a hyperdimensional jump point generator spooling up for activation. At the rate it's generating, it will be active before the station hits the surface."

"Do we care if they jump away?" asked the captain.

"We care because we're gravitationally locked with that station. If she jumps, we could get drawn away with her as well!" said Serosian urgently.

"Can't we just cut off the gravity projector?" asked Maclintock.

"Not with the Hoagland Field operating."

"But if we're unprotected—"

"Yes, Captain, the resulting displacement wave could hit us unshielded."

"Thirty seconds," I said into my com. *Starbound*'s command crew had that much time to make a life-or-death decision. I knew from my experience at Levant what an HD displacement wave could do to an unshielded Lightship.

"How long to reactivate the Hoagland Field if we shut it down?" demanded Maclintock of Serosian.

"Eight to ten seconds," replied the Historian.

"And to shut down the gravity projectors?"

"Five to seven seconds."

"Disengage the Hoagland Field!" demanded the captain, rising from his chair.

I did as ordered. "Hoagland Field shutting down. Twenty seconds," I reported. We couldn't guarantee that there was enough time left to shut down the gravity projector *and* spool up the Hoagland Field. I looked down at my display for options . . .

"Shut off the projector!" shouted Serosian in my ears. I hit the cutoff switch to the coil cannon array and the power levels dropped achingly, second by second, to zero. The link to the station was broken.

"Ten seconds, gravity projector at zero," I reported.

"Refire the Hoagland Field!" ordered Maclintock. It was going to be close . . .

"Peter—" It was Serosian's voice, but I would probably never know what he was going to say, as his voice was cut out by blaring static in my ear com. On my viewer the space station blinked out of our dimension, traveling to parts unknown. The displacement wave was visible as a flash of white light, all-encompassing, and potentially destructive even for a fully shielded Lightship. For an unshielded one . . .

"Brace for impact!" yelled Dobrina.

I did as I was trained to do, crouching at my station, my heart pounding in my chest, saying a silent prayer to Gods I never talked to that the Hoagland Field would come up in time.

7

A minute later I had managed to get myself up off my ass and back to my longscope station. *Starbound* was still in one piece, and the space station where so many of the men and women under my command had died was gone from Jenarus space, hopefully for good.

Dobrina was doing her job, moving rapidly around the bridge, going from station to station, demanding reports on damage, injuries, and systems status. Maclintock was at his chair, the calm in the center of the storm. Serosian was busy poring over a data stream of telemetry on his viewer that was incomprehensible to me. I, for my part, gave my final situation report to the captain.

"The station has left the Jenarus system, sir. No sign of it or its HD signature on any of my monitors, sir," I said.

"Good riddance," replied Maclintock. A few more minutes passed before Maclintock was satisfied that we were really back to normal with no serious casualties, or at least back to nominal. The displacement wave had hit us but we were lucky, or at least good enough at our jobs that the Hoagland Field rebooted in time to protect us from the more harmful effects of an HD displacement wave. Effects such as, for instance, a horrible burning death.

After another ten minutes, Serosian, Dobrina, Maclintock, and I were back in the staff room, there to discuss what had just happened. Dobrina reported first.

"The energy weapons array is offline, thanks to Lieutenant Commander Cochrane. Coil cannons, cutting lasers, antitorpedo batteries," she stated. Maclintock looked to me and then back to his stoic XO.

"What do you mean, offline?" he asked. Dobrina gave me a quick glance, then continued.

"The commander shut down the entire energy weapons array, sir, to zero, rather than just shutting off the gravity weapon," she said. "The result is that those systems have all gone cold and have to be refired from zero, sir."

"How long will that take?"

"Eighteen hours is the standard protocol, sir," Dobrina said. Maclintock turned to me.

"Why?"

I straightened up in my chair. "Sir, shutting down the entire energy weapons array saved us approximately three seconds. As the situation was, we couldn't guarantee that the gravity projector would completely shut down in time for us to refire the Hoagland Field," I stated. Maclintock looked to Serosian.

"He's correct," said the Historian. "By taking this action he saved the ship almost two point eight seconds, enough to guarantee that we would have our Hoagland Field back up before the displacement wave hit. It was a viable option."

"But not one you presented to me," said Maclintock. Serosian merely nodded. Maclintock turned back to me.

"On what initiative did you take this action, Commander?"

"On my prerogative as longscope officer, sir. Under the circumstances I have the authority to take unilateral action to protect the ship. Also, technically, the longscope officer reports to the Historian, sir. Not to you," I said, taking a page from Dobrina's book and staying as stoic and professional as I could.

"But you left the ship defenseless," stated Dobrina.

"I deemed the immediate threat of the HD displacement wave to be our greatest concern, XO," I replied. She crinkled her nose a bit at that, but said nothing more. Then Maclintock chimed in.

"You're correct, Commander, you do have the authority to take unilateral action when the ship is in danger, but a bit of advance warning would have been appreciated," said Maclintock.

"Understood, sir," I said.

"In the end, you did the right thing for the ship, Commander Cochrane. But we're in a tough position without our energy weapons array." He turned back to Dobrina. "You may as well get started with the refire, XO. In the meantime, what other defenses do we have available?"

"Our full complement of two hundred atomic torpedoes, sir. Plus some kinetic energy weapons that we could roll out of mothballs," she said. He nodded.

"Proceed with preparations on all fronts, XO. We are still in what is possibly hostile space and we are severely down on armament. I want all our torpedo tubes loaded and ready to fire at a moment's notice. No telling what else may be lurking out there. And maintain yellow alert, but stand down from battle stations."

"Aye, sir," she replied.

"What's the condition of the Hoagland Field?" he asked her.

"Lieutenant Layton tells me that we came out okay, but suffered some system overloads. She's running at sixty-five percent efficiency at the moment, but the lieutenant says she'll likely need service again when we get back to Candle," said Dobrina.

"Christ, we just left there!" said Maclintock, clearly frustrated. "How long for service on the field?"

"He recommended two weeks at Candle, sir."

Maclintock swore again and then turned to me.

"Last point of business, Commander. I'm relieving you from your shift for the rest of the day and confining you to quarters. You've been through a lot in the last twenty-four hours. I want you to rest and recuperate and do nothing else until your regular shift begins in the morning," he said. "Hell, you can get drunk if you want to. But I want you to *rest*, Commander. Understood?"

I shook my head negatively. "Am I being punished, sir?" I asked. Now Maclintock shook his head.

"No, Commander. I'm only thinking of giving you time off to process all the recent events on this mission. I know if I don't force you, you won't take the time. But I insist that you do. I hope it will give you a better perspective in the morning," he said.

"Aye, sir," I replied. Maclintock turned to the silent Serosian. "Anything to add to the proceedings, Mr. Serosian?"

The Historian looked at Maclintock. "Just that Commander Cochrane's actions did save us precious time and possibly saved *Starbound* from serious damage and heavy casualties. And I did not think of his solution myself in the crisis. He should be commended for that."

"Noted," said the captain, then looked once more around the room. "If there's nothing else?" No one said anything more, and I certainly wasn't going to open my mouth again. "Dismissed," he said with a nod, then everyone stood and left the room, except me. I lingered a moment, sat back down, put a hand to my head and sighed. I was tired.

I spent most of my afternoon off napping while the rest of the crew got us underway back to the Jenarus jump space tunnel. I dreamed of Horlock and especially Private Jensen. Her death disturbed me. I'd never been touching a person at the moment they died, even through an EVA suit. Deaths had happened at the Academy, and in the military it was always a possibility. But I'd never been this close, physically, and my dreams were haunted with how her body felt in my hand. One instant vibrant and alive, the next cold and unmoving.

I shook myself out of my disturbing slumber and made for my cabin workstation. I scanned through my duty reports on the ship's com system, but nothing really required my attention. After our altercations and such heavy human losses, the First Contact mission here at Jenarus was on hold until *Starbound* could get repaired. Again.

I was about to order dinner when I got an entry request chime at my cabin door. I looked at my watch to confirm that the day shift had ended. I figured it was Dobrina, but the last thing I wanted was her company, especially if it came with a lecture. I went to the door and hit the wall com, using the privacy protocol that kept the two-way visual display off.

"Not now, Commander. Let me lick my wounds in private," I said. There was a pause before the reply, and it wasn't Dobrina.

"Request you open the door, sir." It was the deep and scratchy voice of my friend John Marker. I opened the door to see both him and Layton in the hall. "Thought you might need some cheering up, sir," said Marker, holding out a dark amber bottle that had no label. I nodded to them both.

"Come in, gentlemen," I said.

We gathered around my sparse table and Marker poured into three glasses I pulled from my display cabinet. They'd been one of the many gifts I'd been given on my graduation from the Lightship Academy, what seemed like ages ago. Marker raised his glass. Layton and I followed suit.

"To our lost comrades, proper marines, all," Marker said. "May we fare as well when we die." I recognized the unofficial Marine motto.

"May we fare as well when we die," Layton and I repeated in unison. Then we clinked our glasses and drank. It was Quantar scotch, and it was harsh and bitter, much like we all felt, I was sure. I looked at my two companions, young men who had attached their military careers to my own. Right now it seemed like a questionable choice to me.

"I assume we'll get replacements when we arrive at Candle, sir?" asked Marker in a quiet tone. I nodded.

"Replacements, as well as new shuttles," I said.

"We can replace the numbers, but not the people," Marker said. Layton nodded in agreement. A silence descended on us then, each of us in turn thinking about the losses we had suffered.

"How well did you know Private Jensen?" I asked Marker, breaking the silence. He took another drink of his scotch before answering.

"Aydra? Well enough. She was energetic, there was a real spark about her. She was good at everything she tried. First class. I told her more than once she should aspire to be more than just a grunt, but she loved it. Loved the training, the physicality of it," he said. Then his gaze got distant and his eyes turned red.

"Something more, John?" I asked gently. He drank again before replying.

"She was a vibrant lover, sir, and I'm not ashamed to say it."

"You shouldn't be, John, we're all human."

"Her more than most," said Marker. "I try to minimize my associations with women under my command, but she was ... something special, and damned insistent!" He cracked a pained smile and then emptied his glass. I thought about her last moments, John and I holding her by either arm as we struggled to get down the lifter shaft to the station deck, away from the automatons ...

"How are Colonel Babayan and Verhunce handling it?" I asked. Marker shrugged.

"Lena's a stone wall. Verhunce is tough, but we're all suffering a good dose of survivor's guilt," he said. I hadn't had any time yet to sort through my own feelings of guilt and remorse, but the scotch was quickly forcing them out. I drained my glass before continuing.

"Keep me apprised of their performance. And best to put Verhunce on light duty for a while," I said.

"Already done," replied Marker.

I put my empty glass down on the table, my buried feelings coming at me now regardless of my desire to resist them. I was glad I was with not just fellow officers, but with friends. I rubbed my hands through my hair, looking down at the table as if I could bore a hole through it with my eyes.

"This is dirty business. Thirty-three dead out of thirty-seven ..." I trailed off as the impact of those numbers started to hit me. Thirty-three men and women under my command, dead. Thirty-three people who had lives just like Private Aydra Jensen, or Private Kevin Horlock, killed in a fight that we probably never should have started by going up that shaft. Killed because I wanted to explore a possible Founder Relic, to satisfy my own curiosity.

"It's my fault," I said, sighing and leaning back in my chair. "We never should have gone up after that power source."

It was the usually quiet Layton who took issue with my self-loathing assessment. "We're out here to explore,

Peter. Finding out what was happening on that station is what we were all trained to do. You followed protocols and you followed orders," he said. I shook my head.

"All those dead Imperial marines . . . it should have been warning enough," I protested, then sighed again and took the bottle, pouring us all another drink. I continued with my pity party.

"I trust my intuition too much and I don't think practically, and I'm impulsive. This time thirty-three marines got killed," I said.

"You're too hard on yourself," said Marker after emptying his glass a second time. "If it wasn't us, then another ship would have explored that station, a ship likely not as capable as *Starbound*. Serosian's weapons helped us to clear that thing out of here. Now Jenarus is safe. A less capable ship led by less capable officers could have been destroyed, with all hands lost. It hurts to lose so many men and women that I've trained myself, but it's a better outcome than the alternative."

I grudgingly accepted Marker's words as I drank again. He was probably right. A Royal Navy frigate or destroyer wouldn't have been capable of pushing the station toward the surface of Jenarus 4 and forcing it to bug out with the jump point generator. It was small consolation.

"And I think you're forgetting that you may have saved us again today by shutting down the energy weapons array," said Layton. "That wasn't an easy decision. Many times you guess right. And mostly you end up saving someone's life. You have a gift, Peter."

"Do I?" I said. "Or am I just lucky? And will my luck run out soon?" Layton shook his head at that.

"What did you test out at in command school for intuition?" he asked. I hesitated. Only the Admiralty had that information, and me, of course. The testing was required for any officer deemed capable of one day commanding a ship in either the Union or Quantar Royal

Navy. Some said it was the navy's deciding factor in promoting a candidate. These men were my closest friends in the service and in many ways their lives might depend on decisions I made in the future, so in a way they had a right to know, but still, I hesitated.

"C'mon," said Marker, "spill it!" Whether it was the scotch loosening me up or not, I had no way of knowing, but:

"Eighty-four point six," I finally said.

"Jesus Christ!" Marker exclaimed. "You're practically psychic!" The navy didn't officially believe in psychic abilities, but still . . .

"The average is fifty-three point two," stated Layton. "I scored in the fifty-seventh percentile and they gave me command of an entire cadet team! How in the hell can you be *human* with an intuition score like that?"

I thought about that a moment. Maybe genetic traits had fallen in my favor, but I never considered myself better than my friends nor anyone else I served with. And I certainly felt all too human under the current circumstances.

"It didn't help us at the station, did it?" I said. Layton waved me off.

"If I was you," continued Layton, "I wouldn't consider anything *but* my intuition when making command decisions." I shrugged at that.

"I'm still likely to make a mistake fifteen times out of a hundred," I said.

"I'll take those odds any day. Next time we get liberty at Artemis I'm taking you with me to the gaming tables," said Marker.

Then he poured again and we consoled ourselves with stories about the dead marines. Marker knew each one by name, and we remembered them all. By the end of the evening we had gone through dinner and the entire bottle of scotch. I pushed them both out of my cabin at midnight, making sure to take a hangover pill before I crashed down on my bed, not bothering with the covers. Tomorrow was another day, and I would get to return to my duties, for which I was glad. Even the unpleasant ones.

The alert claxon woke me at 0318. I jumped up from my bed stone-cold sober thanks to my meds and grabbed my uniform jacket, quickly pulled on my boots, and straightened my hair in the mirror. Then it occurred to me, was I even on duty?

I called up to the bridge and immediately got Maclintock. "Don't bother asking," he said. "You're reinstated early, Mr. Cochrane. Now get up here."

"Aye, sir!"

I ran out the door and down the hall toward the main lifter, pulling on my duty jacket as I went. I saw Dobrina coming out of her cabin as I ran, and slowed to meet up with her. "Know anything?" I asked.

"Not yet," she said, pulling on her own jacket and then sealing it with a motion of her index finger. I followed suit as the lifter made its way up to the bridge. We were both nearly presentable when the lifter doors opened.

The bridge was on yellow alert. Maclintock was at his station but dressed in just his duty shirt, slacks, and boots. I glanced at Serosian's station, but it was dark and quiet. Dobrina made for the XO's station, but Maclintock motioned me to the longscope.

"If you please, Commander," he said. I fired her up and got under the hood as quickly as I could. "Long-range scan please, Mr. Cochrane. Approximately fourteen AUs toward the jump tunnel," came the captain's voice through my ear com. I did as instructed.

The bridge quickly started filling up with day shift personnel. Layton, Jenny Hogan at Astrogation, Duane

Longer at Propulsion. We had a full crew by the time my 'scope focused and sharpened. I ran a deep-field scan.

"Scanning, sir," I said.

"I'm here as well," came Serosian's welcome voice in my ear. "Monitoring from my quarters, Captain."

"Very good. Let us know when you have something, Mr. Cochrane," said Maclintock. I acknowledged while my scan continued. It took about thirty seconds for the longscope to pick up two targets in the infrared spectrum.

"Two targets have emerged from the jump tunnel, sir, holding in place in our path. By displacement they're similar to the HuK we encountered at Levant," I stated.

"These are of a more modern design, however," said Serosian through the com. "Likely about one hundred and eighty years old, by my guess. They are similar to a known design from our archives but they appear to have some modifications."

"Manned or unmanned?" asked Maclintock.

"Automated," replied Serosian. Maclintock cursed.

"Search and destroy mission, again," said the captain. "How long until intercept?" They were 14.6 AUs distant from us, but we were traveling on full HD impellers, almost .96 light speed.

"I make firing range in one hundred and twenty-seven minutes, sir," I said.

"And if we slow down?"

I readjusted my calculations. The news was not good.

"According to their specs, they'll catch us in three-point-four hours on their full impellers even if we stopped and reversed course, sir," I reported.

"And they're in our way. They know we have to get to that jump tunnel, so they're content to wait for us to get there," said Maclintock.

"Yes, sir," I said, having nothing to add to my acknowledgment.

"Energy weapons status?" Maclintock asked.

"Minimum six hours to complete the bootup, Captain," said Dobrina through the com. Maclintock sighed heavily, then made his decision.

"We go forward, then," he said. "And hope our torpedoes don't let us down."

All division heads were present at the strategy session fifteen minutes later in the briefing room. Myself, Dobrina, Serosian, Layton, Marker, Babayan, Jenny Hogan, and Duane Longer were all spread out around the conference table. As I looked down at them I was reminded of how young we all were. I wondered if this was part of the Grand Plan, to populate deep space not with experienced local spacers, but with young, fresh minds that could be open to the possibilities of newly rediscovered civilizations, and perhaps their technology as well. It was a subject that would have to wait for one of those rare times when Serosian and I could share an evening in conversation rather than making battle preparations.

Captain Maclintock gave us the sitrep. "The situation is that we will face a well-equipped and heavily armed enemy attack force in less than two hours. We are at a disadvantage with our energy weapons array down, so anything we can gain before we engage them is to our benefit. Ladies and gentlemen, I want to hear from each of you as to what your department might bring to the table. I'll start with you, Mr. Cochrane," said Maclintock, looking to his right at me.

He chose me first because as third in command I had direct reports from all of the department heads sitting at the table, and a few more who weren't here. Dobrina would be in charge of ensuring any decisions made by the captain were carried out properly, something her focused demeanor would be of great use for. One thing came to mind immediately.

"We could reengage the hybrid impeller drive," I said. Dobrina looked up from scanning her report plasma and glared at me from across the table.

"The thing is more likely to damage us than help us," she said.

"I disagree." I said. "If we were able to rig it to repeat the power burst we used to escape the jump space tunnel, it could be to our advantage. We could potentially accelerate away from those HuKs, or jump right past them into the tunnel and activate our Hoagland Drive before they could get off a shot, sir."

Maclintock looked down the table to Duane Longer. "Lieutenant?"

Anticipating his question, Longer said: "I can have her hooked up in twenty minutes, sir. Give me another twenty to warm her up and she'll be at your beck and call."

Maclintock nodded. "Good," he said. "That's Propulsion. What about Astrogation, Lieutenant Hogan?"

Jenny Hogan flushed a bit under the captain's gaze, cleared her throat nervously as she always seemed to do, and started in. "If we were to play out the scenario with the hybrid drive, we would have time to spool up the Hoagland and get ourselves into an HD jump bubble within about five minutes of the hybrid drive resetting. I doubt those HuKs could catch us before we jumped, so we would be on our way back to Candle before they could react."

"For what purpose?" The voice was loud and angry, and it came from down the table, from John Marker. "If we jump back to Candle and spend weeks getting repaired, then what? Those HuKs will still be *here*, still have to be dealt with if we come back. What's to stop them from following us back to Candle and attacking us there, or even attacking Jenarus itself? We lost thirty-three marines in this system. That's a lot of human capital, not to mention they were all friends of mine. Are we just going to forget that? Run away while we can? If we do that I guarantee they will be back next time with even more force. This ship is all that stands between our Union and the old empire. If we're planning on turning tail and running every time we face a difficult situation then I'd just as soon surrender now."

The room went dead quiet. His words were powerful and spoken in anger, but I couldn't argue with his logic.

"I agree," I said. "We must do more than just escape this system. We're being tested, and I fear if we show weakness then we'll fall into a downward spiral we won't be able to escape from."

Dobrina took up the challenge. "Fight them when we're not one hundred percent? Put the ship at risk, *all* of the crew, not just the men and women we've lost already? You may not remember, Commander, but I lost an entire ship and crew at Levant. That's something I don't want to repeat, ever. And if they can report that they destroyed us, even a weakened Lightship, that will only embolden them," she said forcefully. Her words stung. I was at Levant, too, and part of *Impulse*'s crew.

"That's enough," said Maclintock. He looked pensive, then leaned forward as he considered everything. After a moment he looked up at George Layton. "Can we engage them using just our torpedoes, Helm? Can we keep them at close enough range?"

Layton nodded. "Our Hoagland Field should protect us enough from their energy weapons to allow me to maneuver us into effective torpedo range. But if they're shielded as well—"

"They have limited shielding, mostly designed to stop energy weapons. They will eventually become vulnerable to our torpedoes, *if* we can stay close enough to them," said Serosian.

Maclintock looked to me again. "Can you keep your torpedo volleys effective against them with their maneuvering capabilities?" he asked.

"I've worked up multiple scenarios in training, sir. I'm confident I can handle them both. Mr. Serosian will vouch for my skills." The captain looked to the Earth Historian, who merely nodded affirmative. Maclintock took this in silently, then looked down the table again to Lena Babayan.

"Colonel, I know your marines have taken a big hit, but can you cobble together teams from nonessential volunteers to strengthen our hand-to-hand defense forces?" Maclintock asked.

"I thought Mr. Serosian said the HuKs were unmanned?" interjected Dobrina. It was a valid question. Maclintock dismissed it quickly.

"If our time in Jenarus has taught us anything, XO, it has taught us that 'unmanned' doesn't mean unpopulated. They could have automatons like the ones at the station aboard," he said. He looked back down the table again to Colonel Babayan.

"Aye, sir. We can put together a full complement from volunteers," she said.

"I might suggest Lieutenant Daniel, the purser," I said. "I saw him shoot before we left Candle. He's not bad."

"He was on my list," said Marker. Maclintock leaned back in his chair again.

"If we're all in agreement—"

"One more thing, sir," I said, interrupting. He looked at me. He was not happy at being interrupted.

"Mr. Cochrane."

"Sir, the energy weapons array is down but the gravity projectors are still installed. They can run off energy from the HD drive, not the ship's weapons system power. If we power down the energy weapons array again and de-link it from the gravity weapons, we could still use the gravity systems in the battle, if we need to," I said.

"Power it down again? Start the whole cycle over?" protested Dobrina.

"That's what I'm proposing, yes," I said. I hated being at odds with her all the time, but I had a responsibility to give my captain every option.

Maclintock looked around the table, then to Serosian, who remained stoic.

"Mr. Serosian?" the Historian answered.

"What the commander says is true. However, I caution you. These weapons are powerful and destructive, and they represent a dangerous escalation that the Imperial forces may not take kindly to."

Maclintock considered that, then, "Do it," he said to me. "Make the hybrid drive preparations and power down the energy weapons array. I'll expect your tactical plan for the torpedo engagement in thirty minutes, Mr. Cochrane." Then he stood and we all followed suit. "Stations, everyone. Let's not fuck this up." Then he strode out of the room, leaving us all behind him.

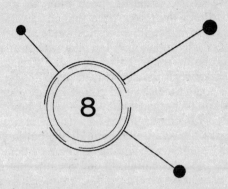

At the Jenarus Jump
Space Tunnel

My torpedo scenarios were fully loaded into both the longscope weapons interface and the captain's tactical computer ten minutes early. I'd gone through multiple scenario tests with Serosian at the Academy, and I ended up simply picking my favorite three. They all concluded with us winning the scenario decisively, with more than thirty torpedoes to spare, minimum. We had a full complement, two hundred, of varying sizes, yields, and mission objectives. But the fact remained that no scenario was ever like a real battle, and I would be relying on my skills, experience, and yes, my intuition, in this one. The captain said nothing, but approved my scenarios without comment. He knew that Serosian and I, linked in through the longscope, were *Starbound*'s best opportunity for success in the coming battle.

We slowed to battle speed when we crossed within .005 AU of the jump space tunnel, 750,000 kilometers out. We would continue to close on the nearly stationary HuKs for about another ten minutes before reaching realistic battle range. Effective speed to fight had to be much slower than speed in transit. Simply put, if you were going too fast you couldn't engage your enemy and they couldn't engage you. They could, however, rip you apart with simple things like scatter mines, essentially massive blocks of metal and debris put in your path, if you chose to try to slip by an enemy. I detected no dispersal of such weapons in our intended path.

"Path looks clear ahead, Captain. HuKs are starting to move toward us at low speed in a stack formation, inverting at forty-five degrees to our ecliptic," I reported.

"I can read my tactical screen, Mr. Cochrane," said Maclintock curtly. "Time to torpedo range?"

"With their current rate of acceleration, two minutes, sir."

"You and Mr. Serosian have the tactical con, Commander."

"Aye, sir," I replied, then switched to Serosian's com channel. I set the scope controls to envelope me under the hood. I wanted no distractions.

"Ready here," I said to Serosian. He started in with his instructions without hesitating.

"These appear to be Mark VII HuKs, developed late in the Imperial civil war, designed to be decisive in one-on-one encounters with enemy ships. They have limited AI capabilities and should follow all preprogrammed instructions. Fortunately for us, our Lightships are much more advanced than the ships of that time, one of the advantages of three centuries of technological research and development. The HuKs will undoubtedly try to split their attack at the last possible instant, take us on from two sides. My recommendation is that we try to divert them earlier than they want with a full volley of fifty-kiloton torpedoes, stepped in their launch sequence so they create a maximum possible wall of both yield and EMP," he said.

"Won't they be hardened against EMP?" I asked.

"They will, but our torpedoes have a magnetic resonance that will have a significant effect on their shield strength. Cumulatively, their shields will eventually fail and we will be facing an unguarded enemy."

I switched to my long-range visual. The two HuKs were still coming at us in their stack formation, one ahead of the other by about a hundred clicks on the same vector. I switched to close-ups and evaluated them individually. The forward one looked much like the HuK we had battled at Levant, a dark cylinder with a forward cannon array glowing a sickly green color. This ship, I decided, was a battering ram, designed to hit us hard and weaken our belly. The second ship had the same basic configuration, but with three additional coil cannons on extended stanchions at equidistant points around the cylinder. This one, it seemed to me, was the real enemy. It would follow on after the battering ram's attack and hit us with multiple coil cannon bursts, trying to get through our Hoagland Field and shatter our hull. I was determined not to let that happen.

I checked the clock. Forty seconds to firing range on the first HuK.

"I believe scenario two is the closest equivalent to what we're seeing here," I said to Serosian.

"Yes, I agree," he replied. "Proceed per that scenario, but be cautious of variables. We don't want any surprises."

"Affirmative," I said. I laid out my torpedo pattern, essentially ignoring the first HuK, which would likely have no luck breaking through our field with just its coil cannon, and I detected no other weapons signatures besides about a dozen low-yield torpedoes in the ten-kiloton range.

I played out my scenario, waiting until the forward HuK in the formation had reached about one hundred kilometers range. The second, and in my mind the more dangerous vessel, was trailing its companion now by a mere ten kilometers.

"They're closing formation, less than a hundred clicks out now. Firing solution locked in," I reported to both Serosian and the captain through my com link.

"Proceed," came the Historian's reply. I keyed in the launch sequence and fired five volleys of two torpedoes each, six seconds apart. The torpedoes accelerated toward the forward HuK, which began evasion maneuvers. The trailing HuK stayed on course and true. I switched to my weapons control display and instantly uploaded my preprogrammed variables to the torpedo warheads. Suddenly and in real time I watched as the two forward-most torpedoes broke off their run at the closer HuK and swerved for the second. She suddenly began evasive moves herself as her onboard AI detected the incoming threat. Then the second group of two torpedoes also broke away from their initial course and targeted the second HuK, then the third pair did the same. As the torpedoes closed on their targets they accelerated at different rates, trying to make a firing solution difficult for the enemy.

Facing an imminent threat, the trailing HuK powered up her three stanchion-mounted coil cannons and fired, disintegrating the forward three torpedoes, but the second group of three came on untouched. The specs had told me she would need 2.5 precious seconds to reload and refire her cannons, and that was all I needed. The first torpedo hit the top stanchion on the HuK square, the resultant atomic detonation blowing the coil cannon off its mounting, even through the thing's shielding. The follow-up pair detonated within half a kilometer of the HuK as she scrambled away, and I watched as her shields blew out completely, overloaded by the detonations.

Serosian was true to his word, the torpedoes did their job. The HuK veered off but I had no doubt she'd be back. Her shielding may have been gone but she still had a pair of nasty looking coil cannon arrays that worked.

The forward HuK was within fifty clicks now, and was facing our remaining four torpedoes in a staggered-spread formation. They were constantly compensating for her evasion tactics, and she was going to have a hard time avoiding them. Then I saw the HuK make her only play; she fired four counter-attack missiles at my screaming torpedoes. They impacted true enough, the small-yield defensive missiles packing just enough pop to detonate my incoming torpedoes. Still, she took a massive pulse hit, and hardened or not, her shields were gone, and she was less than ten seconds away from crashing into *Starbound*'s Hoagland Field. The resultant ramming attempt would dissipate her energy throughout the field and undoubtedly destroy her.

"Brace for impact," yelled the captain from his station. It was a precautionary measure, but any collision of this kind was likely to be far worse for our enemy than it was for us.

My eyes flicked to all my displays as I looked for any potential trouble signs as Layton counted down to impact in the background. At this point, with the speed of the incoming HuK, evasive maneuvers by *Starbound* would undoubtedly be compensated for by the battle AI aboard the HuK. But it didn't matter, we would be more than safe behind our protective Hoagland Field.

Unless . . .

I saw it on one of my frequency monitors. A rise in hyperdimensional energy above the mean. It could only be one thing; a displacement wave, one that had been insidiously cloaked from our scanners.

I heard Layton call five seconds to impact with the HuK.

The next thing I felt was as though I was being sifted,

like my consciousness was in multiple places at once, and my body, Gods know where. I felt and heard an audible crack in my head, as if I had given off an electrical charge. Then I came back together as one and promptly found myself laying on the deck.

Alarm claxons reverberated throughout the bridge and undoubtedly the rest of the ship as well. I jumped up and tried to focus on my longscope displays. The intercepting HuK had been destroyed by its own HD detonation. The second was coming at us fast, her remaining two coil cannons primed to fire.

"The Hoagland Field is down!" I heard Serosian yell in my ear. Maclintock ordered evasive maneuvers from Layton at the helm but I knew it was too late. This was a sophisticated and well-planned attack. The HD displacement wave had temporarily knocked out our Hoagland Field, and it would take the requisite 7-10 seconds to refire. That wasn't my job, though. Protecting *Starbound* was.

"Torpedoes, Mr. Cochrane!" came Maclintock's call in my ear.

"Too close!" I responded, and I was right. Any atomic detonation at this range, with us unshielded, would do as much damage to *Starbound* as to the HuK. I had only one chance, and I took it. With the coil cannon array out of commission, I turned to the already-prepped gravity projector weapon, thankful Maclintock had given the go-ahead to use the system. I hit the fire icon and the system shot out a glittering silver lance of gravitons toward the enemy HuK. The beam hit her head-on as she fired her coil cannons from short range. The instantaneous exchange nudged the HuK just enough to keep her coil energy from hitting us at full force. The glancing blow ripped through *Starbound*'s outer skin near the science labs. No doubt there would be casualties there, but I had no time to think about that. The HuK flew past us at .00002 light, then swung around for another pass.

"Get that field up!" I heard Maclintock yell, and a second later it was, thanks to Serosian. We were now protected from the HuK's coil cannon fire. Her onboard AI picked up on this and she weaved and bobbed, moving evasively away from us. The captain ordered pursuit, but I had *Starbound* already on her track by the time it came.

"She's making for the jump space tunnel," reported Serosian.

"Weapons status, Mr. Cochrane?" asked the captain through the com. I had just let go a volley of four pursuit torpedoes.

"We still have enough torpedoes, sir, but she's quicker than us and pretty smart, too. That HD displacement wave trick shows a sophisticated attack plan, likely programmed specifically for encounters with Lightships," I stated.

"I concur," came Serosian's voice in my com. Dobrina chimed in with systems reports. We were fully nominal at all stations, our only lack being the coil cannons, which would have been the easiest solution to our problem. I watched as my four torpedoes ran out of fuel and began dropping off their pursuit pace.

"We'll need a full pursuit, Captain, full HD impellers to catch her before she enters that tunnel. My torpedoes aren't fast enough to catch her at this range," I reported.

I heard Maclintock give the orders and we began to accelerate, closing the gap with the HuK, but it wasn't enough.

"We need more," I said out loud.

"Solutions?" demanded Maclintock. "That was far too close back there. I want that thing destroyed."

"We could use the gravity accelerator to increase the

HuK's mass and strain her systems, slow it down," said Serosian.

"Can you make that work, Mr. Cochrane?" asked Maclintock.

"Aye, sir, I can," I said. "We'll have to shut down the Hoagland Field to use it, but that still won't be enough to stop her from entering the jump space tunnel. She's going too fast for that. Once inside she could jump out anywhere."

"And take us with her?"

"Unlikely," said Serosian. "The topography of jump space, with us being in normal space, would likely break any link with her. We will be within torpedo range a full thirty seconds before she enters the tunnel, though."

"Can your torpedoes take her out before she enters the jump tunnel?" asked Maclintock. I ran my calculations.

"Uncertain, sir," I admitted. It would be close.

"That's the best you can do?" demanded the captain of Serosian and me. I checked my data one more time.

"Indeterminate outcome," I finally said. There was a pause, then:

"Proceed with the plan, Mr. Cochrane."

I did as ordered.

Thirty seconds later and I had the gravity projector locked on to the HuK, increasing her mass and steadily slowing her as she flashed toward the jump space tunnel. My torpedoes launched as scheduled, but she was still too far away and going too fast for a likely intercept before she made the tunnel.

We all watched as the minutes clicked by, our gravity projector not slowing the HuK enough, our torpedoes lagging behind. She entered the jump space tunnel a good five minutes ahead of *Starbound*.

"Disengage the HD impeller drive," ordered the captain to Duane Longer. Then he turned to me. "At the first sign she's spooling up for an HD jump, disconnect the gravity projector and bring up the Hoagland Field."

"Aye, sir," I said, then checked my board again. We were still out of torpedo range, but there was something else amiss. "Captain," I said.

"I see it," said Serosian through the com. "We're not closing on her anymore, captain. She's accelerating through the tunnel like a snow sled going downhill. She's pulling away from us, but we should be breaking contact with her at this range. The gravity projector—"

"It's locked," I said. "We're locked in with her. I just checked her and she's blowing out neutrinos at an alarming rate, shedding her mass. The neutrinos are bonding with the gravitons in our beam. We're essentially bonded to her, like we're at either end of a frozen rope."

"Will she jump and take us with her?" asked an anxious Maclintock.

"Negative, sir," I said. "Unless she's found a way to completely cloak her HD drive, she's running cold."

"She's not spooling up her HD drive, Captain, she's breaking it down, shedding her mass by depleting her HD crystal and using the neutrinos to bond with our gravity beam. It's brilliant, and quite deadly," said Serosian.

"What do you mean?" asked Maclintock, obviously concerned at this turn of events. The Historian sighed.

"Once we enter the tunnel, Captain, we will both be in jump space and our trajectory will accelerate."

"Trajectory? To where?"

"The Jenarus star, Captain. The HuK has locked with us using our own gravity weapon as a kind of rope to attach to us. Her trajectory will take us through the tunnel and into the Jenarus sun, where she will burn up, and take us with her," Serosian finished, his voice somber and resigned.

"Suicide mission," I said aloud without really thinking.

"Exactly," said Serosian. "Sophisticated and well planned. And deadly to us."

And then the com line between all of us was silent, as we contemplated our impending deaths.

The command team spent the next few minutes exploring possibilities away from the rest of the crew in the briefing room. We stood in a circle freely exchanging ideas. There appeared to be no good ones. The Hoagland Field would be burned out by the gravity projector if we tried to fire it up. Similarly, an attempt to jump without the field would place us in another dimension with no protective bubble of normal space around us, which Serosian assured us would mean our destruction. We had already entered the tunnel and had less than ten minutes before we exited, at the Jenarus star. I could think of only one other possibility.

"We could fire up the hybrid drive again, try to blow our way out of the tunnel," I said.

"With all the neutrinos in the gravity stream, wouldn't that likely result in our destruction?" asked Dobrina. I nodded.

"It would be like throwing gasoline on a fire," I acknowledged. "But the energy from it just might be enough to break us free."

"With no shielding," she said.

"With no shielding," I admitted.

"How much damage would we incur?" asked Maclintock.

"It would be significant," said Serosian. "But before we go there, there is one other possibility."

Maclintock, Dobrina, and I turned our attention toward him.

"We're listening," said the captain.

"I could take out the yacht, separate it from *Star-*

bound to make it a separate entity, fire up its Hoagland Field and then project that field around the ship. That would allow you to use the hybrid drive and break free of the HuK," he said.

"What about the gravity beam?" asked Dobrina. "If we can't use our own field how would the yacht's field be able to protect us?"

"*Starbound*'s defensive field is designed to envelope the ship. The yacht uses a smaller field that can be customized to size. However, I wouldn't be able to protect the coil cannon arrays that we are using to project the gravity beam. They would be lost in any explosion caused by engaging the hybrid drive," the Historian said. Maclintock thought about this for only a moment.

"I'm clearing you for this action, Mr. Serosian. But first, you need to answer me one more thing. What will happen to you?" he said.

"By projecting the field around *Starbound*, the yacht would be exposed to the explosive forces of the hybrid drive."

"In other words, you'd be killed," said Dobrina.

"Most likely."

"Unacceptable," said Maclintock. "There has to be another way."

"We could jump," I said, letting my intuition and impulsiveness get the better of me again.

"How would that help?" asked Dobrina. Serosian looked at me and nodded. I continued.

"Any interaction between our HD jump drives and the yacht's Hoagland Field would automatically expand and extend the field. This expansion is minimal on a ship the size of *Starbound*, but expansion of the yacht's field by even a few meters could envelope it and protect Serosian. There's no guarantee that Serosian would survive the interdimensional shift unshielded in the few moments before the field expanded, but he *could* possibly survive it," I said.

"That seems like a long shot," said Dobrina. Maclintock looked to Serosian.

"Are you willing to risk it?" he asked.

Serosian nodded. "There is a higher probability of my survival, but not much more than for the hybrid drive scenario. I could set a ten-second delay and then try to get forward into the area of the field projector. We have conducted experiments of this type with inorganic materials, but never with an organism as complex as a human being. It's a possibility, though one that's never been tried before."

Maclintock looked at the wall chronograph. "We have eight minutes before we exit the jump space tunnel into the corona of the Jenarus star. Is that enough time?" he said to Serosian.

"If I leave now."

"Go," said Maclintock.

Serosian went.

I was at my longscope monitors, piped in to the command com along with Maclintock and Dobrina, listening to Serosian's status updates. We now had three minutes before our ship exited the jump space tunnel and we were dragged into the Jenarus star by the suicidal HuK.

Serosian had the yacht in position for our maneuver, floating above *Starbound* at about one hundred meters. Jenny Hogan had the Hoagland hyperdimensional drive warm and spooled up for our attempted jump. She had set the initial jump for a nearby uninhabited star system, Skondar, one that had stable jump space that we could move very quickly into, assess our damage, recover Serosian and the yacht, and then make our way home to Candle from there.

"Activating the Hoagland Field," came Serosian's call on the com. I watched as the tiny but powerful yacht extended its protective field around us. As planned, he excluded our coil cannon arrays from the field, but the body of the ship, and the crew, would be safe. We'd lose our weapons pylons in the jump, but since we were locked to the HuK through the gravity projector that damage was unavoidable, and it could save us.

Serosian waited only a few seconds to act. "I've set the ten-second delay," he said. "Be prepared to jump ten seconds from my mark."

"Acknowledged," said Maclintock, then turned to Jenny Hogan. "On my mark, Lieutenant," she acknowledged.

I could feel sweat on my forehead but I refused to take my eyes or hands away from my station. My friend's life was at stake.

"Now," said Serosian. I watched as the field glowed purple, surrounding and protecting the ship, but not all of the yacht. I counted off into the command com. At two seconds, Maclintock gave the order to Jenny Hogan to jump the ship. I tried not to think about my friend scrambling to find any safety he could inside his small yacht, a ship that had saved my life not long ago.

The now familiar but still very disturbing sifting sensation engulfed me and I became disoriented for what seemed like both an eternity and a tiny fraction of time. When I recovered my senses my focus went immediately to my board.

The yacht was still with us.

We were in Skondar space as Jenny Hogan had said we would be. The Field was still active, projecting from the yacht to *Starbound*. We were the worse for wear, though, our weapons pylons sheared off in near seamless fashion. A few moments went by and the Field cycled off per Serosian's clock, leaving both ships floating free in space, now two independent bodies again. I tried to raise Serosian, but there was no response on either the standard or longwave coms. I was about to say something as the yacht approached *Starbound* to reattach itself per Serosian's preprogrammed flight plan, but Maclintock cut me off.

"Commander Kierkopf, secure the bridge. Mr. Cochrane, you're with me." With that, I was out from under the hood of the longscope and on my way down to Serosian's quarters, to see if my friend was still alive.

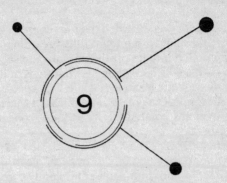

9

I stood outside the Historian's quarters monitoring the inner environment from a wall display. The yacht had docked and the inner rooms were balancing their environment with the rest of the ship.

"Well?" said Maclintock to me. A team of three medical staff, a doctor and two nurses, stood behind us in the galleria hallway, emergency equipment at the ready. The last system on my display clicked over to green.

"She's docked," I said.

"Put in the code to open her up," Maclintock ordered. I was already doing that. Then the doors slipped apart with only the slightest wisp of air as the yacht and the galleria environments balanced. Maclintock was first in, followed by the medical team, and I trailed. We went through the upper deck—library, chapel, and sleeping quarters—looking for our friend, but with no luck. I opened the small stairwell down to the yacht's command deck and we went down in the same order as we came in.

Serosian was sprawled over his console, his breathing slow and shallow, but thankfully breathing. The medical team pulled him up off the console and sat him back in the pilot's couch, reading his vital signs and administering therapeutic treatment while they evaluated him.

"Serosian, can you hear me?" asked Maclintock, leaning over his comrade. I stood back, concerned for his well-being.

He opened glassy eyes and turned to Maclintock, starting to speak quietly. "I'm here," he said. The doctor gave him a shot in the upper arm and he grabbed at the spot where the injection went in.

"What happened?" asked the captain. Serosian gathered himself for moment, then:

"I couldn't make it to my lair. I ended up riding out the whole . . . event, from here," he said. "There were fractions of a second between the jump and the field expansion, moments where I was both places, and neither . . ." He trailed off, then smiled at me.

"Peter . . ."

"I'm here," I said. He looked at me, as if he couldn't focus on me, then said, quite without provocation:

"I lived an eternity in fractions of a second." Maclintock and I exchanged glances and the captain nodded to me to continue the conversation with my friend.

"What was it like?" I prompted him. He looked at me oddly, then said:

"Like a lifetime in hell." Then he broke into a coughing fit and the doctor quickly gave him another injection. He quieted and his breathing became low and heavy; his eyes closed as the orderlies moved him to a portable medical bed.

"I've sedated him," said the doctor, a female commander named Farrington, to Maclintock. "I'm taking him to sickbay for monitoring and recuperation. He needs at least twenty-four hours of full rest, and that is not negotiable, Captain," she said. Maclintock agreed with her and we both waited while the medical unit moved him out of the yacht. The captain and I stood together outside the Historian's quarters, watching him recede down the galleria toward sickbay.

"That is one brave man," said Maclintock.

The next several hours were spent by most of the crew evaluating *Starbound*'s condition. I, however, got the task of sending HD probes back to Jenarus to assess the remaining threat there, if any. The probes tracked the HuK's death spiral by following its shedded neutrinos directly to the star. The whole process had taken only a few minutes after we had broken the lock between us by jumping out. I, for one, was glad the damnable thing was gone. I was learning to hate them. Ships that had men and women aboard tended to act with much more care as to the protection of their crews. Ships without crews, HuKs controlled only by AIs, ran solely on programming. Most were programmed with at least a minimal survival instinct, but these had behaved like they had virtually none. I wondered if the sacrifice of the Levant navy in our last encounter with an automated HuK had somehow entered into the programming of these new HuKs. It was a question I was looking forward to discussing with Serosian once he had recovered.

After duty hours, Maclintock came by my cabin to discuss things aboard ship and just ahead. He sat across from me at my small desk.

"We've been ordered home for repairs. Candle says two weeks to replace our weapons mounts and make refit and repair. And of course there will be new marines. We also lost nine more crew in the HuK attack, mostly in the science labs," he said.

"They took the hardest hit in the attack," I acknowledged. Forty-two men and women out of a crew of 386 were heavy losses, no matter how you cut it. It made me feel sick inside. I leaned forward, staring down at my conference table. "These losses, do they affect you as much as they do me?" I asked.

"They always get to you," Maclintock replied. "No getting around that."

"I promise we'll have her back up and running ahead of schedule, sir," I said bravely.

"Not your concern, Commander." That took me by surprise. Maclintock leaned back in his chair and put his hands behind his head. "You'll be departing Candle for Quantar as soon as we arrive, along with Commander Kierkopf. *Starbound* will get along fine without you during the repairs."

"But, sir, my duty is here," I protested. He smiled, the first time I could remember him doing it in my presence.

"You also have other duties, Commander. Diplomatic ones. And as you may recall before all this started I said you would be going to Carinthia to attend the *Impulse* inquest."

Truth was, it had slipped my mind.

"As part of those duties, Commander, Admiral Wesley wants you on your way as soon as possible once we dock. So while we refit and repair, you'll be doing your part as an interstellar ambassador, representing Quantar and the Union Navy, after a quick briefing at home," he finished.

I didn't like this assignment, not at all, being paraded around as a show toy for the pleasure of the Admiralty. But I had no choice, I knew that much.

"If you say so, sir," I said.

"Not my call, Commander. I'd much rather have you here. But as long as you're going, get Commander Kierkopf to show you the sights on Carinthia. I hear winter in New Vee is lovely."

"Yes, sir," I said. "I will enjoy myself. Sir." Maclintock smiled again at my mocking tone and then stood to leave.

"We jump for Candle at 0800. Take the downtime to relax, Commander. You've been through a lot in a very short time. In fact, I'm ordering you on light duty for the duration of the traverse. Understood?"

"Understood, sir," I said, standing myself. He reached out and shook my hand.

"Good job, Peter. Let's hope our next few missions are less . . . eventful."

"I hope so, sir."

And with that he was gone, and I sat back down and sighed. I *was* exhausted.

Dobrina and I managed only one evening together during the traverse. She was on full duty, not to mention pulling a little extra as she was picking up much of my work, but she seemed not to resent that. We would have plenty of time for recreation later, but we spent the last night of the journey home eating a sparse meal together and then getting straight down to business in bed. It had been a while and we both needed to release some stress, which we did, to our mutual enjoyment.

The next morning I was back to full duty, but Maclintock ordered me to stay off the bridge until 1000 hours. The drop back into Quantar space near Candle would be at 1230. I decided to use the extra time to visit my Historian friend in his quarters.

He had been released by ship's medical and was resting comfortably back in his quarters. I caught him reading in one of his library chairs when I came in.

"Spiritual, technical, or pleasurable?" I asked. He looked up from the leather-bound book as I sat down.

"*The Three Musketeers*, by Dumas," he said, smiling.

"So purely pleasurable." He put the book down and took a sip of tea. "Would you like some?" he asked. I waved him off.

"I've already had my coffee and breakfast," I said. "I just came here to check on you."

"I'm fine," he said. "The effects of the jump were unpleasant, but not in any permanent kind of way."

"Can you talk about it?" I asked. He put down his teacup.

"You know that sifting feeling you always talk about?" he said. I nodded. "It was like that, but each of those 'sifting' events was like a passage to a different reality. It was . . . very disconcerting. Without the field to protect me, it was like I experienced a lifetime in each one of many different dimensions. I felt like I was learning and forgetting all the knowledge of each place as I shifted, then was forcefully thrust back into my own space and time, but my mind was unprepared for my consciousness's return." He stopped there for an uncomfortably long time, staring past me as if I weren't there. Then he refocused and said, "I hope I didn't scare you."

"You gave me some cause for concern," I admitted. He smiled but said nothing. I tried to keep the conversation going. "Perhaps this is something we should be exploring, these other dimensions?" Now he got an ashen look on his face, and his eyes went distant again.

"Have you read the Bible, Peter?" he asked abruptly. That stopped me.

"Some," I replied. "As a child, mostly." Serosian clasped his hands together in front of him, looking in my direction, but not at me.

"There is a story where the apostle Paul is taken up into 'the third heaven' and he sees 'inexpressible things, things that a man is not permitted to tell.' That is what it was like, Peter. And it should not be explored, as to see and experience the things I saw would drive a lesser mind mad." I could see from his demeanor that he was deadly serious. I immediately dropped the conversation and tried to deflect to something else. I cleared my throat.

"Will you be back on duty today?" I asked. He shook himself out of his torpor and looked at me again.

"Not today," he said. "Once we hit Candle I will be spending many of my days filing reports back to the Church. There is much to discuss." Then his focus seemed to drift away from me again, and so I made my excuses and headed toward the bridge early.

I, for one, was glad this mission was over.

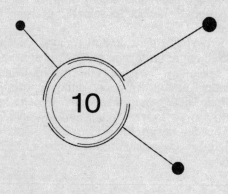

Above Quantar

Our Union Navy aerojet zipped across the New Brisbane skyline, high overhead but still close enough to see the port city in all its splendor. New Briz was located on the northernmost peninsula of Quantar's Southern Continent, in the state of New Queensland. Five and a half million people made it easily the largest city on a planet of twenty-seven million. I pointed to the harbor.

"Twenty thousand containers a year go through that harbor, and if you look downriver from the inlet you can see New Maine Road, the home of my favorite soccer club," I said.

"We call it football," said Dobrina, looking down at the sky-blue and silver stadium. Whatever you called it, it was still humanity's most popular sport, centuries after its invention. She smiled at me. "So you're a big fan?"

"Well, just of New Briz Blues. Further inland you'll

find New Briz United, but any self-respecting Blues supporter just calls them 'The Scum,'" I said. "I was a junior professional for the Blues for two years, before I decided to sign up for the Union Navy. Probably could have been a full-time pro if I'd wanted."

"I see." She was humoring me, I could tell, but I still found it quite charming. I spent the next few minutes pointing out the museums, the public parks and beaches, the different skyline buildings and such while our pilot gave us the full show, circling the city's business district before heading uptown to Government Square.

The government buildings sat on a hill north of the harbor business district. Sometime during the city's founding the civic leaders saw fit to flatten the top of their second-highest hill and build a planetary capital complex in gray marble. The merchants in the harbor always looked up at the watchful eyes of their government, while on Queen Anne Hill, the city's tallest, the richest merchant princes looked down on those who sought to govern them. It was an uneasy alliance, but one that had served Quantar well for most of its five hundred years since colonization.

The government buildings were laid out in the pattern of the Southern Cross, with Government House to the north, Parliament to the south, the New Queensland State House to the east, and Merchant House to the west. The fifth building, offset from the other four, was the Royal Naval Arsenal and Museum, headquarters of the navy and more commonly known as Admiralty House.

Government House had been the official working residence of the highest royal leader, the Director, during Imperial times. Quantar had been without a Director for a century and a half, since the end of the Imperial Civil War. My father had taken the title Duke of KendalFalk at the age of seventeen when his father had passed away, but officially the government was run by an elected parliament and not by the old system of royal peerage. However, the merchant class had always held more control over the government purse strings than the parliament had, so it had become a mostly ceremonial body in post-imperial days, subservient to the wishes of Merchant House. And the richest merchant princes on Quantar were still the Cochrane family.

"Centuries ago," I said, "when the planet was just a frontier outpost exporting hardwood lumber, coal, and minerals from the north, the original syndicate which owned the planetary rights sold them to a company based out of Australia, on Old Earth. The company was called Queensland and Northern Territories Amalgamated Resources."

"Q-U-A-N-T-A-R?" said Dobrina, smiling even broader. "How quaint." I laughed.

"Well, it gets better," I said. "The majority stockholder in QUANTAR was a man by the name of Cochrane. So, for the last four hundred years or so, our family has owned the rights to the seat of power here. And that right was affirmed by the Corporate Empire when it formed."

"So you grew up privileged," she said.

I shrugged. "I grew up in the north, away from all this, at KendalFalk, in a place called the North Palace that our family traditionally used to escape the steamy, humid summers here in New Briz. In recent times there's been a movement among the family to make KendalFalk the new capital, but New Briz always manages to keep its place," I finished. That was true enough. The merchant class hated KendalFalk's bitter winters worse than New Briz's sweltering summers.

The history lesson over for the moment, we made a vertical landing behind Government House on the official pad reserved for the Duke of KendalFalk, Quantar's official Head of State and, coincidentally, my father.

I led Dobrina out into a sunny but brisk day, typical

for winter in the northern latitudes. I descended the
steps first and then held out my hand as my superior
officer, my lover, and the first Carinthian in well over a
hundred years set foot on family soil.

I tilted my head so that our uniform caps wouldn't hit
and kissed her sweetly on the lips. "Welcome to Quantar,
Commander Dobrina Kierkopf," I said.

"Thank you, Peter," she replied. "Or should I say
'Thank you, Viscount'?"

"Peter will do for now."

"And is this kiss a traditional greeting when one arrives on Quantar?" she said.

I smiled. "It is for me."

Then I led her to the waiting ground car and we took
the short ride to Government House together in silence,
hand in hand.

The ground car pulled up at the main entrance to Government House. It was a gray marble building with an
imposing façade, done in traditional British colonial
style. I stepped out into the dimming daylight and
snapped off a salute to the House Guards, then was in-
undated with the sound of clicking cameras and shouted
questions.

I was unprepared for the press contingent to be so
large. They surged forward, taking my picture at every
possible angle and shouting questions. I looked back at
the ground car longingly, wishing I could be back inside.
I turned back and stuck my head in. Dobrina smiled
back at me.

"The triumphant hero returns home," she said.

"You don't have to go through this," I said back, really
speaking for myself. "I had no idea this was coming."

"I know. But it has to happen sometime. It may as
well be now." I resigned myself to her wisdom, then

extended my hand to help her out of the car. She stepped out gracefully and into the waiting mob of press. The questions came at us rapid-fire while we stood for pictures.

"Is this Commander Kierkopf?"

"Are you engaged?"

"Do you have plans to tour the city, ma'am?"

"Will you be staying in the same room?"

I held up my hands to quiet the crowd. "There will be plenty of time for questions later," I started, not really sure when that might be. "But for right now I'd just like to welcome Commander Kierkopf to Quantar on behalf of my family and the people. It's been far too long since we've had a visitor from Carinthia to Government House." I was absolutely stumped then, so I just finished with a "thank you" and took Dobrina by the arm as the press continued shouting after us. I hustled her under a canopy and up the steps to the East Portico where a Guardsman held the door open. We were escorted in to an anteroom and there dispensed of our caps, gloves, and coats. A domestic family attaché named Perkins greeted us there and then took us down the hall to a lifter, where we went up two levels to the private apartments.

Perkins had assigned us separate rooms, across the hall and down from each other, and I wondered if this was my father's doing, protocol and all. I had never really had a particular room here growing up, as "home" was almost always the North Palace at KendalFalk. After a few minutes of settling in, I had the porters unpack my belongings and then made my way down the hall to an open loft, where I found Dobrina and Perkins already fully engaged in conversation over tea and biscuits. I took the chair reserved for me and started in myself.

"I had expected to see my father when we arrived, Perkins," I said.

"Couldn't be helped," said Perkins. "He's detained right now with government business in his offices. He told me to tell you that he'll see you at the reception tonight, at seven o'clock in the East Room." I checked my watch, which had automatically adjusted for local time. Half past four.

"Well then, it seems we'll have time to rest before the evening's activities." I winked at Dobrina but she stayed stoic, ignoring me. Perkins turned to her.

"I've had your closet filled with some fine evening wear, based on your size measurements from the navy database. You should find something quite appropriate for the reception," he said. Dobrina took a sip of her tea before responding.

"Thank you for your thoughtfulness, Perkins, but I am active duty in the navy and will be wearing my dress uniform tonight. If you could have my jacket and trousers pressed I would be most appreciative." Perkins seemed displeased but nodded.

"Of course, madam," he said, then stood to go. "If you'll excuse me." He nodded to us both and then left us alone. I looked at her.

"We have two and a half hours before the reception," I said, smiling mischievously.

"Which I intend to spend in that marvelous porcelain bathtub I saw in my room," she said, standing up and coming toward me. She put her hands on my shoulders and then kissed me on the cheek before turning to go. "I'll see you at seven, Commander," she said over her shoulder as she went.

"Commander will do for now. But you'll have to call me Viscount later," I said after her. She spun and gave me a quick sly smile and then disappeared around the corner and down the hall to her room.

I pulled up an ottoman for my feet and lay back in my chair, soaking in the last of the day's winter sunlight through the window, then crossed my arms in my lap, closed my eyes, and sighed.

"Ah," I said aloud, "home."

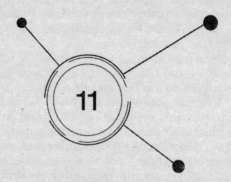

11

I was in my navy dress blues by ten of the hour, freshly showered and shaved, after one of the multitude of house assistants had delivered my newly cleaned and pressed navy jacket and helped me dress, though I hardly needed it. I was out the door with a thank you and then down the brief distance to Dobrina's room, there knocking gently on the door. I got a muffled "come in" for a reply and turned the knob, stepping through.

Dobrina was at her wardrobe mirror, fully dressed in her Carinthian Navy green dress uniform, making some last minute adjustments to her short-cropped military-cut hair. I shut the door behind me and crossed my arms, admiring her for a silent moment while she tussled with an errant curl. She had a pleasant, angular face that positively shone with life when she smiled, which she wasn't doing just now. I contemplated her and my feelings for her as I watched.

I'd seen enough of her taking her frustrations out in the fencing arena and the racquetball court to know she felt a deep sense of personal responsibility for the loss of *Impulse*, even though I constantly reminded her that it was the rogue Historian Tralfane who had betrayed her crew, and me who had actually sent the Lightship on her final course toward oblivion. I knew it didn't help alleviate the individual pain and professional loss she felt at being the sole Carinthian survivor of her doomed crew, besides of course *Impulse*'s original Captain Lucius Zander, but in my mind it did speak to her character, which was simply another thing about her I admired, among many. I also decided as I watched her primp that she didn't need to be beautiful, as I probably loved her anyway, and love, I noted, tended to ignore any flaws of the physical kind.

"You're staring," she said, still moving the curl around on her head and not looking at me.

"It's a hobby of mine. Sometimes I do it when you're asleep, just so you can't complain," I said. She gave me a glance of mild annoyance before finally ending the battle with the curl and turning toward me.

"Will I pass being presented to your family?" she said. I smiled and walked up to her, giving her a kiss on the cheek and a warm hug.

"You'll be fine," I said. "Just don't forget you're representing an entire planet to the royal family of Quantar."

"Oh," she said, "Is that all I have to worry about?"

"For now," I said.

"Are we ready?" she said, pulling back from me. I admired her one last time.

"More than ready." I stuck out my arm and she took it. I escorted her out the door and down the hall toward the stairway to the East Room, two floors down. We walked the first flight in silence, then came around to a long landing, open to the ballroom below. I walked us to the balustrade and looked down. There must have been two hundred people in formal regalia milling about, champagne glasses tinkling as the hum of anticipatory conversation filled the vast room. An orchestra took up one corner of the ornate hall, setting up on a large stage from which there would no doubt be speeches made. Marble columns supported the exterior walls and chandeliers of ancient crystal lit the room in soft, glittering gold tones from above. Multipaned glass doors lined the far side of the hall leading to a patio that overlooked the formal house gardens. Men in military uniforms mingled with finely dressed merchants and political dignitaries, almost all of them with an equally fine lady in attendance. It was quite a spectacle.

"Are none of the merchant class ladies?" asked Dobrina. I shrugged.

"The merchants tend to hand down their properties by heredity, which tends to favor males. The political class, though, is much more egalitarian. Almost a quarter of the parliament is female," I stated, then contemplated that a moment. "Perhaps we're not as modernized as we think. Is it like that on Carinthia?"

She shook her head. "The Planetary Assembly is almost half women, but we have no real merchant class. The Feilberg family runs the military and has the executive powers, and the courts for that matter. The noble class is small, and there are few wealthy independent merchants to challenge the status quo. It tends to cut down on the competition."

"Hmm, very efficient. How much power does the Assembly have?"

"Not much," she admitted. I pulled her back from the balustrade.

"Things are more complicated here. But enough of politics," I said as we made our way to the stairway again. "We have a performance to conduct."

She laughed as we rounded the corner, then stopped me just out of sight of the milling crowd and kissed me quickly on the lips one last time. "For luck," she said. I smiled back.

"You won't need it," I said.

We came down the stairs first to a smattering of applause, which turned into a much more robust cheer. By the time we got to the last of the marble steps and set our feet on the ballroom floor, we were surrounded by well-wishers and we were both shaking hands and fully engaged in greeting the crowd. This went on for some minutes before the orchestra started the Quantar anthem, which brought the hustle and bustle to a stop. We all stood as they raised the flag outside in the garden courtyard behind the dais and I sang along to "On Quantar Fair" with the rest of the crowd, stopping to share a smile with Dobrina as she clung to my arm.

My father, Nathan Cochrane, Director of Quantar, made his entrance at the conclusion of the anthem to another warm round of applause, which we both heartily joined. It seemed unusual to see him out of military uniform, instead wearing the dark civilian suit of a merchant. Madrey Margretson, his longtime secretary at his naval office, accompanied him to the stage, which was a bit of a surprise to me. I had assumed their relationship had ended with the closing of his military service. Apparently, I was wrong.

Grand Admiral Jonathon Wesley of the Unified Space Navy and his matronly wife accompanied my father. Wesley was wearing full military dress regalia. As the applause rippled on my father spied me in the crowd and waved for me to come up to the stage.

"I was afraid of this," I said to Dobrina. "We're not part of the spectacle, we *are* the spectacle." She didn't say anything, but squeezed my arm tightly as we made our way up to a pair of empty chairs. I sat Dobrina down and then turned to my father.

"I'm proud of you, son," he said as the applause continued, shaking my hand and then giving me a big hug.

He was a huge man, and I still felt like a child being embraced by him. I hugged him back.

"Thank you, sir," I said. Then he released me and Wesley was there to shake my hand, but thankfully without the embrace. My father went to the podium and lifted his hands to the crowd to quiet them, then unfolded some papers, which I assumed was a prepared speech. I sat down next to Dobrina, grateful to be out of the limelight for the moment, and took her hand in mine.

"I want to thank you all for coming," my father started, then proceeded with the usual acknowledging of dignitaries and the like that happens in most political speeches. After a few minutes of this he turned to me.

"I would be remiss if I didn't ask you now to turn your attention toward my son, Peter, and his companion, Commander Dobrina Kierkopf of Carinthia. These two are true heroes of the Union and the Navy, and I am proud that after such an arduous journey, which I am sure you have all heard about, they are finally here with us today," he said. He made no mention of our more recent arduous journey to Jenarus and back, but then that was still classified.

What proceeded was a thankfully short speech about the loss of *Impulse*, and how we had both fought so hard to defeat the Imperial dreadnought that had threatened *Starbound*. He welcomed Dobrina formally and she had to stand and acknowledge the crowd while we all applauded.

Then things got more serious. There was to be a medal ceremony, which neither of us had been informed of previously. I made a mental note to have a conversation with Mr. Perkins about that. The parliament had apparently voted to award us both the Quantar Cross of Valor, and Merchant House had approved. One of the parliament members came up with the medals in velvet cases, and everyone applauded as they were placed around our necks and we posed for photographs again. Once we had sat back down, of course my father had to mention the drama film that would be showing the next evening on the digital networks, highlighting our personal exploits in the *Starbound* affair. I covered my eyes in mock horror and the crowd laughed.

"I'm sorry," I whispered to Dobrina, "It's what they do here."

"I can't wait to see who plays me," she said, and we shared a quiet laugh.

At that, Wesley came up and made a brief speech, then gave us another set of medals, the Navy Cross. I had never heard of the Navy Cross, but the Unified Navy was new so I assumed the honor was legitimate and not made up just for the occasion. We both stood dutifully as he pinned the medals on our uniforms. As we made our way back to our seats the orchestra struck up the anthem again and then the dais broke up.

We spent the next two hours drinking toasts and mingling with very important people we would no doubt not remember in the morning. Precisely at ten o'clock I was delighted to find Perkins at my side whisking Dobrina and me into the library where we both sat down heavily in matching oversized leather chairs. My father and Wesley followed a few minutes later, accompanied by their dates. I got my first hug then from Madrey, which was a blessed relief from the evening's events, and something I'd grown used to in my times visiting my father's office at the Admiralty.

"So good to see you again, Peter," she said.

"And you, Madrey," I responded. She kissed me on the cheek as my father and Wesley sat down across from us. Madrey released me and I glanced across at my father.

"Is there something you want to tell me, sir?" I asked. My father smiled as Madrey and Mrs. Wesley ventured off to the far end of the large room, drinks in hand, leaving the four of us alone to chat.

My father took a drink of his brandy. "You may as

well know now, son. I intend to marry Madrey in the spring. It will be announced after Reunion Day, at the turn of the year."

"Congratulations, sir," I said. "And to you, Madrey," I called down to her. She smiled and waved.

"It's been coming for a while, son. I tried to live without her for a few months after I left the Admiralty, but I found I just couldn't function in my new role, in more ways than one. After that it just sort of happened."

"I couldn't be happier for you, sir," I said. It had been eleven years since my mother had passed away, and with the more recent loss of my brother Derrick I was just truly glad to finally see him happy again.

"Civilian life is busy, but in a much different way than in the military. I found I needed a companion to navigate uncharted waters," he said. I felt as if he were trying to justify his choice to me, and it made me uncomfortable.

"I understand completely, sir, really, I'm very happy for you both." He nodded in his silent way of acknowledging things, and then Wesley spoke, turning the conversation to more comfortable topics.

"I've just read the preliminary reports about the Jenarus mission," he said. "I'm glad you both made it back in one piece."

"Thank you, sir," said Dobrina for us both. Wesley continued.

"I understand you're both anxious to return to your navy duties, but there's still much to be resolved about the loss of *Impulse*, at least as far as the Carinthians are concerned," he said. I noticed Dobrina flinch just slightly at this. "And after reviewing the damage reports, *Starbound* likely won't be ready to go for another three weeks. So there is a bit of time yet, and the inquest is coming up next week on Carinthia."

"What should we expect from the inquest process, sir?" I asked. Wesley shifted in his chair.

"The Carinthians have requested a formal inquest into the destruction of *Impulse*. They feel that she was their property, and that it was primarily their sailors who were killed—"

"We don't know that they've all been killed," interrupted Dobrina, emotion in her voice. Wesley nodded.

"I did read your report, Commander. And that's partly what the inquest is for," he said to her. "We've granted their request, and you will both be there to testify, of course."

I looked at Dobrina, trying to reassure her. "I think we're both prepared to tell our story, Admiral. Attending the inquest representing the Union Navy would be an honor, sir," I said. "When would we have to leave?"

"In three days," said my father. "After the holiday but before year's end." I looked to Dobrina, and she gave me a confirming nod.

"We accept, then," I said.

"There is one other point, lad," said Wesley. "This would be as much a diplomatic mission as a military one. The military part is a courtesy to the Carinthian Navy from the Union Navy. The diplomatic part is more about your role as a royal representative of Quantar."

"I'm not trained as a diplomat," I said flatly.

"That's why I've set up some sessions for you with the Ministry of State," said my father. I nodded.

"Great," I said, lying. I was trained as a navy officer, not in diplomacy. And I didn't want my first trip to Dobrina's home world to be filled with protocol and state dinners.

"The fact is, son, that even though you're formally in the navy, you will have to accept other semi-official duties as well," said my father. It was as if he had read my mind.

"I understand, sir, it's just—"

"Things are changing here, Peter," he interrupted.

"It's my intent to take up the old Director's Chair in the new year. That means you'll have to take a new title as well."

"I'm sorry," I said. "I'm not really following you." I looked to Dobrina, who was clearly ill at ease with this high-level protocol talk. At this Wesley cut in.

"Fact is, lad, we don't know yet what the old Corporate Empire consists of. It's possible they are more advanced than we are, militarily anyway. If we were to fight a reinstitution of the old imperial system and lose, the cost could be millions of lives," he said. "And no one wants to repeat the last war."

"Thus we're taking the necessary political steps of filling the old imperial peerage lines, reestablishing our claims to this star system as sovereign family territory, filling in the blanks as it were, in case we were to lose, and the Union was dissolved," said my father. I shifted in my chair, which, soft as it was, was becoming increasingly uncomfortable.

"And how does this affect me?" I asked.

My father leaned forward. "I will be relinquishing the family title of Duke of KendalFalk in favor of the imperial title of Director. I want you to assume the Duke's title before you leave for Carinthia. This will make you the primary title holder within our family, and secure your ascension to the Imperial Chair should something happen to me. If we were to leave the line of succession open, then the emperor could appoint his own lackey to the Chair."

His words surprised me, and not in a good way. I looked to my father and Wesley, and then back again. "What's going to happen to you?" I demanded. At this Dobrina interrupted.

"Excuse me, gentlemen," she said, standing. "I believe I will join the ladies. This conversation obviously doesn't concern a lowly Union Navy commander."

Before I could say anything in protest she was on her way, and I barely had time to stand in respect before she left our gathering. I had been confused. Now as I sat down I was starting to get angry.

"Again," I said tightly to my father, "what's going to happen to you?"

My father shrugged. "Anything could happen, Peter. War. Blockade. Invasion. Anything. And since we are swimming in deep, dark, and unknown waters, I think it's best if we have you out there, in space, separated from our home for the time being. That's the best way I know how to protect you, and Quantar, and our family. That and restoring these old imperial forms of law, whether we think they apply to us anymore or not."

"There's a planned ceremony tomorrow, formally announcing your ascension to the title of duke. It will be televised tomorrow night," said Wesley. "And then our mission will be to get you off of Quantar as soon as possible." I looked at Wesley, my supreme military commander. More and more, I felt his hands working behind the scenes of my life, and more and more I didn't like it.

"I have no choice but to accept, then," I said.

"No, son, you don't," said my father bluntly. I finished my whiskey with a quick shot to the back of my throat.

"I'll be in my room then," I said, "waiting for my instructions." Then I set my glass down a bit harder than I would have liked and walked away.

I quickly caught up with the ladies and took Dobrina by the arm, wishing Madrey and Mrs. Wesley good night.

"I take it that didn't go well," she said quietly as we left.

"It will be fine," I whispered to her as I escorted her from the library.

"I hope you're right," she whispered back.

We slept that night in our separate rooms, and that was fine with me. I was probably too angry for good sex anyway. The next morning I received diplomatic briefings on the trip by protocol wonks from the Quantar Ministry of State. After a morning full of protocol I was glad to take up Wesley's invitation to lunch at the Admiralty. We met and ate in his office, the one that used to belong to my father.

"You'll be happy to know that I've officially assigned Commander Kierkopf to the inquest mission as a temporary Union Navy diplomatic attaché to the Carinthian Court. It's important that the Carinthian Navy see officers from both of our worlds are fully committed to the Union. The fact is that she doesn't really have a permanent military assignment right now, being as her position on *Starbound* is considered temporary," he said. "The Carinthian Navy won't validate her commission transfer to *Starbound* until after the inquest. As far as they're concerned she's still acting captain of *Impulse*."

"I have been worried about her," I admitted between bites of my club sandwich. We were seated across from each other at a conference table that had been converted for our luncheon. "She's done well on her assignment as XO aboard *Starbound*, but I think her strongest desire is to go back to Altos and look for her crew."

"I understand the sentiment," said Wesley, "and she'll get her chance, but that isn't possible right now. We don't have the resources. We're building a new Lightship, *Defiant*, although she won't be ready until next year. The Earthmen are fast-tracking *Resolution* for Levant and the Carinthians are building three more after losing *Impulse*. They don't do anything half-assed, that's for sure. But until they're all commissioned it's just *Starbound* and *Valiant* out there in full operation. I just hope we don't have any more Imperial incursions to worry about until we have a fully functioning fleet."

"And what about the jump gate at Levant?" I asked. He shook his head.

"Shut down from our side and guarded by the fleet, or

at least as much of it as we can spare. We need to understand this ancient technology, whether it's Imperial or Founder-based, much more thoroughly before we try to use it again. And we don't want to encourage any further contact with remnants of the Corporate Empire, automated or not," said Wesley.

"I've had my fill of run-ins with those things recently," I said. "My concern is that the HuKs we faced at Jenarus seemed to have preprogrammed their AI's specifically for fighting a Lightship. If that's so, then they're either getting outside help or there's some kind of super-intelligent fleet AI out there reprogramming the HuKs. I'd like to be part of whatever operation we do to take them out. They've caused enough havoc already."

Wesley stopped eating his meal and looked up at me, then back down to his plate.

"It's not your concern, son. The Union Navy is just holding its own at the moment, trying to consolidate. That's why this diplomatic mission is so important. We need Carinthia in this Union, and Pendax and Levant and Jenarus and many others we haven't even contacted yet. They all have resources that can speed up our naval and industrial development considerably." I sat back.

"And what about this inquest on Carinthia aids in that process?" I asked. Wesley shook his head.

"It should be a formality. We've prepared all of our files for you to take along. The presentation is simple enough. You'll just have to sit there and look official."

"That sounds fine," I said.

"Oh, and one more thing," said Wesley. He got up from the table and hit a button on his desk. At that, a navy medical tech entered the room and began preparing a hypo.

"What's this?" I asked.

"Something I promised your father," Wesley said as he sat back down at the table. "A subcutaneous tracker. Historian technology. It emits a low-frequency longwave that transmits through the Historian ansible network. It should be completely undetectable to our Carinthian friends."

"Should I be expecting trouble?" I asked. Wesley shook his head.

"Not as far as we know. But we wanted to be able to track your location, under any circumstances. You are the heir to the Director's Chair," he said.

"What circumstances—" I started. The tech interrupted me.

"Extend your left arm, please, and roll up your sleeve," she said in a very businesslike manner. I looked to Wesley. He was finishing a dinner roll.

"Don't make me order you," he said. I did as instructed. The tech injected me but I didn't feel a thing. There was a slight trace of blue and green wires under the skin of my left forearm. I rolled my sleeve back down.

"The unique thing about this tracker is that we'll be able to find you in short order if there's any trouble," said Wesley.

"Again," I asked, "are we expecting trouble?" Wesley smiled.

"As I said, Commander, it's just a precaution so your father sleeps better at night."

With that the tech left and we both finished our lunch.

"I've arranged for private transport for you to Carinthia, if that suits you," said Wesley. I smiled at that. Private accommodations beat navy bunks any day of the week.

"It does indeed," I said.

"Good luck then, Commander."

"Thank you, sir."

And then we were done, and I was on my way back to Government House for a further afternoon of protocol training.

The ceremony entitling me as Duke of KendalFalk was blissfully brief and recorded in the late afternoon for broadcast in advance of the *Impulse* drama later that evening. I did my best toy soldier impression in full royal regalia and dutifully followed the script handed to me by Perkins.

That night was Reunion Day Eve, and after a satisfying dinner with Dobrina, Madrey, and my father at Government House's private apartments we exchanged holiday gifts, one only, as was our family tradition. I gave my father an antique sextant that Serosian had found for me at my request in an Earth maritime museum, and Dobrina received a traditional aboriginal dress, no doubt picked out by Madrey. My father gave his fiancé a pair of large diamond earrings. I opened Dobrina's gift to me, an artisan holiday nutcracker-type figure with a pipe called a smoker. My official gift to Dobrina was a native hunting weapon called a boomerang that was ornately decorated with jewels and native art. I planned on giving her my own personal gift later.

As the evening wore on Dobrina and I found ourselves in my suite cuddled comfortably alone on a large sofa, a fire burning, reclining and watching ourselves being portrayed on the digital telenetwork drama of our exploits, and laughing.

"You're quite handsome," she said of the actor portraying me. "But I seem more buxom than pretty." I looked down at her chest.

"Not a completely inaccurate portrayal," I deadpanned. She smacked me on the arm.

"Pervert."

"Yes, ma'am." Then we laughed again, and kissed.

The film ended with me riding a rocket out of the launch tube of *Impulse*, then throwing the rocket at the massive Imperial dreadnought as I drifted away in space, there to meet my fate.

"Did you really yell 'sic semper tyrannis' when you threw that rocket at the dreadnought?" she said, teasing me.

"That's not how it happened," I said.

"As if it ever is." As triumphant music played in the background I switched off the player and kissed her, more forcefully this time.

"Time for bed, madam. And this time I intend to keep you up for a bit," I said.

"Umm," she said as we kissed. "Promises, promises."

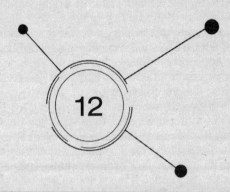

Back to Candle

The next day was full of gift giving, most of which
Perkins had already taken care of for me, a formal
mass at the National Cathedral, and a traditional Reunion Day dinner in the formal dining room with more
military and political dignitaries. I drank too much and
was only allowed a meager bit of time with Dobrina, to
our mutual consternation.

By Boxing Day our departure to High Station Candle
was a welcome relief. We used our time once again
aboard *Cordoba* for some precious privacy, and we were
granted all we wanted. The ship was empty of passengers
this time except for us.

We arrived at Candle the next morning fully refreshed
and ready to begin our next adventure. Once in our suite
we found a waiting message from our transport liaison,
who went unnamed.

The instructions were cryptic, only to meet him for

lunch on the Cloud Deck of High Station Candle at noon. We still had a few hours so we killed time going over the inquest briefings. It was innocuous stuff, and I had a hard time believing anything would come of it. At the appropriate time we headed up a few decks and took our places at a table that had been reserved for us. Our liaison was yet to arrive.

I got restless and ordered mimosas for Dobrina and myself at her insistence, then surveyed the Cloud Deck from the bar as I waited to be served. Every High Station had a Cloud Deck, a place where they could charge exorbitant prices for ordinary things such as dinner and drinks. They called it the "Cloud Deck" because it invariably offered the best view of the prime planet that you orbited, a view of the clouds, so to speak. Unfortunately Candle only offered a view of the yellow and orange sulfur-scarred rock that the station had been carved out of. Not a cloud within several million miles of the place.

Our liaison came through the door at 1205. I heard him behind me first, rather than saw him.

"Jesus, lad, drinking already? It's barely noon."

I turned around, mimosas in both hands, to see the scarred face of Lucius Zander, my former Lightship commander, a man I had rescued from a raging fire inside a damaged shuttle just a few months back. A man who was barely alive the last time I saw him.

"I would like to think you'd at least be respectful enough to acknowledge a superior officer with a salute, lad." The voice was weaker and his speaking pace was more deliberate than I remembered, but there was no doubting the owner of the gravelly rasp. I set the drinks back down on the bar and saluted automatically.

"Captain? Captain Zander, sir?"

"For Gods' sake lad, relax! I'm not Marley's ghost come to warn you on Christmas Eve. Finish your business." I stood frozen looking at him. What I saw shocked me.

He had no hair under his captain's beret. His exposed

skin was crinkled orange and mottled brown, deep lines cut through almost every inch of his face, neck, and hands. He held a titanium cane in his left hand as a balance for his good foot, his right. The left obviously was a hindrance, but not too much. When I looked into his face it was hairless, his right eye a dark brown as if it too had been burnt, and a huge scar ran down his forehead at an angle over his left eye, which was covered by a patch.

"What's the matter, boy? Never seen a man that's glad to be alive?" Then he stuck out his free hand to me and I shook it.

"It's good to see you, sir, but I never expected to see you so . . . soon," I said.

"It's all right to admit the truth, boy, you never expected to see me at all. Well, to tell you the truth I wasn't sure I'd ever make it this far myself. Eighteen surgeries, over a thousand micrografts, and two months in a lung regenerator for five hours a day will make a man want something, anything, he can grasp onto for a better future."

"I don't understand," I said. Just seeing him was a shock and I wasn't tracking our conversation well. He shook his head and jabbed a bony finger at me.

"I didn't do all that rehab just to go sit in a chair on some beach," he said. "I've got a ship! And I'm here as your taxi ride to Carinthia."

Zander strolled over and sat down with us, giving Dobrina a kiss on the cheek that she did her best not to cringe away from, and ordered a beer. Though his appearance was shocking, he was still every bit the crusty navy captain we had known on *Impulse*.

"What an ugly place," said Zander, looking around the restaurant and out the view windows. Then he took a long draught of his beer. He was in the middle of explaining to me about his decision to leave rehab six months early.

"I can grow a new leg anytime, or get another hundred grafts of newskin," he said. "I'll look right and pink then, lad, enough to capture all the ladies' hearts. But it will take two years to grow back hair and fill in the scar for the eye replacement, and I haven't got time to do with that business now."

I took another sip of my mimosa. "So you put in for active duty and they accepted you?" I asked.

"Hells no, boy!" he said. "They wouldn't give me another command, son. Not the way I was broken," he said. "I'm a privateer now. I cashed in every chit I had in the Union Navy to get a Functional Discharge, and they finally gave me one. I work for a trader from Pendax named Admar Harrington. He's rich as the devil, and as ambitious, too."

"There wasn't anything in the Carinthian Navy for you?" asked Dobrina. "I was told our commissions would return to the home navy in the event we left Union employ." Zander looked pensive at this. He eyed Dobrina and then me.

"I had my reasons for not rejoining the Carinthian Navy, missy. They may just be the suspicions of an old man, or they may be more," he said. Dobrina looked concerned at this, as was I, so I pressed him.

"What do you mean, 'suspicions of an old man'?" I asked. He waved me off.

"Forget I said anything."

"I'm afraid I can't do that," I said. "You see, I'm not just a navy commander anymore, I'm also a diplomat on his first mission and a royal duke of the Cochrane House of Quantar, so you'll just have to tell me, because in the real world I outrank you." Zander gave me his best pirate growl before drawing deeply from his beer again. Dobrina took another drink of her mimosa but stayed silent.

Zander sighed. "Just rumors, my boy. Nothing to be concerned about."

"You're evading the question," I said. "Spill it. Need I remind you I saved your life at Levant?"

"No need to remind me of my debts," he bristled.

"Captain, it would be helpful to know what we're getting into," chimed in Dobrina. Zander sighed as if resigned to his fate.

"Very well. Rumors mostly, about Carinthia. Rumors of commanders being replaced at the highest levels. Rumors that *some* in the Carinthian Navy are not all that happy with resources being allocated to the Union. I usually give it no thought, but every loyal Carinthian ship captain I know and trust is now taking his ships in-system through High Station Three. Not Two, and certainly not One," he said. Three was the most distant of the Carinthian High Stations, in orbit around a colorful gas giant two light-hours from primary Carinthian jump space.

"Why just Three and not One and Two?" asked Dobrina. Zander turned his direct attention on her.

"That's where the command replacements are supposedly being made, One and Two. One is in direct orbit over New Vienna. Two is stationed at the edge of the Habitable Zone. That leaves Three as the only remaining outpost for Loyalist commanders. And those Loyalists are staying well clear of One and Two and even Carinthia herself. And High Station Three is no longer being resupplied by Carinthia. They're relying on supplies from Quantar, Levant, and Earth. My new boss on Pendax is anxious to help as well," he said.

"You keep mentioning Loyalists. Loyal to whom, or to what?" I asked.

"Loyal to the Grand Duke Henrik, son, and to the Union," said Zander.

I sat back in my chair, suddenly sobered by the conversation.

"Lucius, we know that *Impulse* was infiltrated from within, by Tralfane, the Historian. He could not have acted alone. There had to be help—"

"From inside the navy, the Carinthian Navy. I know," Zander said. I watched concern play across his mottled face. I weighed my next question heavily before asking it.

"Could this be a sign of revolt within the Carinthian military? Revolt against the Union?" I asked. Dobrina's head snapped around at this.

"It could be. It could be a lot of things. It could be nothing." With this Zander tried a reassuring smile, but it didn't work on either Dobrina or me.

"Why didn't Wesley give us this intelligence before we left Quantar?" I asked.

"He's doing that right now, lad, through me," replied Zander.

"You work for Wesley too?" asked Dobrina.

"In some way, we all do, Commander," he said. Then he sat back and tried to appear relaxed. "In any case, the mission is on. Anything you two can discover about the situation on Carinthia will be well appreciated by the higher-ups, I'm sure."

"So now we're spies," I said. Zander shrugged.

"I'm sure the grand admiral wouldn't call it that." Once again I found myself resenting Wesley's using me for his own purposes. This time, though, he had included Dobrina, and that rubbed me the wrong way.

"Oh cheer up, you two. It won't be so bad. You'll get to go to state dinners and then probably spend one afternoon answering innocuous questions asked by a bunch of naval flunkies. Things could be worse," he said.

"When do we leave?" I asked.

"We're taking on stores for Three right now. We'll be ready for shove-off at 1700 tonight. Dinner in my cabin an hour later, if you please."

"But, Captain—" started Dobrina. He cut her off.

"It's a full day to traverse from the Carinthia jump

point to High Station Three at safe cruising speed. Plenty of time to talk then, lass," he said, then leaned forward. "But for now, let me tell you about my ship!"

"Please do, sir," I said, humoring him. He smiled again.

"I've got a brand spanking new Wasp, the *Benfold*."

"Wasp?" asked Dobrina. Zander shrugged.

"It's just what we call them. They're really line frigates, designed for running military and commercial cargo for the navy."

I sat forward again at this. I was intrigued. "What's her drive?" I asked.

"Two FTL spools and a Hoagland," said Zander. "But she packs enough firepower to turn this rock to ashes and she's faster from point-to-point in normal space than anything in the Unified Navy!"

"Crew?" asked Dobrina.

"Thirty-two," he said. "Three commissioned officers from Pendax, half a dozen private security and a staff sergeant. The rest commercial spacers. We run pork and beef from Pendax to Candle, plus a good lot of your Quantar scotch and shiraz out to Levant and back home. We pick up absinthe and schnapps for the Carinthians in the Union Navy and spread them out among the Union High Stations. We carry military cargo, too. The odd missile battery, anything that will fit in our hold, which is a lot. And if we see anything amiss while we're out in the Great Dark, we have full rein to stop and investigate for the navy."

"Sounds like a nice life," I said. He shrugged again, and raised his beer stein.

"It beats fighting off all the widowed *hausfraus*," he said. Then we clinked our glasses. Dobrina's eyes betrayed her concern to me as we drank.

I smiled politely, and wondered what we were heading into.

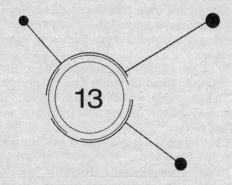

13

To High Station One

Benfold was a cozy ship despite her unexpected size. She was indeed shaped like a wasp, with the cargo holds encompassing her belly while the hyperdimensional drives and Hoagland Field generators were held out well to either side, like wings. She was also a full two-thirds the length of a Lightship and in some ways superior in performance, especially trimmed as she was now in normal space, with low mass in her spacious cargo holds. But she was not so elegantly appointed as a Lightship, with the majority of her interior space reserved for carrying cargo. Nonetheless, her forward third held our sturdy crew well, with an oversized mess hall and a smaller room whose walls Zander could draw closed to create a proper dining room.

It was almost a full day out in normal space to the jump point from Quantar to Carinthia, then another full day's trek to High Station Three, limited as we were by the Carinthian Navy's in-system speed regulations. We had already made the turn inbound and Dobrina and I were getting some rest when Zander's call from the bridge woke us both. I checked my watch. Still two hours to High Station Three.

"Cochrane here," I said into the desk com.

"Just got the call from Carinthian Naval command," came Zander's raspy reply. "They want us to skip our scheduled stop at Three and proceed directly to One first, so I can drop you off. Then back out to Three to deliver my scheduled cargo. And they're assigning us an escort."

"What kind of escort?" I asked.

"By displacement, a Carinthian Navy destroyer. I'll let you decide what kind of company that is."

I looked to Dobrina, who was already up and dressing.

"We're on our way," I said.

We arrived at *Benfold*'s command deck a few minutes later. Flying as we were under the red-and-gray standard of Pendax afforded us some measure of protection, even exception from any importune requests from our escort. The Carinthian destroyer flew side by side with us, to give us a gentle nudge away from our filed flight plan. It was clear that we were not to even consider a stop at High Station Three. Nonetheless, as we passed close by Three on our new vector Zander received numerous greetings from his many friends in the Carinthian Navy by radio and even longwave packet, which was unusual. If there was any sort of warning in those private packets, Zander kept it to himself.

The command deck of *Benfold* was tight and cramped, and really no place for visitors. Only five seats were available, including the captain's, which Zander wasn't giving up. It was really more of a C-and-C, buried as she was deep inside the ship's fo'c'sle, away from the engines and cargo holds. I was reminded again of the fanciful design of the Lightships, with their archaic conning towers with the bridge on top, like an Old Earth sailing vessel. It was a symbol of the openness and freedom of the explorer, a central theme in Lightship design. Such fanciful touches were a direct result of the Historian's gift of the all-enveloping defensive Hoagland Field, given to Quantar and Carinthia more than a decade ago.

We stood on either side of Zander, assessing the situation.

"They've asked us to increase our speed," said Zander. "Obviously they want us to get in-system faster than our original plan."

"To what end?" asked Dobrina.

"Who's to know?" replied Zander.

"No chance they could just be a friendly escort?" asked Dobrina.

"Unlikely with as much offensive hardware as those destroyers carry. A scout or corvette could do the job easily enough, without the show of force," replied Zander.

"The Carinthian government has known we were coming for weeks. Why this kind of act?" asked Dobrina.

"It could be nothing. But it does seem like the powers that be on Carinthia want to show us their fist instead of shaking our hands. I'd take that as a message. Like I said, rumors of unrest in the capital, Commander," said Zander.

"Politics aside, can we defend ourselves if required?" I asked Zander. He looked at me sidelong.

"I'd say yes. They're guided missile destroyers, pack plenty of wallop, including nuke-tipped torpedoes. We're much faster than they are. I don't have as much artillery, but my coil cannons could mess them up right good," he said.

"Let's hope it doesn't come to that," I said. Zander stood, his cane supporting his bad leg.

"This is my ship, but on this mission I'm under your command, Mr. Cochrane. What are your orders?" he said. I thought about that for a second.

"Steady as we go, for now," I said. Dobrina looked up from the tactical board.

"At this speed I make it around five hours to High Station One," she said.

I only nodded in response.

In the end they asked us, in a way that sounded very much like an order, to fly in close formation, making a heading straight for One. I decided discretion was the better part of valor, so we followed without protest. After slightly more than five hours with our escort, we docked at High Station One, far above Carinthia, her blue-green shine glowing in the dark of space as we looked at her on the main display.

"Does it feel good to be home?" I asked Dobrina, trying to cheer her. She nodded nervously but said nothing.

"Watch your back, lad," said Zander as we stood at the airlock of his cargo bay. "Strange goings on these days."

"I'm sure it will be fine," I said, not really sure if I believed that. We said our goodbyes to Zander as the Carinthian soldiers on the other side of the air lock tapped three times on our door in staccato repetition. I verified the environment was stable and then reluctantly opened the airlock. A phalanx of six Carinthian military police, or *Feldjäger* as Dobrina called them, stood facing us on the other side.

"Commander Cochrane? Captain Kierkopf?" asked the tallest one in the middle. We both acknowledged. "Come vis uz please," he said in a heavy Carinthian accent. His tone and manner left no doubt that it was an order, even if he did say "please."

We followed the commandant of the guard through a nearly empty deck on what should have been a thriving military station. No question that High Station One was buttoned down tight. As we approached a more central hub of the station traffic picked up a bit, looking more like what you would expect from an operating military space station. I got more than one sidelong glance from passing officers and enlisteds. I supposed that my choice of wearing my royal family colors instead of my Union Navy uniform had something to do with that.

We were guided into an anteroom that could only be described as plush, with soft velvet-covered chairs and a formal sitting area. The *Feldjäger* were pleasant enough, even though no smiles were on offer, offering us tea and pastries. We ate in silence, avoiding small talk. After about half an hour of this we were escorted into an adjoining, much larger room. It was also done in a rich, formal style, and very much looked to be the type of room that would be used for receiving visiting dignitaries. There were a few servants scattered around the perimeter, but we were offered no further refreshments, nor a place to sit. After about five minutes of this, a man that looked to be some sort of protocol official entered the room and activated a small standing monitor station placed on top of a central podium. Then he came up to me.

"Your codex please, Sire?" he said. I immediately went to my diplomatic pouch and retrieved a small black box, opened it and removed a metal cylinder from the velvet casing and handed it to the officer. He took it to the monitor and slipped it inside the unit. The codex had been given to me by Perkins back on Quantar prior to our departure. The codex had been used for centuries in the Empire as a way of validating the bearer's DNA and ancestral history. It confirmed a royal was who he said he was. These were ancient and very formal protocols, but Perkins had suspected I might need it. The Carinthians, it seemed, stayed much closer to the old royal protocols than we on Quantar did.

After a few moments the cylinder popped back out of the monitor and the officer took it and handed it back to me.

"Thank you, Sire," he said with a head bow, then made for the far doorway as if to depart.

"What's that all about?" whispered Dobrina. I tilted my head toward her.

"Just royal formalities. The protocols of the demigods. Nothing for you mere mortals to worry yourselves over," I said. That got a smile from her despite our obviously stressful circumstances.

When he reached the doorway the protocol officer opened it and then stood to one side. At that signal a tall man, looking about thirty years old and dressed in a highly decorated Carinthian green military uniform, stepped through the threshold and strode purposefully toward us, trailed by the protocol officer. He stopped a few meters away from me and then just stared, as if waiting for something. He reminded me of Serosian: tall, dark hair, but with a slightly rounder face that nonetheless reflected the angular edge of his father, who was undoubtedly the Grand Duke Henrik Feilberg.

The protocol officer stepped up, placing himself between but not in front of the two of us. Dobrina took a step back away from me. I just waited, perplexed by the whole thing. I was wondering if I would have to start the conversation when the protocol officer thankfully spoke up.

"Your Highness," he said to the decorated man, "may I present Peter Erasmus Cochrane, Duke of KendalFalk, Viscount of New Queensland, and heir to the Director's Chair of Quantar." Then he turned to me. "Sire Cochrane, may I present to you Prince Arin Feilberg, Duke of New Styria and New Burgenland, Prince Regent of the Realm of Carinthia."

"Prince Arin," I said, bowing from the neck per the protocol Perkins had taught me.

"Duke Peter," he replied with no real joy in his voice, making the same bow to me. "Welcome to Carinthia."

"Thank you, Sire," I said, then turned to my

companion with a sweep of my arm. "May I present Captain Dobrina Kierkopf of the Unified Space Navy." At this Dobrina stepped out and did a slight dip, which I supposed was what they called a curtsey. The prince did not move to shake her hand, but simply acknowledged her with a slight nod and a single word.

"Captain," he said. She stepped back behind me. The protocol officer took over the conversation again.

"Duke Peter is here in the role of a Union Navy Commander, Highness, attending a Royal Navy inquest on the loss of our Lightship *Impulse* in the Altos system," he said. The prince made a face like this was news to him, but said nothing. There was an air about him of superiority, as if he was looking down on an obviously uncultured young royal from a provincial world. Finally, he spoke again.

"I have been taught by the Historians of Earth that our families were on opposite sides of the old Imperial civil war. How convenient it must be for your people that we are now on the same side," said Arin.

I was puzzled by the comment. "Well, Highness, I am not sure if I would use the word 'convenient,' but yes, the Union has been to Quantar's advantage, undoubtedly," I replied. He gave a quick, humorless smile at that before responding in kind.

"What I meant to say is that Carinthia offers the Union our heavy industry, our machinery and resources, our engineering enterprise. Yet Quantar seems only to offer some inexpensive timber and your noted shiraz wines. It hardly seems a fair exchange to me," he said.

My puzzlement grew. Frankly, I felt a bit insulted, but wanted to avoid an interstellar diplomatic incident, per my recent training.

"We like to think our contributions to the Union Navy have been of some use," I said evenly.

"Indeed, to the Union, such as they are. But not to Carinthia directly," said Arin. Now I was sure I was being insulted.

"It was Quantar lives that were the first to be sacrificed aboard *Impulse*," I said, trying to make a point without starting an argument. He gave the quick half-smile again and then immediately changed the subject.

"Tell me of your family's lineage. I know little beside what I've been taught," he asked. I gave a quick overview of our family's founding of the planet through the QUANTAR corporation, and the emperor's granting of royal titles some three centuries past, before the war.

"So really, you were merchant princes, endowed with your lands historically and then given formal titles as a means of quelling growing support for rebellion against the empire," he said. I hesitated now. Again, I didn't want an argument, but there was no doubt he was trying to belittle me and my family.

"I know little of the reasons for the revolt against the empire, Highness. Only that my family fell on the side of the republicans, in the end," I replied.

"You should be interested to know then that my family lines go back to Central Europe on Old Earth, more than a millennia in fact, and our family includes generous blood from both the Von Drakenberg and De Vere families," he said. I had no idea what he meant by these references, except to show his family's blood proximity to the ruling families of the First Empire.

In the end, a polite "indeed" was all I could manage in response. With that he nodded, apparently satisfied that he had put the rube royal from the hinterlands in his place.

"Enjoy your stay," he said finally with a slight uptick of one side of his mouth. At that, he turned and started to walk out, the formalities apparently ended. I gave Dobrina a perplexed look. Before he reached the door, however, it opened from the other side. A lighter-haired young man, shorter by a full head but wearing the same military uniform, with less decorations, came through the door. The two men had a quiet but intense exchange, and then Prince Arin was gone. The door shut behind him as the other man came into the room and approached us.

"I'm Prince Benn Feilberg, the grand duke's youngest son," he said, extending his hand with a smile. I took it.

"A pleasure to meet you, Prince Benn," I said. He turned to Dobrina.

"You must be Captain Kierkopf," he said, and then also extended his hand to her. She tried the curtsey move again but he stopped her. "No need for that, Captain."

"Thank you, Sire," she said, then returned his handshake. Prince Benn dismissed the protocol officer and had the servants bring over three of the sitting chairs strewn about the room. Then we all sat together in the middle of the large, mostly empty room, our chairs placed on top of the only area rug in the room. Once we were settled, I started in.

"Your brother, the prince regent, seems a rather formal chap," I said conversationally. *Unfriendly* was the word that I was actually thinking.

"A bit," Prince Benn said, with only a slight smile.

"I wasn't aware Carinthia was under a Regency," I said. He bristled at that a bit.

"It isn't, not technically," said Benn. This was concerning. "My brother has assumed the title but without all of the appropriate mechanisms being implemented, the proper levers being pulled, if you will. As far as I and many in our government and military are concerned, my father is still Carinthia's sovereign. That's part of why I'm here today. I'm just passing through on my way to High Station Three." That was the "Loyalist" station, Zander had told us. Now things were becoming clearer. "So I'm glad I caught you. I should be back tomorrow, and perhaps when this inquest is cleared off the books we can talk more freely," he said.

"I would appreciate that, Highness. Can I take your meaning to be that there is some question about the grand duke's, uh, condition?" I asked, I hoped delicately.

"There are moments when he is not all himself, I'm afraid," said Benn. "But he has not ceded power and Arin does not have the authority to take it. Let's just say we are having a vigorous family disagreement about that."

"Speaking of family—"

The prince cut me off. "You must be about to inquire about my sister, Karina. She is in New Vienna. She sees to my father's care on a daily basis," he said. This surprised me. She was a fully trained Union Navy officer, an astrogator, from what I had been told. But I supposed family came first for her.

"Prince Benn, how serious are things here on Carinthia?" I pressed, finally cutting to the point.

"Serious enough," he replied. "That's why I'm heading to Three, to take the lay of the land, so to speak. I wouldn't worry, though. This is about politics, mostly, and I hope to keep it that way." With that he stood and we stood with him.

"I want to thank you, Captain Kierkopf, for your service aboard *Impulse*. It was a shock to all of us when she was lost, but your heroism in the matter, both of you, is well documented. Have no fear about this inquest business. I'm sure it's just military formalities," he said.

"Thank you, Sire. Those thoughts are well appreciated," she said in reply. He gave us a final nod of acknowledgment and with that he said his goodbyes and made his way out, leaving Dobrina and me together in the room.

"Not what I expected," I said, "of either of them." I sat back down but Dobrina stayed standing. "You're unhappy?" I asked, looking up at her. She looked back down on me with concern etched across her face.

"I want off this station, as soon as possible. Let's just get this damned inquest over with and get home," she said. She seemed embarrassed by the disarray she had found her home world and its military in, and I couldn't blame her. I was pleased, though, that she mentioned "home," which I took to mean *Starbound* and the Union Navy, and perhaps even me. I acceded to her request, and we made our way back to the docking area, ready to get on with the business at hand now that the necessary formalities were over.

We were promptly escorted to a military shuttle where we were hustled in and instructed to strap in to safety couches. Our *Feldjäger* commandant and two other guards also strapped in behind us, the rest peeling off of our detail and staying on station. The commandant issued an order in German into his com and the shuttle burned to life. What seemed like seconds later, we were off the deck of the station and back out into space, on our way to the surface of Carinthia. The whole transaction had taken barely five minutes.

"Very efficient," I said quietly, trying to lighten the mood. Dobrina sighed.

"This was not how I wanted you to see my home world," she said, equally quietly.

"You can apologize later. Right now I want this all over with, just like you do," I said. We were quiet then for several minutes while the shuttle descended. Dobrina poked her head up to the shuttle's porthole to look out, then turned back to me, leaned in, and whispered to me.

"This is not the route to New Vienna," she said. "Normally diplomats or VIPs would be received at the Ganderstaad Air Base. We're tracking much further north," she said. I took her hand and squeezed it gently, trying to reassure her.

After another twenty minutes of descent our shuttle landed in daylight hours in an area I could only describe as tundra, far north of any sizable settlement that I could identify during our approach. From the air it looked like it could only be a remote airbase, but even as we landed it looked seldom used and out of date. The sky was gray and dismal, and there was a sizable amount of snow on the ground, piled up and well frozen.

Once we were on the ground the *Feldjäger* commandant personally unbuckled us from our couches while the guards stood watch, hands on their weapons. The commandant silently motioned us to the shuttle door, which had popped open into a frigid day with a cold north wind whipping through the air. More armed soldiers lined our path as we made our way to a ramshackle wood and steel building with a metal pipe on the roof blowing dark smoke into the air. We were silently ushered inside, where a small, bald man wearing a black military police colonel's uniform and circular eyeglasses sat behind a simple wooden desk. He was writing in a paper journal with a pen. He checked his watch once, then wrote down the time, as if he was keeping a log. Then he rose, hands behind his back, and stepped around the desk. He addressed Dobrina first.

"Captain Kierkopf," he said in Standard, albeit with a heavy accent, using the temporary rank she had held aboard *Impulse*. "You will face charges of neglect of your duties before a court-martial, beginning tomorrow morning."

"Neglect of my—" started Dobrina before I cut in.

"There must be some mistake, Colonel. We were told this was to be an inquest only. And the captain here is part of my entourage, and thus under diplomatic protection," I said firmly. The colonel shook his head.

"You do not understand, Commander. There is no 'diplomatic mission.' The captain was given her commission by your Union Navy, but since she no longer has a command in that navy her commission has now been returned to the Carinthian Navy. There will be answers for the murders of the crew of *Impulse*, which had an almost all-Carinthian crew, sir," he said to me, defiant.

"Murders?" said Dobrina. I put a hand out to quiet her.

"I am also Duke of KendalFalk, of House Cochrane of Quantar, not just a navy commander," I said, "and as such that makes this a diplomatic mission, and the captain is part of that mission."

The colonel got angry now.

"This is a navy affair, Commander, and you will both be tried in your capacities as navy officers!"

"But Captain Kierkopf—"

"Captain Kierkopf will stand trial for negligence and dereliction of duty. But you, sir, you will stand trial for much greater crimes. It is *you* who destroyed *Impulse*, *you* who lost her crew. You, sir, are charged with treason, and the murder of the entire crew of *Impulse*!"

And with that he stomped from the room, and I felt the chill wind blow right through the shack walls, the cold sinking deep into my bones.

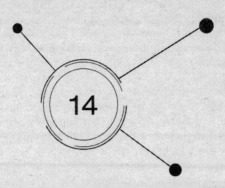

On Trial

I spent the night in what could only be described as a military brig with minimal heat, bedding, or services of any kind. The discomfort didn't matter much as sleep eluded me all night anyway, my mind spinning with the possibilities of my situation, and Dobrina's of course, which ran the gamut from a huge misunderstanding to an outright coup d'état against the grand duke and the Feilberg family. I found it hard to believe that Carinthia's ruling family would want an outright conflict with Quantar, unless what constituted the Feilberg military had taken control of the civilian government and was now hostile to the Union.

There was no doubt that Prince Arin had been at best distant in our conversation, and borderline unfriendly. It was obvious that whatever was happening on Carinthia, it must certainly revolve around him and his attempt to implement a Regency government. That much had been made clear by Prince Benn. The full extent of that attempt, and its peripheral effect on me, was still unclear. I wondered if he was the kind of man who would go so far as to execute another royal on trumped-up charges to further his goals, and who or what might be backing him in these endeavors. Worries about Imperial entanglements came to mind many times over the course of the night.

My worrying of course also encompassed Dobrina. We had been separated immediately after our arrival and I hadn't seen her nor heard anything about her at any time during the night. I feared for her, as I hoped my status as both a Union Navy officer and a Quantar royal would be enough to protect me from the worst of circumstances. But if someone in the Carinthian hierarchy had singled her out for punishment in the *Impulse* affair, then her career was certainly in jeopardy at a minimum. I also feared for her as a woman, one I had more than just a passing interest in.

In the morning one of the *Feldjäger* MPs brought me a rudimentary breakfast of a fried egg, slice of bread, and water. I was then taken out and allowed to use the toilet and a sink to freshen up. When returned from this I was given my Union Navy commander's uniform from my baggage and ordered to put it on. Apparently the Carinthians wanted to try me as a navy officer, and not a royal. From there I was walked under heavy guard to a room with a small window, a simple wood table, and two chairs facing each other. I was instructed to sit down and I did, facing the door. My escorts departed and locked the door behind them.

After several minutes of sitting I got anxious and started pacing, stopping to look out of the high-set window. As I craned my neck to see out, I could see a small patrol of guards in the square outside, a disheveled fence, and an empty guard tower. Beyond was a long, empty run to some very sharp, barren, snow-capped peaks. The guards I could observe seemed casual in their approach to their duties, and I had no doubt it was due to the low probability of escape by any prisoner. Where would they go? If someone left this base alive, my belief was it was surely at the beneficence of its masters.

I was surprised then by a knock at the door. A tall, lanky redheaded lieutenant came through the door wearing a standard Carinthian Navy green uniform. He sat down opposite my chair and pulled several papers from a brief, then set the brief down on the floor. He donned glasses and took to reading for a few moments, then looked up at me.

"Are you enjoying the view?" he asked, his accent coming through strongly.

"Not really," I said, keeping my place at the window.

"Come. Sit," he said, gesturing to my open chair and smiling slightly. I didn't want to go on with this charade at all, to give it any credence, but I decided this moment might not be the best time to fight. "I am Lieutenant Karl Poulsen. I will be the . . . what do you call it . . . lawyer? Yes, the lawyer representing Captain Kierkopf in her defense," he said once I had sat down.

"But not for me?" I asked. He shook his head, shuffling papers.

"You have no standing in our court system for representation. You will have to defend yourself against all charges. However, I thought it might be helpful to the captain's case if I talked with you first, to see if you would be sympathetic to helping her?"

"Of course I would," I said.

"Good, then we can proceed," he said, seeming satisfied. What followed was a series of carefully prepared questions. Whoever this lawyer was, he had done extensive research into the *Impulse* incident. I tried to answer as honestly as I could and to be as helpful as I could to Dobrina's case. At least, that's what I hoped. After about twenty minutes he concluded his questioning and started to pack up.

"So that's it?" I said, starting to get upset. "Nothing about my case, no consultation, not even a reading of the court rules?" He stopped and looked at me in that even, passionless, Carinthian way.

"You are not without my limited sympathies, but I do not make the rules. You will stand trial on your own, although the court proceedings will be held side by side. I will not consult with you nor answer your questions in court. My only interest is in getting Captain Kierkopf exonerated and returned to duty in the Carinthian Navy, nothing more." He stood to leave. I stood as well.

"The Carinthian Navy? Captain Kierkopf is a Union Navy officer," I said.

Poulsen smiled narrowly. "Not anymore. Her commission belongs to the Carinthian Navy, and her knowledge of your navy's inner workings is far too valuable to us to allow her to leave our service again," he said with only a hint of a threat.

"One last question," I said as he turned to open the door. "Your name, Karl Poulsen. Would you be any relation to Claus Poulsen, late of *H.M.S. Impulse*?" He looked at me impassively.

"Claus was my brother, and a good officer, and another black mark on you," he said, then went through the door. I sat back down as the impact of that nonrandom selection hit me.

Nothing was going right here. Nothing at all.

An hour later, I was escorted across the yard through cold, blowing snow to the original building we had been brought to when we arrived. This was obviously to be the trial location. I was placed in a holding room that was slightly better appointed than my previous locale. I sat down on a small couch and was brought tea by a *Feldjäger* MP, which I welcomed. All the *Feldjäger* were kitted out in winter gear. I had just my navy uniform jacket as protection against the cold. After a few minutes of drinking the warming tea and contemplating my situation, I was surprised by the door popping open as another MP came through, followed by Dobrina. The MP then turned and left, locking the door behind him. I was ecstatic to see her. I jumped up and we hugged for a few seconds, almost as much out of a desire for warmth as out of affection, and then we sat together on the couch.

"What the hell is going on?" I asked.

"I wish I knew," she responded, taking my hand. "They didn't hurt you, did they?" she said with some concern in her voice, enough for me to take it seriously.

"No, they've been respectful. Should I be worried about that?" I said. She shook her head.

"I don't know, and I don't know what's going on. My lawyer has told me only that he thinks the court wants to be lenient with me, but that means they want to come down hard on you."

"Your lawyer is Claus Poulsen's brother. It's clear he hates me. He also made it clear that the Carinthian Navy wants to keep you as a resource for information to use against the Union Navy," I said.

"Like hell I'll let myself be used like that. I haven't resigned my commission and they haven't tried to force me to do so. I won't cooperate," she said.

"You should think about that," I replied. "Agreeing to serve in the Carinthian Navy could get you off the hook."

"And what about you?" I shook my head.

"I still have my royal standing. Perhaps it will suffice for them to convict me, hold me for a time, and then send me home in disgrace," I said.

"I wouldn't bet on that." I had no reply, so she continued. "What's really going on? Is what Zander said true? Is Carinthia on the verge of a civil war?" she asked. I shrugged.

"It could be. Some sort of renegade faction within the

Carinthian military. But if it is that, then they have broad control and sweeping powers. They have High Station One locked down, and they have the cachet to kidnap the official representative of both the Union Navy and the Quantar government and stash us here," I said. She looked very concerned.

"I think you have to be very careful in there, Peter. Don't take responsibility for things you didn't do. They want your scalp. Don't give it to them to protect me," Dobrina said.

"What can they do to me really? Hold me here?" I said. "They risk war with both Quantar and Earth if they try anything that brazen. I think this is brinksmanship. In the end they'll find me guilty of something and maybe kick me off the planet, if what they're trying to do is put cracks in the Union alliance. But that's as far as they can go, nothing more."

She shook her head at me. "Don't be so sure." I kissed her then, on the forehead, for reassurance.

"You take care of yourself in there," I said. "Don't worry about me."

"But—" I cut her off with another kiss, this time on the lips, just as a knock came at the door. A *Feldjäger* entered.

"It is time," he said. We both stood and I followed Dobrina out. We were taken back, under guard, to the same room where we had met the unpleasant *Feldjäger* colonel on our arrival. He was there again, seated across the room from us at a long wooden table. He was flanked by two assistants, a young man and a woman. Dobrina was escorted to a table in the center of the room, which had two chairs, one for her and the other occupied already by Karl Poulsen. I was seated at a table by myself. A dozen MPs spread about the room were the only others present besides the court participants. A large table with three empty chairs faced us, flanked by the Carinthian standard black-and-green flag with the double eagle on one side of the table and the Carinthian Navy flag on the other. The room, thankfully, had been outfitted with half a dozen space heaters.

After ten minutes of waiting, an MP went to the main table and rang a naval bell three times. At this we all stood and a back door opened as three Carinthian Navy officers came through. By their looks they were all elderly, no doubt career men, and no doubt picked for their loyalty to the cause, whatever that may be. The one in the center seemed like a rock of a man, with a bristling crew cut of hair that still held some of its youthful black against an advancing army of gray. They all sat down and we followed suit. The man in the center, an admiral by rank, tapped a gavel three times and then spoke in Standard from prepared remarks, not looking up from the text.

"I am Vice-Admiral Commack. I am the presiding judge of this tribunal. Vice-Admirals Sostek and Grunar will serve as associate judges. The charges before this court are severe and carry the heaviest of penalties. Both parties under court jurisdiction will be given a fair trial with the opportunity to respond in their own defense. By Carinthian Navy law Captain Kierkopf is provided with legal counsel. Under that same law, Mr. Cochrane, being an agent of a foreign government, is not extended the same privilege. Do you both understand?" he said, again without looking up.

At Poulsen's prompting Dobrina stood and responded, "Yes," then sat back down. I said nothing and stayed in place.

"Do you understand, Mr. Cochrane?" said the admiral without looking at me. The room stayed silent for several moments. Finally I said:

"I understand, but I do not agree."

"Agree with what?" demanded Admiral Commack, looking up at me for the first time from under wire-rimmed glasses. I stood and absently buttoned my uniform jacket just to make him wait.

"Firstly, sir, if this is a naval proceeding, you will address me by my rank, which is commander. But beyond that, I demand that you address me by the title that I undertook for this mission, which is Duke of Kendal-Falk, in which case you may refer to me as Sire, or Your Highness," I said.

He started to turn red at this. "This court will do no such thing," he retorted.

"Then I want that dishonor noted for the record," I replied. Commack took off his glasses and looked directly at me.

"Look around you, Mr. Cochrane. Do you see a court recorder?"

I scanned the room. There was none. I did note what was undoubtedly an observation camera in one corner of the ceiling, though.

Commack smiled. "May we go on, Mr. Cochrane?" he said. Seeing no other opportunity, I sat back down. Dobrina gave me a displeased frown, no doubt upset that I was drawing the court's wrath on myself, but I was determined to protect her at any cost.

"Colonel Kobin," said Commack to the prosecutor, "would you be so good as to read the formal charges?"

Kobin read the formal charges against Dobrina, which ranged from abandoning her post to malicious neglect of her duty and fraternization. That last one stung and was no doubt aimed at me. He also read an extensive list against me.

"Mr. Cochrane, as the agent of a foreign government, left his post as interim commander of *Impulse* to engage in a poorly planned rescue mission of the damaged shuttles at Levant, a mission which focused first and foremost on the rescue of Captain Kierkopf, with whom he was having an improper sexual liaison in violation of fraternization regulations. This act delayed the rescue of Captain Lucius Zander and his pilot, Ensign Claus Poulsen. This delay led directly to the death of Ensign Poulsen, a fine young Carinthian officer." I watched as Karl Poulsen shifted uncomfortably at the mention of his brother's name. Colonel Kobin continued.

"Ultimately this neglect led to *Impulse* coming under attack by Imperial forces in the Levant system and forcing her retreat from the shuttle rescue operation. Because of this attack, *Impulse*'s Historian was forced to abandon ship in his yacht in order to keep her hyperdimensional drive from falling into the hands of enemy forces." Now this was new. The rogue Earth Historian Tralfane was the major player in the hijacking and destruction of *Impulse* by our view of things. I wondered where this new information could have come from. I shot a glance at Dobrina, who caught my eye before turning her attention back to the charges against me.

"The prosecution will prove that this act of neglect by Mr. Cochrane of the Union Navy led directly to the loss of *Impulse* and the death or abandonment of her entire crew in the Altos system. This act is a capital offense, and carries with it the ultimate punishment. The prosecution will seek said punishment when Mr. Cochrane is found guilty: death," said Kobin in a simple, matter-of-fact tone. Then he sat down. Dobrina's face was full of worry. I tried to calm her with a look of reassurance, but in reality I was stunned by Kobin's statement of intent as well.

Admiral Commack nodded to Karl Poulsen. "Your opening statement on behalf of Captain Kierkopf, Mr. Poulsen," he said. Poulsen rose and straightened his uniform jacket, his lanky frame perfectly erect.

"My client, Captain Kierkopf, has had a fine record of service in both the Carinthian Navy and then following that the Union Navy. Nothing in the charges against her are in line with either that record or her known character. I could bring multiple witnesses of this strong character, but I will spare this tribunal that time and simply note the many references I have already filed in my brief." At this he turned to me. "Let it be stated clearly now and for the record that Captain Kierkopf was the victim of this man"—he pointed at me—"and his negligent actions at every turn. If Mr. Cochrane had followed both his orders and his duty the crew of *Impulse* would still be alive. My brother would still be alive, and Captain Kierkopf would not be here facing these charges. I ask the court to place blame where it clearly lies, in the lap of this man, Commander Peter Cochrane of Quantar." With that he sat down. Dobrina started to speak but Commack cut her off with a wave of the hand.

"You have spoken through your counsel, Captain, and you will not be allowed to speak again unless you designate yourself as counsel, which would be in defiance of this tribunal's recommendations," he said.

She stood up quickly. "I do so request this of the court," she said, barely under control. Commack looked right at her.

"Denied," he said. "Shall we move on to witnesses?" She shot me a look, but I waved her off with a hand gesture. We needed to pick our fights carefully. What happened next, though, was a shock.

Kobin rose and in his even tone said, "Prosecution calls Ship's Historian Tralfane of *H.M.S. Impulse*."

"What?" said Dobrina out loud. We both turned to see a door at the rear of the room open and the primary villain in our comrade's death walk through the threshold. I was on my feet and then being restrained by the *Feldjäger* MPs before I could control my reaction. How Tralfane had found himself in this place as a witness against both Dobrina and me was the main question. We had presumed he was in the hands of the Imperial forces he had given up the crew of *Impulse* to. A presumption that was now clearly incorrect on our part.

He gave his cloak to an MP and then proceeded past

both of us, moving slowly between our tables without looking at us or acknowledging our existence at all, then taking his place at the makeshift witness stand. I was forced back into my chair, each of the MPs keeping a firm hand on my shoulders.

"Bastard!" Dobrina shot out.

"Restrain your client, Colonel Poulsen!" demanded Commack, pounding his gavel. Poulsen forced Dobrina back into her chair and whispered to her vigorously, making firm hand gestures. For my part I simply glared at the man, wishing for all the world I had a coil pistol to dispatch him quickly. But restrained as I was by the heavy hands of the two MPs, such an outcome seemed unlikely.

After the usual requests for the witness to identify himself, Kobin went right into questioning Tralfane.

"On or about the date of 2768.12.30 CE were you involved in the mission of the Lightship *H.M.S. Impulse* to the Levant system?" he asked.

"I was," replied Tralfane. His appearance hadn't changed at all. He still struck a tall, stoic, and heartless figure, one ruled by his own intent, almost as if he was a god deigning to be dragged into the affairs of mere mortals. It wasn't just arrogance, but a firm belief in his own superiority to those he stood before that came through the most, as I'd never seen it before. Clearly, whatever had transpired after he had abandoned *Impulse*, he was none the worse for wear.

"Did Mr. Cochrane, during the series of events in the Levant system, put a fully charged coil pistol to your head?" said Kobin. No pulling punches here.

"He did," replied Tralfane.

"And did he also abandon his post as designated commander of *Impulse* to affect the rescue of the shuttle commanded by Captain Kierkopf?" asked Kobin. Again Tralfane answered in the affirmative. "And to your knowledge, were Mr. Cochrane and Captain Kierkopf, then a commander aboard *Impulse*, engaged in a sexual liaison against navy regulations?" I glanced at Dobrina. The look on her face was one of seething hatred.

"They were, as she was also previously involved with Mr. Cochrane's brother," said Tralfane coldly. That was an outright lie. Our affair hadn't started until our rehabilitation assignment, when we were both officially "on leave" from *Starbound*. I wanted to punch him, to defend my lady's honor, and my brother's. The MPs seemed to sense this and tightened their pressure on me.

"And do you feel this had an impact on the decision Mr. Cochrane made to rescue her first?" asked Kobin.

"Undoubtedly," Tralfane said, almost casually.

"May I speak?" I said, interrupting. This led to a sharp round of gavel pounding by Commack.

"This is not your designated time, Mr. Cochrane. You will get a chance to make your statement when the prosecution has finished with reporting its facts!" Of course those facts were highly questionable, but there was one ring of truth in all this; I did have a budding relationship with Dobrina, and it did impact my decisions, but not to rescue her shuttle first. That part was untrue, and Tralfane of all people knew it.

Then Kobin started in a different direction.

"Please tell us what transpired aboard *Impulse* after the failed rescue attempt by Mr. Cochrane that resulted in the death of Ensign Poulsen," he said.

Tralfane shrugged, a practiced gesture for certain. "With Mr. Cochrane off the ship and Captain Zander either seriously injured or dead, I had to take care of *Impulse* as best I could," he said. That almost made me laugh. Almost. "*Impulse* was experiencing a degradation of her HD containment field, and I had to move her away from the area where she had been attacked."

"Did you consider *Impulse* still in danger?" asked Kobin.

"Yes," nodded Tralfane. "Grave danger."

"Go on."

Tralfane cleared his throat, again in a practiced manner.

"With the containment field in jeopardy of collapse, my first thought was of the crew, of course. I decided to move *Impulse* away from the danger zone and take her closer to Levant to see if we could make repairs. With no shuttles left aboard, rescue of Captain Zander or the commander would have to be a secondary priority, and to be frank I didn't really care what happened to Cochrane, who had taken *Impulse*'s Downship for his own purposes," he said, looking in my direction with disdain. "When we were a few hours out from Levant, the HD drive became critical and I had to start depleting the crystal for the safety of the ship and her crew." I knew this was a lie. The main HD drive had come through the displacement wave attack with minimal damage thanks to my own actions and was running smoothly when I left on my rescue mission.

"Running on the secondary drive was taxing on *Impulse*'s systems, damaged as we were in the displacement wave attack we were led into by Captain Zander. At this point we were then taken over by a tracking control system, something of Imperial design, a relic of the old empire. Debilitated as we were, we were unable to break away from this system and *Impulse* was dragged into the automated jump point generator at Levant prime and propelled to Altos, where her fate was then unknown to me," Tralfane finished.

"And how did it come to pass that you were not with *Impulse* when she jumped?" asked Kobin. Tralfane shifted, his face displaying what I could only conclude was mock guilt for abandoning the crew of *Impulse* to their fate in the Altos system.

"I detached from *Impulse* in the yacht, prior to it going through the gate, to keep the yacht and the HD drive aboard her out of the hands of any potential hostile forces on the other side of that jump gate. *Impulse* still had several days of battery power left, more than enough to keep her going until we could mount a rescue, so it was agreed that I would take the yacht and make my way to the natural jump point of Levant and began a series of jumps back here, finally arriving at High Station Three. Unfortunately, by the time I got here it was too late. *Starbound* had already gone through the gate at the Union Navy's order and then Cochrane here destroyed *Impulse* during the attack by an Imperial dreadnought in Altos space," he finished.

Kobin looked down at his notes, as if considering what more to ask. It was an award-winning performance. "Thank you, Mr. Tralfane," he finally said, then turned to Commack. "No more questions at this time." Commack nodded and then looked to Karl Poulsen. Poulsen took the signal and stood, never leaving the area of his desk. He shuffled through his papers for a few moments as Dobrina and I exchanged worried glances.

"Mr. Tralfane, during the planning aboard *Impulse* for the mission to the Levant system, did you see or observe Captain Kierkopf do anything that implied negligence of her duties?" he finally said. Tralfane struck a thoughtful pose before responding.

"No," Tralfane said, "but the rumors of her tryst with Cochrane were all over the ship."

"That is not the question I asked," said Poulsen sharply. "Did you see anything in the performance of Captain Kierkopf's *duties* that implied negligence?"

"No," Tralfane conceded.

"And would you say that the initial attack on *Impulse* in the Levant system was a direct result of Captain Zander's ignoring of his orders not to engage potential dangers to his ship?" Dobrina shifted in her chair at this. I could tell she was not happy with this line of questions.

"If you are asking my opinion, which is all I can offer, then yes, Captain Zander was responsible for putting

Impulse in the line of fire," said Tralfane. Tralfane had no love for my first captain, that was certain.

"So then this man" — Poulsen pointed at me again for effect — "Peter Cochrane of Quantar, placed a charged energy weapon to your head on the bridge of *Impulse*, in full view of the bridge crew, did he not?"

"He did," said Tralfane.

"And then he left his post, ostensibly to rescue Captain Zander, did he not?"

Again, "He did."

"And during any of this time did you have any contact with my client?"

"No," said Tralfane. "Communications were knocked out in the attack."

"So there is nothing in your experience or observation then that implies in any way that my client was negligent of her official duties?"

"No," Tralfane said again with finality.

"Thank you, Historian," said Poulsen. Then he sat back down. "No further questions."

Commack nodded at Tralfane and the Historian exited the stand, heading directly for the door with a purposeful stride, pausing only to retrieve his cloak. I watched as he went, tracking every step, but the firm hands of the *Feldjäger* MPs on my shoulders prevented me from taking any irrational action. The door flew open and a mix of wind and snow invaded our ramshackle courtroom. The guards slammed the door shut behind the traitor and after a few moments of paper shuffling on the dais I heard the sound of a VTOL jet engine light up in the distance, no doubt a small aircraft lifting off and then screaming away from our desolate base. Tralfane was gone, but he was still alive, and that gave me hope, or at least something to focus on. Nothing drives a man like revenge.

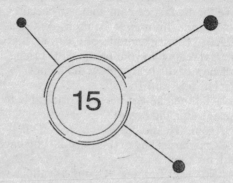

15

The rest of the day was taken up with a steady stream of "witnesses," though none as dramatic as Tralfane, most of them explaining technical details about the attack, my attempted rescue, and even a viewing of the visual record of my assault on *Impulse's* Historian. It was something he no doubt would have had access to from the yacht, and it conveniently had no sound, leaving the whole incident without context. In reality the only witnesses alive were myself, the rogue Historian, and Jenny Hogan, Wesley's niece and the sole survivor from *Impulse* after her piracy by Tralfane. I had talked to Jenny soon after the incident, and she remembered nothing of value, no doubt due to an intentional act of memory wiping before she was left aboard the dreadnought as a "calling card" to the Union.

By the end of the day it was looking grim for me, especially since they were treating me as an agent of a foreign government. Dobrina, though, was faring better, her reputation only sullied by her alleged dalliance with me.

I was sanguine about it all, no doubt in denial about the depth of my real troubles. After a brief rest I was fed dinner as the early winter night closed in, a beef stew with potatoes and a few sparse vegetables. As I ate at my small wood table, under the steady gaze of my ever-present *Feldjäger* guards, I sifted through the day's events in my mind. The most important, I thought, being the sound of the VTOL plane departing. If there were more of those planes at the base, then the prospect of escape was at least minimally available. But I had heard nothing before or since the plane's departure to indicate that there were any other operational aircraft at this base. In fact, only the few officers and military police units I had seen seemed to be present. It was discouraging.

As I poked at my stew, wondering where my appetite had gone, there was a quick knock at the door. The guards each took a step to the side and the door opened out to reveal the hallway and another guard, along with an unexpected sight, Captain Dobrina Kierkopf. They ushered her in and placed a second chair opposite me, along with another bowl of stew, some water in a cup, and a spoon. She sat silently, grim-faced, staring at her food and glancing over her shoulder as the guards left and then shut the door behind them. They were at least being minimally kind, allowing us to see each other. I tried my best to smile.

"Well, this is an unexpected pleasure," I said, trying to be as light as possible.

"One last meal together, I suppose?" she replied. I nodded.

"I highly doubt our keepers are truly allowing us to eat in private," I said, "but the illusion is nice."

I watched as she picked up her spoon in resignation and scooped small bits of food into her mouth.

"You have to eat," I said. "You need to be strong." She looked up at me, then ate a bit more.

"Any chance of escape?" she whispered between bites. I shook my head, then looked to the single, tiny, barred window to the room and the dark, snowy skies beyond.

"I doubt that's possible. This base seems abandoned except for us and our captors. It was likely planned this way, pure isolation. If we escape, we'll freeze in the snow. And there seems to be very little equipment here of note."

"Which means what?" she whispered again.

"Which means everyone here and all the supplies were flown in just for this trial, and then the planes left. We're alone here, and that's likely the way our captors planned it," I said.

"For what purpose?"

I looked up from my stew.

"It seems, to blame me for *Impulse*, to set me up as a criminal. Use my crimes and punishment as a political tool to break up the Union."

Dobrina slapped her spoon down hard on the table. "They can't," she said, loud and more than a little angry. I shrugged.

"It seems like a done deal," I replied, "and you still need to eat." I pushed the bowl closer to her.

"I'm not interested in eating." At that she got up and started pacing. I watched her for a minute, then got up and joined her. She stopped at the window and I came up behind her, putting my arms around her waist.

"This is my problem, Dobrina," I said softly. "They seem willing to go easy on you, you still seem to have value to them, but I doubt they will let you return to the Union Navy. You have to accept that."

"I won't," she said with anger, then pulled away and walked the short distance across the tiny room again. Finally she sat on my bed, her eyes darting across the floor like she was trying to drill a hole in it. After a moment I came and sat down next to her.

"You can't change this, Dobrina. You have to accept it. Take whatever they offer, but inside, keep fighting."

"And what about you?"

"I'll be fine," I said.

"Liar. They're going to execute you." I contemplated that for a long moment.

"That's a distinct possibility," I had to admit. Absently I touched the tracker in my left arm, hoping that my being a no-show in the capital had set off some alarm bells through the system. If not . . .

"You do what I told you, understood?" I said, putting my arm around her and giving her a gentle kiss on the forehead. Then I guided her back to the table and her stew. She sat down reluctantly, but she sat. I went to the other side and finished my paltry portion, washing it down with the last of my water. Then we sat together in silence, with only the howl of the wind as company.

"Tell me it will be all right," she finally said, reaching out a hand to me. I took it.

"I think it will be, for you," I said, not really sure if it would or not. I took a deep breath then and sighed before looking into her eyes one more time.

"As for me, it seems I'll be needing a miracle."

We were back in the courtroom at 0700 hours the next morning. I had hardly slept, my mind whirling with thoughts and fears and anxieties about the court outcome and my impending punishment. Despite Dobrina's continued presence, I felt very much alone.

After about ninety minutes of additional "testimony" in the morning session, Commack finally nodded, half-heartedly, in my direction.

"The accused may make a statement," he said. I sat

absolutely still. I hadn't planned this, but my intuition told me my only chance would be to attack. After a few long moments, Commack finally looked at me and made direct eye contact for the first time. "The prisoner has a right of statement, which you will yield in another five seconds if you do not comply," he said sharply. At this I stood slowly before speaking to the court.

"This case presented here is a sham, a contrived collection of non-facts and outright lies. Principal of these are the statements of *Impulse*'s Historian, Tralfane. The incident you saw between us on the bridge of *Impulse* occurred because he was unwilling to allow a rescue operation for Captain Zander, Ensign Poulsen, whose death I am accused of causing, and Commander Kierkopf. I was determined to mount such a rescue mission because I refused to allow my comrades to die in the cold of space. I think it likely that if Mr. Tralfane had allowed me to act as I initially intended, Claus Poulsen might have survived. Instead, Tralfane attempted to deter me at every turn, and the result was a delay which caused the loss of my friend and personal adjutant, and for that I am truly sorry," I said the last in the direction of Karl Poulsen. He did not acknowledge me, but he stopped taking notes and Dobrina leaned in to whisper in his ear. He nodded very slightly at this. I continued.

"In addition, it was solely Historian Tralfane who commandeered *Impulse* and took her to her demise. Virtually every detail he presented to this court was a lie. *Impulse* was in fighting shape when I left her in his hands, and her hyperdimensional drives were in no danger of collapsing. I admit to leaving my post, but as acting captain in Captain Zander's absence it was within my purview to mount a rescue mission personally, and since I had trained for one and prepared for one, I considered it to be a low-risk operation. No one was better prepared for such a mission than I was, and I believed I was leaving *Impulse* and her crew in safe hands."

"Two minutes," interrupted Commack. I continued as if he hadn't spoken at all.

"The charges against me are a farce, but even more so are the charges against Captain Kierkopf. She is a loyal Carinthian officer and a leader in the Union Navy. No doubt she will have a distinguished career in either service. To hold her responsible for the events of the *Impulse* rescue mission would be unethical of this court.

"Lastly," I said, "this court must consider one other question." At this I looked to each of the tribunal members in turn. None of them looked back at me. "The unjust execution of a royal son of Quantar will bring war on Carinthia. War on your families, your children, and your homes. Is this truly what you seek? Or are there other agendas at work here, and are you willing to sacrifice everything to serve those agendas?"

At this Commack pounded the gavel a dozen times. "The accused's right of statement has expired. This tribunal will adjourn to deliberate. All members of the court must stay in the courtroom," he said. With that the three admirals trundled off. I hoped that my last warning had some impact, if not on Commack, then at least on the other two. It was a slim hope.

After a few minutes Dobrina was allowed to get up. She came over to my table, accompanied by two guards. I stood to greet her, the table between us.

"Brave words. Trying to protect me again?" she asked. I shrugged and gave her a half smile.

"I did what I thought was best for you," I said. "It appears they are willing to be lenient on you, for whatever reason. I just wanted to give them more reasons to do so."

She sighed. "They want what I have, the information in my head. That's my only worth to them."

At that the doors opened and the flag officers came back in, led by Commack. Dobrina was ushered back to her table. After a minute of shuffling papers and official-sounding mumbling between the judges, Commack pounded the gavel three times.

"Captain Dobrina Kierkopf, please stand," he said. She did, as did Karl Poulsen next to her.

"This tribunal finds you innocent of dereliction of duty charges in regards to the *Impulse* incident," he said. That was the most serious charge. I comforted myself that at least she would likely avoid any prison sentence. "However, we do find you in contempt of the Carinthian Navy codes against fraternization with an agent of a foreign government. Your close relationship with Mr. Cochrane is a black mark on your record. Although this violation occurred in your service in the Union Navy, the oath you swore first to Carinthia takes precedence." Legally, they couldn't really do that, but then nothing in this court had the air of legality about it.

Commack shuffled his papers again. "As to the penalty for this violation, your commission in the Union Navy is hereby revoked, and you are to be reduced in rank back to commander. Your post will be transferred to High Station One where you will be a staff officer until a suitable post on an active navy vessel can be assigned to you. Do you understand this tribunal's ruling?" he said, looking directly at her. Basically, they were kidnapping her. I felt great relief, though. At least she would be safe, for the moment.

She addressed the tribunal. "I understand the ruling but I do not agree," she said sharply. My heart raced. She was getting out with her life and her career intact. "I am a Union Navy off—" she started until Commack's pounding of the gavel drowned out her voice and she stopped speaking.

"This tribunal's judgment is final," stated Commack. With assistance from the ever-present guards she was pressed back into her seat. She glanced at me but I gave her no hint of my own emotions. Commack turned to me.

"Mr. Cochrane," he said, "please stand."

"I will not," I said defiantly. "To do so would give this court respect which it does not deserve."

Commack merely nodded and my *Feldjäger* keepers "assisted" me to my feet. Commack then started in. "Mr. Cochrane, you are found guilty on all charges. It is you who this court holds responsible for the death of Claus Poulsen aboard the shuttle. It is you this court holds responsible for the destruction of *Impulse* and the loss of her crew. These actions in and of themselves would be grounds for your execution, but the fact that you are in addition to all of this an agent of our ancient and sworn enemies, the Cochrane family of Quantar, this demands swift and careful justice. You are sentenced to be executed by firing squad. You have one hour to consider your guilt before your execution takes place."

"No . . ." cried out Dobrina. The guards swiftly handcuffed me and took me under the arms, lifting me as they started me toward the door. I couldn't see her, so I shouted over my shoulder, "It will be all right," even though I knew that was a lie. In front of me the door was kicked open and I was dragged into the bitter winter's day. Behind me I heard Commack slam down the gavel and adjourn the tribunal. I could hear Dobrina weeping, but there was nothing I could do. I looked up into the dim gray sky as tight, dry snowflakes fell stinging on my face.

I would need that miracle after all.

•—•——•

The drone of the transport VTOL planes landing at the airstrip came fifteen minutes before my scheduled execution. They were no doubt called in the moment my conviction was finalized. From their sound they were clearly larger than the personal craft I had heard Tralfane depart in earlier. It was also clear this entire court would be hustled away from the airbase and vanish as quickly as they had come once the deed was done.

I tried to control my breathing, but found I couldn't. The shivering I was experiencing back in my tiny shack wasn't only due to the cold. As I contemplated my circumstances, I was riddled with anxiety. I felt totally alone. There seemed very little that could save me now.

My ever-present *Feldjäger* escorts knocked promptly at five minutes to the hour. I was cuffed again and led out into the cold winter day. The snow was as unceasing as my trembling. There was a small contingent of five MPs standing in line as I was led down a short path to a single metal pole standing between two old and battered buildings. None of the court participants were there, not even Commack, though I had no doubt they were watching from the safety of the adjoining buildings. There was no sign of Dobrina or Karl Poulsen either. The duty captain said nothing to me as I went past the firing squad, the MPs dragging me to the pole, then turning me and unlocking one of my cuffs before swiftly reattaching it around the pole behind me. My heart was pounding and my head filled with the sound of the wind, some from the cold winter weather, some from the burning engines of three VTOL transports on the airfield tarmac, and some no doubt from my own blood rushing through my veins. I stared down my firing squad as they took their positions, coil rifles at the side. The squad captain gave his first order, in German.

"*Bereit!*"

They raised their weapons to their shoulders, aiming them at me.

"*Aufladung!*"

They charged their weapons. I waited an eternity, blinking bleary eyed into the wind while the old-style single shooters filled their firing chambers with oxidized ion gas. My thoughts turned to Dobrina, and Derrick, my father and mother, all swirling through my mind in a flurry of confusing emotion. I couldn't believe my life was about to end.

The squad captain drew and then raised his ceremonial sword. I refused to look away. I couldn't. These could be my last moments alive.

The sound of rushing in my ears suddenly accelerated, I assumed from my pounding heart, fighting for its last beats in this reality. I closed my eyes and turned my head away, holding my breath, waiting for the final blow, the blast from the coil rifles. It didn't come. Instead, I heard a roar coming from the tarmac. I opened my eyes again to see one of the VTOL transports rising behind the shooters.

As the squad captain prepared to lower his sword a blinding flash of orange light impacted just behind the firing squad, sending them all scrambling for cover. A single firing squad man's rifle misfired and a shot of coil laser energy singed the air over my left shoulder as I instinctively ducked away. I went into a crouch, or as close to one as I could get to chained to a pole.

The squad captain started shouting orders in German as confusion broke loose around me; *Feldjäger* came scrambling out of the buildings, running past me with their weapons drawn. Soldiers in winter camouflage broke from behind the VTOL transports and started firing at the *Feldjäger*. The VTOL itself hovered up to about twenty meters and started slowly advancing toward me, firing coil and incendiary rounds at anything that moved, quickly taking out an electronics shack and a communications tower as it came. I turned my attention to the squad captain. He had gathered himself as his firing squad had scattered, and now his attention was on me. He came toward me, ceremonial sword drawn. I rose to my feet from the crouch as he started toward me at a full run. He raised his sword to strike and I leaned back against the pole, using my leverage to raise both of my legs and kick him in the midsection as he came, sending him tumbling off to my left. He got up quickly and with a low growl charged at me from the side. I was in no position to defend myself further.

A blur of green flashed by me, then someone in a Carinthian Navy uniform crashed into the squad captain and knocked him to the ground again. The two bodies scrambled at my feet, struggling for control of the sword. I watched as the navy officer snapped back the thumb of the squad captain, who howled in pain, and freed the sword. Then she scrambled to pick it up off the ground before driving it into the squad captain's gut with force. He gurgled once, mortally wounded, then collapsed, dead. The navy officer pulled out the sword amidst a crushing volley of incoming fire from the rapidly advancing Carinthian Regulars. The *Feldjäger* MPs were being routed.

Then the Carinthian officer came up and kissed me hard on the lips.

"Thank you, Captain Kierkopf," I said between scattered breaths.

"My pleasure," she said, then turned and yelled. "Poulsen! Get over here!" I turned to see the lanky figure of Karl Poulsen running through the field of fire, a coil pistol drawn. He rushed up to me, and for a moment I feared betrayal as he charged the chamber, but he lowered the weapon and cut my cuffs from the pole with the laser.

I had my miracle.

I threw my arms around Dobrina and kissed her again, but she pushed me away. "Later," she said, and we ran for cover, although there was precious little of that. We dug in under the crawlspace of a barracks building and waited for the firefight to die down. We didn't have long to wait. Ten minutes later and all was quiet except the shouting of the Carinthian Regulars as they secured the airbase. Then I heard someone calling my name.

"Commander Cochrane!" I signaled to Dobrina and Poulsen and then led them out of our crawl space cover with a nod.

"I'm Commander Cochrane," I said to the nearest

regular. He nodded and called in a report in German, then snapped to action in a defensive mode when he saw Dobrina and Poulsen emerging. "They're with me," I said to the private, and motioned them over. He hesitated a second, as if he didn't quite understand my English, then relaxed a bit as two more ratings came up to support him. We were quickly surrounded by friendly faces and we were then led off the base proper to the tarmac. The three VTOL transports were now secured to the ground with their engines idling. We walked past a row of soldiers who had Commack, Kobin, the prosecutor, and the rest of the tribunal in cuffs on their knees. Only a few remaining *Feldjäger* were among the captured. The rest had met a more permanent fate.

"I should have known you'd get into trouble without me," said a familiar voice coming from the nearest transport. I turned at the sound of the voice as Colonel Lena Babayan stepped down from the VTOL and approached us, removing her pilot's helmet as she came, allowing her flaming red mane to fly free in the wind.

"Colonel Babayan, why aren't you aboard *Starbound*?" I asked in my best mock-authority voice.

"Because she's still in dry dock, sir. And a certain Captain Lucius Zander relayed to me that you might need some help," she replied.

"Nonsense," I said, spreading my hands. "We had everything under control."

"Yes, and if I'd hesitated another second you'd have been coil dust. Very well under control," she said, smiling.

"Thank you for that, Colonel," I said. She hugged me, and then Dobrina. Poulsen stood to the side awkwardly. I thanked him as well for his part in saving my life, but he remained cold and distant to me. Babayan then waved off the privates and we started back to her VTOL plane.

"Come on," she said, "there's someone you need to meet with."

I nodded and then followed her up the ramp and into the VTOL transport, then went forward to a command cabin just behind the pilot's nest. There were three men inside, one seated at a desk. He stood to greet us.

"Commander Cochrane," said Prince Benn Feilberg as he extended his hand to me. "I'm glad to see you again, and glad we got here in time."

"So am I," I said in reply, taking his offered hand and shaking it. The moment passed quickly, however, and things turned very serious again.

"It's essential that we be on our way. This incident is unfortunately not isolated. I'm afraid you've arrived on Carinthia just as we stand on the brink of civil war," said the prince. "That's something I couldn't tell you on High Station One, for obvious reasons. It's best if we take our seats for takeoff."

"Prince Benn, just one question. How did you find me?" I asked, not ready to cede the conversation just yet.

"Your friend Captain Zander relayed to us that you were overdue in New Vienna. Something about a transponder signal?" he said. I gripped my left forearm.

"Apparently very helpful Historian technology," I said. The prince nodded.

"He relayed your location, and as soon as I saw the latitude and longitude I knew you were in trouble. We haven't had operational bases this far north in decades. Now, if you would please take your seats?" he said.

I nodded as the transport began filling with soldiers and we made our way to the nearest flight couches. Dobrina strapped in next to me and held on to my arm so hard I thought she might stop the blood flow. Then the prince gave the order for our departure.

"From the frying pan into the fire," I muttered to Dobrina just as Lena Babayan fired the engines for takeoff.

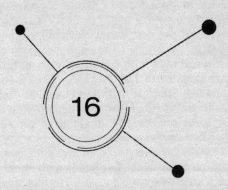

To New Vienna

I was told the flight to New Vienna would take six hours. The air base we were held at was in the extreme north of the primary continent of Carinthia, at least the most populated one anyway. New Vienna was apparently in a more temperate zone, though it was still winter there and I was told we could expect temperatures at or below freezing.

I found it interesting that both Quantar and Carinthia were in winter seasons at the same time. They didn't always match, as Quantar had a 382-day year traveling around its primary star Beta Virginis. Carinthia had a 407-day year as it traversed the mighty Zeta Herculis. Because of a rather unique orbital anomaly, attributed to its companion star, winter tended to be the longest season on Carinthia by a few extra weeks. It was something that I remembered took some getting used to for the first colonists, as well as the 1.15 Earth normal gravity, as opposed to Quantar's rather quaint .92. It seemed we were smaller in every way, except in naval power. I'd put our Royal Navy ships up against theirs any day.

Interestingly, both worlds were about thirty-five light-years from Earth, but only about twenty-four and a half from each other. If we'd had Hoagland Jump Drive capability before the Historians had brought it to us on the first Reunion Day we might have rediscovered each other first on our own.

I sat on the transport contemplating these things with Dobrina on my right, her head on my shoulder, sleeping, and Karl Poulsen on my left. He had stayed silent for much of the trip. I had thanked him for his part in my rescue but he'd remained stoic toward me so far. Prince Benn was ensconced with his military advisors inside his private cabin, and except for the occasional order coming from one of his advisors they had remained out of sight. I had slept some sitting up, with Dobrina and I using each other as pillows. The last few days had taken their toll on both of us. After about an hour of snoozing I woke up and found Poulsen awake as well. I shifted Dobrina to a more comfortable position (for me), and she moaned a bit before settling back down. Then I turned my attention to Poulsen.

"Do you blame me for your brother's death?" I said flatly. No reason to couch it in softer terms. He looked at me, clearly uncomfortable with the question, then leaned forward, staring at the floor, not willing to meet my gaze.

"I don't know," he said through his heavy accent. "It became apparent to me during the trial that the testimony was being manipulated against you, and so was I. It's been very difficult for me to put aside my feelings of blame on you, and I think in the end that made it easier for them to accept me as being sincere in wanting to see you dead. During the trial I tried very hard to close my personal feelings off and just do my job to protect Captain Kierkopf." She stirred a bit at the mention of her name, and Poulsen took his tone down lower. "In the end when the rescue opportunity came, it was clear I was just one of their pawns in the game. I'm not sure that I don't blame you still for Claus's death, but clearly there was more to it than I was initially led to believe."

"I appreciate your honesty, Karl," I said. "Thank you."

"You've done that once already," he replied.

"I know. But when a man comes as close as I was to dying, I guess you just can't say it enough." This time he nodded in silent acknowledgment. "Lieutenant," I said, using his rank for emphasis, "who were those people? What the hell is this all about?" He looked at me and then shook his head.

"I wish I knew," he replied. "There have been changes in leadership going on above me for months. Commanders being replaced, some being reassigned to distant outposts. That sort of thing. I don't know much else."

I nodded. "Thank you, Karl," I said. "I want you to know that I liked your brother very much, and I did everything I could to rescue him."

"Thank you for telling me that, sir," he said formally, but without commitment either way. That put an end to the conversation, and I had said what I needed to say. I moved again and got up to stretch, being careful not to disturb Dobrina, then decided to make my way up to the pilot's nest and see if I could gather any more information about what was happening on Carinthia, and get it from a source who might know more.

"Hello," I said, sliding into the empty copilot's seat. Lena Babayan smiled back at me from under her flight helmet without taking her eyes from the com board. I looked outside the cockpit window to see that we had collected a sizable fighter escort on our journey.

"Hello, sir," she replied. "Happy to see you in one piece."

I exhaled deeply. "You and me both."

"That was a close call back there." I nodded and raised my hand, trying and failing to hold it steady.

"I'm still feeling it," I admitted.

"No shame there," she said. That much was true.

"I'm curious, how did you know where I was?" I asked, quickly changing the subject from my close brush with death. "Last I heard you were still at Candle, recruiting new marines."

"Captain Zander sent a private com to Wesley that you might be in some kind of trouble. He relayed that to Maclintock and he sent me along on the next transport, thinking I could help," she replied in between checking her flight controls.

"That you did." She nodded without taking her eyes from her board. My experience with Colonel Babayan was that she didn't like to leave anything to automated systems if she could put her hands on it instead.

"I had some leave time coming so the captain *suggested* I take it on Carinthia. When I got here the Royal Navy Command put me out on one of their search patrols immediately. The orders came from above to deploy to this location early this morning. We knew we were looking for you, we just didn't know *where* we might find you. I assume someone up the chain of command got an intelligence break. And from the looks of it we got here just in time."

"*Just*," I agreed. "Any idea who *they* are?" She shook her head.

"They didn't look like Carinthian Regulars to me, sir. They were almost all *Feldjäger*," she said. I put my hand to my chin, contemplating.

"What was it with all the MPs?" I speculated out loud, not really expecting an answer. I got one.

"They've been building up the MP ranks for more than three years, sir. It's something that didn't go unnoticed by the Royal Navy Command. Almost like someone was trying to build a small, multidisciplined military force that went across all services," she said.

"Makes sense," I said, "if you're planning a revolt." I leaned in closer to her and spoke softly. "Lena, is civil war really coming to Carinthia?"

She gritted her teeth under her flight helmet. Clearly she was reluctant to talk about this subject.

"It could be, sir," she finally admitted. "And those of us loyal to the Royal Navy and the grand duke are caught in the middle, between our loyalty to him and our service to our world. And for those of us serving in the Union Navy, it's even worse."

"And you don't want to have to make that choice. I'll do anything I can to stop it from happening," I said. She nodded.

"Thank you, sir, I hope things aren't out of your hands already. I work for you and the Union, sir. Hell, I believe in it, but I'm Carinthian first," she said.

"Understood, Colonel," I said.

"Thank you, sir," she said.

With that I patted her on the shoulder, which I hoped was reassuring, and then headed back to the passenger compartment. As I passed Prince Benn's cabin one of his lieutenants stuck his head out the door and invited me in again. I went in and sat down at a desk across from the prince while the other two men stood to one side.

"We have some new information, Duke Peter," said Prince Benn. His face was grim as he talked to me. "Some Loyalist forces have withdrawn from New Vienna and returned to their barracks, and unauthorized deployments have taken place from several airfields in and around the capital. Right now New Vee is under our control, but it's being ringed by apparently hostile forces, trying to contain us. There's no shooting yet, but the city is on edge."

"What type of forces?" I asked.

"Military police and their equipment," said the taller of the two nameless advisors.

"Paratroopers, light tanks, and other armor," said Prince Benn, more specifically. "It appears as if the military is splitting along the lines of those loyal to the grand duke and those loyal to my brother."

"Arin?"

He nodded. "As I explained on High Station One, he's been running the government for most of the last three years. Since our mother died, my father has become . . . somewhat distant. My father still retains nominal authority, but Arin has moved very swiftly, building loyalties, buying favors and alliances. Most of the movement in our military has been to his side, and away from the grand duke and the Union."

"Is he actually challenging your father? Is this civil war?" I asked.

"I don't know," the prince admitted. "But I do know that those men back at that base who had you on trial were loyal to Arin. If it hadn't been for the transponder signal . . ." He trailed off, but I knew where he was going. I changed the subject.

"There was an Earth Historian at my trial. Tralfane, the man who hijacked *Impulse* and led it to its doom. Last I saw of him, he was in the Altos system, and his Historian's yacht was missing. How did he get *here*?" I asked.

"I'm sure I have no idea," replied the prince. I pressed my point.

"He could only have had help from the empire. If Tralfane is in league with your brother's revolt, and working with elements of the empire, then we have much bigger problems on our hands than Arin," I said. The prince shifted in his chair, clearly uncomfortable with this news.

"Be that as it may for now, my experience with Earth Historians is that they are 'in league' with no one but themselves," said Benn.

I sat back at this, to let him know through my body language that I disagreed with his assessment. "One of my best friends is an Earth Historian," I said.

"Yes, Serosian. He is known to us. But he is from a different Historian school than that man Tralfane, and they appear to have competing agendas, neither of which seems to be to our benefit," said the prince.

I thought about this, and admittedly I couldn't really argue with his point, because I didn't know enough about the subject. Serosian had been my mentor since the day Derrick had died, and I trusted him and his motives. I wanted to defend him vigorously, but refrained for the moment.

"If Arin is working with Tralfane, and Tralfane is working covertly with Imperial forces, then it seems highly probable that your brother is being influenced by those forces as well," I said. Prince Benn tapped on his desk with a pen for several seconds.

"The situation is fluid," he admitted. "But my primary concern is for my family first, Carinthia second, and the Union third. If I have to abandon New Vienna to keep our people safe from civil war I will do it. If I have to denounce the Union to keep Carinthia and the royal family safe, I will do that as well."

"And if you have to denounce me?" I asked directly. He smiled, I thought sincerely.

"It won't come to that," he said.

"And if it does?" He didn't blink.

"It won't," he said. I cocked my head, not taking that as reassuring, then changed subjects again.

"If New Vienna is surrounded by potential hostile forces, then how are we going to get this very obvious aerial convoy past them and into the city?" I asked.

"We have a distraction planned," interjected the tall advisor again. Benn nodded affirmation.

"But we also have a massive number of very similar convoys going in and out of the city right now. Everyone is getting in position, but so far no one is interfering with anybody else's flights. There have been no hostilities. Yet," the prince finished.

"And what forces do you have in the city?" I asked. Benn nodded to the smaller advisor, who stepped forward.

"We have heavy armor all around the city, superior in total armament to the Regency force's light armor, though not superior in total number. The Royal Square is reinforced with tanks, mobile infantry, heavy ground guns and antimissile defenses. We have air superiority over the city and control the two most important airfields, Aspern and Leopoldsdorf, as well as the Royal Spaceport. There is a safe corridor above the spaceport through which we are bringing in supplies and moving Loyalist troops back and forth. We have enough food and water supplies for perhaps six months, if there is a siege. So far all the roads into and out of the city remain open, but Regency forces are taking up positions near the roads in the exurbs as we speak, tightening the noose," said the advisor.

"We control the city itself and a ring about twenty kilometers deep around the city. Regency forces hold the next fifty kilometers or so, and then there are pockets all around the countryside where either one side or the other has the advantage," interjected Prince Benn to clarify.

"As you said, fluid," I said. "So if we make it into the city, what then?"

"First and foremost, we get you off Carinthia. Your presence here heightens tensions immensely. If we can't get you off our world then we will try to at least get you to Aspern airbase, where there is a small cadre of Union forces. Get you out of the way. Then, we negotiate, for the good of the royal family and Carinthia," said Benn.

"And the Union?"

"As I said, it's our lowest priority."

I nodded. What more could I say? I couldn't blame

him for putting his world and his people first. It's what I would do in his situation.

"Thank you for the briefing," I said, then stood to leave. Prince Benn watched me leave, then turned back to his advisors as I shut the door behind me. I went straight back to my flight couch, feeling like a helpless diplomat while others around me made the big boy decisions. I strapped myself in with a sigh, then leaned back in my couch and stared straight ahead at the bulkhead, wishing I could be off this world and back doing something that mattered.

I saw Prince Benn's "distraction" from the air about an hour later. A large tanker loaded with fuel had gone down at an airfield about thirty kilometers outside New Vee, in the zone controlled by the Regency forces. The crater it left and the smoke from the crash were visible kilometers into the air. As we looked out the windows, black smoke billowed from the massive wound in the ground. I hoped silently that the plane had been unpiloted when it went down.

We all strapped in securely as our convoy made a high-speed approach to the Loyalist-controlled Aspern airfield. We barely slowed as we hit the ground rolling, the VTOL aspects of our plane abandoned in favor of speed. We rolled directly and at an uncomfortable speed into a large military hangar protected by tanks, coil cannons, and missile batteries, then disembarked quickly. The prince and his entourage got into an armored military vehicle and we—Dobrina, Colonel Babayan, and I—followed in the second group. I filled in Dobrina and Babayan on the situation report as it had been conveyed to me by the prince. Both had strong opinions as we convoyed along the city streets of New Vee, presumably to the grand duke's palace.

"Prince Benn can't abandon the Union. It's our only hope for the future," Dobrina insisted as we were driven to the palace.

"I agree," replied Babayan. "But I'm Carinthian first. I want to see our world protected from harm, and a civil war would cause plenty of harm."

"You can't protect Carinthia by isolating us from Quantar and Earth. We could easily fall under the influence of the old empire again, and I'll be goddamned if I'll allow that!" Dobrina said, her voice rising.

"I understand, but—"

"Look, you both swore an oath to the Union," I cut in, "and right now your commissions are with the Union Navy, of which I am the highest ranking official on this mission. We will act in the Union's best interests. If you have a problem with that, you can resign your commission to me now, or agree to follow my orders on this."

"I don't want to resign," said Babayan after a moment's hesitation.

"Good," I said. "Then we're all in this together, and we have to stay together. Agreed?"

They both nodded and replied "agreed" at the same time.

"Thank you. Now the bigger question is, what happens next? Prince Benn wants me off Carinthia for political reasons, and I can't say I don't feel the same way after the welcome I received here. How are our communications with the Union Navy, Lena?" I asked.

"Not good," she said. "The last time I was in the staff office here was two days ago, and communication was intermittent and not considered secure. High Stations One and Two are controlled by forces loyal to Arin's pseudo-Regency, and they routinely block longwave and diplomatic packets to High Station Three, which is controlled by Loyalist forces. Any hope of getting help in or a signal out to the longwave ansibles is moot at this point. The Regency controls the military communication lines. Commercial lines are still open but definitely not secure."

"What about commercial traffic at the spaceport?" I asked.

"Still coming and going, but heavily monitored and decreasing by the day as conditions deteriorate at New Vee. If we're going to get out that way it's going to have to be soon, I think," she said.

"All right. When we get to the palace I want you to work on securing us transportation off of Carinthia. Anything will do as long as it's not military. Commercial, maintenance, even a garbage run will do fine if it gets us to High Station Three at least, and preferably without us having to stop at One or Two. Clear?" I said.

"Yes, sir," replied Babayan.

"Commander Kierkopf and I will work the diplomatic side," I said. "Dobrina, I'll need you to work your military contacts among the Loyalists. Find out what they have, what they need, and how the Union Navy might be able to help them if hostilities start. Also, take an inventory and find out what we have available in terms of Union forces on the ground here."

"They're liable to be very light," she said. Then they both looked to me.

"I will work with Prince Benn as much as I can to secure a ride off of Carinthia, while offering as much Union assistance as possible. He may not want it. Politically I may be poison to their cause. It seems he'll be glad to get rid of me. Once we get to the palace, start working immediately. Time is of the essence here," I finished. I got two "Yes, sir"s in response and then we were done. I sat back in the vehicle and waited as the armored car's engines droned on to the grand duke's palace.

17

We arrived in a large transport area of the New Hofburg palace, a great marble-ceilinged garage, now filled with military vehicles unloading ordnance juxtaposed with the odd commercial ground truck unloading food and kitchen stores. We were quickly escorted into a wing of the palace reserved for military operations while Prince Benn went along to an administrative area.

I was unprepared for the scale of the palace. It was a magnificent edifice of marble, polished bronze, and ornate gold and silver fixtures and appointments. It had a thick baroque atmosphere that would have smothered a similar building, if there were any, on Quantar. The palace was so large that there were actually moving sidewalks, large glass-walled lifters, and wide escalators to move from one wing or level to the next. We took an underground tram train that went on for several minutes before we got off and headed up to our wing. The Loyalists probably saw the palace as the key piece of real estate in the war of wills between Benn and Arin, but what I saw around me seemed like an unnecessary extravagance that undoubtedly robbed them of men and materiel that could probably be better used elsewhere, especially if this developed into a shooting war.

Colonel Babayan clearly knew her way around the palace and made off on her assigned duties as soon as we exited the tram. Dobrina made her way more hesitantly toward the Carinthian High Command's offices after asking for directions. I was met by a military attaché and an armed guard of two. The attaché explained in broken Standard that I was scheduled for "appointments" in another part of the palace. I took up his offered assistance and we moved off.

It seemed as though we walked forever, our bootheels pounding on the hard marble, before turning down a wide hallway and passing through an ornately decorated arch, topped by an ornamental keystone decorated with an "F" in the old Gothic script. I was then ushered into what appeared to be a large private apartment by the attaché, the guards taking up station at the door. I was about to protest that I didn't need rest when the attaché abruptly turned and left, shutting the door and leaving me alone in the elaborately decorated room. I sighed. I hated playing the part of a royal. Being a navy commander was much more my type of work.

I went to the windows and looked out on the palace gardens below. They were enormous and green, covered by a coat of frost in the winter shade and filled with the bare stems of flowers pruned low for their protection. I thought for a moment of my mother's gardens at the North Palace near KendalFalk, where I had grown up what seemed like forever ago, and got just a tinge of homesickness. My reverie was broken by two massive doors opening into the next room, revealing a still larger apartment inside.

"The princess will see you now," said a matronly lady, gesturing with her arms wide to escort me in. I followed her lead and made my way in, walking a good distance through a ridiculously oversized room to see a petite figure standing at the far window, staring out at the same gardens I had just been looking at. As I approached she turned and gave me a troubled smile.

"Thank you, Gretchen. That will be all for now," she said in a voice that showed no hint of the typical Carinthian accent. I chalked that up to her years of training in the Union Naval Academy, training that would now likely be unused. The attendant bowed slightly and walked away from us, but not entirely, stopping at a reception desk at the end of the enormous room near the doors where I had entered. I assumed we would have privacy nonetheless, by mere distance if nothing else.

I turned to the young woman. She was indeed petite, wearing a formal dress in Carinthian green with trimmings of white lace. She had a pleasantly oval face with tiny features, large dark eyes that seemed a bit on the weary side, and long, straight brunette hair. She forced a smile at me and then spoke.

"I'm sorry we don't have a more formal reception for you, Sire Cochrane," she said, then held out her hand to me. "I'm Karina Feilberg, the grand duke's daughter."

I was uncertain whether to kiss her hand or shake it. Since I was there as a visiting royal and not a suitor, I decided to just grip it gently with both hands and smile.

"I'm very pleased to finally meet you, Princess Karina," I said. She nodded.

"I wish we were meeting under different circumstances," she said, then motioned me to a pair of sitting chairs that faced each other in front of a large lit fireplace that put out a glowing warmth.

"I understand," I replied as we both sat down. "There was a time when I expected we might even meet in the Union Navy."

She smiled the weary smile again.

"I'm afraid those days will never be," she said, then looked away from me, toward the open window. I feared I had insulted her, but before I could apologize she was up again and pacing around the room.

"I understand you've met with my brother, Benn?" she asked.

"I have," I said, then stopped. She noticed.

"And?" she asked, stopping her pacing for a moment.

"And I think he considers me a huge political liability," I offered. The pacing resumed.

"Benn, he is a tad too much the son of a sovereign," she said, smiling bemusedly for the first time. I liked the way it played across her face. "And not nearly pragmatic enough," she finished.

I sat forward in my chair. "Is the situation here as bad as he says?"

"Worse," she acknowledged, her pacing taking her to the window again. She looked out as I waited for her to say more, then turned back to me. "Essentially, we are prisoners here in the city, in New Vienna. The royal family, I mean. Arin controls almost everything coming in and going out of the city except the spaceport, and we have only a narrow tunnel of airspace through which we can make our supply runs. High Station Three is bringing us more and more of our supplies through that corridor. We are getting almost nothing from our own world now. We are relying on your people, the Union, I mean, and their goodwill to help us." She trailed off for a moment at this, then turned back to face me directly.

"If you do anything when you get off Carinthia, you must get us as much food and medical supplies through the port as you can, and soon. I'm sure they'll cut off that avenue any day now. If your Union can do anything for us, that is what we need. Weapons would likely be interdicted, but commercial ships or light military vehicles might still get through," she said.

I was surprised by her tone. She sounded more like an intelligence officer giving a situation report than a royal daughter of the grand duke. I chalked this up to her military training and reminded myself not to forget that point again.

"Those will be my first recommendations to the Union Navy command when I get back," I promised her. She came back to the sitting area with me, still standing with a chair between us.

"Thank you," she said.

"And what of the prince regent? Do you think he will attack soon?" I asked.

"I don't know," she said. "There was a time when I never would have believed him capable of betraying his father, but that time is long past. He is a dangerous man, Duke Peter."

"Please," I said, "Just Peter." Frankly I was much more used to being called commander. She smiled again for a moment.

"Peter, then," she said, and nodded. "Whatever you do, Peter, you must keep the Union out of this war. Arin is desperate to take full power and set my father aside, and to end the treaty relationship with the Union. He'll look for any excuse, as your kidnapping can attest."

I nodded, acknowledging the truth of her words, then pressed on to other matters. "What would he replace the Union with?" I asked.

"That, I don't know," she admitted. "Things started changing here a few years ago, once Arin started assuming regency powers that he was never granted. My father is an old man, and when my mother died, well, honestly, he began slipping. We all became aware of the need for a regent, and eventually my father agreed. But it was never formalized, and soon Arin began his usurpation of powers." This was yet another confirmation of the seriousness of the situation on Carinthia. I decided to press on.

"How is your father's physical health?" I asked. At this she frowned.

"He isn't well. He seems to slip more each day, each week. But he is still my father, and I will do anything to protect him."

"I understand. You were telling me about Arin?" I needed to know more about this new adversary.

"Yes. Once he assumed Regency powers things began changing, as I said. There were soldiers in the palace guard we did not recognize, and more in the city. Many longtime military leaders were replaced, and some were 'reassigned,' and they just disappeared. It was a full year before Benn and I could acknowledge what was going on. We consolidated support around my father, but with limited success. Since then Arin has continued tightening the noose, slowly, month by month," she said.

I still needed more information, but I also needed to reassure her in some way, I could tell that much. "Lady Karina, it is my suspicion, and I cannot prove this, that your brother may be working with elements of the old empire, possibly through an Earth Historian named Tralfane. In my opinion, this man Tralfane is the one responsible for the hijacking and destruction of your Lightship *Impulse*. And I think it is highly likely he is also functioning as an agent for the empire."

Her eyes widened at this. "Do we really have so many enemies?" she said, her voice a hushed whisper. I stood.

"Respectfully, lady, I think you do," I said. She nodded silently, her eyes looking away from me, as if making a decision.

"Benn has called a war council for this afternoon. I think you should be there. But in the meantime, there is someone you should meet," she said.

I looked at her, surprised.

"It's time for you to meet the grand duke."

The walk to the grand duke's private apartment was quite a ways, in another wing of the palace entirely. I now came to realize that the Lady Karina had met me in a working apartment, far away from where the family resided.

There were palace guards ever-present with the lady, and I picked up my original two as well. Security was high and we had to wade through several checkpoints until we were allowed into the family wing. Karina waited patiently while I cleared security at each stop. While I waited at one such point I caught a glimpse through a window of a parade ground adjacent to the palace. It was full of soldiers and their equipment: armor, rotor gunships, VTOL fighters and the like. If someone tried to attack the palace, they would no doubt be in for a ferocious fight.

Once we were finally inside the grand duke's apartment Karina waved off our guard companions and we walked privately down a long hallway, saying nothing. We came to a pair of massive doors—were there any other kind here?—and then up to an attendant in a nurse's uniform. She was seated at a desk and quickly rose and bowed to the lady and me, then began a report to the princess.

"He's had his tea, my lady, but I'm not sure how well he is this morning. He didn't sleep good last night. He had bad dreams again," she said.

"Thank you, Berta. We would like to see him now," said the princess. Berta did as she was instructed and opened the door to the inner chamber.

Grand Duke Henrik Feilberg of Carinthia was sitting in a chair and gently snoring in the dark room, one arm draped over the arm of his chair. He was still in his bed robe, his hair white and disheveled, far different from the vibrant, dark-haired monarch portrayed in all of his official portraits. Karina approached him and gently touched him on the shoulder.

"Damn it, Berta!" he said in a rough voice once she had roused him. "I told you not to disturb me until lunch!" He looked around the room and then back to his daughter, clearly confused.

"Father, it's me. It's not Berta, it's Karina," she said.

He focused his eyes on her more intently. "So it is," he said after a moment, then pulled his robe tighter and shuffled some papers on a nearby table. "I was just reading reports about the latest naval maneuvers. We're in good hands with Admiral Steiner in command of our forces."

I remembered the name. Steiner had been the highest-ranking Carinthian officer in the Union Navy when I had joined the Academy. He had been retired for over three years. Either he had come out of retirement, or the Grand Duke didn't remember he was gone from the military.

"Father, there's someone I want you to meet," Princess Karina said, then motioned me over. I walked up slowly and Karina introduced me. "This is Duke Peter Cochrane, of Quantar. He is here to meet you."

I bowed slightly and the grand duke gazed at me through gray eyes that looked confused but still commanding. "Cochrane, you say? From Quantar?"

"Yes, Father," Karina said. I extended my hand.

"Honored to meet you, Your Highness," I said. He took my hand, then looked at me again.

"You're from Quantar?" he said.

"Yes, Sire."

"Nathan Cochrane's son?"

"Yes, Sire."

He looked around the room, still seeming confused. "I didn't know he had a son," he said flatly.

"There were two of us," I said, slowly and respectfully. "My older brother Derrick was lost in military service three years ago." Something I'm sure the grand duke would have been told at the time. This information just seemed to confuse him more, however. Karina smiled at me uncomfortably, then smoothed out her father's hair.

"I'll send Berta in to get you your morning treatment, Father," she said. "Duke Peter and I have some things to discuss."

He looked back and forth between the two of us. "Yes, yes, that would be fine," he said. Then Karina kissed him on the cheek and he went back to his reports without acknowledging me again. Karina took me by the arm and led me silently back out the door, where she instructed Berta to attend to him. I had no idea what his morning treatments might encompass. When Berta was gone, the princess and I walked slowly together back down the hallway.

"And now you see why I am so concerned, Peter. My father is very fragile and vulnerable, and I will do *anything* to protect him, and that's why I must ask you to do one very important thing for me, and for Carinthia." At this she stopped and turned to face me directly.

"Anything I can do, I will, Princess," I said, looking down at her.

She looked at me with fear and worry in her eyes.

"Get my father off this planet," she said emphatically.

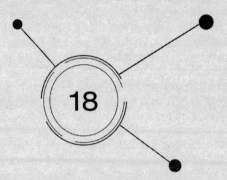

18

Dobrina, Babayan, and I reconnected after lunch. There was a lot to report and discuss. Dobrina started in quickly as I sat across from the two ladies, who were sitting next to each other on the couch.

"The situation here is poor, militarily speaking. I talked to Air Marshal Von Zimmerman directly. He's the head of the planetary air force and low-orbit space forces. He told me they are keeping the corridor to High Station Three open for now, but that he is outnumbered enough that the Regency forces could overcome them in a week and likely shut down the spaceport," Dobrina said.

"That doesn't sound good," I said. "What, if any, hostilities have there been?"

"None yet, but they see them as inevitable. And there's more bad news." I sat back in my chair.

"What now?"

"Von Zimmerman told me that construction on the two new Lightships for Carinthia has been fast tracked. *Vixis* and *Avenger* will likely be ready within ten days. That's in addition to *Impulse II,* which was delivered from Earth last month to the Loyalists at High Station Three," said Dobrina.

I contemplated this. "So in a bit more than a week the Regency forces will have double the Lightship firepower of the Loyalists. And we have just *Starbound* and the Earthmen have *Valiant,* but she's primarily an exploration and First Contact vessel, not a fighting ship. It's not good from a strategic standpoint. Not good at all."

"What about *Resolution*?" asked Babayan, referring to the new Lightship being built for Levant at High Station Quantar.

"She's still three months away," I said. "The ship itself is getting close, but we're training a Levantine crew that's not familiar with our technology. Even when she's ready, it could take weeks to get her up to an effective operating level, and this crisis is on us *now.*"

"Couldn't we put a Quantar crew on her temporarily?" asked Dobrina. I nodded.

"It's possible, though I think Prince Katara would scream loud and hard about being left out of any battle," I said.

"That he would," Dobrina agreed.

"Are you expecting war between the Union and Carinthia?" asked Babayan. I looked at her and saw the worry in her eyes.

"I'm not *expecting* anything," I said to her, "but as a Union Navy officer I have to consider every possibility."

I turned back to Dobrina. "How long until *Impulse II* is ready to roll out?"

"From what Von Zimmerman has told me, she's ready now, she just needs a command staff," she said.

"They could do worse than you," I commented. She hesitated a second. Then:

"Actually, Von Zimmerman offered me the command."

I was surprised by this. Not stunned, but surprised. I stood and walked around our small meeting room, the women watching me, waiting for a reaction.

"You should accept," I finally said.

"Do you really believe that?" Dobrina asked. I nodded.

"Having you as an ally in command of the only working Carinthian Lightship, one that is in the Loyalist camp, would be a huge advantage for the Union," I said.

"There is a complication," she said.

"Yes?"

"They're asking me to renew my original oath. The command offer is through the Carinthian Royal Navy. I will have to resign my Union commission and vow to follow Carinthian Navy orders, not Union," she said.

"That is a complication," I agreed. I came and sat back down across from her. "Dobrina, you know how much respect I have for your abilities, and I know where your true loyalties lie. But having you in command of *Impulse II*, even if it's not commissioned in the Union Navy, would give me great comfort. Wesley won't like it much, but he doesn't like anything much. Right now, Carinthia and the Loyalist cause need you." The look on her face betrayed that she had more to say, but was holding back. I tried to be reassuring without giving my true feelings away. This woman was my friend, my lover, and a valuable fighting comrade. I was going to miss her on many levels.

When I said nothing more she exhaled deeply and said: "I'll tell him I accept."

"Thank you, Dobrina," I said back. Then another thought crossed my mind. "Will there be a Historian aboard?" I asked.

"Yes. A woman named Gracel. I am told she is of the same school as Serosian, and trustworthy," said Dobrina.

"I wouldn't rely completely on that intelligence," I said. Dobrina gave me a quizzical look.

"I've never heard you question the loyalty of the Historians before. What's going on to change that?" she said. I went to the window and looked down at the back gardens again, full of military personnel and equipment. I turned back to her. "Tralfane betrayed *Impulse*. I know Serosian is loyal, but I'm unsure about any unknown members of the Historian sect. There are clearly different schools of thought, and I want us to be as sure as we can of the people we work with. Be cautious," I warned.

Dobrina nodded and I turned to Colonel Babayan. "Have you found a way for us to get off Carinthia yet, Lena?"

"I think so," she said. "There is a reception tonight for the commercial carriers, here at the palace. Obviously they are all concerned about the political crisis escalating into a military one and disrupting trade. I am reliably informed that one of the merchant traders attending will be one Admar Harrington from Pendax. He has a reputation as a formidable force in the planetary trades. Some say he's the most powerful man on Pendax. They don't have a planetary level government formed there yet and aren't ready for membership in the Union, but they're close."

"And he's also Captain Zander's new employer," I said. "Do you think he'll help us?"

Babayan nodded. "From what the intelligence officers said, he's been very helpful to the Loyalist cause. I think he's the one who can get us our passes off Carinthia."

"Can we get an invitation to this reception?" I asked.

"Already done," said Babayan. "They're expecting us at 1900 in the South Wing Reception Hall."

"Have I ever told you how much I admire your efficiency?" I said with a smile, trying to lighten things up.

"Not recently," she said, and smiled back. It was a pleasant sight on her pretty but tough face. I made a note to get to know her more once we got back to our navy duty. I sat down again.

"There is one more complication, from my end," I said.

"What now?" asked Dobrina in an annoyed tone. There was no getting around our circumstances so I started in at the beginning.

"I met with Princess Karina Feilberg, the grand duke's daughter," I started.

"Is she pretty?" interrupted Dobrina. I gave her a cutting glare. "Sorry, I meant prettier than her portraits," she said in response. I ignored her and got back to the serious matters at hand.

"She took me to see the grand duke," I said. This sobered Dobrina up.

"How is he?" asked Babayan. I shook my head.

"Old. Tired. Probably struggling with dementia. Clearly, not able to lead this world," I said. Both Dobrina and Babayan looked away. I doubted any Carinthian would like hearing that about their sovereign. I pressed on. "The Lady Karina made a request of me after our visit. She wants us to . . ." I paused here and took in a deep breath. ". . . smuggle the grand duke off of Carinthia when we leave."

"What?" said Babayan.

"Are you insane?" asked Dobrina, leaning in toward me. She was visibly shaken by my revelation. "We're going to try to smuggle a sovereign ruler off his own world? And take him *where*?" I quickly checked my com monitor to see if we were being surreptitiously observed. The com told me we were in the clear, but I encouraged both of them to speak more quietly with a coded navy hand gesture used for surreptitious conversation. When it was safe to speak again, I started in.

"All I can tell you is that she made the request. As to the details of how it would work, I haven't a clue. I assume we'll know more once we have our transportation secured.

For now, just keep quiet about it and let me handle the negotiations with the princess. Understood?" I said.

Dobrina shook her head. "I can't believe you agreed to this," she said.

"I agreed to help. Now if you don't mind, I think we should end this conversation, agreed?" They both nodded. We started more casual conversation then, in case we were being monitored. A few minutes later, there was a knock at the door. A young adjutant informed Dobrina and me that we were invited to Prince Benn's strategy meeting in twenty minutes. I looked to Babayan once he had left.

"Carry on as if there is no change in our plans, Lena. Let Dobrina and I see what, if anything, this strategy session has to offer. Then prepare for the reception tonight. Nothing has changed because of the princess's request. Nothing is certain," I said. She agreed and Dobrina and I headed out.

"This is getting sticky," I said to her as we walked together down the hall.

"I thought sticky situations were your specialty," she replied. Then she smiled at me, and I fought off the desire to take her by the hand.

"You, madam, of all people, should know better," I replied. Then we laughed a little, but not too much.

◆————◆———◆

The "strategy session" was nothing of the kind. It was a war council, that much was clear.

Air Marshal Von Zimmerman was a tall and rail-thin Carinthian with a thick mustache. Other officers were less dramatic looking but no less important in the Loyalist hierarchy. Dobrina and I found ourselves to one side of the military library with the air marshal while we all waited for Prince Benn. The tension in the room was palpable.

"I'm pleased that you have accepted my offer of command of the new *Impulse*," said Von Zimmerman to Dobrina. Then he turned to me. "And equally pleased that you encouraged her to accept my offer, Sire." I put up a hand to stop him there.

"Please, Air Marshal, I am still just a commander in the Union Navy, and I'm much more comfortable being addressed that way," I said.

"As you wish," said Von Zimmerman. He turned back to Dobrina. "Your commission is already being transferred back to the Carinthian Navy. The paperwork will be completed in a few hours, but I see no reason why you cannot assume command at your discretion."

"Thank you," said Dobrina. "I do have a few questions, though, if you would humor me, Air Marshal?"

"Of course."

"Tell me about the Earth Historian assigned, this Gracel?" she asked. He nodded as if expecting the question.

"As far as I know, she has been approved by the Historian's Guild. Beyond that I know little of her background, but she has been here on Carinthia for a number of years. This is her first shipboard assignment," said Von Zimmerman. Dobrina stiffened a bit at this, her hands going behind her back in a respectful but determined posture.

"I hope you'll understand, Air Marshal, but aboard the original *Impulse* we had several problems with the Historian, the man named Tralfane. I will not tolerate that kind of behavior, that kind of treachery, on my ship. Tralfane was also approved by the Guild and assigned here on Carinthia prior to his assignment to the first *Impulse*, so in my mind that is no guarantee of her good behavior. My relationship with the Historian must be completely transparent, otherwise I will not allow her aboard my ship." Dobrina was agitated at the thought of a repeat of the betrayal of Tralfane, and I understood that given her history with him. One thing I did agree with her on was that the Historians in general were still a puzzle that required more thought.

I stepped in here. "Perhaps, when I get back to Quantar, I can ask Serosian for a review of Gracel's background," I offered.

"That would be helpful," said Dobrina, "if not a bit untimely. *Impulse II* should be in service by then."

"I understand your reticence, Captain Kierkopf, but all precautions have been taken against a repeat of the *Impulse* incident. Now to your other concerns?" said Von Zimmerman. Dobrina hesitated a moment, then continued.

"I will report directly to you in all matters?"

"Yes."

"I can pick my own command crew?"

"Of course."

Dobrina nodded, then turned back to me. "I'd like to have Colonel Babayan as my XO," she said. I was surprised by this request. I didn't think the two of them were particularly close.

"She's a marine colonel," I said by way of argument, though I wasn't really prepared to disagree with her about it one way or the other. "I'd like to keep her for my own team. And besides, her commission is still with the Union Navy."

"It would be a bit unusual," interjected Von Zimmerman. Dobrina got that hard, steadfast look in her eyes that let me know she was going to be insistent on this.

"Nonetheless, I think she's the best choice for the role. She's efficient, I know her, and I trust her. Plus you have John Marker to command your marine units. The rest of the command crew can be assigned as you wish, Air Marshal," she said.

Von Zimmerman shrugged. "I have no objection," he said, then looked to me for final disposition of the matter.

I didn't want to argue with Dobrina, but I also felt I couldn't give in. "I don't want to pull diplomatic rank," I said. "But I'm afraid I must. Colonel Babayan is too valuable to the Union, and to me, to allow it. I understand your desire to have a familiar face around, Captain Kierkopf, but I'm afraid I must decline your request."

"Don't," she replied abruptly. I watched her face for a moment and saw that she was determined to have her way, as I was determined to have mine.

"I'm afraid there's no arguing about it, Captain," I said. "She's too valuable to me at the moment. I haven't even secured safe transport off of Carinthia yet. I can't spare her right now."

She gave me a hard stare. I wanted to help her, wanted to grant her request, but I couldn't spare Lena under these circumstances, not with all the potential skullduggery involving the grand duke.

"I can see that arguing with you about this will be pointless," she finally said.

"It is."

She nodded reluctantly. "Then I withdraw my request. But you will owe me a favor, Commander," Dobrina said.

"That I will."

At that moment Prince Benn and his advisors came into the room and the somber group started gathering around a large 3-D strategy projection table.

"And so we begin," said Von Zimmerman with a sweep of his hand toward the table. We took our places next to him.

There were about thirty Carinthian officers, men and women, gathered around the table, all standing, all with worried looks on their faces. I wondered absently how many of them would be here if they were given a free choice of which side to support in this conflict. None of them, though, seemed the type to violate their oaths.

The prince started in.

"Good afternoon," he said, then immediately paused. I looked up to see the Lady Karina and her attendant guards come into the room and then stop a few feet back from the table. She was dressed in her full navy duty uniform. Some of the officers made room for her and she stepped up to the table, just a few feet from me. We exchanged a glance of recognition as Prince Benn started again, seemingly unfazed by her arrival, which was no doubt unexpected.

"Thank you for joining us, *Lieutenant*," he said to his sister, emphasizing her low rank for his own purposes, no doubt. Then he lit up the 3-D graphics on the table. It showed the city of New Vienna with the vicinity surrounding the New Hofburg palace in the center in green, the rest of the area controlled by the Loyalists in light blue, a buffer zone in pale yellow, and finally the vast holdings of the Regency forces in red.

"As any of you can plainly see, we here in the city are now surrounded by potentially hostile forces. Arin has systematically enclosed us in his net and now controls almost every major military facility outside of the green zone. We have two infantry divisions. He has twenty-eight. We have two hundred and forty armored units, he has seventeen hundred. The only area in which we can even compete with him is the air. We have three hundred and forty fixed-wing aircraft and one hundred sixty VTOLs. He has roughly the same amount, but our pilots are the best of the best, so we have a small advantage there. The High Ground is a problem. We have forty space-ready craft and he has about sixty, but again ours are a bit better outfitted, both in displacement and pilot capability. The Regency holds High Stations One and Two along with most of the low-orbit defense platforms, and we hold High Station Three, the most distant from Carinthia. Our only clear advantage is that *Impulse II* is ready to launch under the command of Captain Kierkopf," he nodded at Dobrina, "and *Vixis* and *Avenger* are still ten or so days out to completion. We do still hold our airspace corridor and the spaceport at Aspern, but our window is narrow. To state it plainly, gentlemen, if it comes to civil war, we can probably hold out for a week, perhaps more, with our air forces, but eventually his ground superiority will grind us to dust if that's what he wants to do." He looked around the table. "Options?"

A gray-haired female air commander spoke up first. "A preemptive strike on his air units would force him to the ground, and we could do serious damage to his ground forces if we have full air superiority," she said. "Plus, we have the heavier armored units."

"Yes, but they could break our supply corridor by attacking the spaceport and bring down their space-based platforms on you from above," said the prince. There were quiet nods all around. "Other ideas?"

"Use the air corridor to evacuate the green zone, protect the royal family and Loyalist forces," said an older, balding army general. "Give the city to the Regency."

"Evacuate to where?" asked the prince.

"High Station Three, of course," he replied. Prince Benn nodded.

"And then what?" he said, hands on hips. I sensed he was growing angry. "Perhaps young Duke Peter here can find us a home in exile on Quantar." I looked at him from across the table but said nothing. The implication that humiliating exile on my world was worse than defeat on Carinthia was clear, and I didn't much care for it. He switched his gaze from me to Von Zimmerman. "Air Marshal?" he said.

Von Zimmerman surveyed the map, then pushed out the view from the city to the region, then the continent, then the whole planet. The display glittered with hundreds of communications and defensive weapons platforms in orbit over Carinthia. "Only one plan that can lead to victory, Sire. Activate *Impulse II*. Use her impeller speed to bypass High Stations One and Two and the forces there and bring her into orbit. From there she destroys the Regency's low-orbit warships and communications network. Simultaneously we use an all-out airborne assault to take out Arin's atmosphere-based aircraft. This is followed by a takeover of the space-based defensive weapons platforms by marines from *Impulse II*. We then turn the platforms on Arin's ground forces and take them out from above with our missiles and coil cannon batteries. We clean up with our heavy armored units on the ground," he said. There was no emotion in it, just pure military tactics.

The prince rubbed at his face. "Use atomic missiles and coil cannons on ground-based military units? What would the casualties be in the city? I'm sure you have that number," he demanded. Von Zimmerman stiffened.

"We estimate three million dead, mostly within the city region of New Vienna," he said.

"Half the city killed? A tenth of the entire population? Unacceptable," said the prince, smashing his fist on the table and causing the display to waver before resetting. "I demand another option!" He went around the table from face to face. There was none.

"Very well," he said. "Then I've made my decision." Heads around the table snapped from the tactical display to focus on the prince. He waited until he had all of his commanders' attention. "We will open negotiations immediately with the Regency command to initiate a peaceful transition of the city into their hands at the earliest opportunity. The green zone will be emptied of all Loyalist troops. All of our units will be returned to barracks. The royal family will agree to stay within the green zone. There will be no bloodshed if I can avoid it. My first priority is the protection of the royal family, followed by the people of the city. All other considerations," he looked at me here, "are secondary. I will not allow a bloodbath in my city over membership in the Union. The transition will begin as soon as I have negotiated terms," he finished.

"Transition?" It was the Lady Karina. "You mean surrender! You have no idea what you're doing, Benn. If you think we will be safe, if you think Father will be safe, you're gravely mistaken. Arin is in league with the old empire, and they will not stop until they control everything on Carinthia, and they will allow nothing or no one to get in their way."

"I'm forced to agree with the princess," I said, then instantly regretted speaking out. Prince Benn looked at me with a fire in his eyes that could bore holes in granite. Since the damage was already done, I continued. "Surrender is no guarantee of safety for your father. He is the icon of the family, the one everyone else in the Union looks to as your leader. If you allow him, and Carinthia, to fall into Imperial hands, he will quickly become an inconvenience. And then how long until you and the princess become inconveniences as well? I have seen the empire at work firsthand, seen their merciless actions in turning the crew of *Impulse* against their own through the use of nanites. They are not the kind of people you can negotiate a peaceful surrender with."

"So what do you suggest?" snapped Prince Benn at me, obviously seething inside.

"Retreat to High Station Three *and* activate *Impulse II* under Captain Kierkopf, as the air marshal proposed. I will return to High Station Candle and call personally for *Starbound* to be deployed to Carinthia. When she arrives, and it may be several days as she is still undergoing refit and repair, we can take out High Stations One and Two and disable the new Lightships before they can become active. The fighting will stay away from Carinthia. Once that operation is complete, the Loyalists and the Union will control all air and space above Carinthia. We can then combine Union and Loyalist units to deal with the prince regent on the ground," I said. I wasn't really sure if it would work, but Von Zimmerman, Dobrina, and the princess seemed buoyed by my plan. Prince Benn, though, merely shook his head.

"Foreign troops on our world, especially Quantar troops, is completely unacceptable. The people would never accept it and half the military still loyal to us wouldn't either. It's a nonstarter," he said.

"But your other options—"

"Are really none of your business, Duke Peter. Thank you for your input, but this matter is finished. We will proceed as I have outlined."

"I will not allow this, Benn!" said the Princess Karina, angry.

"You are not in command here, Lady!" he bellowed at her, his face flushing red with anger. "The decision is made. May I suggest that you focus on getting your young Quantar friend here off of Carinthia as soon as possible? Otherwise I might see fit to use him as a bargaining chip in the negotiations. This meeting is ended." And with that he turned and strode out of the room followed by a host of commanders. Von Zimmerman was not among them. He came up to me.

"Please attend the reception tonight for the commercial traders as planned. At that meeting we will try to negotiate a deal to get you off Carinthia, Sire," he said to me before following the prince out the door. At that moment, getting off of Carinthia was all I wanted to do.

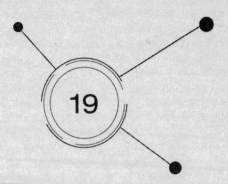

19

"**D**id I make a mistake? Opening my mouth like that?" I was asking the question of Dobrina in my stateroom, a small space with a single bed, lav, and sitting area. Dobrina, Lena, and I were waiting for the reception and the opportunity it presented to get me off of Carinthia, and none too soon for me. Outside the window tiny snowflakes were falling against the panes as a winter night closed in. I was reminded of how cold this world had been to me, in more ways than one.

I sat on one of a set of matching sofas facing the two women across a coffee table. Our dinners sat on the table between us, mostly untouched. I found that under stress, I didn't eat much. Neither did they.

"Protocol-wise, of course you made a mistake," said Dobrina. "Strategically, though, what you proposed was sound. The politics of it, however, are another matter."

"And in politics we are not likely to win," I said, then

rubbed at my face. We were all tired, but our beds had gone unused. None of us could sleep, even though we had all been up through most of a grueling day. A bit over twelve hours ago I was about to be executed.

"So what's our next move?" asked Colonel Babayan. I looked at my watch.

"The reception starts in thirty minutes. You and I need to make our deal to get off of Carinthia, and that's going to be the best place to catch our ride," I said. Lena looked uncomfortable with this.

"And what about the princess's request?" she asked. I sat back to consider this.

"I don't see how we can help her now. Perhaps when I get back to Candle I can consult with Wesley and we can work out some sort of plan, but I'll be the first to admit I'm not good at the covert operations game," I said.

"So we're refusing her request?" asked Lena, clarifying.

"Not directly, no," I said. "Any action will have to be initiated by the princess. I will give her the courtesy of letting her know when I'm departing, but beyond that . . ." I spread my arms open.

"Understood," said Lena. She was clearly not pleased, but we were trapped in our current circumstances, as far as I was concerned.

I looked to Dobrina. "What has Von Zimmerman told you about your assignment to *Impulse II*?"

"We're heading out within the hour, a military shuttle," Dobrina said, then looked to Babayan. "This will be our last meeting together."

I stood then and they both stood with me. "I think that you are very brave, taking command of *Impulse II*. No matter what Prince Benn thinks, this is going to be very dangerous business for you, but I wouldn't want anyone else in command of a friendly Lightship right now," I said to her. Colonel Babayan cleared her throat then.

"I need a moment, if you don't mind," she said. And

with that she disappeared into the bedroom and shut the door behind her, a gesture designed to give Dobrina and me a final, private moment. I pulled her close to me.

"You're doing the right thing," I said. She leaned in and rested her head on my chest.

"I know. But what guarantees are there? Everything is coming apart. We aren't even in the same navy anymore," she said. I said nothing but instead just held her close, the rhythm of our breathing slowing breath by breath until we were in unison. I was getting experienced in saying goodbye to women I cared about, far too experienced for my taste. Whether I liked it or not, Dobrina was leaving my life, and it hurt me more than I could express, so I shared my feelings the only way I could, with a kiss, the kind only lovers share.

She pulled away from the kiss and returned to resting her head on me as we gently embraced. She spoke in a whisper.

"When I was a little girl, I dreamed of marrying a handsome young prince and riding off to some magic land together, to live and love," she said.

"Happily ever after?"

"Of course. But as I've grown up I realized what a foolish dream that was. Princes don't marry the daughters of military men, common girls. They marry princesses and ladies and women so far above my station that I couldn't even imagine. And then I met you, and all of that changed. I'm going to miss you, Peter. Miss the hopes and dreams that I had when we were together. If we were different people, not committed to our oaths, we could be together. But we both always knew that could never happen," she said.

"Dobrina—"

"No," she said, raising her voice just a bit. "It's been enough to be here with you these last months, to taste what the dream could be like. I loved it, and I'm certain I love you. But now it's time for us both to move on."

With that she kissed me again, then pulled away a final time, and I felt her emotional walls go up. "I promise I will miss you, Peter, when I have the time," she said.

She called to Babayan, the two of them joining me at the stateroom door. There we shared a salute and some muted goodbyes, and I watched another former lover walk slowly out of my life, to her duties. Babayan went with her, to see her to her waiting ground car.

When they were gone, I shut the door behind me and poured myself a drink, then sat down heavily on the couch, checking my watch one more time. Then I drank, feeling completely alone for the first time on an alien world.

My companion guards accompanied Lena and me on our way to the reception, but they discreetly disappeared into the crowd once we arrived. The reception hall was ornate, as was seemingly everything involving the Carinthians. Their love of rich, baroque architecture and furnishings was expressed in everything they did, down to the last detail. I marveled a bit as we both took an offered drink of champagne in a crystal glass, then made our way through the crowd, not really sure what our most promising contact, Admar Harrington of Pendax, looked like, or when he might arrive.

We agreed to split up to work the crowded room more efficiently, and I engaged several traders in conversation, gently inquiring about transport to High Station Three and just as gently being rebuffed. From my best guess there were at least fifty merchants in the room, not counting their attendant ladies and assistants, enjoying drinks and hors d'oeuvres courtesy of the Carinthian royal family. There were several conversations about the political situation in New Vienna, and many available trade officers in military garb were there to soothe the nerves of the merchants. All would be resolved soon, they said repeatedly, with more than a glimmer of enthusiasm. Prince Benn, it appeared, would have his peaceful resolution. The question was, at what cost?

After nearly thirty minutes of this I had mingled and conversed with several merchants but had yet to meet Admar Harrington, my former captain Zander's new employer. Lena and I regrouped near the center of the hall.

"Any luck?" I asked.

"No," Babayan replied. "Those who know Harrington say he's not here, and no one else seems interested in cargo or passengers bound for High Station Three. I guess fear of retribution is the best type of blockade."

"Word of the negotiations between the two princes has gotten out, I'm afraid. No merchant trader in his right mind would want to be on the wrong side of a new planetary government," I said.

"Except, we hope, a certain Admar Harrington." I nodded at that and finished my champagne.

Precisely at the bottom of the hour the Lady Karina made an unexpected appearance with a portly gentleman sporting an enormous handlebar mustache and dressed in gray formal military garb, complete with a red sash. I knew little of Pendax, but I knew her flag's colors and could recognize a ceremonial uniform when I saw one. This must be Admar Harrington. He practically reeked of frontier garishness and crude manners.

As I watched the Lady Karina float through the room in a black evening gown, escorting Harrington from merchant to merchant, I patiently waited for my chance. Once he got close, I stepped in and introduced myself as Duke Peter Cochrane of Quantar. Harrington, for his part, was charming and bowed as he shook my hand.

"Honored, Sire," he said in a clipped colonial accent.

"As am I to meet you, sir," I replied. This was one occasion where I thought my rank as a royal could be more useful than my rank in the navy, so I decided to use it to my advantage and not discourage the use of my honoraria. I introduced Lena to both Harrington and the princess, and then we got down to business.

"I understand I may be of some service to you, Sire?" he said. I nodded.

"Colonel Babayan and I need to buy passage off of Carinthia, and quickly," I said in a quiet voice. At this the Lady Karina stepped in.

"No need to buy your way off our world, Duke Peter. The royal family will gladly pay your freight as recompense for what those Regency thugs tried to do to you," she said in a voice loud enough to arouse strained looks from nearby traders. Obviously any show of discord with the current government line was regarded as disturbing to the merchants. The attendant Carinthian trade officers quickly reassured their clients and another round of drinks came by quickly, which I declined.

"Just so you know, Sire, travel to High Station Three is fraught with potential trouble. I've had my ships interdicted at either One or Two, or both for that matter, several times in the last few weeks. Everyone out there is on edge," said Harrington.

"Is there some danger I could be taken captive again?" I asked.

"I've made sure that your safe passage is part of any agreement with the Regency government my brother negotiates," Karina said. That was somewhat, but not altogether, reassuring.

"Can Prince Benn be trusted to keep that agreement? He has no love for me," I replied.

"He can be trusted in this regard," said Karina.

"But—"

"Please, Peter, don't ask me to elaborate," she said.

I nodded acknowledgment. I had to trust someone on this planet. I turned back to Harrington.

"As for your ship—"

"Cargo run," he said, "Nova class, slow and steady, but she should get you to Three in half a day."

I nodded. "When does she leave?" I asked.

"Midnight. You both need to be at the spaceport at Leopoldsdorf an hour before. The accommodations won't be what you're used to, I gather, but they'll do. We'll rendezvous with your friend Zander at Three and he'll zip you home," Harrington said. I checked my watch. Lena and I had about three hours.

"We'll be there," I said. With that Harrington said his goodbyes and trundled off, leaving me with the Lady Karina. "Will we be able to get ground transport to Leopoldsdorf?"

"Of course," she said. "It takes about thirty minutes, so plan for that. I'll make sure you have a proper escort."

I looked to Lena and she nodded. "That should do," I said, then hesitated. "Lady, about your other request—"

"No matter," she said, interrupting me. "The grand duke is safe, for now. I just hope that someday you and I can meet under very different circumstances, and that I can thank you properly for your good intentions."

"What you're doing for us now is more than enough," I said.

And with that she turned and departed the room without another word.

⁌

We were escorted from the New Hofburg Palace at 2230 hours for the trip to the Leopoldsdorf spaceport. We had a convoy of three armored military utility vehicles at our disposal. Lena and I sat in the back of the second one in line as our journey began, taking mostly dark and empty roads. The city of New Vienna was under a 2200 hours curfew during what the news reports called "extremely sensitive negotiations" between the two government factions.

Lena had several coughing spasms in the first few minutes of our trip. "Nervous, Colonel?" I asked. She shook her head.

"I think I've picked up a native virus, sir. Something I'd forgotten about New Vee winters," she replied.

"Thank the Gods I appear to be immune," I said. She smiled a bit.

"Of course you are. What virus would dare attack a royal such as yourself?"

"Hmm." I let things lie for a few minutes as we cruised along the roads at a moderate pace, then asked a question. "Lena, are you all right with my refusing to let you go with Dobrina?"

She shrugged before replying. "The captain and I aren't that close. I've fenced with her once or twice, and taken her measure on the squash court a few times, but socially, we've never mixed. I think she always thought of me as a soldier, not a navy officer. I was surprised when I heard the offer. I supposed she wanted a familiar face around and I was conveniently here. But I made my decision to serve in the Union Navy years ago. I have no desire to change that," she said.

I took her answer as sincere. We were quiet from then on. I looked at my watch at five minutes to the hour.

Our convoy took a turn off of the main roadway and down past a row of low set warehouse buildings. I assumed they were for military overflow and storage. Suddenly the lead MUV in front of us accelerated and pulled away at a rapid pace.

"Is there a problem?" I asked our driver, a Carinthian private.

"I don't know, sir. Should I—"

"Step on it!" I shouted. A second later a rocket-propelled grenade exploded a few meters behind us, shrapnel pinging against our rear armor plating like the sound of hail hitting a metal roof. A second RPG round hit just in front of our trailing escort and the MUV spun and rolled over, crashing into a row of metal bins stacked against a warehouse wall. I turned and saw four Carinthian soldiers scrambling for cover behind the bins, their vehicle on fire.

"Vat should I do, sir?" asked the driver. Ahead of us lay the building where the RPG fire came from. I didn't hesitate.

"Turn us around!"

"Vat?"

"Go back! We have to help those men!" I ordered. The private quickly turned our vehicle and spun us around, weaving his way back to the second MUV and the sparse safety of the bins. We pulled up, using our vehicle as additional cover, then we all jumped out and hit the ground. The four soldiers from our escort stepped up and began firing at the roof of another warehouse building across the road. Their fire was returned.

Our driver, armed with only a coil pistol, joined in the fray. Babayan and I took cover behind the bins, as both of us were unarmed. I felt useless. The firefight went on for a solid two minutes before another RPG hit our vehicle dead on. Our driver was killed instantly, his coil pistol skidding across cold concrete to within a few feet of me.

"Stay here!" I said to Babayan and scrambled for the pistol.

"Sir! You can't!" she yelled at me.

"Stay down!" I ordered her, then zigzagged to the remaining soldiers' position. One of them was wounded badly, his left arm dangling at his side. He was trying to return fire with his coil rifle, but they were heavy and it was hard with only one arm. I quickly swapped weapons with him, handing him the easier to handle pistol. Then I took cover and started returning fire.

"How many?" I asked the soldiers, but they just looked at me, confused. Apparently none of them spoke Standard. After a few more precious seconds of exchanging fire with the snipers, who were ensconced on the roof of the warehouse across the street and forward of our position, I determined that there were two of them. The coil rifle volleys came in pairs, then would drop to a single shooter for several seconds right before an RPG volley would come in. Our rifles had tracker fire on them, and we were lucky to intercept several RPG rounds before they hit our position. But when the next volley came, we weren't so lucky. The RPG exploded against the overturned MUV and sent metal pieces flying in the air. We were all able to duck except the wounded soldier. He took a piece of MUV armor right in the head, killing him instantly. I ran over and grabbed his pistol as we hunkered down behind our burning vehicle, almost our only protection now.

"Lena!" I called, then raised up and sent out three volleys of suppressing fire. She came running and I tossed her my rifle, taking the pistol for myself. I checked the mix chamber: barely ten percent left. I held up my pistol to the nearest soldier, showing him my mix reserve. He made a gesture, holding his index finger and thumb millimeters apart. The other two both nodded agreement.

We were running out of ammo.

"What are we going to do?" asked Babayan. We were pinned down here.

"There's nothing to do. We hold out here as long as we can and pray for help to arrive," I said. "Can you tell them to start rotating their fire, to save as much of our ammo as we can?" I asked her. She shot off a short sentence in guttural German and they all nodded, then started taking turns sending out single volleys. The enemy returned fire with multiple sniper rounds at every turn.

"They haven't fired an RPG in a while," Babayan said. I nodded.

"If I'm right in my count, they have three left. RPGs

come in packs of six. Any more is too heavy for a single man to carry. If this is an assassination squad of two they will be traveling light. They're trying to get us to use up our energy weapons. Then they'll zero in and finish us with the RPGs," I said. I gave a cutoff signal then and we all stopped shooting. The dual coil fire continued for about ten seconds, then it reduced to a single volley. A second after that an RPG round hit our MUV. It went up in flames and we had to scramble back to the metal bins to find cover. We were down to our last line of defense.

We all huddled together as the coil volleys cut holes in our protection, tearing pieces off the slim metal bin with every shot. Another minute of this and they'd probably have us.

"What do we do?" asked Lena. I had no idea.

"Pray," I said.

At that moment the coil volleys fell silent. I could hear the sound of mechanized gears turning and something like the hum of a motor. I motioned everyone to the ground, then stuck my head around the bin to look down the road just as a motorized armored vehicle came around the corner and on to our road. Immediately the coil fire resumed, aimed at the MAV. The MAV had a prominent gun mount of a design I hadn't seen before. It quickly raised up, pointing at the rooftop we'd been taking fire from. In rapid succession an immense volley of ordnance, rockets no doubt, battered the top of the warehouse. It exploded in a burst of flame and sparks and smoke. When the volley ended I looked across and down the long road. As the smoke cleared I could see that the top quarter of the warehouse had been sheared off. I gave the All Clear and our group stood up, walking out into the open as a squad of about a dozen Carinthian Regulars came rushing toward us, much to the relief of our comrades. Lena came up and stood next to me, watching the warehouse burn.

"Well, so much for questioning them," she deadpanned.

I tossed my pistol to the ground as the soldiers came running up to us.

"I can't wait to leave this planet," I said.

•——•——•

We were at the airfield a few minutes later. I thanked the soldiers who had fought with us and the ones who had rescued us, then Lena and I made our way into a waiting room, flopping down on the couch. Lena grabbed us each a bottle of water and we sat silently together, contemplating another near brush with death. After a few minutes of this I stood and looked out over the massive base. I could see many ships that were eager to depart and the crowded tarmac was buzzing with activity, even at this late hour. It seemed obvious the merchants here were all getting off-world as fast as they could in case something went wrong with the peace negotiations. After a few minutes we were escorted to another building by soldiers. Once inside the gritty terminal an attendant with Harrington's flag seal on his winter coveralls led us down a ramp and out into the night.

"Wait here," he said, then went off to talk to some port maintenance workers. I pulled my uniform coat tighter around me against the brisk winter chill. The sky above the spaceport was a dull gray, with just a hint of stars beyond broken clouds. I looked at our transport as it was being fueled and loaded. It was functional enough. It looked like a great whale with a flat head and stubby wings. There was no doubting the twin hydrazine plasma engines could do their work, though. Besides the cargo hold itself they were the largest feature of the ship. The front featured a cockpit and three tiny portholes, which probably indicated the passenger compartment. Absently I wondered how I would get up there. It was a good three stories up.

The rear of the transport was opened upward and

large cargo containers were being loaded into her belly, though this looked like far from a full trip. My guess was that it would be less than twenty-five percent full.

As I watched, three longshoremen finished loading the cargo hold, then set the cargo door in motion to seal it up for our flight. The attendant from the terminal came over then and motioned Lena and me into the hold through a side access door, which he shut behind us. As we entered the transport the great metal cargo doors closed and locked, finishing with a resounding clang. We were directed by one of the workers up an open metal ladder to get from the cargo bay to the passenger compartment while the crew mingled around the deck securing their loads for air and space transport.

Harrington hadn't been kidding about the accommodations. I took an acceleration couch in the back row among a group of six, clustered in two rows of three, near one of the portholes. Lena strapped in next to me. The cabin had a single lav with only a sink and loo for inflight service. A small galley completed the ensemble. Ahead of us two pilots were busy in the cockpit making final checks for the flight. At precisely two minutes to the hour they fired up the engines and after a brief check-in via radio in German, the pilots rolled us away. They seemed to have no interest in me, and I frankly had none in them. I laid back in my seat and closed my eyes, trying to rest.

"You should try to sleep," I said to Babayan.

"I can never sleep on takeoff, sir, and sometimes not even in transit. Gets me too wound up," she said. I opened one eye.

"Control freak," I said.

"Guilty. I'm a pilot," she said, smiling. I shut my eye again and tried to relax.

A shuffling of boots on the metal floor a few minutes later roused me. The three workers from the loading dock strapped into the row in front us as we taxied down the tarmac. I gave them hardly a second thought as the giant transport roared down the runway and into the air, modest turbulence shuffling us around in the cabin.

It took twenty minutes for us to clear the atmosphere of Carinthia, and I looked down on her blue-green globe without a bit of remorse at leaving, privately wishing I never had to go back, though I knew that was probably impractical. The space propulsion system clicked on then and I felt the tug of the plasma engines kick in for space-flight. I closed my eyes tight, trying to block it all out. I was dog tired.

"Are you awake yet, Peter?" came a feminine voice. I stirred, thinking in my mind that it must be Lena. But it didn't sound like Lena. I had no idea how long I'd been dozing. Then I opened my eyes and looked in the direction of the voice, to the row of safety couches in front of me. The Princess Karina Feilberg looked back at me. The longshoremen were gone and Lena was asleep.

"What the hell are you doing here?" I said a bit more sharply than I would have liked. I quickly roused myself and looked again, just to confirm what I was seeing.

"What's going on?" said Lena, waking slowly.

"I'm sure I have no idea," I said to her.

"I'm protecting my father, like I said I would," Karina replied. "Do you have some objection?"

"Wait—what . . . *what* are you doing here?" I said again. She looked at me, wearing the coveralls of a cargo worker, not looking the least bit like the princess of the palace.

"I told you I wanted my father off of Carinthia, and conveniently you provided the opportunity. Arin granted you safe passage in return for Benn's surrender. I couldn't live with that, and I wasn't leaving my father in Arin's hands. So I made other plans," she said.

I looked to Lena and then back again. "I don't understand. Your father . . ." I looked around the cabin just to be sure. "Your father isn't here."

"Oh, but he is, I assure you. Come and see." She unstrapped herself and Lena and I followed suit, trailing her out of the cabin and back down to the cargo hold. It was cold and dark, but she illuminated a pair of overhead lights. I followed her between two of the large containers that had been loaded as cargo. Two longshoremen were standing guard on the containers. The third, I realized now, must have been Karina. The princess used a magnetic key to unlock one of the crates. A control panel slid out and she entered a code, at which point an entire side of the container slid away.

Inside, behind sealed glass, was the Grand Duke Henrik Feilberg.

He was in stasis field, monitor lights flickering his vital signs, which looked steady to me. I was shocked at the brashness of the action, but not surprised, as it was obviously born out of desperation.

"You can't be serious?" I said.

"Completely," she replied. "These crates contain absinthe and schnapps for Carinthian troops on Union bases. As such they were perfect for smuggling my father off of Carinthia. There is a stealth field around the crate which should protect him. With luck, no one will find him, and he will ride with you and me all the way back to the Union. To Quantar, in fact."

"This is insane," I started. "The political ramifications—"

"Are completely secondary to my father's safety. You have to face the facts, Peter. My world is in the midst of a takeover by forces who are working with the old empire. That makes Carinthia your enemy, and that makes it unsafe for all of us, and it means trouble is coming," she said.

"And what trouble will come of Union officers being

involved in the abduction of the Grand Duke of Carinthia?" asked Babayan.

"That's how they'll couch this, you know," I said. "The Union and I will be made the villains, more fodder for war," I said. The princess stepped back, hands on hips, as I had seen Dobrina do so many times. I wondered if it was a Carinthian affectation.

"War is coming anyway, Peter Cochrane, war against the Union, don't you see that?" she said.

I looked down at the grand duke. All I saw was a frail old man in a very dangerous position, and a precarious strategic situation that seemed to revolve around me. All I wanted was to get back to *Starbound*, and to my duties there. That was where I knew my place, not in these roiling waters of politics and intrigue.

"This is insane," I repeated. Then I walked away from her, like I wished I could walk away from all my troubles.

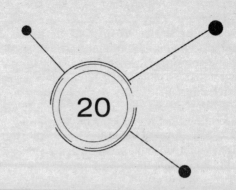

20

On High Station Three

Twelve hours later we were docking at High Station Three. I had slept fitfully and intermittently, and I'd hardly spoken to Karina. She was a resourceful young woman, and I respected her for that, but she had put me in an untenable position, both here in Carinthian space if we were found out, and no doubt back on Quantar when I arrived at the Admiralty with a surprise guest. I resented being put in this position, but I knew those feelings were selfish, and I was trying very hard not to be that way under the circumstances. She was afraid for her father's life, and I understood that. I probably would have done the same thing in her position. And I had promised the princess I would do anything I could to help her. I just hadn't thought it would be this.

Karina was back in her coveralls as we docked and the cargo doors were opened inside the station. I was glad to be back on what could be termed friendly territory, if only marginally so. She stayed undercover with the work crew as the crates were being transferred through the station to *Benfold*, under Captain Lucius Zander's command. Colonel Babayan and I were walking the station's cargo deck trying to locate what berth *Benfold* might be in when I heard a voice call my name from behind me.

"Commander Cochrane?" I turned to find the curly-haired Lieutenant Daniel from *Starbound*.

"What are you doing here, Lieutenant?" I asked, surprised to see a familiar face. Then I glanced at his garb and I had my answer. He was out of uniform and dressed as a merchantman.

"Captain Maclintock sent me," he said. "He thought you two might need some assistance, and, well, I volunteered."

"I see," I replied. I was impressed with the slight young man's desire to be more than the ship's purser.

"Captain Zander and Mr. Harrington would like to meet with you both aboard *Benfold* as soon as possible," said Daniel.

I nodded. "That was my plan exactly. Lead the way, Mr. Daniel." Daniel weaved his way quickly through the crowded loading dock as he led Lena and me down a series of passenger terminal hubs and connectors and then through a large umbilical dock and onto *Benfold*.

Once aboard we walked onto a gangway above *Benfold*'s hangar deck just as the crates containing our secret cargo were being delivered. As I looked down to the deck below a group of six Carinthians were inspecting the crates. Not Loyalist guards, but rather the military police, the *Feldjäger*, the same type of troops I had encountered at the military base where I had been put on trial.

"What's with the MPs?" I asked Daniel.

"While you were in transit a preliminary agreement was reached between the two princes. The MPs were put in charge of station security as part of the agreement," he said. I eyed them nervously.

"This might not be good," I said. As I watched, the MPs were probing each of the crates with some advanced scanning devices, nothing like I had seen before. Karina and the two longshoremen, who I took to be her personal bodyguards, stood to the side as the inspection continued. The bodyguards were getting agitated, though, shifting from side to side every few seconds, something that didn't go unnoticed by the *Feldjäger*. Karina stayed stoic and covered under her hood and mask.

"Stay here," I said to Daniel and Lena. "I'm going down there." I made my way down an open metal stairwell and headed straight for the cargo crates. Against my orders I heard Lena trailing behind me, but I didn't have the time to correct her.

"Say there!" I called to one of the *Feldjäger* military police as I approached. "Those are my supplies!" My yelling seemed to confuse them temporarily as I approached. Then two of them peeled away from the pair of investigators and approached me with weapons at the ready.

"Zeugenstand verlassen!" one of them yelled at me in German as I kept coming, which I took to mean "stand down" or something similar. The second brought his weapon to bear on Babayan as she came up beside me.

"Sir, wait!" I heard Daniel's voice from behind me. I waved him off.

"Get back, Daniel!" I turned and ordered. Just then one of the inspectors was at the crate containing the grand duke. It only took him seconds to sound the alarm. He started yelling something in German and then everything exploded into a flurry of action. One of Lady Karina's bodyguards pulled out a coil pistol and shot both guards approaching me in the back. The first one fell neatly but the second got off a reflex shot that burned past Lena and me far too close for comfort. The second bodyguard dispatched another *Feldjäger* as Karina ran for cover. I scrambled to gather the rifle from the nearest fallen MP and Babayan did the same. We ran for cover, firing at one of the inspectors as we went. A bolt of energy from my rifle went right through one of the inspector's handheld devices and pierced his chest. The second inspector went for cover as the lone remaining MP dispatched one of the princess's bodyguards. The second guard took cover behind some crates, protecting the princess behind him. The problem now was that from either direction the crate containing the grand duke was in the way for one of us. Babayan and I then took up a sniper position behind some barrels. The second inspector was in my sights, but so was the crate just past him. If I missed . . .

Meanwhile the two MPs and the princess's lone remaining bodyguard were exchanging potshots to no avail. We were at a stalemate. This exchange went on for several more tense seconds before I heard the sound of someone calling out and demanding attention.

It was the Princess Karina.

She yelled at the two remaining *Feldjäger* in German, some commands that I didn't understand. She stood up and pulled her hood down off her face so that they could see her. That was all the distraction I needed. The second inspector raised his head clearly into my line of fire and I took him out with a sniper shot. The last MP was so startled at seeing his sovereign that he had dropped his rifle and stood up to surrender, hands in the air. It didn't stop the princess's bodyguard from dropping him with a shot to the chest. I jumped up and ran to the princess.

"Are you all right? What the hell did you think you were doing?" I demanded. It was the second time I'd asked that question of her.

"Giving orders to my subjects," she said. "It worked, didn't it?" I looked around at the carnage on the deck.

"Seven of your 'subjects' are dead, Princess," I said.

"Eight." She pointed behind me. I turned to look. Ensign Daniel lay in a bloody pool, a neat hole the size of a melon in his chest. He'd been cut down by the reflexive coil rifle shot from the fallen MP. Damnable luck. He was a good kid, or at least he had been.

"He was one of ours," I said, but there was no time to waste now on sentiment. "We've got to get these bodies—"

"Get them off my deck!" yelled a voice from behind me. I swiveled, rifle still drawn, to see Lucius Zander and a group of his men rushing to the scene of the shootout. "Lock down the hull! We're breaking station in two minutes!" he bellowed. I went to him as he stood over Ensign Daniel's scarred body. "He was a good lad, just in the wrong place at the wrong time."

"Like us?" I said.

"Not if I can help it," replied Zander. Then he bowed as the Lady Karina came up. "Highness," he said.

"Captain Zander I presume," she said, then removed her gloves and extended her hand and he kissed it. "How long until we can get underway?"

"Thirty seconds if I have my way, Highness," he said. "The station's been taken over by those *Feldjäger* bastards. Part of your brother's 'Peaceful Resolution.'"

She nodded. "Unfortunate. But we have to go. Time is of the essence, Captain."

"I understand, Highness," he replied and then turned to Lena and me. "If you're done shooting up my cargo hold, Mr. Cochrane, perhaps you'd like to join me on my bridge," he said.

I handed the rifle to one of his men. "Gladly, sir. Anything to be out of this star system."

We were rushing on full impellers toward the primary jump point out of Carinthian space. It was still a two-hour trip from our current position. Time enough for trouble to find us.

"What happened to Harrington?" I asked once things had settled down. Zander sat in his captain's chair, ever-present coffee cup in hand, monitoring our progress on his main plasma screens, which included forward visual, longscope, tactical, and infrared. It was an impressive display for any vessel less than a Lightship. I sat next to him in what was clearly a military XO's station, actually quite an array for a "merchant" vessel.

"He got off of Three in his yacht. Not to worry, though; it's better equipped than *Benfold* and a far sight snazzier. I imagine he'll be in touch at some point in the future, once he can create enough plausible deniability about that shootout you had in my cargo hold," he said.

"I am sorry about that," I replied, "but our cargo—"

"Is of the highest priority. I understand that, lad." I sat back in my chair. Lena and Princess Karina and her lone remaining bodyguard were standing watch in the cargo hold over the grand duke. My thoughts turned else-where.

"I didn't even have the chance to thank Harrington for getting me off of Carinthia," I said between sips of some of Zander's famous exotic coffee. This batch was from Levant, and the mere thought of that lush green world and its most beautiful and popular ruler, the Prin-cess Janaan, sent a pang of loneliness through my body. I put those feelings, and the coffee cup, aside for the mo-ment.

"No need to thank him. It was your Admiral Wesley who sent me to pick you up. Harrington was just doing his job," Zander replied.

"Job?" I said. "You mean—"

"Harrington works directly for Wesley and the Union command, lad, as do I. Our merchant status is only a front. Wesley thought he would be useful in an intelligence-gathering role, moving agents about, that sort of thing.

Turns out he was right," said Zander. It made sense, especially the way *Benfold* was trimmed out.

"And what about you?" I asked. Zander shrugged.

"Wesley offered to hire me in the same capacity. Truth is, there's been rumors of trouble with the Carinthians for years. Wesley, and the Earthmen as well, saw the Merchant Marine as a way of surreptitiously supplementing the official navy forces. Of course, when he offered, I said yes. Rather be out in the midst of things than on some glorious Lightship doing First Contact negotiations when trouble hits," he said.

"So there's a surreptitious navy?" I asked.

"As I just said, lad."

I thought about this. It must mean that my father and Wesley both believed that war with Carinthia was a possibility, if not inevitable, and for quite a long time. Ships like *Benfold* didn't just spring up full-born overnight.

"What's this ship's military capacity?" I asked, glancing down at the XO's station console. Zander took a sip of his coffee before answering.

"My Wasp's got the same firepower as a *Hobart*-class missile destroyer, and she's faster, harder, and more nimble by a long ways. Your father and Wesley commissioned these ships as a backstop against trouble with Carinthia, trouble that has now arrived. Since these are classified as merchant ships, they don't count against either Earth's or Quantar's navy allotment, which has to stay relatively equal to Carinthia's. And Harrington runs twenty-two of them for your Admiral Wesley in his merchant fleet," he said.

So these were really warships after all. It was worse news than I was prepared for.

"So the Admiralty has suspected war with Carinthia as a possibility for years," I asked. Zander nodded.

"Carinthia has strong cultural ties to the old empire. Any good textbook will tell you that. They were firmly in the Imperial camp during the civil war, and your two worlds were deeply involved in that conflict, on opposite sides. The Earthmen took a risk when they chose Carinthia and Quantar to be the first two planets contacted for membership in the Union. The old ties would always be there. But things accelerated when you encountered your dreadnought at Levant. Arin and his like are clearly under the influence of the empire, and the black school of Historians," he said.

"Excuse me, the what?"

Zander looked at me. "There is a secret society, even within the Historian order itself, a group that shadows the order, integrates with it, but has its own motives. That's where Tralfane came from. They don't show their faces until it's too late. You should really ask your friend Serosian about all this."

"I will," I said. That was another item to add to my list of worries. "One thing has me curious, though. I thought you were a tried and true Carinthian Navy Officer, not so much a Unionist."

"No, lad, I'm a Loyalist. Loyal to that man down there in that crate. Old Henrik brought Carinthia forward into the Union with the best of intentions. I'd never have been in command of *Impulse* if it wasn't for him. I owe him my career. So do a lot of other officers. We may be Carinthian, but we swore an oath to the Union and to the grand duke, and I intend to fulfill it."

Just then the ship shuddered with an impact, something being deflected by the Hoagland Field, jostling us enough that my coffee dropped off the console to the floor of the bridge. The tactical board lit up with incoming data. From what I could read, we had plenty of unwanted company.

"How many ships?" I asked.

"Looks like three, cruiser displacement," said Zander; then he barked orders at this tactical crew. "You'd better strap in," he said to me. I did.

"Can you handle them?" I asked.

"Any two would be a cakewalk, lad. But three . . ." His voice trailed off as he yelled more commands, then returned his attention to the tactical display. "That was just a warning shot, likely a missile with a conventional warhead. They'll want us to heave to, but I'm not of a mind to give them what they want."

"Are they trying to stop the duke from escaping?" I asked.

"It's you they want, *and* our cargo. They must know the grand duke's on board. If they can capture us they can blame you for trying to kidnap the old duke, really fan the flames for war. My job is not to give them that satisfaction."

"What's going on up there?" came the voice of Princess Karina over the captain's com.

"We have company, Highness, of the surly and not-too-friendly type," said Zander. "I suggest you strap in."

"They can't take this vessel, Captain. They cannot take my father back."

"I understand that, Highness. I swore an oath to your father before you were born, and I have no intention of failing him. Now if you'll excuse me, we are a bit busy up here," Zander said.

"But—"

Zander cut off the com and turned to me. "Can you operate that longscope, lad?" he said, pointing to a small station.

"I am still a Union Navy officer, not just a royal prince with no training," I said, unstrapping again and springing from my seat as the ship rocked with more nearby missile detonations. At least they weren't shooting directly at us. Yet.

Once I was under the longscope hood I piped into the com and was able to send vector and speed status to *Benfold*'s weapons officer, who turned my data into targeting resolutions. *Benfold* launched a counterattack with five tactical atomic multiwarhead missiles. The separate warheads gave the cruiser commanders plenty to think about. Our first volley took out nearly thirty percent of one of the cruisers' tactical capabilities, including weapons. The other two were only slightly diminished, at just five and eight percent lost.

"I'd feel better if we could have knocked one of those cruisers out," said Zander, just before we took our first full-on volley of retaliatory missiles. My displays showed a twenty-two percent degradation in our attack and defense systems, which I quickly reported to Zander. "We need cover," he said to me through the private com.

"I'll see what I can find," I said, and began a search pattern as I'd been taught at the Academy. I quickly had an option.

"Large field of ice and rock planetesimals at point-four-four AU distance, Captain," I said. "Calculations indicate we can be there in three-point-six-six light-minutes at full max."

"Mr. Fraser," called Zander. "Full max on the plasma impellers. Mr. Cochrane will give you our heading."

"Full max," said Fraser, after I fed him the directional telemetry. At our current clip *Benfold* could accelerate to .994 of light speed in about thirty seconds. The Cruisers would of course follow, but I doubted they could match *Benfold*'s acceleration curve. Still, with three of them they could keep us from reaching Carinthian jump space by chipping away at our defenses.

"Recommend you strap in again, lad," said Zander, and I did. After a few seconds of rattling and shaking we hit a safe cruising speed and the ship's hull integrity normalized with the aid of her Hoagland Field.

The passage through open space was tense. The cruisers quickly fell away behind us, but only out of range of their missiles and torpedoes. If they had accurate coil cannons they could still hit us with those. Within a few moments, though, it was obvious they either had none or were unwilling to use them until they could regain their tactical advantage. We were faster in a sprint, but we were still two hours from jump space and we wouldn't be able to maintain our speed for that long.

We were thirty seconds from the asteroid field when Zander cut the impeller drive and we went to maneuvering thrusters. The bridge doors opened a few seconds later and the Princess Karina stepped onto the deck. She had changed into a regular *Benfold* casual duty one-piece uniform, lieutenant rank, and made straight for the weapons station, pushing the merchant sailor there aside.

"Highness, you would be best served to remain in your cabin," said Zander. She snapped around to face him.

"I'm a naval officer, Captain Zander, and probably better qualified at this station than your commercial grunts," she said. "And my first observations indicate your defensive fields are only running at seventy-two percent because your man here is running them off batteries instead of the ion plasma from the sub-light impellers."

"And you can get them up to what, Lieutenant?" said Zander, using her rank. She checked her displays again.

"Eighty-three percent in sixteen-point-five seconds," she replied.

"Do it, Lieutenant. You have the station," said Zander.

"Yes, Captain," she said as Zander nodded the original weapons officer off the bridge. Zander and I exchanged looks, but he only lifted an eyebrow in response. Clearly, the lady was going to have her way.

We arrived in the planetesimal field a few seconds later, and I found us a good hiding place inside a field of five slow rotating ice-rocks composed mostly of magnesium trilite. They would serve as good cover, as they scrambled magnetic sonar signals, which the cruisers likely had as standard search and destroy armament. The cruisers would have to do things the hard way, with visual probes.

"So we've bought some time, but to what end?" asked Zander rhetorically. I joined him at the captain's chair.

"Captain, suggest we power down the Hoagland Field and the coil cannon. It will make it harder for them to detect us in this field," I said.

"But that will leave us defenseless," said Karina, turning from her station and approaching us. "We have to protect the ship." I knew what she really meant, and what she was really protecting.

"The best way to do that is to remain undetectable, Highness," I replied. Zander contemplated the situation.

"And none of that gets us any closer to making the jump point. We can't stay in here forever. If we don't make our stand soon they'll bring in the rest of their deep system fleet and then we'll really be outgunned." He stood silently for a moment, then made his decision. "Lieutenant Feilberg, power down the coil cannon. Reduce the Hoagland Field to fifty percent," he ordered.

"But that won't—" I started. He cut me off.

"It will offer us protection from anything but a direct hit, Commander," he said. "And I owe the princess and the grand duke that much."

"It will leave us more detectable," I stated.

"I'm aware of that, Commander. And one more thing. Since you've both chosen to get involved in this situation on my bridge, you are now both subordinate to me and my military judgment in these matters, regardless of your rank in higher society. Do you understand?" Zander said.

"Yes, sir," we both responded in unison. That made me smile. I for one was happy to be working with Zander again, if only for a short time in emergency circumstances. For her part, Princess Karina, or rather Lieutenant Feilberg, seemed all too happy to be in the midst of things herself as she made her way back to her station, then glanced at me, catching my eye before returning her attention to her board.

The cruisers showed up five minutes later.

I was able to observe them through the longscope, the limitations of magnetic sonar not affecting us with our more advanced equipment. I wanted badly to use longscope probes to view the cruisers in real time, but that would be tempting fate too much. We were in partial stealth mode, but if they looked hard enough and they got lucky, they could find us.

I switched my tactical display to the main viewer and stepped out from under the longscope hood. The three cruisers were performing a search pattern, but with no results. After about thirty minutes of this they backed out of the field and went to station keeping.

"What's this?" asked Zander.

"Either they're waiting for reinforcements with better scanning equipment or they've got something else in mind for us," I stated.

"Or both," said Karina.

We watched as they formed into a triangle formation and then suddenly, without warning, one of the cruisers launched a missile. It streaked into the planetesimal field and exploded against a rock in a nuclear fireball about sixty kilometers from us.

"One kiloton warhead, no impact on us," I reported from my station. The bridge stayed silent. A second cruiser launched an identical missile, then the third ship launched one. None of them were near us. We watched as they regrouped, changing formation, then repeated the pattern and shifted position again. I watched my readouts, then grew alarmed.

"Captain, I think—"

"They're triangulating on us," said Zander. "Using neutrinos in the atomic explosions to bounce off of our Hoagland Field to create a shadow effect. They may have to do it thirty times, but eventually they'll find us. And once they do they'll cut us to pieces, bit by bit," he said.

"What do we do now?" asked Karina. Zander looked to me.

"We take our chance," I said. "Let me launch three longscope probes to triangulate on the nearest cruiser. We make our run at her, take her out. Then we accelerate back up to full max and make our run for as long as we can."

"Aye, lad," said Zander.

"And how long is that?" asked Karina. I glanced at my display readouts.

"Based on our fuel and power outputs, one hour forty-seven minutes, most likely," I said to her. "Then we would have to back off to keep the drives from melting down. If we lean her out at that point and run at point-three-eight max capacity we *could* beat them to jump space."

"Could?" said Karina. "That's not good enough to gamble my father's life on."

"We're doing that staying here, Lieutenant Feilberg," chimed in Zander. "And the commander's plan just might work."

"And if not?" demanded Karina.

"If not we stand and fight. Smash them in the mouth with all of our missiles and torpedoes, and hope we have enough power left at the end to make the jump," he said. "And if we don't, then heaven help us."

I launched my probes, and from that data I was able to calculate that a thirty-three second thruster burst would get us out of the planetesimal field and into open space. From there Karina would have to fire a mixed volley of multiwarhead missiles and single-warhead torpedoes to take out the target cruiser. We'd have probably a sixty-second advantage if we were able to disable it. That was enough time to accelerate away from the other two cruisers and hope they didn't get any backup help. I calculated our prospects of making it unscathed to jump space at roughly fifty-fifty.

When we were ready Zander gave the orders and we swung into action.

The latest volleys from the cruisers provided us with some cover, as the blasts would almost certainly scramble their scanning equipment for a few moments. We used that advantage to go right at the nearest of the three cruisers. Ten seconds in to our attack run, they began to react, changing their vector to try to put more distance between them and us and get closer to their companion ships. Karina's firing sequence was spot-on, however, and the first blast from a fast-moving missile caught them broadside with a fifty-kiloton explosion from five ten-kiloton warheads. This was followed by a volley of a dozen single-warhead torpedoes with five-kiloton yields, enough to crack their Hoagland Field and expose the hull to direct assault. The result was satisfying enough. I couldn't tell if the cruiser had been disabled or destroyed, but it didn't matter, we had our breakout and we were on our way.

Zander cut the sub-light impellers back to .38 light at forty-five minutes from jump point space, leaving us a few minutes to spare just in case we needed a reserve. The two chasing cruisers had abandoned their third partner and were steadily closing on us, their slower acceleration curve working to our advantage. All was well for the next half hour, and I began to believe we would make it to the jump point when I had to deliver the bad news.

"Captain, the impellers are diminishing in performance. We can't maintain this speed," I said. "The burn ratio from the ion plasma is just too great."

"What's our lead?" Zander asked. I ran some swift numbers.

"Relatively speaking, our lead is down to six minutes at this pace," I said.

"And how long until we reach optimal jump space?"

"Fourteen minutes, sir."

"What's our power reserve, weapons officer?" he demanded.

"Thirty-two percent," replied Karina. "We need twenty if we're going to be able to spool up the HD drive and still keep the Hoagland Field strong enough to survive the jump, sir."

"So if we borrow too much power from the battery reserve to maintain our speed, we'll lose the ability to jump safely?" asked Zander.

"Correct, sir," she said. He turned back to me, arms folded across his chest.

"What's our speed, Commander?"

"Point three-five-eight light and dropping, sir," I said. Zander's hand went to his scarred pink chin.

"How much time would the power transfer buy us, Commander?"

I checked my calculations. "Not enough, sir. At our current use rate we'll fall four minutes short," I said. He didn't hesitate.

"We'll do it anyway, we have no other choice. Transfer battery power to the impellers, Lieutenant Feilberg," he ordered.

"Yes, sir," she said. I went back under the hood and activated my private com to the captain.

"You do realize we'll be in full range of their weapons, missiles, torpedoes, even coil cannons, for that full four minutes?" I said.

"I understand, Commander," he said. Then went silent.

It would be the longest four minutes of all our lives.

We came under fire immediately once we were within range of the two remaining cruisers. First with atomic missiles, single-warhead, thankfully, then torpedoes, all with lesser yields than our own. But we couldn't fire back. That would require turning and risk losing our momentum, and our goal was singular: to reach jump space and get out of the Carinthian system.

Two minutes from jump space we took a direct hit from a ten-kiloton missile on our Hoagland Field. Weakened as she was by our run of desperation, the field shut down, setting off alarms throughout the ship. The resultant surge of excess power from the shielding system being redistributed throughout our power systems overloaded our impeller drive and it cut out for its own survival, but it left us a sitting duck, drifting on our course on momentum only.

"We've lost the Hoagland Field and our ion impellers, Captain," I reported grimly. "Only eighteen percent in power reserves. Not enough to spool up the Hoagland Drive for a jump."

"And one more direct hit and we'll be destroyed," stated Karina from her station. Zander stood and stiffened his back, stretching as tall as his diminutive frame would let him.

"So now we find out if their orders are to capture us or to kill us," he said.

"The result may be one and the same," said Karina as she stepped away from her now useless weapons station to join the captain. I stayed at my longscope. The two remaining cruisers closed to an optimal firing range, then went to station keeping, coming no closer but paralleling us.

"What are they waiting for?" asked Karina.

"Orders, probably," said Zander.

I looked at my board one more time. The two cruisers had us in their sights, dead to rights. But then another blip appeared on my tactical display.

"Another ship coming in range, sir," I called out. "Large displacement."

"Imperial dreadnought?" asked Zander, alarm in his voice.

"Calculating," I responded. "Wait, no. Too light in mass. From her signature . . . she must be a Lightship."

"Is it *Starbound*, laddie? Did she jump in to save us?" asked Zander. I ran my numbers again, then shut down my display and came out from under the longscope.

"Negative, Captain," I said as their faces fell in disappointment. I went over to join them. "From her course vector she must have come the way we came, from High Station Three. It must be *Impulse II*."

"But isn't your . . . friend, I mean Captain Kierkopf, in command of her?" asked Karina.

"She is," I said. "But she is now a Carinthian Royal Navy officer again, and if I know her at all I know she will follow her orders and take us back to Three, if that's what she's been instructed to do."

"I have to agree," said Zander. "She's one of a kind, that woman." I looked at Zander but he was focused on the tactical screen. Karina eyed me but I could say nothing to comfort her. We had given it our best shot, and we had failed her and her father.

"I'm sorry, Princess," I said. She looked at me but said nothing. We stood together at Zander's station, watching our failure play out as the imposing figure of *Impulse II* loomed ever larger on the main visual display.

Suddenly there was a burst of light from *Impulse II* as a crackling wave of coil fire shot across open space and struck the closest cruiser. It disintegrated in a flash of light, the explosion rocking our ship. A second later a similar blast hit the second cruiser, but it had been ready, its Hoagland Field absorbing the tremendous shockwave that sent it tumbling. A second later and she had righted herself, turned toward us, and fired.

A single torpedo was coming right at us. We all scrambled back to our stations.

"Do we have enough power to bring the Hoagland Field back on line?" said Zander.

"We have the power," I said, "but not the time." We watched as the missile streaked toward us, only seconds separating us from the impact and our likely deaths.

"Five seconds," I said. The bridge went silent.

A lance of coil cannon fire intercepted the missile two seconds later, the explosion of energy rocking our ship beyond what our inertial dampers could bear. We all went tumbling about the deck.

But we were still alive.

When we got back to our stations we saw a surprising sight, two more Wasps guarding us. They must have come in through the jump point in the last few seconds, intercepting the incoming missile. We never saw *Impulse II* destroy the second cruiser, but we knew what her fate was. I got our main display back up, and our com, but we only had visual and ship-to-ship; no tactical or telemetry was available. It took only a few seconds for us to receive the visual call from *Impulse II*.

The face of Captain Dobrina Kierkopf filled the bridge on our main display and all of the station display plasmas as well. It felt like there was a hundred of her on the bridge of *Benfold*.

"Captain Zander, Commander Cochrane. It appears from our scans that you are in need of resupply and repair. Can we be of assistance?" she said.

Zander stood and let out a deep sigh.

"That you can, Captain. That you can," he said, a toothy grin crossing his scarred pink face. "A quick question, though, Captain. I somehow doubt that your departure orders from the air marshal included destroying your own cruisers?"

"Goddamn my orders," she said. "I swore an oath to protect the grand duke and his family long before I signed up for this job. It's just too bad that those cruiser captains disobeyed orders and tried to destroy your vessel instead of capture it, Captain Zander. Admiralty law forced me to intervene on your behalf. At least, that's my story, and I'm sticking to it."

Then she looked at me and winked, and I laughed for the first time in days.

It felt good.

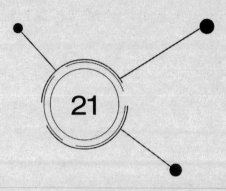

Home

Admar Harrington had ordered his Wasps through
the jump point immediately upon his return to
Pendax. Their arrival and timing was pure luck, or fate,
depending on what you believed. They offered to escort
us home, to Candle, and we accepted.

Dobrina was kind enough to send over a repair team
to refuel and reenergize our engines and batteries before
releasing us to go on to the jump point. Then she went
on her way to an uncertain destiny. She said she had a
loyal crew and a plan for reporting the three cruisers
destroyed, confirming that we had taken one of them out
in the planetesimal field. The rest I was hopeful she
could make a good case for.

Still, parting with her again was difficult. Though I
wasn't sure that I loved her in a way that would preclude
any other romance in my life, we had a strong bond; of
that there was no doubt. I hoped that she would be safe

as I watched *Impulse II* go. We were at a critical tipping point in the Union's brief history, and whether it would survive this crisis was more of a question than ever.

We left the battlefield in a hurry after recharging, and once our fleet of Wasps reached jump space we made the instantaneous leap back to Quantar without incident. That didn't mean, however, that there weren't going to be incidents aboard her. We had the reigning Grand Duke of Carinthia, our ancient adversaries, stashed away in our cargo hold in a stasis field disguised as booze. That could be problematic.

Once in Quantar space we gave thanks to our escorts, who turned and left for Pendax. At this point Zander proposed, and I agreed, that we should make straight for High Station Quantar and skip stopping at Candle. My navy duties aboard *Starbound* were still foremost in my mind, but we had other duties to attend to first.

As we passed near Candle I sent a com packet to Maclintock, being deliberately vague about my real responsibilities but insisting to him that I still had diplomatic duties to attend to before I could return to naval duty aboard *Starbound*. He replied with a simple acknowledgment of my packet, the equivalent of a nod of assent, and with that we were off to Quantar. By now *Starbound* would be well under way with repairs, and this political complication didn't concern her or Captain Maclintock. I found myself again stuck with the difficulty of having to make decisions as a royal at a very high level, but seeing others from my position as a Lieutenant Commander in the Union Navy. It was a conflict I hadn't completely resolved yet.

During the traverse time my only plans were a brief dinner followed by a solid eight hours of sleep. There was no telling how much or how little I would get after arriving home, and by home I meant the North Palace at KendalFalk, not New Briz. I had no intention of telling my father about the grand duke, at least not just yet.

I begged off Zander's offer to join him at dinner and ordered straight from the galley. My food arrived promptly and not five minutes into my meal there came a chime through my privacy lock. I quickly wiped my mouth and hit the voice-only com in my sparse stateroom. To my surprise it was Princess Karina.

"May I come in?" she asked through the com. I got up and quickly opened the door.

"My pleasure," I said, inviting her in with a sweep of the hand. She came in and sat at the small table where my meal sat steaming.

"Gods, that smells good," she said.

"Chateaubriand," I said. "Captain Zander will put up with nothing but the best cuisine onboard."

"So I see."

From the way she looked at my dinner I could see that the evening meal had been an afterthought for her. I quickly ordered her the same meal from the galley, along with a bottle of Quantar shiraz. We made small talk until it arrived ten minutes later, then we both ate rather voraciously, I thought. Once we had finished, I refilled our wineglasses and we both sat back, pleasantly full.

I looked at her for what seemed like the first time, reevaluating her under our new circumstances. She still wore her Carinthian Navy uniform, rank of lieutenant, with the appropriate Union patches. I took this to mean she intended to act for now as a military officer and not as a princess. Her hair was let down, and it was straight, smooth, long, and black. I remembered one of her father's nicknames was "The Black Duke," and she looked every bit the part, though her pleasant face held none of the harshness of her father's. I could see that she had also freshened up with a bit of makeup. I thought she was very attractive, but in an entirely different way than what I had experienced with other women, especially Dobrina, who was taller, more lean and athletic. Karina

was petite and rounder than most, although that round-
ness complimented her form in every way. She smiled as
I finished pouring the shiraz, then we made our way to
the stateroom's small sofa.

We sat on opposite sides and I cleared my throat, unsure how to start the conversation. I looked into her face.
It was elegantly oval, with a pixie nose separating her
large brown eyes. She smiled, and must have noticed me
examining her. I looked away and took a sip of my wine
before starting the conversation.

"So tell me more about your family," I said. "We really didn't get the time to talk socially back on Carinthia." She took a drink herself before answering.

"Do you mean my parents and siblings, or the entire
Feilberg family history?"

I laughed. "I meant your immediate family, of course,"
I said. She pushed back one of the long bangs from her
face and then answered.

"Well, you know all about Arin," she said. "And I
have to warn you, don't underestimate his military acu-
men. He has been well-trained in strategy and tactics
since his youth."

"Noted," I said, and filed that thought away. "I was
speaking more about your upbringing."

She nodded. "My mother died when I was sixteen. I
don't think my father ever got over that loss. Benn, I
think, would rather be a diplomat than deal with all of
this political wrangling. I, of course, had hoped for a career as a navy officer. That seems a faded dream now. I'm
the youngest by five years. And you?"

"I had an older brother, Derrick," I said. "He was
killed in Union Navy service three years ago. So I'm the
only one left. My mother died when I was nine. My father is just now getting remarried. I think he married my
mother rather late in life and at the insistence of his parents. I never knew any of my grandparents. They had all

passed away by the time I was old enough to remember them." She got a very serious look on her face then.

"So you're practically an orphan," she said. I thought the comment was a bit odd.

"Actually, I've never thought of it quite that way," I said. She leaned in toward me on the sofa.

"What I meant was that I have a large extended family," she said. "Cousins, aunts, uncles. I can never remember celebrating a birthday or a holiday alone. I guess I was very lucky. It seems like we were raised very differently."

"Yes, I suppose we were," I said. "But I never felt deprived of love. I was always well taken care of and I had good friends growing up."

"Girlfriends?" she said with a smirk, catching me in the middle of a sip of wine.

"Um, yes, some," I said. "But mostly after I left school."

"So at the Academy?"

"Well, yes, there was one there, actually, Natalie, but she was killed in the initial incident at Levant. Part of the First Contact mission with Captain Zander aboard *Impulse*," I said.

"I'm sorry," she said. "Did you love her?"

I pondered that. "I'm not really sure. It's just another one of many difficult losses I've had to deal with in my life. I'm not sure where to place her in all that," I said, then sighed. That was true enough. Karina reached out a hand and touched my arm, to comfort me. I let that linger. Then she pulled back and said:

"And what of Captain Dobrina Kierkopf?" Suddenly, I didn't much like this line of questioning.

"What of her?" I said, eyeing her directly. She got a pensive look on her face and then continued.

"It's obvious you have, or had, a relationship with her," she said. "I've read the intelligence reports."

"I see," I said. "I thought we hid it better than that." She shook her head.

"We Carinthians are somewhat famous for finding out secrets. I've learned myself in the last few years not to evaluate people merely as I see them, but to look beyond their outer façade and see what they're like on the inside. When I saw the report on you it all made sense, but I really didn't know until I met you. It's obvious that you have feelings for her. Your actions on Carinthia were very protective of her."

Now this was getting a bit too close to home for my comfort, so I decided to try to bring this line of questioning to a conclusion. "Circumstances have now changed, Princess, perhaps permanently. She is staying in the Carinthian Navy service and I am here," I said.

"So you're available?" she said. Again she caught me in the middle of a sip of shiraz and despite my best efforts I coughed and hacked until I was red in the face. This made her laugh. When I had regained my composure she was smiling at me, but not backing away at all, either physically or emotionally, it seemed. I looked for a safe course of action through these troubled waters.

"Pardon me, Princess, but I'm a bit at a loss for words at that question," I finally got out.

"Forgive me for putting you on the spot, but you haven't answered my question yet," she said.

I looked at her from across the sofa. From what I had seen of her so far in our brief acquaintance she was clearly intelligent, resourceful, and deeply caring, especially about her family. I was deciding whether to add cunning to that list. I thought for a few moments and then formulated my answer.

"Forgive *me*, Princess, but I haven't really thought on that subject, what with the near civil war on Carinthia, the pending breakup of the Union, and the fact that I have your family's sovereign in stasis in the cargo hold. Perhaps this isn't the time," I said.

"Perhaps you're right," she quickly responded. "All of these things will be sorted out in time. I apologize for sometimes thinking too far into the future."

"Apology accepted," I said, then yawned. It would have been a good way to deflect the conversation if it hadn't been so spontaneous.

She smiled at me again and said, "You're tired," then rose to leave. I got up with her. "I should let you rest."

"Thank you, Princess. I'm sure tomorrow, and the days after, will be better times to discuss all of these matters. At least for me," I said.

"Thank you for the dinner and the wine," she said, then smiled and made for the door. I followed her and opened it from the inside for her, as a courtesy. She took one step out and then turned back to me.

"I'm glad to know you, Peter Cochrane. Glad to know the kind of man you are, and that I can trust you. I have one request, though. I think it would improve our relationship immensely if you would stop using my title. Please call me Karina from now on," she said.

"I will, Prin—" I caught myself before I finished the word. Protocol was a hard habit to break. "Karina. And thank you. I enjoyed our evening." With that she was gone out the door, and I turned back to my tiny bed, which looked like the most luxurious thing I had ever seen.

The landing at the North Palace went off without a hitch. The pad had been built there primarily for personal shuttles and the like, mostly for use by the royal family, not for military vehicles, but *Benfold*'s "commercial" drop shuttle fit quite nicely on the pad.

We had come down with just the single cargo container holding the Grand Duke Henrik in stasis, plus myself, Karina and her guards, and a single pilot. High

Station Quantar had requested that we stop there first, but I had countermanded that, using my royal standing as authority. It made perfect sense that a planetary royal would want to get straight to his family vacation home without stopping for unnecessary checks and protocols. It also made perfect sense that he would be carrying a cargo container full of Carinthian liquor and other delicacies.

Benfold for her part had docked at High Station and began unloading her regular cargo. Zander had offered to come down when he had cleared everything, but I told him to hold off until I called him. I was fairly sure I would need his help regarding our unexpected guests.

The ground was covered in snow, as was typical for the Northern Continent in January. As we had come down to land I had pointed out the city of KendalFalk, covered in winter white and snuggled up against the Nandewar Mountains, to the princess. It had a population near 500,000, with most inhabitants working in the mining and timber industries, or in work related to the palace and other royal facilities. Our family's presence here on an annual basis for several decades had turned the town from a dusty, cold outpost into a much more cosmopolitan city.

When we disembarked from the shuttle it was midmorning on the local clock. I made sure the princess and her father were safely ensconced in the palace before calling on the necessary medical and technical personnel to begin the process of bringing the grand duke out of stasis. It was a complex but well-defined procedure, and I didn't want the medical staff to know who they were dealing with until they got here. I asked the princess to list what kind of assistance she would need to care for her father, then assigned the proper staff to see to her needs. I also swore the staff to secrecy about our guests, as a precautionary protocol.

I then excused myself and met with the captain of the

Royal Guard, a man named Walther, in the palace library, to see to heightened security arrangements.

"How many men do you have on duty currently, Captain?" I asked. He looked at me for a moment, like it was an odd question, then answered.

"We have two hundred men in palace barracks at any one time, Sire. Fifty share the active duties of the palace and grounds on six-hour rotations," he said.

"Do you have reserves in the city?" I asked. Again he hesitated before answering.

"We rotate troops from the city garrison on a weekly basis, Sire. There's sixteen hundred total at the royal barracks in the city," he said.

"Good. Call them up to the palace immediately, save two hundred for the city garrison. I want a hundred soldiers on duty inside the palace itself and another seven hundred patrolling the grounds at any one time. Two twelve-hour shifts. Do you have a plan to go to a heightened state of readiness at my command?" I said.

This time he answered quickly. "We have three levels of heightened security, Sire, above where we are currently. What level did you have in mind?"

I just gave him my exact desires rather than wait for a list of the different security levels. "I want barricades erected at the palace perimeter with constant patrols. All vehicles coming in or out of the palace are subject to search. Shut down the military airfield in KendalFalk and no units except the city garrison come in or out. I also want armored vehicles on the roads with multiple checkpoints between here and the city. All navy or army air units in the city are to stand down and go cold until further notice. Tell them this is all on orders of the crown prince," I finished.

"Yes, Sire. Immediately, Sire. Is there anything else?" Walther said, his pace of speaking and tone indicating he got the message that this was not a drill of any kind.

"Yes. Set up an encrypted line to New Briz,

Government House. I'll be speaking with my father directly. Have it ready in an hour. That's it," I said.

"Yes, Sire," said Walther. Then he saluted, pivoted, and moved quickly out of the room to carry out his orders.

I went to the library's working desk and pulled out my encryption key, then entered my royal security code. It spat out a sequence of numbers and letters, which I then keyed into the main computer plasma display. Once inside the royal network, I began a search for nearby military units, especially navy ones. After just a few minutes of this I was interrupted by one of my guests, the Princess Karina.

I stood and greeted her. "Please come in, Karina," I said, making sure to use her proper name as she had requested. "What can I help you with?" She smiled at me. She seemed to be getting more comfortable with me every day.

"I just came to tell you that my father is awake in his stateroom. He's groggy and a little confused, but physically he's doing well," she said.

"I'm pleased," I replied. She glanced around the room.

"I have noticed there is increased military activity around the palace," she stated.

I nodded. "I think it's necessary. Things are very delicate with the grand duke here, and we can't take any chances," I said. She eyed me pensively.

"Surely you're not worried about an attack on us here, are you?" she asked, a worried frown crossing her face.

"There are legitimate security concerns, Karina. I don't think at this point that we can afford to take anything for granted," I said.

"I see," she replied. I turned back to my desk.

"I was just about to call my father and request that he come up to the palace as soon as possible, to meet you and your father."

She smiled wryly. "I hope that won't be too uncomfortable for you," she said.

I smiled back. "It shouldn't be. I'm slowly getting used to making bigger and bigger decisions."

"I'll leave you to it, then," she said. We said our good-byes and she left, and I returned to my analysis of navy materiel in the area of the city.

There were about fifty aircraft at the combined military airfield in KendalFalk, a mix of fighters, escorts, VTOLs and personnel craft, with some Light Aerial Vehicles as well. There was also a reserve Royal Infantry unit of five hundred soldiers and light armor stationed at the airfield. Those infantry units were part-time volunteers and we had more armor and full-time soldiers in our Royal Guard units, so I was comfortable that we had what we needed to defend the palace for the time being.

Sixty clicks away, though, was Laverton Airfield, the main military base on the Northern Continent. She had a full complement of soldiers, aircraft, a spaceport, and both light and heavy armor. If a foreign power decided to launch an assault, either overt or covert, on the North Palace and KendalFalk I was confident we could defend anything short of an atomic attack.

Walther chimed in then with my encrypted channel to Government House in New Briz, some two thousand kilometers to the south. "Your father on line three," he said, then signed off. The royal crest on my screen was replaced with an image of my father, bordered in red to indicate the encryption security was active.

"Hello, sir," I said. He nodded back at me. I could see he was taking my call from his official office, not the private apartments.

"Hello, son. I was surprised to hear from you so soon. I thought you'd still be on Carinthia soaking up some of their infamous hospitality," he said lightly. His look changed when he took a longer look at my expression. I couldn't help myself. Things were serious. "What's wrong?" he said.

Clearly Wesley had chosen to keep him in the dark about my misadventures on Carinthia. "Sir, we have a serious situation here in KendalFalk, one I think is of the highest import to our family, Quantar, and the Union. I need you to come up here straight away," I said.

"To KendalFalk? In *January*?" he replied. When my look didn't change he quickly regrouped. "What's happened, son?"

I shook my head. "I can't tell you that over this channel or any other. You need to come here and see the situation firsthand, to see it for what it really is. Carinthia was an ambush, sir. Rogue elements of their military put Dobrina and me on trial for losing *Impulse*, tried to blame me for her destruction. They tried to execute me, and they nearly succeeded." The part about *Impulse* struck close to home for me as I was at least partly responsible for her demise, but not for her being put in that position in the first place.

"I can't believe this. The Union—"

"The Union is in grave peril, sir, and Carinthia is on the verge of civil war," I said as plainly and emotionlessly as I could. "You must come here immediately. There are things here you have to see for yourself that I can't explain over any open channel, encrypted or not."

He looked shocked. "But Admiral Wesley hasn't told me about any of this. How can that be?" he said. I had a ready answer.

"Because for whatever reasons, he didn't want you to know," I said.

"I'm going to call Jonathon and get to the bottom of this," my father said.

"Sir, that would be inadvisable at this time. Have the admiral brief you on the way up. I need you to see things here for yourself in order to make proper decisions. Please, sir. This is vital to Quantar, the Union, to all of us." He looked shaken at this, but finally nodded his head.

"I'll do as you say, son. Expect me there by the early evening. But I'm going to want an explanation when I arrive," he said.

"You will get that explanation, sir, I promise. Thank you, sir," I said. We said our goodbyes then and I broke the encryption link. I stood up from the desk and walked to the window, looking down on the assembling palace guard.

"And now the hard part begins," I said out loud, to no one in particular.

22

At the North Palace

My father's plane touched down at 1815 hours local time. I had him escorted by military convoy directly to the palace without incident. I was there to meet him as the military ground car pulled up to the palace's back entrance.

I nodded to the guards as the car came to a stop and one of them peeled off and opened the car door. My father stepped out into the cold January air, quickly followed by Admiral Wesley.

I turned to Walther and waved the guard detachment, four armed men in all, forward to the car to bracket my father and Wesley.

"Has the admiral filled you in about Carinthia?" I asked my father. He nodded.

"And I've chided him for keeping me in the dark about your situation," he said by way of explanation.

"He's got some very important new information about the situation on Carinthia."

"Not as important as the information I have, I'll venture," I said back. I was angry at Wesley for keeping my father in the dark, but I also realized that both of these men still regarded me as a junior navy officer, one whom they could order around as they pleased. Perhaps it was fighting the dreadnought at Levant, or the automatons at Jenarus, or my narrow escape from execution on Carinthia, but I wasn't that young officer anymore, and they were both about to find that out.

I turned to Walther. "Escort the admiral to the library. The Director and I will be along shortly."

"What's this?" demanded Wesley as two palace guardsmen stepped up.

"Peter? What are you doing?" said my father, clearly unhappy. I held up my hand to stop him. There would be a time and a place for this discussion. My father didn't challenge me further, and at my signal the guards escorted a fuming Wesley through the doors and into the palace. I turned back to my father, the royal Director of Quantar and my superior, both militarily and in royal standing.

"What I have to tell you is for your ears only at the moment. If you'd like to join me, I have a lot of explaining to do, about a great many things," I said.

He continued to look unhappy but said, "Very well," and followed me inside.

We dispensed with hats and coats in the foyer and made our way down the long hallway toward the library. I walked next to my father with a guard escort a few steps behind.

"Explain yourself, son," he said to me as we walked. I didn't hesitate.

"A great many things happened on Carinthia, sir. I want you to know that not all of them were under my control. I need you to trust my judgment on what is happening here at the palace," I replied.

"And what is happening here?" he said. That stopped me.

"Something that will determine our immediate futures, and possibly the future of the entire Union," I said. He looked at me with what I thought I could read as respect.

"I'm still in charge on this world, Peter."

"I understand that, sir. But I'm asking you to trust me on this, and let me work things out as I reveal what is going on here at my own pace and time," I said. He hovered over me, still bigger than me by far, both in physical size and personality. But I read a sense of pride in him as we engaged as near-equals in these matters.

"I'll let you carry on for the time being, son. But I reserve the right to take over at my own discretion," he said.

"Thank you, sir." With that we started down the hall again and went into the library. Walther and two of his guards were at the closed door. They opened it and we went inside. Wesley was seated alone in a large leather chair, looking angry. I motioned my father to the next chair over. Walther shut the library doors so that we could talk privately.

"Now what's this all about, boy?" said Wesley, trying to take the initiative away from me. I crossed my arms and leaned against the library desk.

"You'll know that presently, Admiral. The Union has allies on Carinthia, but not many. Some of those allies were in great danger after my escape, and we were forced to help extract some of them off-planet," I said.

"I never authorized that action, for you or Zander," started Wesley. "Listen, son, I am your supreme commander—"

"You are my supreme commander in the Union Navy, Admiral," I interrupted him. "But please understand that in these matters I was acting as crown prince in the interests of the royal family, and I am therefore *your* superior in this particular matter."

He looked frustrated at this, but then he stood up, followed by my father.

"I think it's time for you to tell us what this is all about," Wesley said.

"I agree," said my father.

"Very well," I said, standing again. "But I think it's better to *show* you rather than tell you so that you can make your own judgments."

I opened the library doors again and then signaled to Walther to dismiss the guards. The four of us then departed the library and went to the utility service lifter, quietly loading into it and then making our way up to the third floor guest apartments. I stepped out and asked them to follow. We went to the main suite, where I knocked on the door. A military nurse opened the door and escorted us into an anteroom, and then I dismissed both the nurse and Walther.

"What you're about to see is why I came here to the North Palace instead of New Briz. What's inside that room changes everything," I said, motioning toward the double doorway. My father and Wesley exchanged glances but said nothing, so I opened the doors and stepped through, followed by my two superiors.

Inside the Princess Karina of Carinthia stood by a large fireplace in her Union Navy uniform while her father, the Black Duke, Grand Duke Henrik Feilberg, slept in a side chair next to the fire, snoring gently.

Wesley took a few steps into the room, then looked back at me, furious.

"By the Great Gods, boy!" he said. *"What have you done?!"*

We sat in the anteroom together a few minutes later: Karina, myself, the fuming Wesley, and my father. I made the introductions and we started talking.

I told the story of my capture, trial, near execution, and attempted assassination on Carinthia. Karina told the story of how she got her father off of the planet, and why it was necessary. After a few more minutes of back and forth, we got down to the business at hand: what should we do now?

"You've put us in a pretty pickle, son," said Wesley. "We've been getting reports of unrest in the Carinthian military for several months, but nothing this extensive. But taking the grand duke off-planet—that could be seen as an act of war."

"I'm his daughter and a crown princess, Admiral. I will vouch for the necessity of our actions in bringing my father here," said Karina.

"That might not matter, Princess," warned Wesley. He rose and started to pace. "If your brothers both present a solid case for their actions, it's you who could be seen as being in the wrong by the Carinthian people. It's clear this Prince Arin wants Carinthia out of the Union, which means any provocation could be used to justify their exit and canceling of the Concord Agreement. You may have just provided them with that provocation, Princess."

Karina bolted up from her chair, standing up as tall as she could to Wesley. "There are three worlds in this Union, Admiral. If the Earth Historians withdraw their support, Carinthia will be at a tactical and strategic disadvantage," she said.

"Not if they replace the Earthmen's technology with assistance from the old empire," retorted Wesley. Then he looked to my father. "This is your call, Nathan. How do we proceed now that your son has participated in the kidnapping of Carinthia's sovereign?"

"I would appreciate it if you wouldn't couch things in such terms, Jonathon, even in private," said my father, more than a bit testily. He sighed, a sign of the stress we were all under. "I will contact the Historians' Guild on Earth and advise them of the situation. Princess Karina, if you could get your father into a state where he can speak for himself, perhaps even record a statement for the people of Carinthia, that could be of great use. Our primary goal must be to try and slow things down. Right now it seems that events are accelerating out of our control, and that's always a bad thing. The admiral and I will return to New Brisbane while we work the diplomatic and military channels. I'll ask the Historians to set up a protocol for open negotiations with the new government on Carinthia as soon as possible. Perhaps we can defuse this situation before it blows up in our faces," he finished.

Karina was indignant. "What *new* government? My father's is the only official government on Carinthia."

"With respect, Princess," said my father, "your father has been only a figurehead for some years now. Whether it was fully legal or not, your brother Arin has assumed the *de facto* power of the Regency and has become the real power broker on Carinthia. We will have to deal with him on those terms. But right now my only goal is to settle things down and see about your father's safe return to his home as soon as possible."

"You can't do that! We just escaped from there!" Karina said. "You don't understand, sir. Arin will kill him." My father looked pensive at this.

"Obviously, that's not the desired outcome, Princess. But these actions you've taken, you and Peter, they've brought us to the brink of war, perhaps even pushed us over it already. If I can stop this war before it starts by sending him home I will do so, despite what my personal feelings might be about the matter." At this he stood and went to the door, preparing to go.

"Sirs, I request permission to return to *Starbound* immediately and resume my duties there," I said.

"Denied," snapped Wesley. "Right now you are a spark to the kindling in this situation, young man. It would be best if you stayed out of sight, at least until *Starbound* is ready to go out again. And I can't think of a better place for you to stay out of sight than here in KendalFalk. That is, of course, if you wish to place yourself under my command again and rescind your royal authority over these matters?"

His meaning was clear enough: follow my orders or resign your commission. It would have solved a number of political problems for him if he could stash me away and get me out of the navy, but I wasn't ready to be done with my military career quite yet.

"I understand and accept your orders, Admiral," I said.

"Good," he replied. And with that both he and my father were out the door. I looked to Karina, feeling helpless.

"I'm sorry," I said.

"Don't be," she replied. "It's not your fault. And at least I know that for now my father is safe."

I thought about that. "How safe are any of us now?" I asked rhetorically.

"I want to stop the war, too, Peter. But not the way they think to do. My father is still beloved by the people of Carinthia, and he is our greatest asset. It seems as though you and I may still have to take matters into our own hands," Karina said. Then she returned to her father's suite, leaving me alone to contemplate what she meant by that.

⋆ ⋆ ⋆

I spent the next day kicking around the North Palace, doing nothing and feeling useless. Neither my father nor Wesley sent an update all day, and my calls to my father's office were taken by his office secretary but not returned.

They were clearly letting me know where I stood in their eyes at the moment, and I didn't like it at all.

I checked in with Karina and the nurses a couple of different times. Her father was still very incoherent, and that was worrisome. The stasis field had had residual effects on him, and he still hadn't fully recovered. I did manage to get her to have dinner with me in the private family dining room on the third floor, but it was a somber affair. We both were very down about being cut out of the decision-making process, perhaps permanently.

We were waiting on dessert when Walther interrupted us.

"Sire, there's an urgent communiqué for you in the library," he said. I glanced up at Karina.

"May I—" she started.

"Please, join me," I said. "This concerns you, too." I asked the servants to bring us coffee in the library and then we and Walther went out of the dining room and made for the nearest lifter.

I sat down in front of the desk plasma console and keyed in my private code to de-encrypt the transmission. It was a text-only message from Zander aboard *Benfold*:

"Have made the run to Candle and back. Arrival expected at 1900 hours your local time."

I checked my watch. Thirty minutes from now. I resumed scrolling the message.

"Harrington aboard with urgent news regarding Carinthia. Request permission to land at Palace and consult with you directly."

I replied in the affirmative and sent the coded packet back to Zander with the palace landing coordinates, then passed the arrival time on to Walther. I shut the library doors again and turned to Karina.

"Zander says Harrington has urgent news about Carinthia. I hope it's good, but I doubt that it is," I said.

"I agree, I have my doubts," said Karina. "Should we consult with your father and Wesley?"

I thought about that for a moment. "Not just yet. They haven't exactly been forthcoming about keeping us in the loop, so I would prefer to handle this first myself. Zander is requesting to consult with both of us, not them. But I'll have Walther set up the link just in case. We can decide after we hear what they have to say," I said.

Zander was ten minutes late on his arrival time, and for a man as diligent to promptness as he was, it was almost an offense. I nodded to him as he arrived at the back entrance to the palace, with Harrington in tow as promised. I led them both into the library where they greeted Karina again, poured them both a warming drink of brandy, and we sat down together.

I looked to Harrington. "So tell me your news." He looked grimly down into his glass.

"There is nothing good, I'm afraid. The reports about the grand duke's 'abduction' have been made public by the Regency. They are blaming it on 'anti-Carinthian agents' and have vowed to track down the perpetrators and bring them to justice, that sort of rhetoric. There is no mention of you, Princess, but it is very clear in the government-controlled media that they are pursuing young Cochrane here," he said, then turned back to me. "They are doing everything but blaming you directly for the abduction. They are making it very hard for anyone associated with Quantar or the Union to do business with Carinthia, so much so that as of today I have suspended my merchant operations there and withdrawn my people. I won't be going back any time soon," he finished.

"So now I'm a criminal?" I said. Harrington nodded.

"At least on Carinthia you are."

"I have to make a statement," said Karina. "Get a message to my people, tell them why we're really here. Can you get a message broadcast in Carinthian space, Mr. Harrington?" He looked to Zander.

"Aye, it can be done, Princess. We'd have to jump in,

drop a longwave ansible and jump back out again. The message would be picked up on any media device that has a longwave receptor, which if I'm guessing right is pretty much every Tri-Vee, personal communicator, and plasma network on the planet. You'll get to most of the people that way," Zander said.

"Would it be dangerous?" she asked. Zander shrugged.

"It might be, a bit. But danger and I are old friends, Princess. And we're not at war. Or at least we won't be until you make this broadcast," Zander said.

Then they looked to me. "I think it's best if we bring in my father on this now," I said. I called Walther in to set up the encrypted longwave link to Government House on the library's main wall plasma display. I sent the communications packet with an urgent request, and this time it was answered. I navigated around my father's secretary and she agreed to get him on the line. His image came up a few seconds later. He and Wesley were seated in his office.

I introduced Harrington and Zander and the merchant proceeded to fill in the two leaders on what he had just told us.

"We're aware of the government line on Carinthia," said Wesley, "and about the blame being placed on young Peter. So far they have refused all Union overtures, either from us or the Earthmen, on diplomatic negotiations. They are threatening withdrawal from the Union, but we're not sure what else they may be planning."

"Then let me fill you in, Admiral," said Harrington. "I've withdrawn all my merchant operations from the Carinthian system. Doing business there has become impossible. They are interdicting all foreign cargo ships that dock at the High Stations under the guise of a search for evidence on the abduction, then taking the cargo and rerouting it to Carinthia."

"Hoarding supplies," said Wesley, nodding his head.

"For what?" I asked.

"For war, son," answered my father. "Prince Arin is threatening military action against any planet found to be harboring these so-called 'anti-Carinthian agents.' Carinthia has demanded the return of all their sailors and soldiers to their home bases. Some are already going. We don't know how many will stay with the Union. We're on the verge of war."

We all took that in soberly.

"There will be a formal war council tomorrow at 0900. It will be up there, at the North Palace," said Wesley. "It would be helpful, Princess, if your father could participate."

"I understand," she said.

With that we agreed to wait until morning for further action and cut the link. I made arrangements for apartment suites for Harrington and Zander, then said my good night to the princess. It had been a long day, and tomorrow was likely to be much, much longer still.

I tossed and turned for more than an hour, exhausted but unable to turn my mind off. I got up around midnight and picked up a novel with an interesting cover from the collection in my room and sat down to read. It was from an author named Swenson, what they used to call "science fiction," an antiquated genre. I remembered reading it as an adolescent and enjoying it. I was barely fifteen minutes into my reading when there was a knock at my door.

"Come in," I said. The doors parted and Karina came in, wearing a pink robe over a flowing white nightgown, which trailed her across the carpet as she came in, and shut the door behind her.

"That gown looks a bit long for you," I said, smiling as I put the book down. She smiled back.

"Short girl problems. I'm only a hundred and fifty-six centimeters," she said. I tried to run the conversion in my head.

"Five-foot-one?" I said.

"Five-one and *a half*," she replied. "In your quaint outmoded measurement system." She came over and sat next to me in a side chair, the gown fabric flowing onto the floor. She wrestled with it, trying to figure out what to do with all the extra fabric.

"We'll try to find you something that fits better tomorrow," I said by way of apology. She smiled again.

"They did their best. No doubt some normal-sized second lieutenant of the royal guard is out her favorite nightgown," she said, then continued. "I saw your light on. I couldn't sleep either. There's so much on my mind."

"And mine," I agreed. I sensed there was something more, but hesitated to ask what it might be, so I let the silence hang in the air for a while. She looked at me as if she was unabashedly evaluating me, but for what? Finally she spoke.

"I hope you would agree that these are not normal circumstances, Peter, and that we've been forced together in a way that neither of us would have chosen," she said.

"I *would* agree with that," I said. *Now where is* this *going?* I thought.

"Then perhaps that will make you open to some more . . . unorthodox solutions in regards to our current predicament?"

I shifted in my chair. This could be trouble. "What's on your mind, Karina?"

Now it was her turn to wiggle uncomfortably in her chair. "You would agree that the problems on Carinthia, with my brother, are now threatening to envelop the whole Union?" she said.

"Yes, that's obvious."

"And if we could put pressure on Arin in his position

as Regent, force his hand, if you will, it might create a crack in my world's desire to follow him down the path to leaving the Union," she said. I thought about that a moment.

"Which side will your people come down on?" I asked.

"My people are dedicated to my father. They trust his rule, and his judgment. Arin is not so well liked. He's never been popular with the people. There has even been a movement to petition my father to make Benn the legitimate heir, though my father never considered it," she said. I thought for a moment again.

"My hope has been that you and your father will be able to make your broadcast to the Carinthian people. Won't that help the situation?" I said. Now she moved in closer to me.

"Help, yes, but will it be enough? Arin could just maintain that the kidnappers were forcing us to make the broadcast. And he doesn't care about his popularity, whether they will believe him. He just wants control," she said.

"Go on," I replied, trying to stay as neutral as I could manage.

"So to my mind," she continued, "we need something more decisive than just the message. An act that will force both sides on Carinthia to choose who they will follow, my father, or the Regency," she said. The look in her eyes was very intense now. It was time for me to find out what she had in mind.

"All right. What are you proposing?" I asked. She leaned in close and took my hand in hers. Whatever was coming, she was very serious about it.

"Marry me. Now," she said.

I could only stare blankly at her, so she continued.

"My father will condemn Arin and declare a government in exile, a union of our two families. It will split the Carinthian people *and* the military in two."

"Karina—"

"Please, Peter. Can't you see this is the only way? My father is fading fast. Once he's gone Arin will have total power, and the Union will be at an end. Only by our two families being joined can we hope to mount a challenge to his authority. Only that bond could sway popular and military opinion enough to save Carinthia from civil war and the Union from dissolution. You have to see it. It's the only way," she said.

She had surprised me again. No, shocked me, with her boldness.

"You're not saying anything," she said. "Is it such an audacious proposal? Or is it just that you don't fancy me as much as your daring Lightship captain?"

I had no idea what to say to *that*. I hadn't even considered this as a possibility. A marriage for political purposes was something I had always been faced with since the death of my brother; I just hadn't thought of it as a solution to this current crisis.

"I think we should consult with my father and Wesley," I said. "This could actually spur on a civil war on Carinthia." Karina shook her head.

"That won't happen. If our wedding is as popular as I think it will be, the people will clamor to stay in the Union, and the military will not act in discord with the people. I'm not saying it won't be dangerous, but I believe there are enough good men left in the Carinthian military to stave off a civil war, and we will be the catalyst for them to stand down, even in the face of Arin's orders," she said.

"But—" I didn't get to protest as she continued to talk right over me.

"As for your father and the admiral, they will discourage it, and Carinthia will pay the price. Our people will fall under oppression and my father will die in exile of a broken heart on a world light-years away from his home. I want to save my world, Peter. I've thought it through, and this is the only way. I'm asking you, not as a young navy commander, but as a royal son of Quantar who will one day inherit his own planetary title. Unite our two worlds. Marry me. Help me to save Carinthia," she said. Her grip on my hand was ever tighter, and she was on the verge of tears. I looked at her and knew she would not be dissuaded from this path. I had to decide, one way or another.

I broke free of her hand, went to my room com, and called down to Walther.

"Listen very carefully," I said.

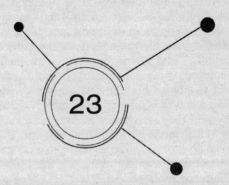

23

I walked into the palace's map room on the third floor at 0850, dressed in my full royal uniform, indicating both my rank and decorations as Duke of KendalFalk. I chose this over my regular navy uniform for obvious reasons; the decisions being made in this room were going to be of historic importance.

The map room was the only one big enough to accommodate the more than forty people required in the council that also had the plasma displays and 3-D projectors necessary for strategy and planning. The main table had a dozen seats around it, and I had instructed the stewards to place me on the wall side, facing the windows, third from the head, where my father would sit. Spaces were reserved next to me on my right for both the grand duke and his daughter. I hoped Karina could get him prepared enough to both attend the council and be coherent enough to make decisions.

Next to my father would be Wesley on his right, followed by a Royal Navy Admiral and Union commanders in descending order of importance. It seemed to me that I had chosen the proper side of the table to sit, next to our allies and not in opposition to them. Harrington would be on my immediate left and Zander was placed next to him as his primary military consultant. Essentially it was the Quantar and Union Navy on the window side and the foreigners, except for me, on the wall side. As the principals began filtering into the room I sat down and then poured water from a crystal pitcher into a glass, as did many others in the grim-faced crowd. Those not anointed with a seat at the table took up strategic positions around the room, standing against the strategy console or sitting in chairs brought up from the family dining room.

My father came in three minutes early, trailed as always by Wesley. They sat down together, engaging in hushed conversation. I was soon joined by Harrington and Zander and their subordinates. My father glanced over at me from his notes, perhaps curious that I had chosen to sit on the wall side, then looked to the two empty chairs next to me reserved for Karina and the Grand Duke Henrik. He cleared his throat.

"Let's begin," he said. I looked at my watch: still two minutes early.

"Pardon me, sir," I said to him. "But could we give the grand duke and his daughter another two minutes? We are starting early."

My father looked at the wall clock and nodded while Wesley gave me a cold glare from across the table. I stayed calm and sipped my water.

At precisely 0900 the Grand Duke Henrik and his daughter came into the room, and everyone stood and gently applauded. His gray-streaked hair was clean and styled, his black military uniform was pressed and properly pleated, and he strode through the room as if he had been in such situations thousands of times. Indeed, I supposed that he had. Karina was at his side and guided him by the arm to his chair, where he sat with the kind of dignity only a lifelong royal could muster. Karina, dressed in her green Carinthian lieutenant's uniform, sat down between us. She smiled at me and gripped my hand quickly under the table before letting go. Then everyone else took their places except my father, who stood and addressed the duke.

"Grand Duke Henrik, let me be the first to officially welcome you to Quantar, and to wish you many blessings on your visit here," he said.

The grand duke nodded, acknowledging my father, but said nothing while the crowd applauded politely again. My father sat down then and looked my way a second time, but again said nothing to me. Then he started in.

"This council is called to address the great threat before the Union, the possible secession of Carinthia from our alliance, and all the implications thereof, up to and including the possibility of war," my father stated formally. "I will ask Grand Admiral Jonathon Wesley of the Union Navy to give us the latest tactical report." Wesley stood, cleared his throat, and then nodded to an assistant who activated the main plasma display taking up almost the entire near wall. The Union Navy Linkworks logo appeared as we all looked down the table to the wall display.

"About nine hours ago we received a distress signal via longwave from *H.M.S. Valiant*, on a survey mission in the Sandosa system. She reported that she was under heavy attack from unknown forces, but was seeking to avoid the conflict and find safe haven. About two hours ago we received an update packet from *Valiant*, containing the following visual recording. I'll let the room assess what it shows," Wesley said, then nodded to the assistant who played the recording.

The display showed a formation of ships attacking *Valiant* from at least three sides. I couldn't be sure but the vessels looked like the type of automated HuKs both *Impulse* and *Starbound* had faced before. The grainy images showed *Valiant* avoiding and escaping from the buzzsaw-like attacks. Then suddenly the field of view cut to a deep field scan that I recognized as being generated by a longscope tactical screen. It showed a large-displacement ship jumping into the fray very close to *Valiant*, and her moving evasively to avoid the rising hulk.

"Imperial dreadnought," I said out loud, more muttering to myself than anything else, but Wesley overheard me.

"Since you're the only one in this room who has seen one up close, Commander, we'll take your word for it," he said, then waved to the assistant, who shut off the screen. "An Imperial dreadnought. From this point *Valiant* was able to use her sub-light impeller drives to escape to the jump point and make a direct jump to Pendax before the pursuing ships caught her, but she burned out her HD impellers doing it. I think you can all see the implications of this attack. The Imperial Navy is operational, and is now hunting our Lightships. They will eventually figure out where *Valiant* jumped to and pursue her. If they do, the Pendax system will be under real threat." I looked to Admar Harrington, who looked more than a bit upset at these potential circumstances, and I couldn't blame him. Something else occurred to me, though, so I spoke again.

"According to the tactical display we saw, that dreadnought jumped directly into the battle scene, Admiral," I said. "That indicates the dreadnoughts don't need to use jump space to ingress and egress our star systems anymore."

"And that means they're a goddamned menace to the whole Union," said Wesley. "No one is safe from them.

And the larger implication of this attack is that we may be facing a war on two fronts."

"Or a single front with two enemies," Karina said. Wesley shrugged.

"Either way, it's not good news, Princess," he said, using her royal rank rather than her military one.

"What will we do about *Valiant*?" I asked. "Rescue mission? Reinforcements?" Wesley waved at the assistant again and the display reactivated, bringing up a link to *Starbound*'s command briefing room, where I was heartened to see the faces of Captain Maclintock and Serosian appear.

"*Valiant* was intended as a survey and First Contact ship, and her captain and crew are not trained for serious battle situations. She will need to be reinforced and brought up to battle trim, and quickly," continued Wesley. "I don't think I need to introduce Captain Jonas Maclintock or Historian Serosian of *Starbound* to most of you, but I'll do so as a courtesy to the grand duke and to you, Princess."

"Thank you, Admiral," Karina said for them both. Then I noticed that she had to give her father a gentle nudge as his eyes started to close. He responded by tapping her hand to thank her.

"What's your status, Captain?" Wesley demanded.

"Fit, trim, and ready to rumble, Admiral," Maclintock said. That set off a round of low-level laughter. "All repairs are complete. We just need our longscope officer back aboard and we'll be ready to head out to Pendax." That was a nod to me and I appreciated it.

"That's good news, Captain, and I do have your departure orders," Wesley said. I looked to my father, but his attention was fixed on the screen. Wesley went to his briefcase at the table and pulled out some papers, shuffling them a couple of times before continuing. I was beginning to worry that I might get left out of the coming battle. Perhaps I had gone too far and now both Wesley and my father saw me as a liability to the navy. Wesley cleared his throat again.

"*Starbound* is hereby ordered to the Pendax system, there to provide protection for the local populace as well as to relieve the command crew of *Valiant*. You'll need to get her on a battle footing quickly, Jonas," he said. Wesley then turned to Admar Harrington. "Mr. Harrington here has a flotilla of merchant frigates, or Wasps as he calls them, five in all, deploying throughout the Pendax system now. They aren't Lightships but they pack a solid punch and they're faster than anything those Imperial thugs have. You'll coordinate with the Wasp fleet commander to set up a systemwide defense. Understood, Captain?"

"Yes, Admiral," said Maclintock.

"Good. Captain Zander will follow you in with a battle group of seven more Wasps deployed from Candle, and the remaining ten are going to be split equally between defense of Levant and Quantar, though we here likely already have enough in-system firepower to hold off anything but a full-scale invasion. The Earthmen, of course, need no help with planetary defenses. You should note that those additional seven Wasps will likely take another twelve hours to reach you after *Starbound* makes her jump, so you can't count on them until they show up."

"Understood, Admiral. But I have a question: if Captain Scott of *Valiant* and his command crew are to be relieved, who will be taking command of her?" asked Maclintock.

"Believe me, that's been a question here," replied Wesley, setting the reference paper back down on the table and then returning his attention to the display.

"I can't recommend Commander Devin Tannace highly enough, sir," said Maclintock. Tannace had been *Starbound*'s XO before Dobrina and I had been assigned to her at Levant. Since then he'd been the military attaché in charge of training the Levantine crew of their Lightship *Resolution*.

"Your recommendation is noted, Captain, but I've already made Tannace captain of *Resolution*. He left for Earth this morning, and the Levantine crew is going to be replaced with experienced Earth spacers. The ship itself will likely not be ready for another week, but we're rushing to get her in the game." At this he took in a deep breath. This situation made me want to get back to my own ship to help as soon as possible.

"With apologies, Admiral," started Maclintock, "but who—" Wesley stopped him with a raised hand. He came back to the table and pulled a small box out of his briefcase. He looked at the box briefly, then set it down and slid it across the table.

To me.

I looked at the box, then reached out and opened it. Two matching gold captain's bars for my collar.

"Mr. Cochrane will command *Starbound*. He's the only command-level field officer besides you with battle experience against the empire, and he's familiar with your ship," said Wesley. This sent a ripple through the crowd. I looked at the bars again, and started to get nervous. Wesley turned his attention back to the display screen.

"But, Admiral," said Maclintock, "Captain Zander has—"

"Lightship command experience, yes, I know, Captain. But he's not in the Union or Carinthian Navy anymore. And besides that, I believe Mr. Harrington here would prefer that Captain Zander protect Pendax's interests, since that is what he's paying him for," said Wesley.

"As you say," said Harrington with a nod.

Maclintock looked nonplussed at this turn of events. "Understood, Admiral," he said. I looked down the table at Harrington and Zander. Zander winked at me, which

I took to mean that he had given Wesley a recommendation in my favor. Wesley continued.

"Captain Maclintock, you will take command of *H.M.S. Valiant* once *Starbound* reaches Pendax. You may take any three command-rank officers with you, but the rest you'll have to parcel together from the existing crew and any locals from the Wasp crews," Wesley said.

"I can give you a list of capable men, Captain," came Zander's scratchy voice from down the table.

"Appreciated, Captain Zander," replied Maclintock. Wesley turned back to me.

"Commander Cochrane," he said. I snapped to my feet. "You are hereby placed in field command of *H.M.S. Starbound* from your arrival in the Pendax system until further notice. Do you understand and acknowledge your orders?"

"I understand and acknowledge, sir," I said. He gave me a nod and I sat down again. It was a field command, something that could be rescinded at a later date, but it was a command. What I did now and in the days ahead could impact thousands, if not millions of lives. The reality of that hit me hard, and quite frankly it felt like a rock had taken up residence in my gut.

"Further to your orders, gentlemen, are the following mission assignments. Captain Maclintock will defend the Pendax system with *Valiant*. Upon change of command, Captain Cochrane"—that sounded strange—"will take *Starbound* with all possible speed to the Levant system where your orders are to destroy the artificial jump gate ring above that world and the generator station on the second moon, L-4b. We don't want that gate to be used as a portal to jump a fleet into our backyard. The value of the jump ring to us as ingress to the Altos system is less than the danger it poses to the Union," he said.

"Understood, sir," I replied.

"Good. Once your mission is complete your orders

are to return to Pendax with all possible speed and rendezvous with the defense fleet there. Are we clear, gentlemen?"

"Yes, sir," both Maclintock and I said in unison. Wesley nodded.

"One question, sir," I said.

"Yes, Captain?"

"Why is *Starbound* returning to Pendax? Doesn't Levant or Quantar need the protection of a Lightship as well?" Wesley shuffled his feet and turned slightly toward me.

"Pendax is the key, Captain Cochrane, because from there any attacking ships could jump directly to either Quantar or Earth, and we have to prepare for that eventuality. If we hold Pendax, we can force them to fight station-to-station, and we can rally all our forces to the battlefield," Wesley said.

"But if the dreadnoughts have the ability to jump directly into a system—" I started.

"As far as we know that capability is limited to having spatial coordinates confirmed by support ships like the HuKs, and *they* still have to navigate using jump points. We hope."

"Understood, sir." I thought that was a risky assumption, but I wasn't running the council meeting, so I kept my mouth shut.

"And now to the Carinthian situation," Wesley said. "Mr. Serosian, if you would be so kind as to update us on your latest intelligence?"

Serosian leaned forward on the massive plasma screen. "Intelligence reports are sketchy at best, Admiral. Most of our observers in the Carinthian system have been neutralized, and by that I mean their ability to communicate with the Order back on Earth is minimal. The last reports we received, which are nearly twenty-four hours old now, indicated that all three Carinthian

Lightships were operational and that they and a substantial support fleet had made for the jump point, and from there jumped to parts unknown," he said.

"They left no substantial forces in-system?" asked Wesley.

"It doesn't appear so, Admiral."

Wesley paced around the room and then looked to my father. "It seems as though they are massing for an all-out attack, Nathan," he said.

"Yes, but when and where?" said my father. "This whole business with Grand Duke Henrik"—the duke brightened a bit at the mention of his name—"has given the Regency propaganda cover for any kind of action they want, even war with Quantar. If we commit all of our forces to defend Pendax we could be leaving ourselves wide open for an attack. But to not defend an associate member of the Union which is soon to become a full partner would be a catastrophic mistake."

"If I may suggest," came Serosian's voice from the screen, "I think that is exactly what they want, to split us, to isolate Quantar from the other Union worlds, and neutralize her power."

"These new Carinthian Lightships," I asked, "are they joining up with an Imperial fleet?"

"Possibly," replied the Historian. "But all we know for certain is that they haven't hit Pendax yet."

"What about diplomatic efforts?" my father asked. Serosian looked grim.

"All diplomatic overtures to Carinthia have been rebuffed and communication channels have broken down," he said.

"And what of your government? Where do they stand?"

"The Historian Order is officially neutral in this, Director Cochrane. They will support the Union against an outside threat by the Corporate Empire, but not necessarily Quantar in an internal conflict against Carinthia. However, I can reassure you that *my* loyalties are with both the Union *and* with Quantar. I couldn't serve aboard *Starbound* if they weren't. As to my brothers and sisters on the Carinthian ships, though, I'm afraid not all of them are of the same school of thought as I am."

"And if we have to fight those Carinthian Lightships?" I asked. Serosian, my longtime mentor, looked down at me from the screen.

"The one advantage you have is that both *Valiant* and *Starbound* have the upgraded weapons systems we gave you after the Levant incident, including both the gravity weapons and the improved coil canon firepower. Those weapons will give you an advantage in any direct conflict with Carinthian Lightships," he said. I looked at him, then to the admiral, then back.

"Some of my friends are on those Lightships, Mr. Serosian," I said. "That's little consolation if I have to use my weapons against them."

"We get your point, Captain," said Wesley. At this Karina reached under the table and gently squeezed my hand again, which I appreciated, but it was sparse comfort. She knew I didn't want to face Dobrina on the battlefield.

"Rules of engagement are as follows," said Wesley. "Any Imperial ship is to be regarded as an enemy and may be attacked and destroyed with impunity. Special emphasis should be placed on destroying enemy HuKs, as they seem to be the units coordinating attacks with the dreadnoughts. Any Carinthian ship that fires on a Union ship may be engaged. The first objective should be to disable Carinthian ships, not destroy them. Use of mass-destruction weapons against Carinthian ships is only authorized if either *Starbound* or *Valiant* are under imminent threat of destruction. Understood?"

Maclintock answered quickly. I hesitated just a second before giving an affirmative. Wesley turned to me.

"Is there going to be a problem with the engagement rules, Captain?" he asked. I looked him in the eye.

"No, sir."

"Good. Mr. Harrington, what does your network have to report?" Harrington shifted in his chair and then spoke up.

"My last ship got out of Carinthia last night, Admiral. She sent a copy of a coded packet that was sent from Prince Benn to all Loyalist personnel. Once we decoded it, it was essentially a final message that said all Loyalists should remember their original oaths and comply with their orders, as long as those orders did not violate said oaths," Harrington said.

"He's telling them to follow orders, but making war against the Union would be a violation of their oaths. He's giving them cover to disobey Arin's orders," said Karina. All eyes in the room turned to her. "The Loyalists may be cooperating, but they have not given up. If we can sway the people of Carinthia—"

"With apologies, Princess, but the Regency military controls Carinthia," interrupted Wesley.

"They control the ground, Admiral. They control two of the three Lightships, but *Impulse II* is commanded by Captain Dobrina Kierkopf, and we know where her loyalties lie," countered Karina.

"And where would that be?" asked Wesley.

"With us. With the Union and with Quantar." She looked at me then. "Carinthia is not gone, Admiral. She is being controlled by forces that do not have popular support. We have that advantage, because we have the grand duke on our side."

"Apologies again, Princess. But isn't the time for propaganda long gone? There is a Carinthian military force massing for an attack somewhere out there," said Wesley.

"The Carinthian people will rally to their duke, Admiral. If we can turn their hearts back to him, we can break Arin's base of support at home and we can force him to return or lose that base. That's what can stop this war, or at least give us only a single front to fight."

Wesley looked fatigued by the conversation once it departed from a military focus. He looked to my father.

"It's your decision, Nathan. I'm not sure this proposed broadcast can help at this point. Prince Arin's operatives can just say it was done under duress and that the Royal family are prisoners here on Quantar. It may even hurt us with the Carinthian people," said Wesley.

My father contemplated this, then started to talk. "Princess, I have to agree this may not be the best time—"

"Nein!" The grand duke slapped the table for emphasis.

My father was taken aback by this as the room grew hushed and all eyes turned to Henrik Feilberg. "This message is critical," he said, slowly and deliberately, in good Standard but with a noticeable accent. "My daughter is right. The people still hold sway on my world, they are still loyal to the Crown. Arin has . . ." He trailed off here and his voice grew quiet, as if it pained him to say the words. "Arin has . . . confused the people. Once they hear from the three of us, they will see that I am still their sovereign, and that our two worlds are meant to be united, not split apart."

My father looked confused. "Apologies, Highness, but you said the message would be from the three of you? But there is only yourself and the Princess Karina. Perhaps you meant to include Prince Benn, but he is not here," he said.

The grand duke turned a steely stare on my father. "I may be old, and heartbroken, and frequently confused, Director Cochrane, but I meant what I said. Myself, my daughter, and her new husband will record the message. Their marriage will unite our worlds, and give my people new hope."

"What's this?" said Wesley, looking from the grand duke to Karina, and then to me.

"Marriage? Husband?" said my father, clearly

surprised. Then he too looked at me. I stood up, as did Karina. The grand duke stood and came between us, joining my right hand to Karina's left in front of him. He addressed my father.

"May I present your new daughter-in-law, Director Cochrane. Princess Karina Feilberg of Carinthia, the new wife of your son, Peter," the grand duke said. "They were married early this morning, by your Vicar of KendalFalk, and they have my blessing." Then he put his arms around both of us, and kissed his daughter on the forehead.

I extended her hand, showing my father the ring I had given her. It was a beautiful silver ring with a central blue sapphire and diamond setting that had belonged to my maternal grandmother. I wore my paternal grandfather's silver diamond wedding band. Both had been pulled from the family jewelry archive at the palace.

The room was stone silent.

"Our worlds are now united, permanently," the grand duke concluded.

My father looked at me, the tiniest hint of a smile of admiration creeping up one side of his mouth.

"You don't do anything halfway, do you, son?" he said.

"No, sir," I replied. Then he stood and began clapping, and the room filled with a rising wave of applause. The grand duke hugged his daughter again, then released her. My father stretched out his hand across the table and I shook it. Then I turned to Karina and pulled her close to me.

The room filled with cheers and "huzzahs!" and, for the first time in a long time, everyone in the room was smiling.

24

We recorded the message an hour later, and I was glad to get it done. The Grand Duke Henrik was stretched to his limits, but he finished the job. Karina had written the script and introduced me in German. I spoke my part in Standard and was told that German subtitles would be added. Barely thirty minutes later and the message was gone with Zander, who would drop it by ansible into the Carinthian system to be broadcast at a preset time.

Karina took her father back up to his apartment while I briefed for my mission with navy personnel in the library. My father had already gone back to New Briz, but Wesley stayed behind to coach his new charge, ready to make his first team debut. It was a daunting task, but after more than two hours of coaching on the ins and outs of commanding a Lightship I felt ready.

"Certainly, this wasn't what anyone planned, lad," said

Wesley. "But we wouldn't have done it if we didn't feel you were up to it."

"Thank you, sir," I said as the briefing was breaking up.

"Do you have an XO in mind?" That only took me a second to ponder.

"Lena Babayan, sir. She's extremely resourceful. I know she's currently a marine colonel, but I'm requesting that her commission be conveyed to full navy commander, sir," I said.

"Done," he replied. "Now just one more thing, Captain. Don't break my ship. I'll be wanting her back when we're done."

"I promise, Admiral."

"And rely on your Historian friend, Mr. Serosian. His advice will be vital."

"Of course, sir," I said. I had negotiated to keep most of *Starbound*'s command crew, with George Layton getting an overdue field promotion to lieutenant commander as my third, John Marker moving from marine sergeant to master chief so I could broaden his duties, and Duane Longer becoming my junior lieutenant commander. Everyone else would retain their previous duties, at least on this mission. And there was one more personnel issue that Wesley brought up.

"You take goddamn good care of my niece," said Wesley in his gruff tone.

"I will, sir," I replied. He shook my hand then.

"Congratulations, son. Be careful out there."

"Thank you, sir. We will, sir. I assume I have a shuttle to catch?" Wesley eyed me slyly, then looked at his watch.

"Not until 1900," he said. I looked at my watch, which said 1520 hours.

"That's nearly four hours, sir. I thought time was—"

"It is, Captain. But time isn't everything. All the wheels are in motion, so we can afford to wait a few more hours to get you airborne. Mr. Harrington reliably informs me has a *very* fast shuttle waiting for you at High Station," he said.

"But, sir, I don't understand, I was under the impression—"

He cut me off again. "You're needed upstairs, Captain," said Wesley, nodding toward the library's high ceiling while he pretended to look at military reports. Now I was completely confused.

"Upstairs? For what, sir?" I asked. He smiled just a bit, but said nothing.

I looked up at the ceiling, then back down at Wesley. It finally came together in my mind. "Oh," I said.

"Even in a crisis, Captain, we can't forget our humanity," Wesley said. I nodded, nothing more needing to be said, then made my way to the lifter for the family apartments.

My room had been transformed into a glittering candlelit retreat, the curtains drawn against the late afternoon winter sun. The bedding had been freshened and there were flowers everywhere, even rose petals on the bedsheets. A handwritten note left on my night stand instructed me to the shower, instructions which I followed to the letter.

When I returned to the bedroom, Karina was there, standing by the bed in a flowing white gown which actually fit her, her long dark hair hanging down her back.

"Welcome, husband," she said.

"Thank you," was all I could manage in reply. It was an awkward situation, and I found myself unsure of what to do next. She extended her hand to me, and I took it, then gently pulled her to me, where we met with a kiss.

She was small in my arms. Her personality was so big and daring that I had somehow never equated her physical size with it. She had always seemed much larger to me, except now when I held her close.

We went hand-in-hand to the bed, where she untied the gown and let it fall to the floor. Once again I was surprised. Although she was petite, that was not a word I could use for every part of her body. She helped me out of my bathrobe and soon we were lying together in bed, softly kissing. It was awkward, we hardly knew each other, but in due course what came naturally to young men and women came naturally to us.

Afterward, we lay together, caressing.

"I've never been with a man before," she suddenly said. I kissed her forehead and then her lips. "Did I please you?" she asked.

"Of course you did. I should think that would be obvious," I said with a small chuckle. She smiled at me.

"I want you to come back from this mission, Peter," she said. "I know this probably isn't what you had planned for your life."

"Actually, I've never really had a plan, except to serve in the navy. And don't worry about the mission. We have the best ships in space, and we will get through this crisis," I reassured her. She looked into my eyes and smiled, then kissed me again with more passion.

After the kiss she looked up at me for a long time, her head on the pillow. I thought about her as we looked at each other: really, we were just getting to know one another, and the fact was that I did not love her, but I would be lying if I said there was no affection between us. Our marriage was a reality that I would not and could not break. I decided that she would make an excellent wife, if we ever got the chance to be together long enough to behave as married couples do.

"I think you should know I'm ovulating," she said out of the blue.

"What?" I said, and sat up on my elbow. "That's a hell of a thing to say on our wedding night. Or day."

"I'm sorry. I hope you're not upset, but it's something I thought you should know. At least there's a possibility."

"So you're not on pregnancy repressors?" I asked. She shook her head.

"I never have been. As I said, I've never been with a man before, and thus, no real need. What about you?" she said.

"Well, not regularly. And I didn't know until last night that I would be getting married," I said. "It kind of slipped my mind." She pulled herself in close to me, and a warm wonderful softness enveloped me. I lay back down next to her.

"I just wanted you to know. It's not something we have to worry about right now," she said. I rolled over on my back.

"Absolutely. The Union is splitting up, the old empire is attacking, I just married a princess, I'm heading into a war zone and, oh, hey, maybe you just made your new bride pregnant. Nothing like that will cross my mind out there, I'm sure," I said. She smiled and rolled her body on top of mine.

"There are circumstances we can't control, Peter," she said. "And like it or not we have been brought together, now. Is it too much to ask to just let your worries go, and be in the moment with me?"

I looked up at her. She was beautiful. "It's not too much for a wife to ask of her husband, no," I said. Then she smiled, and I kissed her, and felt my passion for her begin to rise again.

⸻

Roughly fourteen hours later I strode onto the bridge of *Starbound* at High Station Candle, and greeted Maclintock and Serosian, as well as many others of the crew. Maclintock didn't waste a minute getting us underway to Pendax.

It would be a short two-hour traverse to the jump point using the HD impellers on full max, and from there the jump to Pendax. It would be a 48.5-light-year jump, and thus we would be in a hyperspace bubble for about sixteen hours. All of us would undoubtedly be worried about the situation during that time, but there was nothing we could do about it but prepare.

Maclintock called a staff meeting fifteen minutes after we left Candle in the Command Deck Briefing room. Serosian was noticeably absent, but all the major department heads were present and seated around the oval table: Babayan, Layton, Marker, Jenny Hogan, and Duane Longer along with me. Missing were several important section chiefs who would be joining Maclintock on *Valiant*. What was also missing in the room was any sign of Carinthian officers besides Babayan. Most had left for home, some had simply removed themselves to barracks on Candle, staying loyal to their Union oaths but not willing to fight their countrymen.

Maclintock cleared his throat. "First order of business, congratulations to Mr. Cochrane, both on his promotion and his recent, unexpected nuptials," he said. There was applause around the room. I fingered my new wedding band.

"Thank you all for the good wishes," I said. "I just wish the circumstances were different."

"As do we all," said Maclintock before continuing. "Mr. Marker, did you get your replacement marines aboard?" he said.

"Aye, sir," replied Marker. "Full complement of sixty, trained and experienced, but not a one from Carinthia."

"Can't say as I blame them," said Maclintock.

"Nor I," said Marker.

"Do you anticipate any problems getting the new recruits integrated?" Marker shook his head.

"None, sir. All of them to a man and woman volunteered, even after what happened at Jenarus. I had more trouble sorting through all the applicants to pick the best mix of skills than worrying about recruiting or getting them to work together," he said.

Maclintock nodded. "Good," he said, then looked down the table to Lena Babayan, who was functioning as our intelligence officer on this portion of the mission. "What's your latest report, Commander?" Maclintock asked, using her new navy rank.

"We've received regular updates from Pendax. All is quiet there, eerily so. It's like they're waiting for us to show up before they attack," she said.

"And how would they know when we're coming? Either they have very sophisticated detection equipment we know nothing about or they're telepaths, which I doubt," said Maclintock.

"We do know their dreadnaughts can jump into a star system without using jump points," I said. "Perhaps they have other capabilities as well."

"There is one other possibility that I feel I should raise," said Babayan.

The captain looked at her, waiting for her to finish.

"There could be spies aboard *Starbound*." We all contemplated that for a long moment. Maclintock looked down the table to Marker.

"Marine details on all critical ship's systems, Master Chief. Security alert for the duration of this mission. Passes and personnel checks required at all secure stations," he said.

"Aye, sir. May I also recommend silent running and a catchnet over all com traffic?" said Marker.

"Noted and logged, Mr. Marker. I'll leave it to you and Commander Babayan to implement."

"Aye, sir," they both said.

"Anything else to report?" said Maclintock to Babayan. She nodded affirmative.

"Admar Harrington's network has reported that while we were waiting for Mr. Cochrane to arrive a courier jumped in to the Sol system from Carinthia on a diplomatic mission to High Station Earth. The courier ship had one passenger, Prince Benn Feilberg. He was sent with the Union Secession papers drawn up by the Carinthian Regency government. Those papers were rejected by the Union Council because they were not approved by the grand duke himself, which is a requirement of the Concord Agreement that has never been amended," she said.

"Political posturing," I said. "What of Prince Benn?"

Babayan looked to me. "He immediately caught an Earth shuttle for Quantar. Apparently there was no return ticket to Carinthia on the courier ship."

I felt bad for the prince, who was now clearly in exile. But I took comfort that Karina would at least have some family support soon at the North Palace.

Maclintock took reports from the rest of the officers present and then turned to me last before addressing the room at large.

"As you all know, Commander Cochrane here is set to take operational command of *Starbound* once we reach Pendax. However, I think that is too long to wait. Nothing like getting a few extra hours in the Big Chair, in my opinion. Therefore . . ." At this he stood up, and I stood with him. I hadn't expected this.

"Commander Peter Erasmus Cochrane, I do now solemnly and without reservation, relinquish command of *H.M.S. Starbound* to you, pursuant to orders issued by Grand Admiral Jonathon Wesley on Union date 01.26.2769. Do you accept command?" Maclintock said.

"I do, sir," I replied. He shook my hand.

"Congratulations, Captain."

The other officers stood and applauded then, and Maclintock did, too. I stepped up to the center seat.

"Prepare for the jump," I ordered. "All stations to be locked down fifteen minutes prior to green-go. And since we have sixteen hours in jump space, expect a full inspection of all stations en route." I looked to each face around the table, especially to Marker and Layton, Babayan, Longer, and Jenny Hogan, my friends.

"Dismissed!" I snapped, and they were gone.

Maclintock shook my hand one more time.

"Good luck, Peter. I pray we won't need it," he said.

I met with Serosian after completing one formal inspection of the ship and two informal ones. Maclintock was staying out of the way in his stateroom and letting me run the ship my way, and for that I was grateful. I entered the Historian's quarters after my last run-through, after ordering the command staff to take a full eight hours' break before their duty shift tomorrow when we arrived at Pendax.

Serosian greeted me in the outer room of his chambers, the one furnished like a library. I sat down heavily in a leather club chair and he joined me.

"And how was your first day in command?" he asked, cheerily enough.

"A task. One that I enjoyed thoroughly," I said, smiling.

"And you should," he replied. "You won't ever have a first day in command again."

"True enough." I leaned forward and rubbed at my eyes. I was tired. In the last forty-eight hours I'd gotten married, been given command of a Lightship, traveled the length of my home solar system, and was now halfway to a star system I'd never been to but was probably going to have to defend. And then there was the small point of my mission to Levant and the orders to destroy the artificial jump ring there.

"You've had a busy day," Serosian commented dryly.

"Is it still the same day? I'm not even sure."

"It doesn't matter. You should get some rest at any rate."

"Noted," I said. Then things got quiet again. I *was* tired.

"Do you remember why you came here?" Serosian asked.

"Yes," I said, nodding. "I wanted to ask about the gravity weapons systems. Will they be available to me?"

Serosian nodded in reply. "All of them. At their full capacity."

"And if we have to use them?"

"I will make them available at your command, Captain."

"Good," I said. "Let's hope it doesn't come to that."

"You must be concerned about having to face Dobrina on the battlefield," he said. As usual, he read my concerns easily.

"Of course I am. But I have no intention of using mass-destruction weapons on her, or on any Lightship. Those ships are Union property, and we'll do all we can to protect them and their crews. But I have no such problem with using them on Imperial ships, if and as necessary," I concluded.

"You sound very clear."

"I am."

He went silent at this, usually a sign of his disapproval or of his opinion that I had missed something important. "What?" I finally asked him.

"So the human crews on the dreadnoughts, they have no value to you?" he asked. "Or perhaps just less than Union lives?"

I replied quickly. "The Imperial ships have shown no regard for *our* lives. Are you forgetting they took the entire crew of *Impulse* and turned them against us? They're an aggressor, an enemy, and until they show us a different face I will regard them as such."

"Human lives are, perhaps, too precious a thing to waste," Serosian said. I had no idea what that meant, and now it was my turn to go silent. After a moment he added, "I just want to make sure you aren't acting out of some sense of revenge for *Impulse*, and for the lives you lost at the Jenarus station."

"I'm acting based on what behavior I have seen from the enemy. Until that changes, my approach will remain the same," I snapped.

He nodded, which signified clarity if not assent. "Perhaps we should discuss more pleasing subjects. How are you feeling about your sudden wedding to the Princess Karina?" He was probing me. I sat back in my chair.

"And now you sound like my psychology professor at the Academy," I said back. The fatigue was getting to me. When Serosian said nothing more I continued. "Marrying Karina wasn't what I had planned, but I knew the possibility of a political marriage was always out there. I made the same commitment to Janaan at Levant and I would have kept it had things worked out differently. But they didn't. And now I have Karina, and we have each other."

"And Dobrina?"

I shrugged. "My feelings for her were never the issue. Were I left to choose, I might have chosen her. But that's over now, and we all have to move on." At that I stood to leave.

"We may need every weapon at our disposal to win this battle, my friend," I said.

"I will do all I can to help you, Peter," Serosian said.

"Thank you," I replied, then paused, looking at my friend. "Have you been all right since the jump incident at Jenarus? Resting well?"

He smiled slightly at my concern. "My mind, my decision making, has been unaffected. But I'd be lying if I said that the experience hasn't affected my emotions. It's as if my subconscious mind is still sorting through the experience. My dreams are troubled, my body rhythms disturbed. But I am able to function. There will be time to sort it all out after the crisis is over," he said. I found myself unsure if he was being truthful to me. He looked tired, but then we all were, not least of all me.

"I hope that's so. Good night, Serosian," I said.

"Good night, Captain." Despite my fatigue, I smiled one last time at that, then headed out the door to my cabin, to rest.

25

At Pendax, and Levant

We jumped into Pendax space sixteen hours and six minutes after our entry into jump space at Candle. Jenny Hogan was her usual efficient self.

I sat in the captain's chair with Maclintock on my right, as my guest. Officially he was about to become commodore of the fleet, and I his underling. But for the moment, I was the ranking officer aboard.

I ordered us in to the rendezvous with *Valiant*, and after an hour we met near an outer gas giant of the Pendax system and Maclintock made the transfer over via shuttle. It was strange seeing our two Lightships together, but we were not alone. Harrington's Wasps and merchant destroyers had set up a picket line of defenses between the main planet and the still-under-construction High Station Pendax, situated near the jump point. She was marginally operable from a military standpoint, but months away from being ready for commercial traffic.

We would surely be outgunned by a combined Imperial and Carinthian fleet, especially so with my orders to leave Pendax and take *Starbound* to Levant to destroy the artificial jump gate apparatus. But those were my orders, and I intended to follow them.

Once Maclintock and his crew were aboard *Valiant* we said our goodbyes via longwave, and within the hour I had us back on course to the jump point, where we made our hyperdimensional transformation again. I had mixed feelings about returning to Levant. I had made a good friend in Prince Sunil Katara, and an even closer one in his sister, the Princess Janaan. I wondered what her reaction would be to my wedding to Karina.

I spent the traverse working the crew steadily, but not too hard. We needed the rest that traverse space provided, and we would likely not be getting many breaks once we got to Levant. I hoped for a quick and easy mission, just get in, destroy our targets, and get out.

That's what I hoped for, anyway.

The crew was ready when we jumped in to Levant space, all personnel at battle stations and the ship on full alert.

We found the system quiet and empty of traffic except for the Levantine home-built defensive destroyers and the five Wasps deployed to protect the planet. I immediately opened a visual longwave to High Station Artemis and General Salibi, the commander of Levant's defense forces. His familiar dark and ruddy face appeared on the main plasma display of the bridge.

"Good to hear from you again, Commander," he said in his ever-improving Standard.

"It's captain, now, General. *Starbound* is mine, at least for the time being," I replied over the com.

"Congratulations! That's fantastic news! I'm afraid the prince will be disappointed, though. I think he had you in mind to command *Resolution*," said Salibi.

"I'm afraid the prince may be disappointed in much

of the news we're bringing," I said. I then filled him in on the tactical situation at Pendax, and more importantly, my mission orders for Levant. As I expected, he wasn't happy.

"Of course we'll clear traffic around the jump ring and the base on Tyre. Are you sure you have to destroy them? I'm sure Prince Katara doesn't want to lose such a prized asset," Salibi said.

"Unfortunately, those are my orders, General. The Admiralty feels the gate could be used for ingress of an Imperial fleet into your system, and that's a risk we can't take right now," I said.

"Understood, Captain. How much time do we have?" I looked to Duane Longer. He showed me six fingers.

"Six hours, General. We have a new hybrid impeller drive that gets us around in normal space much faster than before. We'll commence combat operations as soon as we arrive at Levant." Salibi looked unhappy at that.

"We'll be ready. Our defense forces will be deployed to protect the planet," he said.

"Acknowledged. Just be sure we have clear firing lanes."

"As you say, Captain." And with that we said our goodbyes and the line was cut.

I gave orders to the crew to begin firing drills on both the Tyre (or L-4b) and jump ring scenarios. I wanted us to be prepared so we wasted no time in completing our mission. Pendax was where I wanted to be, for a whole host of reasons. The optimal scenario had us sweeping past Levant's larger outer moon, L-4a, and taking out the jump gate ring above Levant itself, then picking up the inner moon, L-4b, and destroying the projector to complete our mission.

After two solid hours of firing drills that hit close to 96.2 percent efficiency, I ordered a thirty-minute break and then left Babayan the con with orders to repeat the drills again until we got it completely right. From the bridge I headed to the captain's stateroom. When I arrived, my belongings had been unpacked and placed around the room, no doubt the work of one of the yeomen. A proper captain's jacket was laid out on the bed, and I tried it on. It fit nicely; the two captain's bars at the collar and three gold bands at the wrists felt right. I hung up my old commander's jacket in the closet just in case, but I hoped I'd never have to wear it again.

After a quick lunch I downloaded the latest intel packet from the Admiralty, but it really contained nothing new. Everything was as it had been, and everyone was on pins and needles, waiting.

A few minutes later and my com chimed in, a private communication was incoming from the planet, from Prince Katara. I smiled. I knew what was on his mind.

"Good to hear from you again, Highness," I said cheerfully over my desk com.

"Don't try to flatter me, *Captain*," he said the last with emphasis.

"What can I do for you, Sunil?" I said.

"You can damn well get me the Lightship I was promised! Keeping us out of the fight to save the Union was never part of our agreement!" he said.

"*Resolution*'s not ready," I replied. "It's really as simple as that. She's almost operational, mechanically, but her crew isn't ready yet. You know that."

"All I know is what *you* tell me, Peter. Our sailors are the best in space!"

"Well, that may be, Sunil. But learning to run a Lightship is a much bigger task than being aboard one of your Levant Navy destroyers. It's a steep learning curve for the best of them," I said.

"Spare me your platitudes, Cochrane. You're doing everything you can to keep us out of this fight," he said. I could tell his ego was taking a hit.

"You're right about that," I said. "But believe me, this is one fight you want to avoid as long as possible. Let us do our job and secure your world."

"But you're taking away our greatest asset!"

"The Admiralty considers the jump gate and generator on Tyre"—I deferred to the local name for Levant's inner moon—"to be more of a threat than they are an asset, Sunil. It has to be disabled, unless you want an Imperial fleet jumping into your backyard?"

"Of course we don't. But our planetary defenses—"

"Are strong enough to fend off anything they have: HuKs, destroyers, perhaps even a dreadnought now that we've hardened your weaponry. But you can't fend off a full fleet. You know that," I said again.

"If we had *Resolution*—"

"Then *Starbound* wouldn't need to be here. But you don't, so we have to be." The line got quiet then and I could practically feel the prince's somber mood. He hated being left out of the fun and losing his precious Founder Relic.

"And how is the Princess Janaan?" I said, breaking through the silence.

"She doesn't know you're here. Or about your promotion. Or . . ." his voice trailed off.

"Or about my marriage. But you know, don't you, my friend?" I said.

"We have a good intelligence network, Peter."

"Indeed you do." The prince hesitated a second before asking the next question.

"Will you be happy with her? This Carinthian princess? More than you would have been with my Janaan?" he asked. I didn't know how to answer that. There was no right answer.

"I don't know," I finally said. "But what's done is done, and we all have to make the best of it."

The line stayed silent again for several moments.

"I'm sure she would want to hear from you directly," said Sunil. I sighed.

"I'm not sure that's possible," I said honestly. "Time being what it is—"

"There is always time for what's most important, my friend," he said. "Call her. She will need to hear it directly from you."

I didn't want to do it, but I knew it was the right thing to do, for her anyway. "If you'll send me her longwave contact ID—"

It popped up on my display screen before I was finished speaking.

"Good luck, Peter. I expect you to be here when we christen *Resolution*," he said.

"One way or another, I will be, Sunil. I promise. And good luck to you as well." With that I signed off, leaned back in my desk chair, and sighed.

I called up Janaan's longwave ID and activated the com, sending a signal with my personal ID directly to the princess's line. After a few seconds she answered.

"Hello, Peter," she said. "I understand congratulations are in order, on many fronts." Apparently the princess had as good an intelligence network as her brother.

"Hello, Princess," I said.

"Please, Janaan."

"Hello, Janaan. This isn't easy to say—"

"Stop, please. Before you go on, I have to see your face." A request for a visual connection popped up on my display. I accepted it and the face of the Princess Janaan of Levant appeared on my screen. The screen was dark and grainy, but even through the distance and local interference I could still see her features. She was as beautiful as ever.

"Princess," I started. I told her all that had happened, as truthfully as I could. She listened patiently and without comment until I had told her everything. The war. My command. Karina. Then it was her turn to speak.

"I understand your choices, Peter, but I had hoped for a different outcome. Please understand that I will always care for you," she said. She looked downtrodden at the news.

"And I for you, Princess."

"Thank you for saving my people," she said. "We will always be in your debt."

"And I will always be in yours, Janaan," I replied. She was having a hard time holding back tears, and frankly, so was I.

"Do you love her?" she finally asked. What could I say to that?

"Not yet," I admitted. "But that doesn't change my commitment."

She wiped away a tear at that, then quickly said her goodbye, and I let her go. It seemed the least painful thing I could do.

I rubbed at my own tired eyes, then pulled up the latest drill reports. 97.5 percent. Still not good enough. I called up to Babayan and ordered her to run through the firing drill again. Then I went to my water basin and ran warm water over my face, trying to rub the tears out of my own eyes.

We received the all-clear from the Levant Navy and Artemis Station twenty minutes before we reached optimal firing range on the jump gate ring. In our last run of drills we'd taken out the jump gate ring and then the generator base on L-4b within twenty minutes of each other. But that was a simulation. I hoped for a similar result in real life.

At ten minutes to firing range on the jump gate ring I ordered us to battle stations and all nonessential personnel to stand down in place. I wanted no distractions. Serosian preferred to wait things out in his cabin, only coming to the bridge if he was needed. I would have preferred him to be there, but his habits were his own, and often hard for me to fathom.

We used the gravity well of the outer moon of

Levant's pair, Sidon, the bigger of the two, to swing us around to the planetside face of the ring construct. It was kilometers across, big enough for a small fleet, and I doubted a round of coil cannon fire could destroy it, so I had opted for a volley of multiwarhead low-yield atomic torpedoes, fired in a mix of ten every thirty seconds for two minutes. The resulting detonations should provide sufficient yields to break the ring into at least four pieces, enough to take it out of service permanently. Historians and Union Navy technicians had mapped the ring technology, so we could put it to use in the future if need be, but only if there was a certainty that we could control it.

The main bridge tactical display showed a clear view of the ring as we swung out of Sidon's shadow and into optimal firing range.

"Five minutes, sir," called Lena from her station.

"Thank you, XO," I replied. I switched my coronal overlay to show me an infrared view, and the screen looked dark, cold, and quiet, just as everything had been since *Valiant* was attacked at Sandosa.

I switched back to the visual display just as everything changed.

I did a double take at what I saw. The ring lit up with a blinding white light as it powered to life.

"Did we—" started Duane Longer.

"Red alert!" I jumped to my feet. "Defensive fields to maximum!" I shouted. The visual display switched automatically to a tactical view as the ship's battle AI rushed through the adversary ship catalog to identify the intruder. It did.

"Imperial HuK! Accelerating toward us, sir!" called Layton.

"Lock forward coil cannon, Mr. Marker," I ordered. My Master Chief was doubling as my Weapons officer and marine commander.

"Aye, sir," replied Marker. "Cannon locked on, sir."

Just then a second flash came from the ring.

"Second HuK, accelerating rapidly," called Layton from his station.

"Keep the lock on the first, Commander. On my order, Mr. Marker!"

"Sir!" replied Marker.

"Fire!"

An orange wave of coil cannon energy lanced out at the Imperial ship and hit her head on. The small ship's shielding buckled and overloaded at the impact of our improved power and weaponry. The small ship absorbed a heavy blow, but not a killing one, yet.

"Recalibrate on the second ship," I ordered to Marker. "Mr. Longer, straight on to optimum firing range on the jump ring. I want full impellers, and engage the hybrid drive!" Now we knew why this ancient construct was so dangerous. It had to be destroyed.

"Aye, sir," said Longer. "Three minutes forty seconds to optimum range."

"You have a firing solution on the second HuK, XO?" I said.

"Affirmative, sir. On tactical," replied Babayan.

With a wink my coronal overlay switched to the tactical display. We had a dead-eye lock on the second HuK.

"Execute!" I ordered, just as yet another flash came from the jump gate ring. I scanned the tactical display again.

Now there were three.

"Orders, sir?" asked Babayan.

"Carry out the attack, XO."

She didn't acknowledge me but instead forwarded her firing solution to Marker, who immediately set and fired on the second HuK. The result was the same as the first, destruction of her shielding, but she still maintained her maneuverability.

At that moment, *Starbound*'s Historian came bounding onto the bridge.

"Did I miss anything?" he said. I gave him a glare but said nothing as he took his station directly behind me.

"Transfer weapons control to the Historian's station," I ordered. Marker complied. "Status of the helm please, Mr. Layton," I said.

"The third ship is moving off away from us, sir. None of them seem to be much interested in attacking us," he reported.

"Longwave scans indicate life signs aboard the HuKs, sir," reported Babayan. I was faced with the prospect of taking human life. I didn't hesitate. These ships were the enemy. I scanned the tactical display again, the three HuKs moving rapidly to equidistant positions.

"Serosian—" I said.

"They're triangulating on us!" he called from his station.

"Feeding stellar coordinates via longwave to a dreadnought, just like with *Valiant* at Sandosa," I said calmly.

"Likely," replied Serosian.

"Torpedoes, Mr. Serosian. Take out those HuKs," I ordered.

"It's probably too late to stop them from sending the coordinates," he said.

I snapped around to my friend and former mentor. "I want them gone now," I said. I had no hesitation when it came to protecting both my crew and the world below us. "Fire at will." He had to know by now that I was his former student, and was now firmly in command of *Starbound*.

He fired.

Three separate sets of torpedo volleys branched out from the ship in different directions. Those volleys used up most of the supply of atomic torpedoes that I had planned to use to destroy the jump gate ring.

I sat down and strapped myself into the captain's couch. The tactical screen showed our torpedoes syncing in on the HuKs, which without their primary shielding were probably doomed. A second later and their destruction was confirmed.

"Prepare for incoming fire," I commanded. Commander Babayan looked back at me from her XO's station.

"From where, sir? My screen is clear," she asked. Right on cue, a massive Imperial dreadnought winked into existence, barely ten kilometers off our starboard side. Our Hoagland Field absorbed most of the hyperdimensional displacement effect, but we still rattled and rocked. And she was closing on us.

"She's arming weapons!" called Serosian.

"Evasive maneuvers, Mr. Layton, but keep us on course for that jump gate ring," I ordered.

"Aye, sir!" Layton struggled with the helm as the dreadnought battered our shielding with a mix of coil cannons and atomic torpedoes. They ignited against our field, but we managed to hold our course. For the moment.

"Repressing fire, Mr. Serosian. Commit all remaining torpedoes to the dreadnought," I said.

"What about destroying the jump gate ring?" he asked.

"We'll have to use the coil cannons."

"But we can't guarantee destruction—"

I swiveled in my chair. "Carry out my orders, Historian, or I will return control of the weapons system to Chief Marker!" I demanded. Serosian gave me an emotionless look, but nodded and programmed the launch sequence.

"Ready, Captain," he said.

"Fire!" *Starbound* emptied her torpedo launchers in a steady stream of ordnance, both torpedoes and short-range missiles, some fired directly broadside at the dreadnought, some having to course-correct and pursue. I checked the tactical board for damage to the dreadnought.

Our combined torpedo and missile barrage hit her on all sides; more than a hundred explosions rocked her massive edifice. I watched as her shields absorbed much of the ordnance, but then a second wave broke through her outer defenses and exploded on her hull. It would have been enough to take out a High Station in a single attack, but it barely slowed the dreadnought down.

"It looks like our Imperial friends have made some improvements. Do they have a functioning Hoagland Field?" I asked Serosian.

"Not exactly," he said, "but something of a similar nature, it appears."

"Mr. Longer, what's our course and speed relative to the dreadnought?" I asked.

"We're pulling away, sir. Accelerating past her ability to catch us. That doesn't mean we aren't in her missile range, though, sir," Longer said.

"Noted," I replied. "Mr. Serosian, recalibrate our coil cannons forward. Target the jump gate ring."

"We can't destroy the ring with just our cannons *and* fight the dreadnought at the same time," he said.

"I'm aware of the tactical situation, Historian. My intent is to disable the ring since we can no longer destroy it with our torpedoes. It may not be to the letter of our orders, but the effect will be the same, at least temporarily," I said.

As our attack ended, the dreadnought resumed its barrage of *Starbound*, but against our hardened defenses the practical effect was negligible. It couldn't stop us from destroying the ring, but we couldn't stop *it* using only our non-atomic weapons. It was a dilemma.

"Time to the ring, Mr. Layton," I asked.

"Twenty-five seconds to optimal firing range," replied Layton. The ship shuddered with the effect of another nuclear missile from the dreadnought exploding hopelessly against our Hoagland Field.

"Take us as close to dead center as you can, helmsman. I want two cannon bursts, Mr. Serosian, one each from port and starboard. We'll break the ring at two points, which will disable it from use by either side until it can be repaired. Are my orders understood?" I said.

"Yes, Captain," replied Serosian. Babayan confirmed and then counted down the seconds to firing range, and I gave us two seconds extra before I ordered the cannons to fire. The effect was perfect, the ring being split widely in two places, half a click apart as we shot past the inside perimeter of the ring. The broken section of the ring drifted off into open space. We had disabled the threat, for now.

The dreadnought was still pursuing us, but losing ground, and we were now out of her effective missile and coil cannon range and accelerating away. She was still a threat to Levant, even if they now had a protective planetary Hoagland net to defend against the anti-graviton plasma disintegrator *Starbound* had fought against the last time we were in this system.

"Track the dreadnought, Mr. Layton. She may follow us all the way to the jump point but she'll never catch us. If she changes direction, I want to know immediately," I said.

"Aye, sir," said Layton. "Where will you be, sir?"

"In the Command Briefing room, with Mr. Serosian," I said. Then I turned and walked off the bridge, not looking to Serosian but expecting him to follow me, which he did.

"Do we have a problem?" I said to Serosian as soon as the Briefing Room door was shut behind him.

"I don't think so," he said back to me, his jawline firmly set in a way I had seen many times before. I continued.

"Three times you either refused to execute my orders

immediately or you questioned them in front of the crew. Three times, Serosian," I said.

"I did," he replied, then went silent again.

"Why?"

"My role is to give you options, remind you of your duties and command orders, as I have always done," he said.

"Circumstances have changed," I said flatly. "I'm no longer your student and you are no longer my mentor. I am captain of this ship, and when I give an order, especially on the bridge of my ship in a battle situation, I expect it to be followed. Do you have a problem with that?"

"No," he said. I nodded.

"Good. The time for bringing up questions on my strategies and carrying out my orders is not when we're in a combat situation. It's now, at times like these, when I welcome your insight. But once I've chosen a direction and we are on that bridge, I expect you to follow my commands without challenging me," I finished.

"Yes, Captain," he said to me with respect in his voice. I went over to the table and sat down in a chair, motioning for him to join me, which he did.

"We have a dilemma," I said.

"Yes, sir."

I rubbed my face. "We've disabled the jump gate ring, so we've accomplished part of our mission. But I don't fancy our chances of getting to the jump point generator if we have to deal with the dreadnought all the way," I said.

"I agree."

"As it stands we can't really leave Levant with the dreadnought still here. Their planetary defenses are adequate for a standoff but it would take a fair sized conventional fleet to take the dreadnought out."

"Also agreed," he said.

"Therefore I have determined we must destroy it," I

said. Serosian eyed me, but said nothing for a long while, so I continued. "It's my intent to use our gravity-based weapons to achieve this goal. Only that way can we leave Levant safe and free ourselves to join up with the Union fleet at Pendax."

Finally he responded. "But the dreadnought is chasing us, not threatening Levant," he said. "It is just as likely that they will follow us through the jump point, possibly to some Imperial-held system."

"Or possibly to Pendax, where we will have to fight them again, along with Gods know how many other ships. We have to get back to Pendax, Serosian, and I can't leave Levant to defend itself against a dreadnought, nor can I allow that dreadnought to join in an attack at Pendax. In my mind there's only one choice," I said.

Serosian's jawline began to twitch at this. He obviously disapproved, but I didn't have time to argue with him.

"There are ten thousand souls, human souls, on board that ship, Peter. You'll be snuffing out their lives with impunity," Serosian said.

"But they threaten thirty million souls on Levant, and countless others if they get to Pendax, or Quantar," I retorted.

"You don't know that!" he said, angry. Things were escalating now. "They might just make for their home base!"

"And how likely do you think that is?" I challenged him.

"Peter, if you do this, you'll have to live with this decision for the rest of your life. You saw how precious life is at Jenarus, don't you feel *anything* about killing that many people?" he said. I had a ready answer.

"The men and women I lost at Jenarus were my friends, Serosian. These people are my enemies, by their own actions. In my own mind, I can't equate their lives. They started this. We didn't," I said.

"And how many 'enemy' lives can humanity afford, Peter? There are threats out there, threats that may be greater than the empire by a long way, and we may need all of humanity to face those threats," Serosian said. I looked at him. What he was saying now was something important, but something I didn't have time for.

"I acknowledge your warning, Serosian. But my course is set and my decision made. The enemy we face right now is the empire, and perhaps Carinthia. That is all I can base my decisions on. I have to defend Levant at the moment, and then likely Pendax. This dreadnought stands between me and those goals," I finished.

"Is this really about Levant, Peter? Or is it about one *woman* on Levant?" That stung. I cared for Janaan, but I wouldn't let that affect my decisions.

"Whatever you think my motivations are, Serosian, I can't take the risk. This is a war, and they started it," I repeated. He looked at me, unwilling to back down, but keeping whatever he was now thinking to himself.

"I've made my decision," I continued. "We'll use the enveloping gravity plasma. If you can't follow my orders in this regard then I'll take care of it myself from my station," I said.

"I will make the weapon available to you, Captain, as I've promised, but I would prefer not to be the one to use it," he said.

"As you wish," I said, then stood to go back to the bridge. I stopped at the door and turned back to him. "One more thing. If you cannot follow your captain's orders, then I would prefer you not be on the bridge at all when they are carried out."

He looked at me, and I could see that this argument was causing him pain. But I couldn't prioritize his pain over my judgment as captain of *Starbound*.

"I understand, sir," he said.

And with that I went back to my bridge.

Five minutes later and I was under the hood of *Starbound*'s longscope. Per Serosian's promise the weapons displays showed all the gravity-related tech at my disposal, unlike at Jenarus when I only had the one option. But at Jenarus I was still a lieutenant commander, not the captain of *Starbound*.

I had ordered Layton to turn us around, to backtrack to the dreadnought. For its part it hadn't wavered at all on its intercept vector toward us. I preferred to think of the great vessel as an automaton, but I had no reason to question Serosian's assessment that it had a crew of some ten thousand. All the Imperial ships we had encountered had been nothing but hostile toward the Union since our first encounter, and I had no sympathy for the crew of the dreadnought. Following orders or not, they were the enemy because they had made themselves so, and they threatened many people I cared about both on Levant and elsewhere.

The display showed a simulation of our attack, and I ran it three times to be sure. The gravity plasma had a range of ten thousand clicks, close enough for them to reengage us with missiles but too far for energy weapons. I ran the sim one last time and it generated a 99-percent probability of success if we fired the weapon at eighty-eight hundred kilometers or closer.

I came out from under the hood of the longscope.

"Mr. Longer, estimated time to reach eighty-eight hundred clicks range of the dreadnought on an attack run?" I asked. Longer looked down to his board at his station and ran some quick calculations.

"Seven minutes, sir, if we begin attack deceleration in the next thirty seconds. But we'll be in range of their missiles for at least three minutes of that time," he said.

"Understood. Bring the Hoagland Field to max and

take us on an intercept course for the dreadnought. Begin deceleration at the thirty-second mark," I ordered. Commander Babayan came up beside me then.

"What's our play, Captain?" she said. I looked at her, then activated the shipwide com on my captain's couch.

"All hands, this is Captain Cochrane," I started. "In the next few minutes we will engage with the enemy dreadnought. Our mission, and my decision, is to destroy this ship with a mass-destruction weapon provided by the Historians. I don't intend for any of you to be involved in firing this weapon, except as may be required in the normal function of your duties. I want you to know I have not taken this decision lightly, but we are at war, and many difficult decisions may come in the days ahead. Man your stations, perform your tasks to the best of your abilities. I or the XO will inform you when this action is complete. Until then, things might get a bit bumpy, but rest assured the dreadnought cannot damage us with our Hoagland Field active. Captain out." I cut the com line.

"I want you to know I trust your judgment, sir," said Babayan.

"Thank you, XO," I replied. Nothing about this was easy, but I appreciated the support.

I took my seat again and transferred the gravity weapon firing control to my station. I didn't want anyone else but me being responsible for using it.

The ship rocked and rolled as we absorbed missile after missile from the dreadnought's seemingly endless supply. I watched on the tactical screen as we crossed the eighty-eight-hundred-click range. I ordered us to full stop.

"All stations, prepare to fire," I commanded. Babayan went to her board.

"All stations report green, sir," she said.

"Standby," I ordered. I took one last look at the dreadnought on the visual display, the lights of her decks illuminating dark space. There were people on her, no doubt, but I didn't hesitate. I couldn't. "All hands stand down," I said to the bridge crew. The order made them put their hands to their sides. This would be my act, and my act alone. I hesitated only a second longer.

"Firing the weapon," I said out loud.

The bridge lights dimmed just a bit as the twin coil cannon ports released the gravity plasma. The plasma accelerated outward, coming together in a silver-tinged bubble. I watched as it closed on the dreadnought, taking only seconds to reach first impact, and then seconds more to envelop the entire behemoth. The plasma closed down on the great ship, and I saw its shape begin to deform under the mass of ten thousand suns projected into a confined space. It was like watching a slow death ballet as the great ship twisted and turned, collapsing under the stress. The dreadnought then imploded before bursting outward in a blinding flash of light that was quickly smothered by the dissipating plasma.

The bridge was silent.

"Not reading anything out there at all, Captain. Not even debris," said Babayan quietly.

I stood up from my station. "All hands, resume full duties. XO, inform Levant that the threat posed by the dreadnought has been eliminated," I said.

"Aye, sir."

"Mr. Longer, engage the hybrid drive. Mr. Layton, take us back to Artemis Station. Inform them that we'll need a restock on atomic torpedoes ASAP. Once we're reloaded, get us to the jump point with best possible speed. Lieutenant Hogan, if you can calculate a trip that will shorten our time in traverse space to Pendax, please do so," I said. There was a round of quiet acknowledgments of my orders. I turned to Babayan.

"XO, you have the con. Inform me when we've completed restock on the torpedoes and are headed for the jump point. And have the crew stand down from battle stations and get some rest. I doubt we'll be getting any once we reach Pendax," I said.

"Acknowledged, sir," said Babayan. "I have the con."

I made for the lifter, my knees a bit unsteady and my hands shaking, but firm in my belief that I had made the right decision.

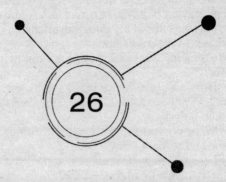

26

Three hours later I was informed by Commander Babayan that we had accomplished the restock and were headed back to the jump point to Pendax at best possible speed. I had inherited a very efficient crew. Artemis didn't have a full complement of torpedoes for us, but the fifty they did have would come in handy in any battle. The delay to restock cost us nearly ninety minutes of travel time, but I felt it was worth it.

We made our run to the jump point in what I was sure was record time, but there was no one there to record it and to me it was irrelevant. I just wanted to get my ship to Pendax. Nonetheless, I made a notation in my log to have it verified once the crisis was past. I wanted my crew to receive any due credit for their accomplishments.

We made the jump into traverse space quickly and without issue. Jenny Hogan was making no promises about our time in the jump bubble, but secretly I hoped she had something up her sleeve. I returned to my state-room, leaving Babayan in command. A few minutes later there was a buzz at my door. Surprisingly, I opened it to find her on the other side.

"Come in," I said. "Everything running smoothly up-stairs?"

"How else do you think I could leave Layton in charge?" she said. We laughed, and then sat down. She looked pensive.

"What do you think we will encounter at Pendax?" she asked straight away.

"I wish I knew. Best guess is some kind of combined Imperial-Carinthian fleet," I said.

"Dreadnoughts *and* Lightships?" she said, concern on her face. I shrugged.

"With our new weaponry and upgraded Hoagland Field, we should be able to hold them off. It would take quite a barrage of power to destroy us or *Valiant*," I said.

"But we know they have everything from displacement-wave weapons to that anti-graviton weapon. Those could be big trouble."

"They could, but we're ready for them. The only question is, what's their game plan? We don't have enough total firepower to fight off a combined fleet for a long period of time. The best we could hope for is a standoff. So far these battles have just been a series of small skir-mishes, and we've won all of those," I said. Babayan got quiet then.

"What?" I asked her. She sighed.

"Sir, it's no secret on the bridge that you and Serosian disagreed on destroying the dreadnought. I think it would be helpful to morale if you two were at least able to patch things up on the surface, for the crew's sake," Babayan said.

I looked at my XO. "I'm sure it would be helpful, but I'm not sure it's possible. Serosian has agreed to follow my orders for the moment but he is still his own man, and not under my direct authority. The Historian Order is independent of the Union Navy. I can only do as much as he will allow me to. As to patching things up, that seems impractical at the moment," I said.

"With apologies in advance, Captain, but you're certainly not going to be able to patch things up sitting in your cabin."

She had a good point. "You're probably right. I suppose I do owe the Historian another visit," I admitted. Babayan nodded.

"For what it's worth, sir, the bridge crew all think you did the right thing."

"Thank you, Lena," I said, then stood to indicate our meeting was over. We said our goodbyes and then I got myself together and made my way out of my cabin, walking through officer country, and then down the galleria toward Serosian's cabin. The crew were more than willing to acknowledge me as I went. Some even congratulated me on the outcome of the battle at Levant. I took it all in as I walked, thankful to have the crew's support. It didn't help my trepidation as I rang the chime on the Historian's quarters.

He let me in without a greeting; the door just opened automatically. When I came in he was standing at the library's map table, a 3-D display of nearby star systems projected above it.

"What's this?" I asked.

"Latest intelligence from our longwave probes. Scans are about six hours old," Serosian said. As I approached I could see he was moving from system to system with just a wave of his finger through the display, the visual view following his motion and bringing up any system he desired.

"Six hours ago we were fighting in Levant space," I said.

"I receive these updates from Earth automatically," he said. As I watched he pushed in on a star, which zoomed in and expanded to reveal the Pendax system. A sweep of the fingers and it expanded again, showing *Valiant* and a dozen Wasps in a defensive formation in close proximity to the system's ingress jump point. There was neither an Imperial force nor a Carinthian one present. "That's where the next battle will be staged," he said. "Within a few light-minutes of the jump point."

He swept his hand again and blew the view back out, then closed in on a familiar yellow-orange star. I recognized Quantar immediately. It showed five Wasps in a defensive tactical array, as well as multiple Quantar Navy ships. Our system certainly looked well defended.

"You can see all this in near real time?" I asked. He nodded.

"Yes. Our longwave probes send periodic updates or as needed on request, through our ansible network. Right now the system is sending hourly reports, but I can't receive them in traverse space," he said.

"Well, I'm just glad our enemies can't see these," I said.

"They can."

"What?"

Serosian looked at me for the first time since I had entered the room. "We all can. The Historian Order is officially neutral in any internal conflict like this, Peter. These reports go out to any Historian working on any Lightship, so that means the Carinthian ships are receiving them, too."

"So you're saying that the Carinthian fleet can see all the defenses we have set up on any system scanned by your probes?" I said.

"No. I said the *Historians* are receiving them. What they choose to do with that information is for them to decide. The captains of those ships may not be seeing these displays. It's at each individual Historian's discretion."

I found that troubling. "Somehow I doubt that if

Prince Arin is working with Mr. Tralfane that he is not receiving this information," I said. He shrugged.

"Perhaps, perhaps not," Serosian said.

None of this was good news to me. The idea that Historians on a Lightship could be making their own decisions on what information to share with their captains was disturbing. My relationship with Serosian was no doubt strained right now, and frankly, part of me wondered if I could trust him completely. "Sixteen hours in traverse space is a long time. You could be sending us into a trap at Pendax," I said. He turned his attention back to the star display.

"Six hours ago Pendax was clear and the Carinthian Fleet was stationed somewhere beyond our longwave probe network's ability to detect. As of now, any battle with Imperial forces should result in a Union victory, and any conflict with the Carinthian Fleet should be a standoff, if you follow the rules of engagement." He said the last like a pointed barb, and I didn't like it.

"I came here to see if we could find common ground again," I said. "But I can see that common ground is not something that Historians seem willing to find, with anyone. It appears you and your order have your own agenda, Serosian. Mine is protecting this ship, my world, and the Union. And it seems as if I will have to conduct myself on my own in that regard," I said. I turned to leave the room.

"Will you use the gravity weapons on Carinthian ships, Peter?" he asked as I reached the door. I turned and glared at him.

"Not if I can avoid it," I said.

"And if you can't?" I didn't hesitate.

"Then I'll use whatever I weapons I have at my disposal to win this battle. If you disagree with that, feel free to remove yourself from my ship at your earliest convenience," I said, and walked through the door without another word.

Ten hours later we were ready to drop out of traverse space and into the Pendax system at the jump point, unsure of what we would encounter there. I had my crew on max alert for the last thirty minutes. A traverse drop wasn't a precise thing. Technically, when you shut down the hyperdimensional drive, you would just "drop" out of hyperspace, traverse space, and into the nearest jump point in normal space. But it wasn't exactly like point-to-point jumping, where you could actually calculate a spatial coordinate for a jump point based on a coordinate grid synced to the galactic plane of the elliptic. Technically, as Jenny Hogan had explained it once to me, you were moving with some forward momentum through hyperspace, and you could drift some distance from the precise jump point coordinates. That momentum might last only fractions of a second, but it could result in "drift" of up to half an AU from the jump point. But Jenny prided herself on being precise, and she was damn good at it.

"We're free to disengage the jump drive at any time in the next ninety seconds, Captain," she said from her station.

"Thank you, Lieutenant. Please pick an optimal time and count down from there," I said. We all braced for the drop, safety straps locked down on our couches. She looked down at her board, made some manipulations of the data, then started counting down from ten. When she reached zero the ship shifted out of hyperdimensional traverse space and into Pendax jump space, and we all got the fragment of a second of interdimensional disorientation before we settled back into normal space-time.

"Position, Lieutenant?" I asked.

"Point-oh-three-five AU inward from the jump point, sir," she replied instantly. Pretty damn close.

"Sitrep, XO?"

"Point-five-five AU from the battle zone, sir," Babayan said. *Battle zone.*

"Switch to main tactical display," I ordered, unstrapping myself and standing to view the display. *Starbound*'s main display screen lit up with the tactical situation. Two Imperial dreadnoughts and half a dozen HuKs were taking on *Valiant* and the Wasp merchant frigates. I only counted nine Wasps, which meant three had already been destroyed.

"How fast can you get us there, Mr. Longer?" I asked. *Starbound*'s propulsion officer looked at his board.

"With the hybrid drive I can get us up to point-two-two light. That will have us in the battle zone in twenty-one minutes, fifty-six seconds," he said.

"Do it," I ordered. "Can you raise Maclintock?" I called to the com officer, a young female ensign whom I didn't recognize.

"Those dreadnoughts are putting out too much long-wave interference, Captain. We can't get through," she said.

"Keep trying, Ensign." I noticed her nameplate. It said Layton. I leaned down to my helmsmen's station.

"The sister you mentioned, George?" I whispered.

"Aye, sir. Lynne. She came aboard during the personnel exchange at Candle," he said.

"It'll be your job to keep her safe," I said.

"Was always planning on that, sir."

I ordered us up to full battle trim and the ship hummed powerfully as we accelerated through normal space faster than any other ship on the battlefield with our hybrid HD drive. I used the remaining time to the battle zone to coordinate a tactical plan with my XO. The two dreadnoughts were keeping *Valiant* pinned down while the automated HuKs were bashing away at Zander's Wasps. I noted, though, that his flagship *Benfold* was still in the game, which meant Zander was, too.

Commander Babayan and I plotted a strategy that

would take us past a group of three of the HuKs, close enough to level our coil cannons at them. This was part of a group Zander was engaged with. I intended to give them a helping hand. I looked to my Master Chief and Weapons officer, John Marker.

"Forward coil cannons on the HuKs, both port and starboard, Mr. Marker. The XO will feed you the firing solutions. I want to destroy them if we can or disable them if we can't so that Zander's men can do the cleanup. Then I want all our torpedoes on the first dreadnought," I said.

"Aye, sir!" snapped Marker from his station. I for one was glad to have him on the bridge. It was Babayan's idea, and a good one. Without Serosian on the bridge he was the most experienced weapons officer available.

"And the second dreadnought?" Babayan asked.

"We'll deal with her after we get that first one off of *Valiant*," I said.

"Where are the Carinthians?" George Layton asked. I gave him a worried look.

"I wish I knew. Ensign Layton," I called.

"Yes, sir," said the helmsman's young sister eagerly from her com station.

"Any luck raising Captain Maclintock on *Valiant*?"

"Not as yet, sir."

"Are you trained on the longscope com systems, Ensign?" I asked.

"Yes, sir!" she replied.

"Then get up here." I motioned to the 'scope. "Prepare a com probe. We'll have her trail a longwave back to us and then bore an HD tunnel through to *Valiant*. Understood?"

"Yes, sir," she said again as she took up her position under the 'scope. George went to assist her, but I waved him back.

"If she's trained, she can handle it," I said quietly to my helmsman. "I need you on your board."

"Understood, Captain."

We waited the remaining minutes until we reached the battle zone. I had Longer decelerate us to a fraction of our top impeller speed so that we could engage the HuKs.

"Do you have the firing strategy loaded, Mr. Marker?" I said as we approached the battlefield.

"Aye, sir!" he said.

"On my mark then," I said. I watched as we entered firing range on the first HuK. She was trying to evade us, but we were too quick for her. "Starboard coil cannons, fire!" I commanded. The coil cannon array, a cluster of three rotating cannon ports, fired a two-second energy plasma burst, each cannon expunging her load and then cycling back to recharge her mixture of gas and plasma while the next port cycled through.

George Layton had to keep the ship on course in conjunction with the cannon port's targeting limitations to keep a firing solution on the HuK. After the first volley the HuK went critical, her defensive systems overloading and her propulsion reactors breaking under the stress of our cannon fire. A second volley resulted in a satisfying explosion from the ship, the last two bursts hitting empty space or debris where the enemy ship had been.

"Hard to port, helmsman. Port coil cannons on the second HuK, Mr. Marker!"

"Aye, sir" came from both men in unison, and they both did their jobs to perfection, *Starbound* twisting her way through the debris field of the first HuK and targeting the second. A few seconds later and the second HuK had also gone up in flames. I watched as Zander's Wasp *Benfold*, now free of the opposition that had been pinning her down, accelerated like a gunshot toward her third HuK tormentor, firing a barrage of missiles. In a few seconds she had turned the HuK into a pile of burning debris as she vented gases into space. I didn't want to think about the possibility the flames might represent oxygen for a human crew, but ultimately, again, it didn't matter to me. They were the enemy.

Zander wobbled his wings at me as he crossed our path a few hundred clicks in front of us. That elicited a round of unexpected laughter from the crew as he gathered his comrades and they made a run for the second battle group of HuKs.

"Let it be noted that Captain Zander still has his sense of humor," I said, smiling. But now it was back to grim business. The closest of the two dreadnoughts was dead ahead.

"Time to intercept on the first dreadnought, Mr. Longer?" I asked.

"Two minutes seventeen seconds to coil cannon range," Longer replied.

"But she's in range of our torpedoes now, correct?" I asked.

"Yes, sir."

I nodded. "Mr. Marker."

"Sir!"

"A volley of torpedoes, if you please. And let's not play games here. Use the fifty-megaton warheads," I ordered.

"Yes, sir," said Marker, who turned back to his board while Commander Babayan fed him targeting coordinates. I walked over to the longscope station.

"Ensign Layton, status of my longwave probe?"

"Ready when you are, Captain," she replied. I looked to George Layton, who smiled, proud of his little sister.

"Launch the probe, maintain contact, and let me know when you have the commodore on the line."

"Aye, sir!" she said enthusiastically again. I walked back to my chair, passing Layton as I went.

"Were we ever that young, George?" I whispered. He smiled.

"Two years ago, sir," he said. I wanted to laugh, but . . .

"Captain Maclintock on the longwave, sir," said

Ensign Layton from the longscope station. She'd done a good job.

"On the main display screen please," I said. A jagged, grainy view of Maclintock on the bridge of *Valiant* appeared.

"Glad you could make the party, Captain," he said.

"Glad to be here," I responded. "We had a surprise waiting for us at Levant."

"Carinthians?"

I shook my head. "Dreadnought. Same field configuration as the one that attacked *Valiant* at Sandosa, sir. And she came in using the direct jump method, triangulating on us with HuK support ships," I reported.

"What happened?" he asked.

"The enemy was dealt with, sir. Levant is safe," I replied. The screen broke up then, but the ensign got the signal back quickly.

"If you can get one of these things off my ship, I would appreciate it, Captain," said Maclintock.

"Unfortunately, *Starbound* is too close to use the mass-destruction gravity weapon Captain Cochrane used at Levant." The words came from behind me. They were spoken by Serosian, who had come onto the bridge at some point during the conversation. The Historian took a step closer to the screen, walking in front of me on my own bridge. "I cannot recommend their use again," he finished.

"Noted, Historian," said Maclintock. "*Valiant*'s Historian Virinius concurs that we are in too-tight quarters to use those weapons. What are our options for pushing these things back out of the system?"

"Limited," I said, stepping between Serosian and the main display. "If we continue at this pace, we'll be out of missiles before we can do enough damage to force them to retreat. Then it becomes a shooting war with energy weapons. Our defenses can hold them off indefinitely, but . . ."

"But we can't keep fighting them that way forever. Understood. Do you have an option, Captain Cochrane?"

"I do, sir, if you'll let me—" At that instant the signal was cut off. I turned to the longscope station.

"Ensign?"

"Longwave probe destroyed by enemy fire, sir," she said. "I can prepare another."

"There isn't time. We'll be engaging the nearest dreadnought in less than a minute. Clear the longscope station, Ensign," I ordered, then took the station myself, bringing up the weapons display.

"Ready with torpedoes, Captain," said Babayan in my ear com.

"Fire at will, XO," I ordered, then went to my weapons display. All systems were available to me. I pulled up the gravity weapons display.

"You could destroy *Valiant* if you use the gravity plasma this close to her," said Serosian in my ear com. He had taken up his bridge station.

"I'm aware of that. It's not my intent at this point," I replied.

"Then what is?" I let the line stay silent between us. On my display the high-yield torpedoes impacted against the defensive fields of the dreadnought. Even hardened against such weapons, the dreadnought took a pounding as layers of skin and metal debris peeled off her massive sides from the explosions. It had the desired effect. She turned to close on *Starbound*.

"And now the game begins," I said into the com, so only Serosian could hear.

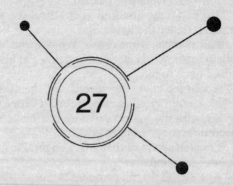

A Battle at Pendax

I had no intention of taking on the dreadnought head-on. We were a match for each other in terms of defenses but the Imperial ship had superior torpedoes in both number and yield, and we had superior energy weapons, but relying on those would be like trying to kill an elephant with a pocketknife. It could potentially go on forever. We had a nearly unlimited source of power for our defensive field and energy weapons via the ship's HD crystals, but there would come a time where continuing the battle would no longer be an option. We had to get this over quick, and I had a plan.

"Is the dreadnought still closing on us?" I called to Babayan on my com.

"Aye, sir. Fifteen hundred kilometers and closing," she replied. "She'll need to get closer to fire her torpedoes. At this distance we could pick them off with our coil cannons."

"Range to *Valiant*?" I asked.

"Twenty-eight hundred clicks, sir," she said. I came out from under the longscope.

"Full reverse, Mr. Longer. What speed is the dreadnought making?" Longer looked down at his board, then turned back to me.

"About ten clicks per second, sir," he said.

"Make our speed twelve, Helm," I ordered.

"Sir, with the hybrid drive we can make much better speed than that," Longer said.

"I'm well aware of that, Mr. Longer. Please follow my orders," I replied.

"Aye, sir." Babayan came up to me.

"What's your play?" she said.

"Get them as far away from the battlefield and our defending ships as possible," I stated.

"And then?"

I turned to my XO. "Snuff them out of existence."

Our ploy went well enough for five solid minutes, always pulling the dreadnought away from the battlefield. Tactical showed that Zander had lost another Wasp, but they had taken out a fourth HuK and were working on the other two. Then things changed.

"Sir, the dreadnought is breaking off, returning to the battlefield," reported Babayan. That was the news I was waiting for. I went to the longscope and pulled up the gravity weapons display, then selected the gravity tow field, essentially a beam of gravity plasma that would attach itself to the dreadnought and pull her in the direction I wanted. I fired up the weapon and activated the beam. It took only seconds to impact the dreadnought. The effect was instantaneous. The dreadnought was under my control. I came out from under the longscope hood.

"Helm, set course for the jump point. Propulsion,

what's our best speed with the dreadnought under tow?"
I asked. He ran calculations on his board again.

"About point-zero-zero-zero-eight light, sir," said
Longer.

"Do it. When we reach one hundred thousand clicks
from the battlefield, let me know," I ordered.

"That will be about seven minutes, sir," he said. Then
Serosian was at my shoulder, and I knew what he wanted
to talk about.

"You could drag the dreadnought back to the jump
point. Give them a chance to escape," he said. I turned
to face him, speaking quietly but firmly.

"And how do we know they'll take it? This is an enemy
that seems to only respond to brute force. I can drag them
all over this system but I can't make them jump out of it,
and at this point, what incentive do they have? They can
keep us at stalemate forever until they get reinforcements, and then they'll finish us. Right now we have one
advantage, and I'm going to use it," I finished.

"You'll destroy the dreadnought. Again," said Serosian.

"That is my plan."

"Ten thousand more lives on your head, Captain?"

"If that will save as many Union lives, then yes. There
is always a chance that the other dreadnought will see
the wisdom of retreat, and maybe we'll have a chance to
save the souls on *that* ship."

"I'm disappointed in you, Peter," he said.

"Then perhaps I'm not the man you thought I was."
He looked at me, impassive.

"Perhaps you're not," he said.

Six minutes later and we had reached the 100,000 click
mark. I put my plan into motion. Serosian had left the
bridge, and that was fine with me. I didn't have time to

worry about the deterioration of our relationship when I still had a battle to fight.

I disengaged the tow field and switched to the gravity-implosion weapon.

"Range to the dreadnought, Mr. Layton?" I asked.

"Nineteen hundred clicks, sir," he replied.

"Give us some distance, Helm. I want a five-thousand-click bubble at a minimum," I said. That wasn't as difficult as it sounded. The dreadnought, once released from our tow, was now able to maneuver and she was turning slowly to make her way back to the battlefield and *Valiant*. Our speed was pulling us away from her, and the distance between us started to grow rapidly.

"Four thousand," called Layton. I activated the gravity-implosion weapon and started the firing sequence.

"Forty-five hundred."

I had a yellow light on my board. Not quite ready yet.

"Five thousand, sir."

"Acknowledged," I said. I was still yellow.

My board went green at six thousand. I fired the weapon at sixty-five hundred.

The dreadnought warped, collapsed, imploded, and then disintegrated in a shower of silver sparks. I shut down the longscope station. Everyone in the Pendax system would have seen that light show. Whether the remaining Imperial units survived or not depended on what they did next. It took thirty seconds for their response.

"Captain Maclintock on the line, sir," said Ensign Layton.

"On the bridge display, please," I said. Maclintock appeared from his bridge.

"The remaining dreadnought is bugging out, making for the jump point. She's ceased all communication interference," he said.

"And the HuKs?" I asked.

"There's only one left, and Zander won't let it escape," said Maclintock.

"Understood, sir." I couldn't blame him. He'd lost four ships today. "What's your status, sir?"

"We have fifteen dead here, Peter. Our Hoagland Field was penetrated by some sort of vibrational frequency fluctuation weapon they were using. It cut small holes in the field, but when you're fending off atomic weapons and coil cannons . . ."

"Understood, sir. Do you need assistance?" I asked.

"No, Captain. But I do need you to parallel that dreadnought to the jump point and make sure it goes through. This is no time for complacency and we're still picking up the pieces here."

"Aye, sir," I said. "I will report when she's gone, sir."

"Carry on, Captain. Maclintock out."

With that I ordered us to parallel the dreadnought at 60,000 clicks distance, just to be safe. Thirty minutes later we were still tracking her and she wasn't showing any signs of changing her tack. Perhaps the Imperial fleet had learned their lesson. At her slow pace we were still another thirty minutes from the jump point. It looked like the Battle of Pendax was over, but looks could be deceiving, I reminded myself.

Right on schedule, things changed.

"Captain, detecting hyperdimensional displacement wave signatures coming from the dreadnought," yelled Marker from his weapons console. "She could be arming a weapon."

"Hoagland Field to max," I ordered, then checked the tactical display. She was indeed resonating with a higher dimensional frequency, but was showing no signs of turning to attack *Starbound*.

"What's she doing?" said Babayan, looking at the same data I was.

"There's only two reasons why you'd match frequencies with a higher dimension. One would be to charge an energy weapon. The other would be to jump," I said.

"But she's not close to the jump point. We're still half

an AU out," said Babayan. At that instant the dread-nought winked out of our existence and into hyperdimensional space.

"Exactly, XO," I said. "She already had coordinates to jump to. She didn't need the jump point. She's just showing us what she can do," I said.

"Jumping without needing a jump point?"

I nodded. "Turn us around, Mr. Layton, back to the battlefield," I ordered.

"Sir!" It was Marker again. Something in his voice brought me to full alarm. I looked down to his station.

"What is it, Master Chief?" I said.

"If I'm reading this correctly, sir, the whole damned Carinthian Navy just came through the jump point," said Marker.

I looked at my tactical board. Three Lightships. Ten heavy cruisers. Destroyers, scouts, even battlefield auxiliaries. Thirty-two ships in all.

"Ensign Layton," I said to the young com officer. "Get me Commodore Maclintock back on the longwave, now!"

•———•———•

"Keep your distance, we're coming to you," was Maclintock's last order. That had been ten minutes ago. Behind us the Union fleet was closing to 300,000 kilometers. In front of us the Carinthian fleet was coming at us at .0005 light from the jump point, but decelerating all the way to establish a battlefield. We were maintaining a cushion of just ten thousand clicks from the Carinthians as we retreated toward our own forces.

The Carinthians were arrayed in a tight "I" formation, with *Impulse II*, and Dobrina, on the forward point, a second Lightship, *Avenger*, close behind, and the third, *Vixis*, trailing the formation. The rest of the ships formed flanks on either side with their heavy cruisers outside and the weaker destroyers and scouts inside.

We were outnumbered three Lightships to two, and we had only eight battle-damaged Wasps in our support flotilla. We did have our enhanced Hoagland Fields and higher-powered coil cannon arrays, but no one wanted to use them on our own ships, or at least ships that had been in the Union Navy only a few days ago. My best guess was that Prince Arin was commanding the attack from *Vixis*, as she'd been the Lightship docked at High Station One in the Carinthian system.

We had our engagement rules: only fire if fired upon, no use of mass-destruction weapons unless either *Valiant* or *Starbound* was in imminent danger of destruction. It wasn't perfect, but it would have to do.

Maclintock hailed us again on the voice-only com.

"Stand by, *Starbound*," he said. "I want you to slow your retreat to us. We're closing fast, faster than they are. But we need to see their intentions before we act."

"Aye, sir," I said. "We'll have to let them get within three thousand clicks for coil cannon range, fifteen hundred for torpedoes."

"Understood, *Starbound*. Those are my orders. We'll be three minutes behind you," said Maclintock.

"*Starbound* out," I replied, then took my seat and strapped in. I called battle stations over the shipwide com, then ordered Duane Longer to slow us to .0005 light to match our speed and timing with both fleets. We'd be in firing range of *Impulse II* for three minutes before *Valiant* arrived on the scene.

I started to sweat as the clock wound down to contact with *Impulse II*. The last thing I wanted was to do battle with Dobrina and her world, which was my world now, too, by virtue of my marriage to Karina.

"Thirty seconds," called out Babayan.

"All weapons on hold. All defenses on maximum. We'll be able to absorb *Impulse II*'s first volley without damage, so hold your stations, regardless of how hard she kicks us," I said, trying to encourage the crew.

At ten seconds I gripped the arms of my safety couch. At five seconds I dug my nails in.

At zero the ship rocked from the impact of *Impulse II*'s coil cannons on our Hoagland Field, our inertial dampers kicking in as she readied a second volley. The support ships weren't close enough to us for an attack, so for now it was just one-on-one. *Just like it had been on the fencing court so many times*, I thought. I had always lost.

Her second volley really jolted us and we lost our longwave com to *Valiant*. "Get it back," I yelled at Ensign Layton. Then an internal alarm claxon went off.

"Sir, we have a hull penetration, deck nine, amidships," said the XO.

"How is that possible through our Hoagland Field?" I demanded of Babayan.

"They must be using—"

"The vibrational frequency modulation weapon," I said. "Ensign!"

"I've got the longwave back, sir! Voice com with Commodore Maclintock!" Lynne Layton said.

I hit the button for the fleet com link. "Jonas, *Impulse II* is using the vibrational frequency modulation weapon you talked about. They're able to penetrate our Hoagland Field in small localized areas," I said.

"Goddamn it!" came his angry voice over the com. "Somebody out there wants a full-scale war."

"Commodore, under the rules of engagement—"

"Granted, Mr. Cochrane. Defend yourself at all costs," said Maclintock.

"Aye, sir," I said, then cut the com. I looked to my console and brought up the weapons display. The gravity weapons were offline. I thought about calling Serosian, then thought better of it. We were going to have to win this on our own.

"Seventeen seconds to mutual torpedo range, sir," called Marker from the weapons station.

"With that frequency modulator they'll be able to pierce the hull with an atomic blast," warned Babayan.

"So we won't give them that chance," I said. "Arm the coil cannons. Full force burst on my mark, Master Chief. Target their torpedo tubes."

Marker responded affirmatively and I watched as the power curve on the coil cannons loaded.

"There's no guarantee we'll break through their field with the first volley," Babayan said.

"I'm aware of that, XO," I replied. The weapons display went all green. "Fire the cannons, Mr. Marker."

He did.

The orange coil energy lanced out at *Impulse II* from both port and starboard. They cut straight through her hull and destroyed her torpedo launchers. Then there was an internal explosion, which was undoubtedly one of her own torpedoes detonating inside the hardened protective shell.

"What the hell?" said Layton.

"Was her field activated?" I demanded. Babayan searched for the answer.

"Her power outputs are at minimum, Captain. Just enough to fire the cannon. No defensive fields engaged, minimal life support. And . . ." she trailed off.

"And what, XO?"

"Our attack has pushed her off vector. She's not in a position to hit us again, sir, drifting further off course every second," said Babayan.

"Confirm, Helm!" I demanded of Layton.

"Confirmed, sir. She appears to be drifting," he said.

I unstrapped myself and jumped to my feet.

"Stand down weapons! Get Maclintock back on the line!" We had one minute to avoid disaster. *Valiant* and the Wasps were bearing down on a defenseless fleet.

"Maclintock here," he said over the voice com.

"Commodore, it is my belief that this Carinthian fleet has been automated for this attack in order to draw our fire! *Impulse II* has no defenses, repeat, no defenses active. We have to break off. They *want* us to destroy the fleet, sir!"

There was no response for a few moments. I was close to panic.

"Commodore, do you copy my last?" I said. Again no response. I looked to Ensign Layton at com.

"The longwave interference has returned, sir. We're cut off," she said.

"What do we do now?" said Babayan.

"Propulsion officer, max on the hybrid drive," I ordered, then turned to George. "Get us between *Impulse II* and *Valiant*," I said. He nodded.

"I'll try, sir."

We used nearly twenty seconds positioning *Starbound*. There were less than thirty seconds left to attack range for the *Valiant* flotilla. If we didn't stop them, they'd turn this engagement into a shooting gallery, and Dobrina and thousands of her countrymen could die.

"*Impulse II* is coming right at us now, sir," reported Marker.

"Will she clear us?" I asked.

"Perhaps by a hundred meters, sir. If we're lucky," he said.

"All stop," I ordered. "Stand down weapons. Stand down on the Hoagland Field."

"You can't cut the field, sir!" protested Babayan.

"It's the only way to show Maclintock she's adrift and not a threat, XO. The only way to save her," I said.

Commander Babayan and I stood together on the bridge as we watched *Impulse II* approach on the tactical screen, her vector varying only slightly from a direct collision. I ordered a switch to visual as she got closer. We watched, holding our breath. Then *Impulse II* slipped by us, barely forty meters off our bow. I watched as *Valiant* closed, then held her position relative to *Impulse II*.

Impulse II didn't move to attack or make any move off of her current course. *Valiant* let her slide by as well.

A cheer went up from the crew.

"Engage the hybrid drive, Mr. Longer. Match our course and speed to *Impulse II*, Mr. Layton. Mr. Marker, prepare shuttles for boarding and make sure you take emergency environmental support with you."

"Aye, sir," said Marker, heading for the door.

"Captain." It was Duane Longer.

"Hold it, John," I said. Marker stopped his exit from the bridge. "Mr. Longer?"

"Sir, it's the third Lightship, *Vixis*. She's under power and making for the jump point at max speed, sir," he said.

"Why?" asked Babayan. "I mean, why only one ship with power?"

"Because that's the ship that Prince Arin commands," I said. "And he set this whole thing up. He tried to get us to destroy his own world's fleet."

"Sir," said Ensign Layton, "I have Commodore Maclintock again. The longwave interference is gone."

Maclintock's voice came up on the com. "Good work, Mr. Cochrane."

"Thank you, Commodore. Request permission to lend aid and assistance to *Impulse II*, sir," I said.

"Denied," he said. "Captain Zander has first dibs on that duty."

I crossed my arms. "Of course, sir. May I recommend we make sure the rest of the Carinthian fleet is disarmed?"

"It's my first priority, Captain. What about *Vixis*?" he asked.

"My belief is that Prince Arin or his agents are aboard her, sir, and they set this whole scenario up," I said.

"But why?" asked Maclintock.

"To destroy the Carinthian fleet, to weaken the

Union. To make it seem like an act of aggression *against* Carinthia by the Union, to turn the people against us."

"What would they gain from that?"

I thought about that for a second. "Locking Carinthia permanently out of the Union, and preparing the populace for alliance with the empire," I said.

"But if their fleet is destroyed, or worse, how will Arin be able to hold Carinthia?" asked Maclintock.

"I can only assume he'll have Imperial help, as he did here."

"Wait," said Maclintock over the com. "New communication being patched in from *Impulse II.*" The line was scratchy for a few seconds, and then the unmistakable voice of Captain Dobrina Kierkopf came on the line.

"Commodore, Peter, you've got to go after *Vixis!* You've got to go now!" she said insistently.

"Dobrina, why? What do you mean?" I said, responding before Maclintock could.

"I mean he's going to attack Carinthia, his own planet, and blame it on the Union! Arin and the empire—you've got to go now!" she said.

And then it hit me. Attack the Union. Send in a fleet of powerless Carinthian vessels on preprogrammed attack. Blame their destruction on the Union. Attack Carinthia under a false flag. Instantly the Union would be ripped apart, both politically and militarily. It was brilliant.

And evil.

"Commodore, request permission—"

"Go," said Maclintock. "We'll be right behind you."

"Mr. Longer, full max on the hybrid drive!" I ordered. Then I sat back down in my chair, seething inside at the people, known and unknown, who had plotted this, and vowing revenge.

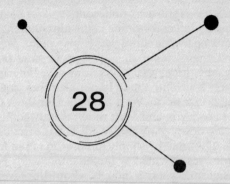

28

A Battle at Carinthia

We were twenty minutes behind *Vixis* when we started our pursuit, but that vanished, along with *Vixis*, before we reached the jump point. She had the jump point generator technology just as the dreadnoughts did, and it was now clear that she had gotten it from the empire.

We, unfortunately, had to wait another thirty minutes to reach jump space, even with our hybrid drive. Our transition was near-instantaneous, as Pendax was within the thirty-five light-year radius of Carinthia, so we could use our point-to-point jump capabilities and avoid traverse space. When we arrived in-system at Carinthia we found High Station Three still operating but in a shambles. They hailed us, begging for help, but we could only offer consoling words and a promise of greater assistance coming behind us.

The trek inward to Carinthia proper was agonizing. I

gave the crew breaks, but even with the hybrid drive at max it was still a six-hour journey. Two hours in we were able to detect the other Lightships jumping into the system one by one through the jump point. *Impulse II* came first, then *Valiant* and *Avenger*. *Impulse II* tried hailing us, but there was heavy longwave interference, most likely from automated Imperial probes along the path to the home world. We'd have to clear them out later, but for now, Arin and *Vixis* were my only goals.

No doubt *Vixis* had avoided all the trouble of communications flak by simply jumping in to predesignated coordinates provided by Imperial forces. My anger seethed inside me when I thought about the level of betrayal exhibited by Prince Arin and the Regency forces, and what promises could have possibly motivated them to fall into league with the empire. But those were questions for another day.

We passed High Station Two. It was in pieces. We couldn't have stopped to offer help anyway. Our goal was to try to get to Carinthia to stop an attack. If we could.

An hour from Carinthia we detected the attacking fleet in orbit.

Three dreadnoughts were in equidistant orbits around the planet, performing crossing maneuvers, gridding the planet, doing Gods know what. Even with the longscope we couldn't get reliable readings at this distance. *Vixis*, for its part, was in geostationary orbit above New Vienna. We could identify her easily enough because she hadn't bothered to turn off her Union IFF—Identification Friend or Foe—beacon. It was the height of arrogance.

Thirty minutes out and the dreadnoughts started moving in our direction, setting up a picket line between us and *Vixis*.

"What do you suppose *Vixis* is doing, sir?" asked Babayan. Our target was still hovering over New Vienna, not moving.

"Raiding the treasury, pretending to be protecting the populace, who's to know?" I said to her. Then I turned to Ensign Lynne Layton at the longscope. "Give me a situation report on Carinthia, Ensign," I ordered. We were now in close enough proximity to receive reliable data. I waited a few seconds while she updated her status checks under the hood; then she broke free of her station and reported to me at the captain's chair. Babayan, standing to my side, watched her come with trepidation. Layton cleared her throat and I turned my attention to her.

"Longscope scans indicate more than thirty atomic detonations on the planet's surface, sir. At least ten civilian targets, port cities, industrial facilities, and large farming collectives have been hit. The rest are military targets, air bases, forts, and the like, sir," she said. I heard Lena stifle a cry at this news; no doubt there were tears present as well. I gave her the dignity of what privacy she could muster on the bridge by not turning toward her. Ensign Layton continued.

"Almost all military space platforms have been destroyed, sir, along with most of the civilian satellite communications array. The atomic weapons used by the dreadnoughts have matched their yields with Union specs, sir, likely in order to blame the attacks on us by masking their Imperial origin. *Vixis* remains stationed over the capital, broadcasting on emergency channels, the only source of information for the populace, claiming she is defending Carinthia from us, sir," she concluded.

"Bastard," said Babayan. "Why hasn't he attacked New Vienna?"

"Likely because he plans on ruling from there, at some point," I said to my XO without turning.

"But three dreadnoughts and one Lightship can't hold off the entire Union fleet, sir, not with our new weaponry," she said. I turned to look at her. Her eyes were rimmed with red but she otherwise maintained outward composure.

"Then it seems likely he doesn't plan to hold Carinthia for now, but abandon her to us and return later, likely with an overwhelming force," I said.

"But where would he go?" she asked. I shook my head.

"That we don't know, but what we do know is that this was well planned in advance, as I'm sure is his escape," I said.

I sat back down in my captain's chair.

"We can't wait for the rest of the fleet to arrive. They don't have the added benefit of the hybrid drive, so they're too far out to help. We have to act now, try to save what's left of Carinthia." Babayan took her station next to me. "Status of the closing dreadnoughts, XO," I said.

She looked to her screen. "They're tracking between us and *Vixis* now. We'll have to go through them to get to her. We'll be within firing range of the gravity weapons in nine minutes, coil cannon in twelve, missiles and torpedoes in fifteen," she said.

"Distance to *Vixis*?"

"Twenty-two minutes max at flank speed, Captain."

"Mr. Longer." I looked down at my propulsion officer. "Flank speed. Everything we've got," I ordered.

"Aye, sir!" replied Longer.

I looked down at George Layton at the helm. "Mr. Layton, plot best course to intercept the *Vixis*," I said.

He hesitated, then said, "It will have to be through those dreadnoughts, Captain."

"I'm aware of that. As I've ordered, Commander."

"Yes, sir," he replied. A few seconds later and the optimal course was up on our tactical display. I turned to my longscope officer.

"Ensign Layton, prepare the enveloping gravity plasma weapon. Signal me when she's ready. I'll take the longscope station at that time," I ordered.

"Aye, sir," she said, and made for the 'scope.

"I'll be relying on you to command the deck while I'm under the hood, XO," I said, turning to Babayan. "As soon as we're free of the dreadnoughts, I want *Starbound* to make straight for *Vixis*."

She nodded assent. "Understood, sir. Will we have the Historian's support for this attack?" I looked to his dark and empty bridge station.

"Unlikely."

"And if he tries to block the attack from his quarters?" she asked. I looked at her dead on.

"Then eject the yacht from the primary hull, XO," I said.

She didn't waver. "Understood, sir."

Then I got the signal from Ensign Layton at the longscope, and took her place there.

The scale of the attack I was planning was unprecedented. I had gauged up the gravity projector to envelop all three dreadnoughts at once with a plasma field almost ten kilometers across. I could see from my display that Serosian was monitoring my station, watching as I calculated the needed power outputs, but he hadn't communicated with me and I didn't expect him to.

The dreadnoughts maintained a close stack formation. This made no sense to me as it made them vulnerable to a multiship attack. My only thought was either they had a secret attack plan that I couldn't begin to guess at, or they were under orders from Arin. The latter scenario seemed most likely: protect *Vixis* at all costs.

Using the power curve I was planning on would drain the ship for several minutes, even with the replenishing power of our hyperdimensional systems. We would be vulnerable for as much as two minutes, but we'd be out of range of *Vixis*'s weapons during that time. At least the ones we knew of. I forwarded the battle plan to the XO.

"This consumes all of our system power, even reserves. Everything but the emergency batteries," she said to me through the command com channel.

"We'll only be vulnerable for two minutes, Commander. An acceptable risk. And *Vixis* is out of range to attack us," I replied.

"What if we don't get all the dreadnoughts?"

I hesitated a second before answering. "We will," I said. "Call battle stations, XO."

"Aye, sir."

My longscope tactical display showed an eighty-seven percent predicted success rate, and that was good enough for me. Babayan announced to the crew that they were to stand by battle stations, and that the attack would be only my responsibility. I waited as she counted down precious seconds to the minimum range of the gravity plasma. When she reached zero, I didn't hesitate.

"Firing the gravity plasma weapon," I said to her over the command com. I watched as *Starbound*'s coil cannon arrays rose to firing position and ejected the glittering silver plasma from their gun ports. The drain on the ship's systems was immediate. When I came out from under the hood, the bridge was dark and dim with the blue emergency lights the only illumination. I watched as system displays slowly came back up one by one as we replenished our power reserves. Then the main tactical display lit up.

The gravity plasma was enveloping the helpless dreadnoughts. They were almost completely enclosed when . . .

"Sir, I'm reading a weakening of the gravity plasma field," said Babayan.

"Weakening? How?" I watched her scan her station monitor quickly.

"Uncertain, sir, but they appear to be punching holes in the plasma. Currently five percent dissipation, sir," she said.

I went to my display station and pulled up the tactical

telemetry. She was right. The dreadnoughts were piercing the plasma. I checked the power wave signatures.

"They're using the frequency modulation weapon to punch holes in the plasma," I stated. I watched for a few more seconds.

"Can they disperse the field?" asked Babayan. I looked at the rate of penetration. Then I sat back down in my chair.

"They don't have enough time," I said simply. Babayan joined me in sitting. We watched in near-silence, only the quiet hum of our operating systems as ambient sound. The gravity plasma made contact with the first of the dreadnoughts. In quick succession all three of the behemoths warped and imploded under the massive gravity field, then a quick succession of three bright white explosions, like fireworks, filled the screen.

Three dreadnoughts destroyed. Thirty thousand men and women. Human beings.

I found myself devoid of feeling for them. They were just the enemy now, an obstacle in a greater, much larger battle.

"Mr. Layton," I said. "Recalculate and optimize our course for *Vixis*." He responded immediately.

"Done and done, sir," he replied. "Seventeen minutes to intercept, sir."

"Good," I said, then silently resumed monitoring my personal tactical panel.

We were nine minutes away from engaging *Vixis*, which was busy spooling up her Hoagland hyperdimensional drives to jump, when Duane Longer at Propulsion called me down to his station.

"I think I have an option, sir," he said to me and Babayan as we leaned on the railing looking down on his station.

"Explain," I answered.

"I think we can use the hybrid drive, a controlled intermix detonation like the one at the Jenarus jump space tunnel, to jump ahead and engage *Vixis* early. Surprise her, sir," he said.

"You *think*?" questioned Babayan. I held up my hand to allow Longer to finish.

"It will be hard to calculate exactly, and we're much closer to *Vixis* than we were to normal space at Jenarus, but if I can use that detonation to calculate how much of an intermix we need, it could jump us into firing range early," said Longer.

"Or blast us completely out of range." The voice came from behind us. We all turned to find Serosian had returned to the bridge.

"I'd be glad to have your help, Historian," I said formally.

"And I've come to offer it," he replied. "The odds are slim we can control the intermix that precisely, but if you are willing to turn the process over to me . . ." He trailed off. I looked to George Layton.

"How long until *Vixis* is ready to jump, Lieutenant?" I asked.

"Looks like seven minutes, sir. They're not rushing," he said.

"Prince Arin has a flair for the dramatic. He wants us to get close before he jumps out. Show us his superiority," I said. I nodded to Serosian.

"Go," I said. "Everyone prepare for the intermix jump. Lock down the ship, XO," I ordered.

"Aye, sir," she replied, a skeptical look on her face.

I took my seat and commed in to Serosian at his station, speaking quietly. "Can our inertial dampers handle this kind of force?" I asked.

"Likely," he said. "They are designed for much greater stresses than this. I can't guarantee that you won't be thrown around your bridge a bit like in those popular

Tri-Vee dramas you liked so much growing up, but *Starbound* should hold together."

"That's comforting," I said. Then I asked the real question on my mind.

"Why are you back on my bridge?"

He didn't break from his preparations while answering. "Your use of the gravity weapons on the battlefield has been a great escalation and marked a moral compromise against other human beings which I could not condone. I have no such moral compunctions where Prince Arin is concerned."

I took his answer as an honest one.

"Seven minutes to attack range. Five until *Vixis* can jump," announced Babayan.

"It's now or never, Historian," I said into the com. A few seconds passed until he said, "Ready," then stood down from his station. He came and took the third chair next to me.

"Mr. Longer?" I asked.

"Intermix calculated and fed into the impellers, sir," he reported.

"Status, XO."

"Locked as tight as she'll go, Captain," she said.

I pulled up the gravity plasma projector weapon on my station panel. It was still warm and ready.

"You'll only get one chance at this," said Serosian. I nodded.

"Understood. Commander Layton, as soon as we complete the intermix jump, I'll need firing coordinates on *Vixis*," I said.

"You'll have them in five seconds, Captain," he said. I looked back down at Longer.

"Count us down from ten," I ordered.

He did.

There was a good deal of thrashing about the cabin as the inertial dampening system tried to compensate for our violent acceleration. After a few seconds we were stable again and Layton quickly fed me *Vixis*'s location.

"We're less than a hundred clicks from her!" said Babayan.

"Understood, XO." I plugged in Layton's calculations and fired the gravity plasma. Then I stood up, watching the tactical display with the rest of the crew as the plasma expanded.

"Are you sure this will work through an active Hoagland Field?" I asked Serosian.

"There is no greater force in the universe than gravity," he said by way of answering.

"Report, Commander Layton," I demanded.

"*Vixis* is running, on full impellers, sir, straining to keep her distance from the plasma," Layton said.

"He'll lose," said Serosian. Something, my intuition, told me that wasn't so sure a thing.

"Sir," cut in Babayan, urgency in her voice. "*Vixis* is raising her HD frequency modulation much faster than she should be able to. She's almost ready to—"

"Jump," I cut her off. And with that *Vixis* was gone from our dimension, her destination unknown. The plasma field intersected with her last known position a few seconds later, heading out into open space, there to harmlessly dissipate.

I sat back down. "He was playing with us," I said.

"But, sir," insisted Longer, "I swear he didn't have time to spool the HD drive enough to create a working torsion field!"

"I'll take you at your word, Lieutenant. Apparently the empire's new jump technology has more features than we anticipated," I said.

And with that, I ordered us into geostationary orbit above New Vienna. There was much to do there, first and foremost to convince the survivors of the atomic holocaust that the Union was not their enemy.

Prince Arin would have to wait for another day.

Dénouement

Once we established orbit, we began to see the damage done to Carinthia firsthand. High Station One was completely destroyed. Almost every usable low-orbit military platform or station had been ripped apart. Three major cities had been destroyed by atomic attack.

New Vienna was spared, perhaps for only the reason that Arin intended to return there one day to rule. Radiation levels were too high on the planet, and there was a dense cloud of debris in the lower atmosphere, obscuring many of the major cities. The prime agricultural areas of the planet had been scorched by coil cannon fire and small-yield atomics. Casualties would undoubtedly be in the millions.

Carinthia had been devastated.

We had boots on the ground inside an hour, targeting major infrastructure hubs around the remaining cities, starting with New Vee. Power, water, food: it was all about the basics now.

At first the military and police resisted us, and there were a good number of skirmishes. But we began broadcasting the truth to the Carinthian people over low-band frequencies, and slowly they began to accept our help. It was in our favor that many of the voices telling people the truth were Carinthian, including Prince Benn, Karina, and their sovereign, the grand duke.

Admiral Wesley had the Union fleet mobilize all the forces at their disposal to help Carinthia. Four worlds, Earth, Quantar, Pendax, and Levant, reached out to help their brothers and sisters in need. It did not go unnoticed by the people, or their rulers. Indeed, Arin's plan seemed to have had the opposite effect on the morale of his planet than what he had intended. But it was clear to me that his first aim had been to cripple Carinthia, the industrial giant of the Union, and he had achieved that. His political goals were secondary, and I suspected he believed achieving them in the near future with the help of the empire was a foregone conclusion.

Within a week, Admar Harrington had antiparticle ships from Pendax scooping the atmosphere clean of contaminated debris. It was something they had to do regularly on their own world, with its frequent volcanic eruptions. It went on this way for weeks, the Union worlds rallying to aid Carinthia, and it made a difference. My time was consumed in humanitarian efforts. I coordinated Quantar's aid program to Carinthia at my father's request, focusing on rebuilding critical infrastructure such as salvageable utility and industrial plants. It was daunting and exhausting work.

Then one day I was called back to the capital, to the New Hofburg palace. I washed and slept, something none of us had done much of in weeks, all under orders of the Admiralty. The next morning I was escorted downstairs into the palace's huge drawing room, and there found it full of dignitaries.

The Grand Duke Henrik, my father, Prince Benn, Wesley, Karina, Dobrina, Serosian, Harrington, Zander. . . .

They all greeted me and thanked me for what I had done. I had been through so much, though, that I felt completely disassociated from them and from my royal responsibilities. I was first and foremost in my mind a Lightship captain. Everything else came second.

After a few minutes of idle chatter I found myself drifting into a corner chair by a fireplace, drinking tea in the cold morning sun and staring out the window.

Then Dobrina came up and joined me, tapping me on the shoulder before sitting in an adjacent chair.

"How are you, Peter?" she asked.

"Numb, I think," I replied with a weak smile. Numb was a good word, but underneath that numbness was a searing pain. I felt deeply depressed at what had happened. I'd lost thirty-three marines under my command and taken fifty thousand lives destroying the dreadnoughts. Enemy or not, that was a heavy burden, and not what I'd thought would happen in my navy career.

Dobrina took my hand and rubbed at my wedding band, bringing me back to reality.

"I'd almost hoped it wasn't true, these stories of your wedding to the princess. But I understand. It's my folly for believing the daughter of a soldier could ever marry a prince."

I sat up. "It was no folly," I said. Dobrina smiled bravely.

"We both know that it is. And right now both our worlds need you and Princess Karina to inspire hope again," she said, "and they need me in command of *Impulse II*. No regrets, Peter. We had our time."

"We did," I agreed. I focused hard on her, this brave woman who had touched my heart, who I would never be able to be with again except on the battlefield. Those emotions were all raw and right on the surface. I couldn't hide them anymore. I didn't want to.

"I love you, Dobrina," I said. She squeezed my hand.

"I know. And I love you. But that's not enough in this world, this Union. Not now," she said. "In a different reality, perhaps . . ."

"Nothing will ever change how I feel about you," I said. And that was true. If I'd been born a navy brat, instead of in a royal house, we could have been together.

"Goodbye, Peter," she said. "I'll always treasure what we had." Then she rose, and in a moment she was gone into the milling crowd. I stood and went to the window again, staring out at the still-frozen back gardens of the palace, teacup in hand, trying hard to keep my eyes dry. My emotions had been rubbed raw, right to the surface, and they were hard to contain. A gentle hand on my shoulder brought me back to reality.

I turned. Karina, my wife, reached out to me. She put her arms around my waist as she pulled me close to her and held me.

"It will be all right, Peter," she whispered. "Everything will be all right, in time."

The next day, after a much-needed night of rest, I was feeling more myself. There was a series of meetings, one cluster with the leaders of the Union: Prince Benn, the grand duke, my father, Harrington, Serosian. I even caught a glimpse of Sunil Katara of Levant through an open door. He waved at me and I waved back, but I was headed for another meeting, one I was much more comfortable with, a military council with Grand Admiral Wesley and the Lightship captains.

I shook hands with Devin Tannace, new captain of the Levant Lightship, *Resolution*. I met Wynn Scott of Earth, a tall, sinewy, African man. The captain of *Avenger* was there as well, Air Marshal Von Zimmerman's son, Dietar. And of course Dobrina and Maclintock.

Wesley cleared his throat and we all sat down at the table. "Let's get down to business. The first item is assignments. We currently have six captains, but only five in-service Lightships," he said. I assumed this was where I would lose my field command. "But that problem will soon be rectified. The Historians have informed us that three new Lightships will be delivered to the Union Navy within a month."

"Can they build them that fast?" Captain Tannace asked. Wesley smiled.

"Apparently we've been a bit misinformed on that front. The ships to be delivered have been completed for some time. Seems the Earthmen were just humoring us, letting us build them ourselves. One each will be delivered to Quantar, Carinthia, and Pendax, as a condition of her joining the Union. Counting Levant and Earth, our fledgling Union now has five members, and many more resources. But we'll need three more captains," he said. "Permanent captains."

I tried to stay calm, and he continued, turning to me. "Mr. Cochrane, your performance aboard *Starbound* as her acting captain was exemplary, no other way to put it. You made very difficult decisions, but ultimately it is my judgment and the judgment of the Union Council that you saved lives, which you seem to have a knack for."

"Thank you," I said. "I appreciate that. But I couldn't save Carinthia from attack."

"Not your job, Captain," he said gruffly. "You did all you could. Let any guilt over Carinthia go, that's an order."

"Yes, Admiral," I replied. That would be a hard thing. Wesley continued.

"Now, getting on with business, I'm afraid Captain Maclintock here wants his ship back, so I'm ordering you to give *Starbound* up. But I'm prepared to offer you one of the new Lightships in her place. Will you take permanent command of *Defiant*, Captain?"

Defiant. If ever there was a name that matched how I felt right now. "I will, Admiral, and I hope to do her name honor as her commander."

Wesley nodded, then continued. "Carinthia will be receiving her new ship, designated *Fearless,* from the Earthmen. Air Marshal Von Zimmerman will be making the call on that assignment. The third new Lightship captain was chosen by Admar Harrington, who speaks for the government of Pendax. He's requested that their new ship, *Vanguard*, be captained by none other than Lucius Zander."

We all had a good laugh at that. "He'll be impossible to deal with!" said Maclintock. Wesley nodded again, smiling.

"I had a good long drink when I heard that request, but I can't blame them. He's as experienced as they get, and he'll be an asset to this team." He paused before continuing. "Now there is one more assignment that I need to announce. Since we will soon be eight in number, and not all orders can come from my office, I've decided to name a fleet captain. Jonas Maclintock will be your new commanding officer and take up the permanent rank of Commodore, reporting only to me. He will be in charge of all fleet assignments from here on out. Jonas?"

At that Wesley stood and shook hands with Maclintock, handing him a pair of crown insignia for his collar. We all stood and applauded. Wesley then went through the other changes being made. All the members of the Union would be mass-producing more Wasp-class frigates on a war footing, and they would be in charge of defending the home planets. There would be new First Contact missions to Jenarus, Sandosa, and places I'd only read about in history classes: Minara, Pharsalus, Ceta,

Veridian, Spartak, Skondar, and Caledonia, plus one more.

"We've got to grow this Union, ladies and gentlemen. Make it stronger, more able to confront the revived empire. And there's one more mission that's only in the planning stages. I'm sending *Resolution* home to Levant, where she'll commence work on repairing the jump gate ring. We're going to Altos, people, there to find out if our enemy still lives there, and if she's left us a gateway to Corant," Wesley said.

"We're taking the war to the Imperial home world?" I asked.

"Not tomorrow, lad," he said. "But soon enough. Soon enough indeed."

After two days of meetings, the leaders of the Union emerged united and set to one purpose: confronting the enemy wherever we found them, and making them pay for what they had done to Carinthia.

The next day I stood behind the curtains in an upper room of the palace, dressed in my finest princely regalia. Navy blue tunic, sash of orange, family crest and a cluster of honorary medals I was sure I hadn't earned. It wasn't something I wore often, and I was definitely more comfortable in my navy uniform. But today I wasn't merely a Lightship captain. Today I was also to be a prince.

In the square below, a hundred thousand people had gathered on a sunny but brisk winter day. They were still hurting, still shell-shocked over what had happened to their world. But they had come here to see their sovereign, and their princess and her new husband. We were here for one reason, to give them hope.

I stood on one side of the grand duke, Karina on the other. Together we each took him on one arm and helped him pass through the curtains and onto the balcony of the palace. The people in the square cheered their duke boisterously. He smiled and waved, accepting the adulation of the crowd. Once we had him safely to the podium, Karina and I stepped back as he spoke in German to the crowd. I didn't understand a word of it. I could have used a translator module for my ear com, but I knew the gist of what he was saying: words of healing, words of prayer for his world. He was weak, of that there was no doubt, but he forged on, and I admired him for it.

Halfway through his short speech Karina reached over and took my hand. She looked beautiful in the cold winter sun, her oval face framed by a luxurious fur coat covering her formal dress. My admiration for her was growing by the day. We both had much work ahead, but we had each other, and that meant something.

As the grand duke finished his remarks, he turned first to his daughter, and then to me. He took our hands and joined them together above our heads, and symbolically led us to the front of the balcony, then stepped back. This set off a frenzy of cheering, and we couldn't help but smile. Then the duke patted my shoulder, smiled broadly, and encouraged us to take the center stage.

We both stepped forward to the balcony's edge. I looked to my bride, a woman I didn't love yet, but certainly could with time, then down at the jubilant crowd and waved. When I looked back at her she smiled at me with pride, and in that moment I was taken away by a sudden urge of spontaneity. I leaned in and kissed her sweetly on the lips.

The crowd roared.

ACKNOWLEDGMENTS

Shout outs for this one go to my editors, Sheila Gilbert at DAW, who is indispensable, and Michael Rowley at Ebury/Del Rey UK, for his insights into the nuances of the Europe/Rest-of-the-World market.

Big thanks to my agent Joshua Bilmes, who constantly makes my work better, and lastly to my friend Tony Daniel, who I will continue to find new and interesting ways to kill in the future.

Available early 2017,
the thrilling third novel of
The Lightship Chronicles
from Dave Bara:

DEFIANT

Read on for a sneak preview

and mine, *Defiant*, were docked here at Candle in our home system of Quantar. The other captains were spread out far and wide across Union space, a bubble about forty-eight light-years across centered on Sol that the Union Navy had agreed to defend as home space. There were only about sixty G-type spectral stars, humanity's preferred type for colonization, within that bubble. Of those systems, only a few had been colonized in the early days of Imperial growth, many of them not having suitable planets with the right climate conditions and atmosphere. We knew of nineteen historical colonies and a handful of industrial bases within that bubble, and our Union, at the moment, represented only five.

I looked at the massive star display on the far wall. Beyond Union Space (the stars identified as yellow dots) the G-type stars of the Imperium were identified as red. That red bubble extended out from about fifty light-years to one hundred light-years from Sol, and while it seemed the two contrasting areas of space between Union and Empire were nearly identical in size (in terms of light-years) the fact was that there were some 448 potential stars with habitable worlds within that Imperial red bubble, nearly eight times as many as in Union Space. The stellar topography greatly favored our enemies in terms of potential numbers of colonized worlds. That was an advantage they could use to crush us if we didn't get stronger and more numerous, and soon. The Historians told us that there were some 350 known colonies in the Old Empire at its peak, before the war, and as we now knew, less than twenty of those on our side of the line. Whether the old Empire had ever colonized beyond that hundred light-year bubble was an unknown.

I turned away from the star display and back to the conference monitors, which were slowly flickering to life. We now had eight operational Lightships in the fleet if you counted *Vanguard*, Pendax's ship, which was near enough to ready. I feared that wouldn't be enough ships, despite my confidence in both our Lightships and their captains.

Valiant, commanded by Wynn Scott of Earth, was conducting the long-delayed First Contact mission at Jenarus, which I had previously visited when I was third in command aboard *Starbound*. *Resolution*, commanded by Devin Tannace, Maclintock's former number two, was on station in her home system of Levant. *Fearless* was captained by Mehzut Ozil, a Carinthian of Turkish descent whom I had met briefly on Carinthia during the incidents there. *Avenger*, commanded by Dietar Von Zimmerman, son of Carinthia's Air Marshal Von Zimmerman, was stationed in its home system. Neither *Fearless* nor *Avenger* had ventured very far from Carinthia since the attack on her.

Impulse II, captained by my former lover Dobrina Kierkopf, was at High Station 3 in the Carinthian system, prepping for a survey mission to a system called Skondar for possible First Contact. Skondar had been a robust mining colony in the old Imperial days. It was unknown if the colony was still inhabited, but it was known that she had been a treasure trove of metals such as lithium and magnesium, not to mention the less exotic but nonetheless valuable gold and silver repositories.

There would be one addition to our virtual table, though; Captain Lucius Zander, my first commanding officer aboard the original, ill-fated *Impulse*, was joining us today as the future captain of the Lightship *Vanguard*, from the Union's newest member world, Pendax. *Vanguard* would be joining the fleet in another month or so as our eighth commissioned Lightship.

As the techs finished up their work I took my seat at the conference table next to Maclintock. We faced a broad, curved plasma in the office's conference work area, just a part of the massive facility the Commodore had at his disposal. One by one the five Lightship captain's faces appeared on the big screen, hanging above us. When the last connection, that of Grand Admiral Jonathon Wesley in his office on High Station Quantar was made, the techs departed the room, leaving Maclintock and I alone with our virtual group.

"Ladies and gentlemen," Wesley started, "I hope all is well where you are." There were nods and general acknowledgments all around. "Good," he continued. "Let's get on with it then. First order of business is new deployments, of which I have three. Captain Ozil, I'm uploading an order packet to you outlining your new mission, which is a first survey of the Ceta system."

"Thank you, Admiral. We're anxious to get back out," said Ozil.

"I'm sure you are. This one will be standard survey protocols; stealth running, observe and catalog, but do not engage nor participate in any activity that might arouse interest in *Fearless*. And at any sign of Imperial forces in the system you are to bug out and return to station immediately, no exceptions," finished Maclintock.

"What are our rules of engagement?" asked Ozil. Wesley looked up sharply from his desk display, staring right into the camera.

"There are none, Captain. You are to bug out, period," he said. The fact was that the Lightship fleet had had no interactions with the Old Empire since the battles at Levant and Pendax almost six months ago. Wesley apparently wanted to keep it that way.

"Understood, sir," replied Ozil. I could see he was disappointed, but Wesley's orders were probably prudent. The Union was looking for as many allies as we could find, but if a system was already under Imperial influence, regardless of proximity to Union space, our orders were to leave that system alone.

"Admiral," came another voice, this one from the other Carinthian captain, Dietar Von Zimmerman. "*Avenger* has been passed over twice now for missions away from home. Can I ask why?" he said in his Carinthian accent.

It was lighter than most, and I hadn't found it a problem communicating with him at all as his Standard was very good. Wesley nodded to Commodore Maclintock, who had operational command over deployed Union forces, for an answer to the inquiry.

"The fact is, Captain Von Zimmerman, that I would like to send you out to get your feet wet. Unfortunately, Carinthian Navy Command has insisted that at least *one* Lightship remain in-system at all times until *Bismarck* is commissioned next year. As of this time, that ship has been designated as *Avenger*," replied Maclintock. What he was really saying was that Von Zimmerman's father, the Air Marshal of Carinthia, was keeping his boy close to home. It didn't sit well. Von Zimmerman got a sour look on his face, then said:

"So Lena and Dobrina get to have all the fun again, and I get to go back and forth between High Stations, never leaving home."

Maclintock shrugged. "They both have battle experience with the Empire, Dietar. And I think we should all be using any quiet time in this conflict to our utmost advantage."

"Aye, sir," Von Zimmerman said, with more than a trace of resignation in his voice.

"Next up, Captain Tannace of *Resolution*," said Wesley, comfortable with overseeing if not running the meeting.

"Aye, sir," replied Tannace. He was an agreeable man in his mid-forties, a bit old for a Lightship command, but he had been Maclintock's loyal number two for a number of years. His appearance was always spit-polish clean, and that's the way he ran his ship, so I was told. He was a by-the-book commander, and every fleet needed its cache of those, to balance out the more risk-friendly types, like me.

"Afraid it's the milk run to Carinthia again, Devin," said Maclintock. "There's another shipment of food goods from the bazaar at Artemis. Live goats, I've even heard, part of the rebuilding efforts. It's not glamorous but if you manage to pick up some Carinthian schnapps on the way back through and drop it off here at Candle, well, I'm sure you'll get a good evaluation on your next rating."

Tannace laughed and responded with an "aye, sir." Then we were on to the next issue at hand. Wesley cut in then and asked for and was given a report on the Jenarus negotiations by *Valiant*'s Captain Scott.

"The Jenaurians are real shits to negotiate with, sir," said Scott frankly. He was a tall and sinewy African man, born on Earth, and darker than anyone I had ever met. We had our share of aboriginal descendants from the Australian continent on Quantar, but none like him. When he spoke it was with authority and experience. "They want massive concessions from the standard Concord Agreement, and I'm not of a mind to give in to them. The biggest hurdle is establishing a representative democracy. They have an authoritarian bent to their planetary government, and there are three or four other nation-states that also want a seat at the table, so negotiations may take a while. Still, whenever I tell them we'll come back at another time when they're in a better mood, they rush to give in on things. It will take time, Admiral, but I expect they will eventually come to agreement with us."

"Good news, Wynn. Please keep me informed of your progress, and remember the Union Council has the Jenarus system at the top of their list for expansion," said Wesley.

"Will do, Admiral," said Scott.

Wesley yielded the floor back to Maclintock, who turned his attention to Zander to give a report on *Vanguard*'s progress. Zander's transformation over the last eighteen months, since the attack on his shuttle at Levant, was nothing short of miraculous. He now had two eyes again, his skin was a smooth pink, and he even had wisps of white hair hanging down to his shoulders, Bohemian style. It was a far cry from the charred face I had pulled into *Impulse*'s Downship that day.

Vanguard was officially three months from being commissioned, but Zander already had her crewed up and ready to go. In a pinch, she could be prepared for a fight in days or weeks. I figured Zander could launch her in twenty-four hours if he wanted.

"My intent is to take her out next week on a traverse run to Minara. It's forty-two light-years, so that should be a good test of the traverse drive system," said Zander in his gravel-rough voice.

"Sounds good, Lucius. No contact with the locals, if you please, but you might find your way clear to leave your IFF signal beacon on for a while. The tech survey team said the Minarans seem to have a high level of technology and may have even detected our probes. So don't be afraid to let them know you're there, and friendly," said Maclintock.

"Aye, Commodore," replied Zander.

"Captain Kierkopf," said Maclintock. "All ready for the Skondar mission?"

"Ready as we'll ever be," said Dobrina. "Skondar is close to the borderline with Empire space. I have my doubts based on the Historian's longwave probe reports that we'll find any kind of functioning colony or camp there. But we'll investigate it thoroughly. We've added another thirty marines to our complement and dropped our Downship in favor of the reinforced marine gunships the Earthers offered. If anybody is alive down there and wants a fight, they'll get one."

Maclintock looked up at her image, unsmiling. "The mining operation is on Drava, the moon of the fifth planet in the system. We need to find out if that operation is still intact and can be exploited. In Imperial times there were valuable minerals there. They may not be valuable to the Empire today, but likely it's different for us. That's my way of saying don't blow anything up you don't have to, Captain." That set off a round of low chuckles.

"Understood, sir," she replied. I could see from her stone-faced look on the display that she wasn't amused. At all. I could still read her moods.

Then Maclintock turned to me.

"Lastly, as for Captain Cochrane and *Defiant*," he started.

"Ah, yes, the Golden Boy," chimed in Zander. This drew another round of laughs from the other captains.

"Thank you, Lucius," I said, to a few more chuckles.

"Well, he has drawn the plum assignment," said Maclintock, turning to me. "You're ordered to take *Defiant* to High Station Pendax, there to rendezvous with a certain merchant named Admar Harrington. The mission is First Contact with the government of Sandosa. They are already in contact with our survey team and anxious to meet us face-to-face. And since your ship carries both a Duke of Quantar and a Princess of Carinthia, it seemed to the Admiralty that you were the best option for this mission, diplomatically speaking," said Maclintock.

"Understood, sir, but why will we be taking Mr. Harrington?" It wasn't that I minded the man, he was a likable enough chap and a great negotiator. I just wasn't sure I wanted his company aboard my Lightship.

"Pendax and Sandosa had a very strong trading relationship under the Old Empire. Harrington would like to get first shot at cracking the market. And since Pendax is our newest member, the Union Council had a hard time saying no to him."

"Understood, sir," I said again, but I didn't really like it. Still, diplomatic missions had their bonuses. They tended to be full of state dinners and lots of merrymaking. The negotiations were more tedious, but I found I was able to distance myself from the hard-core horse trading more easily as time went on, using both my royal standing and my position as a Lightship captain to avoid the tough work.

"Full contact protocols will be sent via communications packet, along with a history of Sandosa and any relevant information from the survey teams. Departure from Candle will be at 1000 hours on 02.19.2770. Understood, Captain?" Maclintock finished.

"Yes, sir," I said. That was the day after tomorrow. More than enough time to prepare my crew and go. We hadn't been out in nearly a month, so the space time would be a welcome break from our leisurely port schedule. When Maclintock was finished with me he turned things back over to Admiral Wesley.

"Last orders, Captains," the Admiral started. "The criminal Prince Arin is still at large. The Empire is still out there, a threat but we don't know how big. Until the prince is brought to justice and the Empire's intentions are fully known, we are on a war footing. If you encounter Empire forces, disengage, contact the Admiralty, and we will organize a response. If you sight Prince Arin or the *Vixis*, your orders are shoot to kill. No mistakes, Captains, and no mercy for our enemies."

"Aye, sir," I said, as did all the other captains.

Dave Bara

The Lightship Chronicles

"Totally convincing space navy…check! Perfectly realized characters complete with depth and heroism…check! Plus a fascinating story with an Ahab of a captain determined to complete his mission, and a fledgling lieutenant who comes into his own in the midst of interstellar conflict. Oh yeah: exploding spaceships…double check!"
—Tony Daniel,
author of *Guardian of Night*

"This guy is the next Jack Campbell; it's that good."
—T.C. McCarthy,
author of the *Subterrene War* series

Impulse
978-0-7564-1066-7

Starbound
978-0-7564-1067-4

and now available...

Defiant
978-0-7564-0998-2

To Order Call: 1-800-788-6262
www.dawbooks.com

DAW 215